THE EVERSPRING

THE EVERSPRING

BOOK TWO OF THE TORIN TEN-TREES SAGA

JOSHUA GILLINGHAM

CROWSNEST BOOKS

Crowsnest Books
www.crowsnestbooks.com

Distributed by the University of Toronto Press

ISBN: 9780921332824 (paperback)

ISBN: 9780921332831 (ebook)

Cataloguing information available from Library and Archives Canada

Cover design and illustration by Helena Rosova.

Map illustrations by Tiffany Munro.

Typeset in Norse, designed by Joël Carrouché, and Adobe Caslon, designed by Carol Twombly.

Printed and bound in Canada

For Hazel – Those who wander wide are sure to discover the hidden magic of this world.

CONTENTS

◇ PREFACE ◇

It is my distinct pleasure to welcome you back to the realm of Noros to continue the adventures of Torin Ten-Trees and his companions in *The Everspring*. The book that you are holding in your hands is the second installment in *The Saga of Torin Ten-Trees* and, while it can certainly be enjoyed on its own, it will be greatly enhanced by first reading *The Gatewatch*. Rest assured that, at the time of this writing, the third and final book of the saga is in the late stages of editing and will hopefully be available for your enjoyment soon.

For any who have not yet feasted in Fjellhall alongside the troll hunters of Noros or explored the underground caverns of the mysterious *nidavel*, I offer here a short introduction to this tale. It may also serve those for whom the names, places, and events of the first book have faded.

Torin Ten-Trees and his closest companions, including Grimsa, Bryn, and Wyla, had come to Gatewatch to perform their duty as troll hunters in service to King Araldof Greyraven. After meeting Gatemaster Gavring and Keymaster Signy, an unexpected misadventure sent the companions far out into the wild woods beyond Gatewatch where they were captured by trolls. As prisoners, they learned that an ancient giant from the far north, named Ur-Gezbrukter, had come to crown himself as the Troll King.

With the help of two *nidavel* named Bari and Brok, they escaped to Myrkheim, the city of the dwarves. Mastersmith Ognir, the ruler of that underground city, aided Torin and his companions by gifting them a chunk of Sunblaze, a metal that burns as bright as the sun. The party then returned to Gatewatch, just in time to give warning of Ur-Gezbrukter's impending attack. At great cost, they defended the city against the trolls and used the Sunblaze to defeat the Troll King.

And now, Torin's adventure continues…

Sincerely,

Joshua Gillingham

October 9th, 2021 (Leif Erikson Day)

◇ A BRIEF GUIDE TO NOROS ◇

Torin's world is greatly broadened in the course of the upcoming adventure; following the wise advice of my editor, I will provide a brief guide to the primary races in the realm of Noros which may serve as a helpful reference for the reader throughout.

Madur are humans. Some, like Torin, hail from Noros in the far north. Other *madur* kingdoms, such as Armeah, exist much farther to the south.

Nidavel are dwarves. Greatly skilled in magic and metalcraft, they live in underground cities such as Myrkheim, from whence they seek jewels, and rarely visit the surface.

Jotur are giants. However, unlike the many folkloric traditions in which they are portrayed as unintelligent oafs, these giants are instead akin to those of the Norse myths: immortal (though not invincible), exceptionally wise, and wielders of extraordinary magic. They hallow Yg, the ancient world tree, and their forebearer Ym, whose body was rent and cast upon Yg's boughs to form the world.

Asyr are immortal beings hailed as gods by the *madur*. Foremost among them are Odd the Wise, Orr the Thunderer, and Fyr the

Fierce. They are despised by the *jotur* because of the terrible wars they fought against them long ages before the present tale.

Huldur are mysterious creatures which are most comparable to elves or fairies. They are not immortal but live long lives as guardians of the forest. They sing enchanted melodies which help the trees to flourish and which ward off evil beings such as trolls.

Nornir are ancient beings who sit at the base of Yg, the world tree, and weave the fates of mortals and immortals alike. They are the oldest beings known to exist and are often depicted as three women: one young, one middle-aged, and one elderly.

◇ A NOTE ON VERSE FORMS ◇

No consideration of Viking Age culture is complete without a mention of their favorite pastime: poetry. Viking poets, or *skalds*, used specific poetic forms to craft epic tales which were told in the fire-lit halls of ancient Scandinavia and later recorded in writing. I have adapted some of the rules of skaldic verse in an attempt to capture the force and rhythm of the original forms. This adaptation, not as viciously rigid as *dróttkvætt* (court meter), bears similarities to more forgiving forms such as *málaháttr* or *fornyrðislag* where the emphasis is on internal rhyme and alliteration rather than end rhyme. The adapted verse form used in this book is based on three rules:

1. Every line must have exactly six syllables.

2. Every odd line must contain *full rhyme* (e.g. sail/whale) while every even line must contain *half rhyme* (e.g. wind/land).

3. Every pair of lines must contain three cases of **alliteration**, twice in the odd line and once in the even line (e.g. 'wrong' and 'ring').

As a demonstration of the form and as an incantation for the telling of tales, I offer these verses:

Flee the frigid *sea*storm
Foul and deadly *howl*ing
Here *a* while *lay* anchor
All *your* troubles leave *there*

Come shed your *cloak soak*ed through
*Cast frost*y helm aside
Keep sharp s*words* safely st*ored*
Guests here *scarce* need a blade

Now *light* logs to *bright*en
Longhouse d*im* and gl*oom*y
Let *long* flames grow *strong*er
Like *red* wolves *wood* licking

Fetch *more* furs *for* comfort
O'er cedar benches fold
Wrap *thick* hides 'round you *quick*
Be **r**id *of* this *grave* chill

Bring *here* **beer** in barrels
Fill every horn **b**rim-*full*
Also *fine wine* **a**nd mead
Till throats *are* dry no *more*

Foul **w**inds of winter *howl*
Harsh seas *slosh* icy **waves**
Yet let them yonder rage
Now **you** m*ust* but l*ist*en

◇ PRONUN⟨IATION ⟨UIDE ◇

Certain words in this book are based on Norwegian and Icelandic, both descendants of Old Norse in which the myths were originally told. These words are not always direct translations but are meant to give the text a phonetic flavor that is distinctly Scandinavian. However, certain consonant combinations that roll smoothly off the tongue in these languages are phonetic tripping hazards by the rules of English. In words like *fjell/fjall* (Norwegian/Icelandic – 'mountain') the 'j' makes a 'y' sound. Instances of 'skj', 'sk', or 'sj' should be pronounced 'sh' as in *skjold/skjöldur* (Norwegian/Icelandic – 'shield'). The combination 'kj' is pronounced 'ch' as in *kjekk* (Norwegian – 'handsome'). For ease of reading I have altogether avoided the use of 'æ', 'þ', 'ð', and any letters with diacritics (e.g. 'ø' or 'å').

1

◇ AN OATH FULFILLED ◇

A GRIM FIGURE sat alone at the end of a long wooden bench in an empty hall lit by nothing but crackling embers. The scent of burning cedar was sharp in his nose and smoke stung his eyes. The dim glow of the fire barely reached the rafters towering high over his head. In the flickering shadows, those great wooden beams hovered over him like a gathering of enormous black ravens.

He sighed and swirled what little mead was left in his drinking horn. Some of the sweet frothy liquid ran into his beard as he tilted the vessel back and slurped the last mouthful. He eyed the empty horn for a moment then tossed it over his shoulder. As it skittered across the stone floor, he wiped his face on the sleeve of his tunic and let his gaze settle again on the dying fire.

The doors at the far end of the hall flew open. All along the hearth the embers lit up as a brisk rush of air blew past the lone figure's face. A large man stumbled through the doorway and braced himself against the end of the long table. In the red glow of the fire, the man seated at the bench silently watched the newcomer blink and squint into the shadows.

A gruff voice called out. "Torin Ten-Trees? By the gods, drinking without me?"

Torin dropped his head down to the table and let his arms sprawl out across the rough cedar planks. "Go away, Grimsa."

The iron door hinges creaked again as another entered the hall. The newcomer's footsteps were light, and they spoke in a whisper. "Is anyone here, Grimsa?"

Torin recognized the voice. It was Signa, Keymaster Signy's daughter. Signy held the key to that mighty hall in which Torin sat and it was rare indeed to find that she was not there. However, nearly every person who called Gatewatch home was out in Stonering Keep enjoying themselves at the Spring Festival.

"Look who I found!" said Grimsa. "Torin Ten-Trees drinking all by himself in Fjellhall."

Signa peered into the darkness. "Torin? What are you doing here?"

Torin lifted his head off the table and winced at the sharp rays of daylight coming in through the door. "What does it look like? Drinking. What are you two doing here?"

Grimsa had stepped closer and now Torin saw a blush rush over his friend's face. Signa grinned and grabbed Grimsa's arm. "Just a bit of privacy. The rest is none of your business. Did you know that Grimsa is going to ask my mother tonight at the festival?"

Signa held up her left hand so that it caught a streak of sunlight. On her finger glimmered a ring, polished silver inset with sparkling green gems. "Emeralds," she said, "My favorite colour. They remind me of glittering dew on fresh spring grass."

Grimsa blushed a darker hue of red, nearly purple, and smiled ear to ear. Torin had wondered if Grimsa would work up the courage to speak with Keymaster Signy about marrying her daughter before the Spring Festival. Apparently, he had.

After the festival that night, all the Gatewatch recruits that had arrived two years earlier, Torin and Grimsa included, would be released from their oath of duty. Most would return home to the life and the family they had known before. A select few would be offered a permanent place among the Greycloaks, the veteran troll hunters of Gatewatch. Grimsa had always been keen on achieving the latter and had become more so now that his engagement rested on it.

"Well," said Signa, "So much for privacy." She hopped up on the bench and kissed Grimsa. "I'll see you two at the festival." With that, she turned toward the door while humming a lively tune to herself and skipped out of the hall.

Torin pushed himself up off the bench. "That's quite a ring. She seems happy. So do you."

Grimsa cleared his throat, his ears still as red as wild cherries. "A few months back I sent word to Bari to have it made in Myrkheim."

"Bari's here?"

"He just arrived. I didn't know he would bring it himself!"

Torin nodded and smiled. In his mind he could still see Myrkheim, the underground dwelling of the dwarves, or *nidavel* as they called themselves. That colossal underground city, with its strange hexagonal columns locked together like a puzzle, was still as clear in his memory as it had appeared before him the day he had arrived there. That was nearly two years ago. He thought often of the mysterious Mastersmith and of Bari's uncle, Brok, who had hosted them. Then the smile fell from Torin's face, and his eyes softened. "So, you're going to stay?"

Grimsa shuffled his feet and stared at the long bed of embers in the hearth that ran down the middle of the hall. "What would I do if I went back? Start a farm? Become a trader? I don't have the head for that sort of thing. But I can slay trolls. And Signa is here." Grimsa let a quiet moment pass then shifted his weight and crossed his arms. "You?"

Torin shook his head. "I don't know. I guess that's why I'm drinking here in Fjellhall by myself."

Grimsa scooped two horns up off the floor and trudged over to where Torin sat. He tilted the nearly empty mead barrel at the end of the table to fill both vessels and then sat down. The bench creaked as Grimsa let his weight rest on it. He passed one of the horns to Torin then sipped his own.

Torin stared down into the mead and frowned. "What if I stayed? What if I didn't go back to Ten-Tree Hall and instead lived the rest of my life here with you and Signa, with Wyla and Gavring, with Keymaster Signy and all the others?"

Grimsa shrugged. "You could. Besides, your father could remarry. He could have another child."

"No, he is old. And he won't remarry. He told me once that he never will."

"Couldn't his nephew, your cousin Varik, take up his seat in Ten-Tree Hall?"

Torin grimaced. "It would break my father's heart. Varik is a spineless, conniving weasel and the hall would go to ruin."

"What does Wyla think?"

Torin took a swig of mead then wiped his lips on the sleeve of his tunic. "I'm not sure. She's not speaking to me right now."

Grimsa stood to refill his horn with the last bit of mead in the barrel. "Is she still sore about losing that game of King's Table last week?"

"No, no, it's not that. It's because I haven't decided whether or not to stay." Torin's shoulders slumped down further. "She said that if I'm leaving, she doesn't have another word to say to me anyways."

Grimsa sat down again and shook his head. "That's Wyla alright. Well, damn the rest of them. What do you want to do?"

Torin swirled his mead a moment more before he answered. "I'd like to dig up Ten-Tree Hall plank by plank and move it up here to Gatewatch."

"Imagine that." said Grimsa. "You could rebuild it a little way up the valley, perhaps right beside Frostridge Falls. What a view you would have."

Torin and Grimsa lingered a moment more over the mead, then toasted the Gatewatch and emptied their horns. In some ways, Torin felt as if he had just arrived. In other ways, he felt he had always been a troll hunter patrolling the wild woods beyond the rugged town of Gatewatch. Outside the hall they heard voices and shuffling feet as more of the townsfolk made their way to Stonering Keep for the festivities. Torin looked at Grimsa, who gave one firm nod. Together they walked out of the hall to the Spring Festival, arms over each other's shoulders, partly as a sign of brotherhood but mostly for balance.

It was late in the afternoon and the sun was sinking into the wild forests beyond Stonering Keep. Torin raised his arm to shield his eyes from the sunset which spread across the western horizon in brilliant streaks of red-golden light. Then he looked east up the valley to Shadowstone Pass and saw the blinding glint of two snow-capped ridges, Frostridge Mountain and Ironspine Peak.

Stonering Keep sat at the very western edge of town. Along with several towers and sections of stacked stone, it formed a wall that stretched across the valley. Beyond it lay many dangers: wolves, boars, bears, giant cats, and, of course, trolls. Trolls were the worst of all, for the most part dim-witted, but always foul and cruel. It was the sworn oath of all those who joined The Gatewatch never to let those creatures pass by the rugged wall to wreak havoc as they had in ancient times. As Torin leaned on Grimsa's shoulder, he realized that he would soon be offered freedom from that oath, though some part of him wanted to join Grimsa in keeping it.

But that night was not one for grim thoughts of foul creatures or dreaded decisions; the Spring Festival was one of the greatest celebrations of the year. It was the equinox, so from that night forward the days would outlast the nights. Already, the last snarling nips of winter were giving way to the lush, green spring.

At the festival there would be music and dancing, salted meat and pickled vegetables, fresh loaves of hearty bread and plenty to drink. The home-brewed spirits made by the folk of the village had strengthened all winter and now would be uncorked with great anticipation. Better still, a friendly competition between local brewers led to some innovative concoctions. Torin still remembered his two favorites of last year: a sweet wildflower mead and a savory pickled spirit.

As Torin passed under the gate into the wide-open courtyard, he remembered the first time he caught sight of Stonering Keep. Back then its walls were crumbled, its ramparts cracked, and its crooked towers lined with tattered banners. In the time since, the towers had been rebuilt, the wall fortified, and the stone courtyard levelled until it lay perfectly flat. New banners, tightly knit and intricately woven, hung down from the towers in a proud flutter. Captain Gavring had ordered the restoration himself when he was appointed to lead the Greycloaks of Gatewatch two years earlier. Now that monumental task was nearly complete.

Grimsa left to find Signa, so Torin wandered through the festival at his own pace. He had hardly passed the first booth when a voice called from the crowd. "Torin! Torin!"

Torin turned around but could not make out the voice. He squinted and frowned but still did not see anyone calling his name. He stood up on his toes and peered over the crowd. Then a tug came on his cloak near his knees.

"Torin! There you are."

He looked down and saw his old friend, Bari, a *nidavel* from under the mountain. "Bari! By the gods, it is good to see you, my friend."

Bari chuckled and grinned wide. "Torin Riddlesmith. Look at you! I cannot believe how much you *madur* change from year to year. And your beard! Soon it will be as long as mine."

"I saw the ring you brought from Myrkheim. Grimsa already gave it to Signa, and she seems more than pleased."

"My uncle Brok forged the ring himself," said Bari. "No doubt it will be the envy of every woman here in Gatewatch!"

"Grimsa didn't ask you to put any enchantments on it, did he?"

Bari fought down a smirk and winked. "Well, if he did, let's say they were not the kind of enchantments we *nidavel* know how to place on rings."

Captain Gavring appeared atop the wall with a host of Grey-cloaks on either side, the veteran troll hunters of Gatewatch. The captain's wild red hair had been strapped back with a length of leather, and his beard, for once, was trimmed. Even among the Greycloaks he stood a head taller than most. Torin saw Gavring wave his hand to signal the drum. As the pulsing bass boom rang out, the crowd fell silent.

Gavring cleared his throat. "Greycloaks, recruits, and towns-folk of Gatewatch! I am honoured to stand here before you all on this spring equinox. It has been almost two years since Ur-Gez-brukter, son of the ancient Troll-King, Gezbrukter, stormed this very keep. His army of trolls tore down the walls, but we have built them up stronger than ever before. In that battle many Greycloaks fell, but we have bolstered our ranks and tomorrow we may add to our number again." He motioned to the Greycloaks that stood alongside him on the wall. "I have here nine grey cloaks, thick and warm and finely made. Nine of the recruits that joined us two years ago will be invited to join The Gatewatch permanently and commit their lives to the defence of our beloved realm of Noros."

Whispers rippled through the crowd at Captain Gavring's announcement. Torin's stomach turned and twisted like a caged dog at being reminded of the decision before him. Most years only two or three cloaks were offered, so nine was highly unusual. Torin felt many curious eyes fall on him and so focused his attention on Captain Gavring.

"But first," said Gavring, "We celebrate the passing of winter! Forget those dark days and frozen nights. Let us feast and drink to welcome the spring! Long live The Gatewatch!"

The crowd cheered at Gavring's words, more for being short and to the point than for being well spoken. Then the whole keep was filled with the sounds of ringing laughter, of draughts being poured, and of toasts as mead horns were drained in gulps. Torin slapped Bari on the shoulder and pointed toward an ale-wagon nearby. "Come, my friend. Let's get a drink!"

Somewhere nearby, a group of musicians whipped up a lively tune. The melodies plucked from their strings flitted through the crowd like a flock of nimble sparrows. Cheers and laughter came from all directions as the festival goers hailed the musicians. When Torin and Bari approached the owner of the ale-wagon, perhaps the brewer herself, she held out two brim-full horns.

"Torin Ten-Trees," she said, "A troll-slayer if there ever was one! You'll be offered a Greycloak for sure." Her eyes widened when she saw Bari standing beside him. "And a *nidavel*? What strange company!"

Torin took both horns and handed one to Bari. "Thirsty company nonetheless!"

The *nidavel* bowed slowly, careful not to spill the ale. "I am Bari, nephew of Silversmith Brok." He raised the horn, laughably large in his small hands. "To your health, lady brewer!"

She smiled at Bari and bowed in return. "My pleasure, Master Bari."

Torin and Bari both threw back their heads and gulped down the ale, each racing to finish it before the other. As Torin was lowering his head, Bari was doing the same so that neither could be declared the winner of that first contest. They both grinned as their horns were refilled and took the second draught of ale in sips to enjoy its fine flavour. For some time, they related their more recent adventures and asked one another about them, each having two more questions for any one that was answered. Then, from the corner of his vision, Torin saw Wyla stumbling toward them.

"Bari," said Wyla, "So it's true! You made it." She embraced the *nidavel* with both arms and lifted him right off his feet. What little was left in Bari's horn spilled out over the stones. All three roared with laughter as they called for more.

Torin raised his horn again. "Here's to old friends, as it seems you're speaking to me again."

"It's not me speaking," Wyla said, "It's the ale. But *skal* all the same!" She accepted another full horn of ale, then steadied herself on Torin's shoulder to drain it in one long gulp.

A disturbance in the crowd behind them caught their attention. Grimsa was dancing along to the music, twirling back and forth with surprising grace. In his arms he held Signa, whose own arms were wrapped tightly around Grimsa's tree-like neck.

Grimsa stopped when he saw Torin, Wyla, and Bari. He set Signa down and threw his hands high up over his head. "She said yes!"

Wyla scratched her head. "Signa? We all knew she would say yes."

"No, no," Signa said. "My mother, Keymaster Signy!"

They all embraced the couple one by one. Tears welled up in Grimsa's eyes and Signa joked about how smiling all day had made her cheeks ache. For some time, the company of friends wandered from tent to tent and cart to cart sampling the brews and tasting the best of the preserved meats.

Signa suddenly swung around and grabbed Torin's arm. "Torin, I nearly forgot! My mother wants to see you. She's waiting for you in Fjellhall."

Torin felt himself sway a bit but caught his balance. "Me?"

Signa frowned. "Yes, I thought she had a strange look in her eye. She said it was very important."

"Alright. I'll go see her right away." He embraced Grimsa and Signa once more, one in each arm, then wandered through the crowd toward the gate back into town.

Not a soul stirred in the winding streets of Gatewatch. Though it was a clear night, the moon was just a sliver and shed only a little light on the rough cobblestone road. A cool breeze whistled down the lanes and ruffled the thatched roofs of the smaller houses. However much it grieved him, Torin began to suspect that he had no choice but to leave. After all, he was his father's only son and heir. So Torin turned his mind to the warmth of his childhood home, to the sound of his father's voice, and to the earthy smell of the glowing hearth in Ten-Tree Hall.

Soon he came to Fjellhall. Torin gazed up at its towering stone walls and carved wooden rafters. This was the place he would miss most of all. Though it was different in many ways from Ten-Tree Hall where he had grown up, the well-worn benches had a homey feel and there always seemed to be a bit of heat left in the hearth. The great wooden door creaked on its iron hinges as he pushed it open. He relished the familiar scent of pine and charcoal as he breathed in through his nose and stepped across the threshold.

Fjellhall was still dimly lit and at first Torin saw no one else there. Then, as his eyes adjusted, he saw a figure seated at the far end of one of the long benches. It was Keymaster Signy, alone. The old woman sat facing the fire and was stroking her long single braid of silver-grey hair as she hummed a quiet, mournful tune. When Torin stepped closer she did not look up but kept her eyes fixed on the glowing bed of coals in the hearth.

Torin sat on the bench beside Signy and rested his feet on the warm hearthstones. With a sigh, he leaned back on his elbows against the table. Then he slowly craned his neck back to look up at the shadowy rafters high overhead, and grinned. "You know, sometimes I think this place feels more like home than Ten-Tree Hall."

Signy smiled and turned toward Torin. A sadness encircled her pale grey eyes like the glow around the moon on a frigid winter night. "I want to speak with you alone, Torin."

Torin raised one eyebrow and turned his head toward the Keymaster. "To me? Is this about Grimsa and Signa?"

The old woman smiled and shook her head. "No, not about them. I know love when I see it and their souls are already entwined at the roots." Her smile faded and she frowned, as if the words were hard in coming. "I want to speak to you about your mother."

"I wish I could tell you something about my mother," said Torin, "But my father only ever told me so little. He said he lost her when I was just a child. That's all he would say. I'm not sure if it was an oath he pledged or the pain of losing her, but he refused to marry again. He's lived alone ruling the lands around Ten-Tree Hall ever since."

Signy nodded. "Well then, it's time you learned the truth. Your father, Einar Ten-Trees, did lose your mother, though not in the way you might have thought."

Torin looked over at Signy. Her steel grey eyes were set on him, her voice like an iron blade against a whetstone. He instinctively pulled his head back a little, so fierce was her look, and his eyes widened.

"Torin, tomorrow Gavring will offer you a place among the Greycloaks, I know it. Then you'll have to decide whether to stay or to leave. I'm sorry you've had to wait so long to know the truth. Your mother did not die. She is alive." Signy took a deep breath and exhaled slowly. "She is me."

Torin said nothing. He blinked and shook his head. Then he stared blankly into the face of the woman in whose hall he had feasted and mourned and sang. He forced a stilted chuckle and pulled his mouth into an awkward grin. "Keymaster Signy, are you drunk on your own stock? Or did you pick a patch of bad mushrooms?"

Then Signy's jaw clenched so tight it trembled and he could see that her hands, as they rested on her lap, had balled up into fists. Torin felt his heart beat faster as her manner betrayed neither deceit nor humour. He suddenly felt an urge to dash away but his eyes were fixed upon the old woman in front of him.

"You can't be telling the truth."

She nodded; her eyes still set firmly on Torin as a single tear slid down her wrinkled cheek.

"It can't be. Not after all this time."

Signy's gaze did not flinch. "It's true."

When Torin stood she grasped his arm. He jerked it out of her grip and took a step back. Signy did not rise from where she sat but instead took another deep breath and tried to let down her shoulders.

"You can leave," she said, "If you like. But you have questions and I have answers. You can choose to believe me or not, but you won't get the truth from anyone else in Gatewatch."

Torin took a few more steps toward the door. A rage-like fire seared the inside of his chest and he desperately wanted to break something. Then he felt a tug within himself, small at first, but persistent, which urged him to turn around and hear what the old woman had to say.

He flexed his jaw as he slowly turned to face her. "Alright then. I'll play along. Though I must say that if this is a joke, it is a savage one."

"What do you want to know?"

Her question put him off balance. After a lifetime without a mother, he had a mountain of questions that had long been festering in his chest. Torin cleared his throat and shrugged. "Well, if you're my mother, then why didn't my father say something?"

"Before you were born, we agreed that, should I bear a son, you would be raised as a Ten-Trees and remain so until you had come of age. If you had been a girl, you would have grown up under the rafters of Fjellhall as the heir to this key." She fingered the ornate silver key that hung off her belt. "We were young then and thought it best that you find out once you were free to decide your own fate. Now your oath to The Gatewatch is fulfilled and you can make your own choice whether or not to stay."

"All my life I've lived without a mother! I thought she had died. All my life my father lived alone and refused to marry." Torin shook his head. "Why wouldn't you live your life together?"

Signy nodded, a distant look in her steel-grey eyes. "It could never be. I was to inherit the key to Fjellhall from my mother and he was to take his father's seat in Ten-Tree Hall. Though he loved me, and I loved him, our paths had already been chosen for us."

Torin's heart was caught between anger and relief. He threw up his hands and then buried them in his hair. "How? How could I have grown up never knowing this?"

"Torin, please, sit down," said Signy.

In truth, Torin wanted nothing more than to storm out of Fjellhall, but his curiosity was too ravenous. The questions that had swirled in his head all his life as he lay awake at night might finally be answered. He leaned back against the wooden bench with his arms crossed tightly over his chest.

Signy sighed, the tight coil of tension in her sturdy frame unwinding just a little. "I can still remember the day your father first entered this hall. By the gods, he was such a mess that day, his hair in tangles and his shirt all muddied. But he was handsome, yes he was." Signy smiled and closed her eyes then shook her head. "We were young then, so young, and I had not yet been given charge of this place. We treasured every moment we had together over the two years he was sworn to serve King Araldof Greyraven here as a trollhunter."

Signy's eyes fell and her brow tensed. "Summer had just passed when I told your father I was carrying his child. I tried to convince Einar to steal away with me at night, but that was not his way. He confronted my mother about our child and my leaving. She was furious. My mother refused to release me from my inheritance and promised a dreadful curse upon us if he should take me from Gatewatch."

Signy's eyes dropped and her wrinkled forehead softened as the memories flowed. "That same summer news reached him that his brother was attempting to usurp his seat in Ten-Tree Hall. He refused to let that happen. I could not go, and he could not stay. He left Gatewatch the next day wrapped up in a whirling storm of anger. I haven't seen him since."

Signy raised her eyes to Torin and winced. "See, you were born in secret during a particularly bleak winter. Though it tore the very sinews of my heart, I had sworn an oath to Einar that our child, should it be a son, would grow up under the roof of Ten-Tree Hall rather than here in Gatewatch. All through those long nights and well into spring I nursed you here, under the rafters of Fjellhall. By the end of that summer, you were weaned and your father's most trusted men, the same ones who had been troll hunters with him here in Gatewatch, came to take you back to Ten-Tree Hall." She paused and drew in a shaky breath. "I can still remember the day they took you away from me. I watched from the top of the East Gate tower as they galloped away up the road to Shadowstone Pass on horseback with you tucked into the saddle. I sat up there in the gatehouse and cried all the rest of that day."

Signy's face hardened and she pursed her lips tight. "After that I refused to speak to anyone. I wandered through the fields east of Gatewatch and cared nothing for myself. I often slept in the grass under the stars or took shelter beneath the stony outcrops along the mountain ridges when it rained. No one could console me or quell my grief. In the fall there came a terrible early snowstorm.

I found my way back to the East Gate, but the wind howled so loudly, and the snow fell so hard that I could not hail the watchman. The next morning, they found me nearly frozen to death outside the city gate."

Torin's eyes were wide, and his throat knotted up tight. The story of his life, like a spool of yarn unspun before him, began to fill some void in his chest that he had barely known was there. Yet the filling of that space seared like fire, like a red-hot iron that cleanses a festering wound.

"They carried me here, back to Fjellhall. My mother used all the knowledge she had of herblore and healing runes to bring me back to health. Though I did not have the strength to wander the fields any longer, I still spoke to no one."

Signy looked up at Torin. "My path took a strange turn then. A Greycloak by the name of Torvid lost his wife that winter during the birth of their twins. The two children were named Signa and Siggam. After I had recovered from the storm, Torvid was attacked by a troll in the wilds and torn to pieces by the beast."

"When news of this reached Gatewatch my mother brought the orphaned twins here and laid them down beside me in the night. When I woke up and saw them, I spoke for the first time in months. I asked her who they were and why they were here. She told me they had been orphaned and I declared right then that I would adopt them."

Torin thought about the day his own father adopted Grimsa as a foster son, and then of how he had adopted Bryn too, a year later. Had he, like Signy, adopted them to fulfill his empty dreams of children that would never be, brothers for Torin that Signy could have borne? Yet fosterage in Noros happened only after twelve winters had passed and the child had come to know their birth family. Signa and Siggam would have only ever known Signy as their mother. Did they know, Torin wondered, that they were adopted, or had they grown up in blissful ignorance?

Signy continued her story before Torin could ask. "From that day on, though my heart still burned with the loss of you, I had them. I often wondered if I needed them more than they needed me. They were young, not even a year, and had no memory of the loss of their parents. Caring for them helped me to find myself again, to find a new purpose. As I watched them grow, I thought about you often. So many times, I wondered how you talked or how you looked when you smiled."

Signy sat back against the bench and let her gaze fall upon the fire. "And so, the oath that your father and I swore to each other is fulfilled. You have come of age and now you know." A moment later she looked into his eyes and stretched her hand out toward his. He pulled away.

"I'm sorry, Torin. I am so sorry. You should never have grown up without a mother."

Torin said nothing but stood up and stormed out of Fjellhall into the shadowed streets.

2

◊ THE DELEGATION ◊

TORIN WOKE UP in a stack of hay piled outside East Gate. The sun was already high in the sky and its bright rays amplified the throbbing headache that threatened to split his skull right in half. His throat was parched and as he stood his knees shook terribly. However, Torin managed to stumble over to a creek a little way from the road. He dropped down to his chest and lapped up the icy water. After slaking his thirst, his headache began to fade, and his limbs stopped shaking.

With the sun overhead Torin knew it was late in the morning. The mountain air was crisp and the towering ridges on either side of the valley stood sharp against the pale blue sky. Spring had warmed the ground and the songs of many birds came in chorus from all around the valley. Beside the trickling creek, no longer frozen by winter's frigid breath, wildflowers peeped out between lush green grasses with dewy faces of red and blue, of purple and yellow, of orange and white. As he rolled onto his back, Torin could feel dampness through his shirt. For a while he did nothing but smile as he took in the sights, the sounds, and the scents of spring.

The events of the previous night returned to him slowly. There was Grimsa in Fjellhall and there was the ring on Signa's finger.

Bari had been with him at the Spring Festival, and they both drank far too much. Then Wyla found them, and they drank even more. Where had he gone after that and how had he ended up outside the East Gate? He frowned a moment more before it came to him all at once: Signy's confession.

A twinge of nausea gripped his stomach and his chest cramped up tight so that he had to gulp down air in gasps. Something within him had rejected the notion that his mother could still be alive, still more that she had willingly let him go to live away from her in secret. Yet there was also the possibility of knowing, after all these years, the mother he thought was lost forever to the shadowy halls of the dead.

Torin's mind was still racing when he heard the sound of voices and the slow clop of horse hooves coming from up the valley. Springtime in Gatewatch was usually the time of year for departures, not arrivals. At first Torin thought he should greet them but then realized he was in a miserable state, damp with dew and mired in mud. Instead, he ducked down behind a rise of turf and watched them approach.

Half a dozen figures rode down the trail of packed earth on horseback with about twice that number following behind them on foot. As they approached, Torin realized that many were not from Noros. He thought they must be foreigners of some kind, such as he had seen in his father's hall on rare occasions. Few people travelled to Noros from abroad and those that did would not dare trek all the way to Gatewatch. He had heard no murmurs of foreign business or of a visit. An odd feeling stirred in his stomach, a mix of excitement and suspicion at such an unexpected arrival.

As the company drew closer Torin saw that they were led by a Norosi man, who was mounted and clothed in rich furs. Two foreigners of spectacular appearance followed him on horseback. One was a young man, perhaps Torin's age, clothed in fine crimson fabric underneath a carved chest plate that glinted like gold. The second, thin and gaunt in the face, looked stranger still. He carried a polished wooden staff in one hand and wore a robe of black and red cloth with glittering stones sewn into the hem. A few of those that followed were Norosi, but most seemed strange and foreign in appearance.

Torin heard them speak as they drew closer to the East Gate. To his ears the language sounded smooth like swirling cream. It lacked the harsh percussive consonants of his own tongue and instead flowed out of their mouths in a stream of fluid vowels. They also spoke from their noses instead of deep in their throat as people did in Noros. This gave their speech a nasal quality which made Torin grin. But soon they were so close that he thought they might spot him, so Torin dropped down from his elbows and laid flat on his stomach.

Soon the foreign company stood at the East Gate. Through blades of tall grass Torin saw a wide smile on the face of the young man in the golden armour. A look of disgust crossed over the older foreigner's face as he inspected the rugged walls of Gatewatch and its crude watchtower.

The Norosi man on horseback called out. "Hail, Watchman! I am Jarl Bor, Lord of Valehold in Stagwood Forest. I have with me a delegation from a faraway land."

The Greycloak atop the gate peered out from her tower and inspected the foreign company with wide eyes. "We have not been told of a delegation."

Jarl Bor lifted a fine metal chain which hung around his neck. From it dangled a silver ring inset with enormous rubies that sparkled in the late morning light. "Around my neck I have the signet ring of King Araldof Greyraven himself. It is by the order of his closest advisors, the elders of the Grey Council, that I have led this delegation here from the king's hall in Ravensnest. Our business is of the most urgent nature! Now open the gate, then send for food and drink! We have travelled a great distance in little time."

The Greycloak paused a moment more before she disappeared behind the wall. The figure robed in red and black made a comment in his own tongue that Torin could not understand, but he could see it made many of the speaker's foot-weary countrymen chuckle. The mounted man in the carved armour was not one of those who laughed at the remark; he frowned at his companion and shook his head. Then the gate winch creaked and squealed as the iron-bound timbers inched upwards.

While the delegation passed under the stone archway into Gatewatch, Torin recalled something his father had told him long ago, tales of a distant country called Armeah. It was a fair land, or so he had heard, so green and lush that the hand of winter hardly touched it. There were fields, bogs, and rolling hills, but no majestic mountains like those around Gatewatch. His father had spoken of white sands and beaches with blue waves that stretched on as far as one could see.

A merchant who once visited Ten-Tree Hall said that the Armheans were great lovers of horses, jewelry, and wine. He claimed that King Araldof Greyraven's ready supply of rare stones, secured through bustling trade with the *nidavel*, had enticed many Norosi captains to brave the journey to Armeah in the last few years. Still, Torin thought it was strange that they should come all the way to Gatewatch. And he doubted that good news would have brought them all so far.

The creak and groan of the gate winch began again as the heavy timbers were eased down. Torin ran up to the wall and slipped under the door just before it closed. The Greycloak who stood in the tower, still staring up the street at the foreign company, did not seem to notice him dash around the corner and along a crooked alley.

The streets were quiet. Torin suspected that most of the towns-folk were still sleeping off the indulgences of the previous night. This silence stretched so far that when Torin arrived at the barracks on the north side of town he could hear Jarl Bor announce himself and his company in front of Fjellhall. Their arrival would cause quite a stir once the rest of Gatewatch woke up, he thought. Though Torin was eager to meet these strangers, he could not present himself in his current state. He gripped the latch of the heavy barracks door and gave it a well-practiced shove to open it as quietly as he could, careful not to let the rusted hinges creak.

Either Grimsa had already left the barracks, or he never returned to it after last night's festivities. The furs strewn across the great man's bed were no more messy than usual and did not show any signs of recent disturbance. Against the opposite wall was Torin's bed, still tidy with the furs tied up in rolls by leather straps near the foot of the wooden bedframe. Throughout the rest of the long stone room, which tunneled deep into the mountain, recruits lay snoring, each sprawled out either over or under their wool blankets and furs. Torin pulled out a clean cloak and tunic from under his bed, tucked them under his arm, and left those asleep to their dreams.

In his two years as a troll hunter, Torin had explored nearly every side alley in Gatewatch, so he knew a shortcut to almost any place he wished to go. Across town, carved into the sheer rock face that marked its southern edge, lay the entrance to an under-ground hot spring which served as the local mineral baths. After a night spent under the stars, he desperately needed a wash. With well-practiced steps he wove his way through town until he stood at the entrance of the steaming spring.

The steps in the tunnel were damp and covered in moss. Torin took his time, careful not to slip on the uneven stairs that led down the passageway. The walls were lined with patches of crusty lichens, both orange and yellow, that clung to the rough rock.

At last, after one hundred steps or so, the tunnel opened into a wide cavern that reached even higher than the rafters of Fjell-hall. The room would have been completely dark except for the tiny luminescent mushrooms that ringed the edge of the bubbling pool, their glow a soft eerie blue. Crystal-white deposits from the mineral spring had left a layer of silt, smooth as polished marble, around the pool and along its floor which stretched into the dim recesses of the cavern.

"Torin! Come join us!"

Torin turned toward the familiar voice. As his eyes adjusted, he saw Bari and Wyla neck-deep in the water near the edge of the bubbling pool. Torin laid down his clean clothes, threw off his mud-stained tunic, and slipped into the hot spring.

Bari waved as Torin waded over. "There you are! After you left to find Keymaster Signy last night, no one could find you."

Torin pushed the conversation with Signy from his mind. "I'm not sure where I got to. Perhaps they are making the home-brews a little stronger these days? Anyways, I woke up outside the East Gate this morning."

Bari's dark eyebrows shot up and he chuckled. "Oh? I didn't sample anything that strong last night. How did I miss it and where can I get some?"

"I figured you had already left for Ten-Tree Hall," said Wyla. "You're quite eager to leave us all behind, aren't you?"

Torin shook his head and sighed. "I wish I could stay."

"Then stay."

"I can't."

"Why not?"

Torin shrugged. "Duty, I guess."

"To who? Your father? You didn't choose to be his son. You've paid your debt to the Greyraven and now you're a free man. You can do what you want to. Duty doesn't make decisions, people do."

Torin felt this conversation sliding toward the same inevitable end it always had. Already he saw Wyla's blood beginning to boil as her face reddened, her brow creasing tighter and tighter.

Torin pushed out into deeper water and sank down to his ears. "You know, if you are going to miss me so much, you could just come with me to Ten-Tree Hall."

Wyla raised one eyebrow. "To Ten-Tree Hall? As what, a retainer? There'd be no one living in those soft green hills worthy of even sparring with me, much less to put up a fight. I would get bored. So will you."

Torin scratched his beard, a small grin tugging at the edge of his mouth. "Actually, I was thinking you would make an excellent cup bearer."

Wyla's eyes shot open and, though she tried to feign offence, she couldn't hold back a smile. With a swing of her arm, she soaked Torin in a wave of steaming water. "Damn you, Torin Ten-Trees. I'd sooner be lobbing a goblet at your head than serving you wine."

Torin sputtered as the water ran over his head and trickled down his face. "Point taken."

Wyla sat back in the water and shook her head. "Well, let's hear more from you, Bari. It's not every day a foreigner comes to Gatewatch."

Torin nodded as he wiped the water from his eyes. "True enough! But Bari won't be the only foreigner in town tonight."

Bari tilted his head to the side and frowned. "Other *nidavel*? I didn't hear of any other party from Myrkheim travelling to Gatewatch."

"No," Torin said. "By their appearance and their speech, I'd bet my best silver they were from Armeah."

Wyla's eyes widened, and she leaned in toward Torin. "Armeah? By the gods, where is that?"

Torin waved his hands as if he were drawing a map in the air. "Noros is here, north and far to the east. If you sail south and west, past the Shrieking Cliffs and through the Grim Isles, and then keep to the coast eventually you will find that land they call Armeah."

Wyla frowned. "How do you know of it? I have never heard of such a place."

"My father hosts travelers of every description in Ten-Tree Hall. I remember once, when I was a young boy, a trader came from Armeah. His speech was smooth, and his clothing was strange to me. As I hid in the grass and watched these foreigners approach this morning, they reminded me of that trader."

Wyla's eyes opened wider with every word of Torin's description. "This is the first I've heard of foreigners travelling to Gate-watch and I've lived here my whole life. What business could they possibly have here?"

Torin shrugged. "Well, I doubt they are here for the Cloaking Ceremony this afternoon. A Norosi man named Jarl Bor led announced their arrival at the East Gate. He claimed to have been sent by Araldof Greyraven on very grave business."

"Do you think it's true?"

"He had Araldof Greyraven's signet ring on a chain around his neck."

Wyla jumped up and started back toward the edge of the pool. "By the gods! Then what are we waiting for?"

Torin and Bari chased after her and scrambled to pull on fresh clothes. They wasted no time hurrying up the stairs out of the baths, down the street, and round to Fjellhall.

Several townsfolk were already gathered around the entrance to Fjellhall when they arrived. Torin thought of Signy again and what he might say to her. Before he could protest, Wyla grabbed his arm and pushed her way through the crowd, bringing him with her. She shoved the heavy oak door open and slipped inside as Bari followed close behind her. A warm breeze rushed out of the hall and carried with it the scent of roasted meat, rising bread, and bubbling vegetable stew. Torin closed his eyes a moment, took a deep breath, and stepped inside.

In all the time Torin had spent in Fjellhall over the past two years, he had never seen it in such a state. Hall hands raced back and forth between the tables and the kitchen with silver platters, iron goblets, and carved-bone cutlery. Celebratory banners hung from the walls, all made of fine silk in gold and green and silver. Table runners of spruce-green cloth ran down each table, each inlaid with knotted patterns of silver thread. Torin also noticed that, in addition to the half dozen beer casks stacked near the back of the hall, a wine barrel had been rolled out from the cellar.

Amid the bustling crowd of hall hands, he nearly overlooked the foreigners at the far end of one of the long wooden tables. Captain Gavring was there with a cup of wine in hand along with a few other Greycloaks as he spoke to Jarl Bor and the young man in gilded armour. There was also the thin, aged figure in the robe of red and black; he was completely bald, and his beard tumbled over his chest in curls of wispy white hair. Torin thought that the slumped shoulders of the old man made him look like a grumpy old crow perched upon the bench.

The rest of the foreign company had their eyes fixed on Captain Gavring as he spoke. Though it did not seem that most of them understood his speech, the gigantic red-haired man towering over them certainly had their full attention. Some of those closer to Gavring leaned back ever so slightly at every boisterous wave of his arms, both of which were as thick as tree trunks. Then the young man in the gilded armour started laughing while the others simply nodded with small, nervous smiles. The old man in the dark robe rolled his eyes and sneered.

Wyla grabbed one of the hall hands by the arm as he passed by. "Fetch me a cup of wine, friend." She motioned toward Torin and Bari. "Then bring two more for them." The hall hand nodded quickly. Wyla let go of his arm and he hurried off.

Gavring saw the three of them and waved with his huge freck-led, calloused hands. "Ah, here they are. Come! Sit with us."

Then Torin saw the foreigners up close. The younger man with the scarlet robe and the gilded armour met Torin's gaze with sharp green eyes. His proud cheeks hovered high over his angled jawline which drew together to a neat point at the end of his chin. Above his brow there fell curls of thick black hair which spilled down over his head and onto his shoulders. His cheeks were speckled with dark stubble, a few days' growth at most. Most striking was the stranger's expression, which seemed to rest in a kind of smirk that Torin found both disarming and unnerving.

Gavring chuckled. "Come, all of you, join us. These guests are a special delegation sent by King Araldof Greyraven himself."

Wine in hand, Torin, Wyla, and Bari sat down beside Gavring and opposite the foreign company. Then the old Norosi man that Torin had seen at the East Gate stood up and addressed them. "I am Jarl Bor, son of Gjoll and Lord of Valehold in Stagwood Forest. This foreign delegation has journeyed far in response to the Grey Council's call for aid, all the way from the land of Armeah. By the order of the King's closest advisors, I have escorted them from the Grey Tower in Ravensnest to Gatewatch with all haste."

A translator whispered to the Armeahan company, his speech a strange light echo to the heavy Norosi words. Jarl Bor lowered his head and his tone became gruff. "The king is deathly ill and no remedy within the realm of Noros has cured him. Believe me, he has endured them all."

Wyla nearly spilled her wine. "The Greyraven? By the gods! What sort of illness?"

Jarl Bor grimaced. "No one can say for sure, but it is a disease of the mind. He raves and screams like a madman one day, then lays motionless the next. Some days he is of full mind and on others even the members of the Grey Council are strangers to him."

Bor cut his description of the king's illness short as the young Armeahan in gilded armour shifted impatiently. "But first, of course, I must introduce the members of this delegation, which was sent by King Ghezelweir of Armeah to aid us in finding a cure. This is Prince Azalweir, the third child of King Ghezelweir and the swiftest rider on horseback to be found in all Armeah. And beside him is Lorekeeper Aldrin, a man of great knowledge who knows much magic. He is a keeper of history, a translator of tongues, and a healer by trade." Both Azalweir and Aldrin nodded in greeting.

Gavring cleared his throat and opened his hand toward Torin, Wyla, and Bari. "Let me also introduce two of our finest young troll hunters: Wyla White-Blaze and Torin Ten-Trees." Prince Azalweir's eyebrows shot up at the sound of their names as if he recognized them. Gavring paused awkwardly for a moment as he motioned toward Bari. "And this is Bari the *nidavel*. He is, um, a cousin to someone or other."

As Gavring's words trailed off into a mumble, Bari cut in. "I am Bari Wordsmith, nephew to Brok the Silversmith who is, in turn, cousin to Mastersmith Ognir. I have come from Myrkheim, the city of the Mastersmith himself. I bring greetings to both of you on his behalf." Then it was Aldrin's eyebrows that rose sharply at the mention of Myrkheim, the *nidavellish* city.

Azalweir spoke their language, but with a smooth accent which softened the harsher syllables. "Torin of the Ten Trees and Wyla Bane of Wights? I've heard many tales about you two. You are lovers, are you not?"

Both flushed flame red in their cheeks and Wyla nearly spit out her wine. "By the gods, no. Where did you hear that?"

Azalweir laughed, a glint of mischief in his eyes. "I meant no offense! In all the tales we hear of you there is a great romance. The passion with which you kiss after the Troll-King is slayed is so vividly described, I thought it must be true."

"Tales?"

Azalweir shook his head, his mouth hung open in surprise. "Well, of course! Many stories have been told in Armeah of your adventures, both in the busy markets and in royal castles. I thought they were all made up by travelling bards, but here you two are."

Wyla narrowed her eyes. "Well, the only bit that you've recalled so far is, in fact, made up."

"What about the riddles? The underground tunnels and the magic apple?"

Aldrin placed his hand on the prince's shoulder. "Prince Azalweir, enough nonsense. Troll stories can wait. We have business to attend to." Torin was surprised to hear the Lorekeeper speak Norosi so fluently with such perfect pronunciation.

Azalweir sighed and shrugged. He raised his glass toward Torin and Wyla. "Later you must tell me the whole tale exactly as it happened. I've always dreamed of travelling to Gatewatch to meet real troll hunters, so I won't squander this chance."

Jarl Bor nodded. "I'm sure there will be plenty of time for telling troll stories over a horn of mead. But first we must speak of our errand."

Aldrin's sunken eyes stretched wide with disbelief. "A mere errand, Jarl Bor? That makes it sound like a trifle. Our purpose and destination are far more serious than that. It is a task, a quest, to be undertaken by none but the staunchest of souls."

Jarl Bor shifted in his seat. "Call it what you like, Lorekeeper."

Aldrin glared at Jarl Bor for another moment before Azalweir broke the silence with an easy laugh. "Jarl Bor, forgive my mentor. He is a bit brash and rather particular in most everything. I know that I have never met his expectations in any subject of study."

Aldrin shook a finger at the prince. "Of course! Because one must be particular in the field of history and in magic. Failure to do so can have terrible consequences." Torin did not like the way Aldrin said the word 'terrible'; there was almost a hint of glee in it.

"And you, my dear prince," said Aldrin, "while quite peculiar, are the least particular person I know!"

The Lorekeeper saw that he had everyone's full attention. "Well, now that you are all listening, I will relate the task before us. I have evaluated King Araldof Greyraven's sickness and found it to be severe. It seems to me to have aspects of dark magics, perhaps from some source here in the north, to which my skills are unaccustomed and unattuned. Therefore, no botanist's concoction or herbalist's tonic will heal him. Bleeding will only weaken him further. Charms and talismans have proven far too weak to affect a disease of this severity. I fear that our only hope to save your celebrated king is a desperate one."

"Remember, Lorekeeper Aldrin, that we here in Gatewatch hunt trolls for a living," said Gavring. He motioned toward Torin and Wyla. "You are sitting at the same table as a woman who brought down an entire horde of trolls with a single Sunblaze arrow and a man who cut the head off a giant. We do not shy away from such tasks. Tell us what must be done to save the Greyraven, and we will do it."

Aldrin narrowed his eyes. "Be careful, Captain, not to underestimate the challenge before us."

Azalweir groaned. "Enough theatrics. Come on, Aldrin, tell them already."

Aldrin shot a glare at the prince then continued. "The only hope, as I see it, for the Greyraven to recover from this terrible malady is to drink a draught from the Everspring."

The tension around the table snapped like an anvil hung on twine and the entire table burst into uproarious laughter. Gavring's shoulders shook like a rumbling earthquake and Wyla nearly doubled over as she wiped a tear from her eye.

"Really," Wyla said, "is that what you came all this way for? A fairytale?"

Jarl Bor slammed his first down on the table. "Silence!" The others fell quiet even before the echoing boom of his voice faded into the upper reaches of Fjellhall. "I may not always get on well with this bookish scholar, but unless anyone else knows of a remedy to cure Araldof Greyraven, we must try what he says. Honour compels us to pursue every possibility. Remember also that the Grey Council has sent us here. If anyone considers themselves wiser than the closest advisors of King Araldof Greyraven, let them speak!"

No one did.

Aldrin's face tightened; bitterness drawn across his lips. "Many years I have spent learning what I could of both lore and history. I am convinced, from what I've seen so far, that there are more books in my personal library than in all of this frigid wilderness you call a kingdom. Know that I share my knowledge at the request of my king, the great and mighty Lord Ghezelweir. It is for his sake alone that I have suffered the misery of this journey!"

Those who sat around the table stifled chuckles and fought to straighten their faces. Aldrin adjusted the collar of his robe then continued. "As I said before, a draught from the Everspring is the only thing, rumoured or known, that might have the power to undo whatever evil has taken hold of the Greyraven. Ancient texts speak of men who travelled far to trade with the *jotur*, those ancient immortal giants of the frigid north. They spoke of an immense power at the source of all the world's rivers: the Everspring. Some accounts claim that all diseases could be cured by it, that aging could be stopped or even reversed by it, and that even the most grievous wounds could be closed up if soaked in its waters."

"Of course, we've all heard of the Everspring in tales," said Captain Gavring. "But does it actually exist?"

Aldrin grinned and nodded. "I also had my doubts. At least, until I received a visit from a stranger." The room, already quiet, grew quieter still, as if the walls themselves were leaning in to hear the Lorekeeper's words.

"This all happened about two years ago. I was working late at night in my study, one of the many side rooms in the royal palace of Armeah. I heard the shuffle of feet behind me and, having thought that I was alone, I turned to see who was there. Before I could draw a weapon or utter a curse, I saw the shape of a man standing not five paces away. He was a strange figure, towering tall with a long grey beard, but in a hooded cloak so that I could not see his face. Despite his apparent age, he stood at nearly twice my height and did not slouch or stoop. He spoke to me in a low, rumbling voice, not in Armeahan but in Norosi. As the figure drew back his hood I nearly fainted. It was Araldof Greyraven himself."

All the smirks and grins had been wiped clear of the faces that surrounded the table; now only blank, awed expressions remained. The wizened scholar peeled his lips back into a smile. "So, there I was, with King Araldof Greyraven of Noros standing before me. He said he had a gift for me. What gift, I asked, would he have travelled so far to grant a humble scholar. He handed me a leather hide wrapped in wool thread. I brushed aside the old manuscripts I had been studying and unrolled it across my desk. It was a map sketched out in blue ink on a canvas hide. He suggested, indirectly, that I might need it someday, then turned and disappeared as abruptly as he had come. Of course, I thought this was at the request of King Ghezelweir. It was not. I later discovered that no one else had seen the Greyraven come or leave. If not for the map, King Ghezelweir would have thought I had lost my mind."

Gavring frowned, a streak of doubt smeared across his face. "How did you know it was him?"

"I never forget a face," Aldrin said. "Especially that face. Years ago, when Araldof Greyraven first travelled to Armeah to make peace with Ghezelweir's father, Kzalweir, I saw him. Indeed, when

Ghezelweir was just a boy we listened to the Greyraven tell of his
newly forged alliance with the *nidavel*. Oh, the jewels he had to
display! The King of Armeah still speaks of the Greyraven's visit
with wonder."

Torin recalled the first and only time he had seen King Araldof
Greyraven. Of course, Torin had been a child then, no more than
ten winters old. The King of Noros had galloped up to Ten-Tree
Hall on a dark steed with a silver-mane under a clear blue sky after
a fresh snowfall. Torin's memory of the Greyraven, broad-shoul-
dered and stern-faced, was still as crisp as the snow beneath the
horse's hooves that wintery day. Aldrin was right when he said
that the Greyraven's proud face was not easily forgotten.

Wyla leaned forward. "The map, did you bring it?"

Aldrin's teeth gleamed with a glint of orange in the blaze of
Fjellhall's hearth. "Of course, Wyla White-Blaze. That is exactly
why I have come. I must verify its accuracy."

Aldrin's bony hand slipped inside some secret pocket within
the folds of his cloak. The Lorekeeper pulled the map out slowly,
as if he were unsheathing an ancient weapon. The bundled hide
rolled open easily. The map itself was made of animal skin, thin
and well treated, and its features were drawn in strokes of brilliant
azure ink. Torin could not read the words around the map, but
he recognized the letters well enough; they were *nidavellish*. Bari
jumped up on the bench and leaned over the table. His mouth
moved silently as he read the swirling lines of text.

"So, Master Bari," said Aldrin, "It is most fortunate that I found
you among this rugged company. I have studied what *nidavellish* I
could from the scant collection in our library, but we need a native
speaker of the tongue to interpret the map."

Bari frowned. "The instructions and directions are all in
riddles."

Aldrin nodded. "I have translated the literal meaning of every
phrase and it is mostly nonsense without a wider understanding

of *nidavellish*." Bari continued to puzzle over the map and said nothing.

"However, there is one peculiar quality of this strange gift that I believe we might be able to discern. The clue is this. Please, Master Bari, forgive my pronunciation." Aldrin cleared his throat then spoke the words in *nidavellish*, followed by a translation into Norosi.

> *When red wolves lick the bloodless skin*
> *The flesh roots find which place they're in*

"What do you make of that, Master Bari?"

Bari stroked his beard. "The *red wolves* are no doubt flames of fire as that is a common comparison in the old *nidavellish* riddles. *Bloodless skin* usually refers to a cloak made of hide but this is a map and not a cloak. As for the nonsense about *flesh roots*, I've never heard anything of that sort."

Aldrin turned toward Torin. "What do you make of it, Torin Ten-Trees? You are famous for your mastery of riddles, are you not?"

Torin pondered the riddle a moment. "Well, if the *bloodless skin* is the map, then *red wolves licking bloodless skin* must mean that fire has some effect on it. And *flesh roots*? I suppose those are the roots of the body which are the feet. But how your feet can find the place they are already in, I'm not sure."

The Lorekeeper nodded. "That was my conclusion as well. It seemed unwise to test this theory until I had further affirmation of the verse's meaning. Now I suppose there is only one way to find out for sure."

Aldrin gathered up the map and walked over to the hearth. For a moment Torin's heart lurched in his chest as he thought the old man meant to toss it straight into the fire. Instead, he held it just close enough to let the flames sweep over the bottom. As he turned back to the table, he threw it down in front of the gathered company. "Look! What do you see?"

Torin's heart beat faster as the dim blue ink started to glow, not all over but in one particular spot, almost as if it were burning through. He recognized the place, a tiny dot just west of Shadowstone Pass. The letters around it flared up like blue flames except that no smoke or scent of fire rose from the hide.

In a loud voice, as if to conclude his case, Aldrin shouted to Bari. "Now tell us Master Bari, what do the flaming letters read?"

Bari looked up and swallowed. "Gatewatch."

3

◇ SILK & SKOG ◇

TORIN WATCHED THE FLICKERING BLUE LETTERS of heatless flame crackle and fade as if they had never been. He blinked and rubbed his eyes, almost unwilling to believe what he had just witnessed except that Wyla and Bari and all the others had seen it too. As he looked around the table, Torin saw the gaze of his companions darken while Aldrin's expression grew nearly giddy.

"Brilliant!" said Aldrin. "Just as I had hoped!"

Bari buried his fingers in his hair. "By the Mastersmith, where did you get such a thing?"

"I told you! From Araldof Greyraven himself."

"And where did he get it, I wonder?"

Jarl Bor grunted. "Isn't it obvious? The language is *nidavellish*."

Aldrin smirked and raised a bony finger. "No, Jarl Bor, in that you are incorrect. We may call it *nidavellish*, but it is in fact an ancient language that was once commonly spoken in many places. Until I encountered my first *nidavellish* text I considered it to be a dead language. Now only the *nidavel* continue to use it, as far as I know."

"How then, Lorekeeper," said Jarl Bor, "did those ancient people know to call this place by its current name, Gatewatch? Answer me that! And if you can't, then I think we can exclude them from the list. Besides, who other than the *nidavel* would have the magic to craft such a thing?"

Bari frowned. "We *nidavel* are skilled in metal-craft. Our smiths work with metal because it is strong enough to bear the enchantments and pliable enough to be shaped. Stone is too rigid to be properly honed. Wood is brittle and only good for scratching a few lucky runes or a petty curse. I have never seen such a deeply enchanted object forged by the Mastersmith or any other *nidavel* that was not made of metal. So no, I don't think this was made by *nidavellish* hands. Hide is too weak a material for our magic."

Aldrin stroked his beard. "Well then, if the hide is too weak for the magic of the *nidavel* then perhaps it is an enchantment of a more delicate sort. Who else in the realm of Noros might possess such skill?"

An ache started in Torin's head. His mind raced back to memories of Ur-Gezbrukter, the ancient *jotur* who had led a horde of trolls against Gatewatch two years prior. Ur-Gezbrukter had magic, dark and powerful. And then there were the old stories of other *jotur*, mighty frost giants, living far in the north.

Captain Gavring opened his mouth as if to speak, then closed it again. With a narrow gaze he eyed the enchanted map and tugged at his wiry red beard. After another moment of silence, he spoke in growling syllables. "I don't like this thing."

The others waited for him to expand on those blunt words, but the captain simply stood up and crossed his enormous arms. "The Cloaking Ceremony is in just a few hours. You are all welcome to attend, of course. We'll speak of this again later tonight." Without another word, he lumbered down the length of the hall and out Fjellhall's mighty doors.

Aldrin's face twitched with irritation as he watched the doors slam shut behind Captain Gavring. Jarl Bor looked haggard, the creases in his grey-crested forehead deep and tired. Wyla and Bari were still lost in their own thoughts about the enchanted map.

Azalweir leaned back on the bench and stretched his arms up over his head. Torin wondered whether the Armeahan prince was constantly smirking or if his lips simply had a natural curl. "Well, I guess that concludes business for today. So, onto the troll slaying stories?" Aldrin flashed a glare at the young prince like the glint of a knife blade, but Azalweir ignored it. "Servants! More wine. No, wait! Not wine." He leaned toward Torin and whispered loudly. "What do troll hunters drink?"

Torin chuckled. Perhaps he was going to get along with this prince after all, he thought. Just as he was about to say ale, Wyla cut in.

"*Skog,*" she said, "And lots of it."

Azalweir raised his finger high in the air. "*Skog* it is! A round for the whole table." The hall hands, who had forgotten their duties because of the enchanted map, stared at each other blankly. The prince raised an eyebrow then reached into his pocket and drew out a few gleaming gold coins. He held them up, his grin nearly as bright as the glimmer of the shining metal. "I am good for it."

Wyla clapped. "Come on! You heard him. A round for the whole table!"

Tensions dissolved as *skog* splashed into horns and goblets. Those gathered at the table broke into lively conversation over the enchanted map, each with their own idea of how the Greyraven had acquired it, who could have made it, and why such a treasure had come to Gatewatch of all places. Though Torin could not make out the flurry of Armeahan words spoken by the newcomers, he could see that some shook their heads with worry while others bounced with wide-eyed excitement.

A few of the older Greycloaks at the other end of the timber-board table whispered among themselves. Magic meant trouble as far as most who called Noros home were concerned. While petty charms and runes for luck were common among village folk and some were known to dabble in fortune telling, most of it amounted to little more than superstition. But Torin had seen real magic before, and he knew without a doubt that the magic of the Greyraven's map was very real.

At last, everyone had a hornful of bitter, pine-scented *skog*, all except for Aldrin who had gagged at the smell and called for more wine. While some of the Armeahans fell into coughing fits over their first sip, the Greycloaks at the end of the table waited to drink.

Azalweir looked at Torin and frowned. "Are you angry with me?"

"No," said Torin, "But we might be if we have to wait much longer. You purchased the round. We won't drink until you make the toast."

"Of course," said Azalweir. "Of course. By my father's royal scepter, I have always wanted to do this." He cleared his throat and stood up. "Long live The Gatewatch!"

A hearty roar came from the Greycloaks down the table followed by the sound of slurps as *skog* slipped down their throats. One of the Armeahans, startled by their sudden outburst, jumped up from his seat and nearly fell off the bench. The prince spoke to him in their smooth-syllabled language and his message seemed to reassure the pale man, though not entirely. With that, Azalweir took a full mouthful of *skog* from where he stood.

Azalweir's eyes stretched open, and he fought to swallow the fragrant liquid like a seabird wrestling a thrashing fish down its gullet. Nevertheless, he managed to swallow it down before he drew in a gasp of air. "By the king's sword! That is powerful stuff."

Wyla threw back another swig. "I'd say it has some rather delicate notes," she said.

Azalweir took another mouthful, a bit more cautious this time. His face twisted and contorted at the pungent mix of bitter herbs.

Torin laughed. "It's better in sips. You really get to savour the flavour that way."

"You think this is foul?" said Bari. "Then you've never tried to distill liquor from mushrooms. Imagine the taste when your starting ingredient is fungus!"

Azalweir forced a smile as Wyla toasted him again and drained her vessel. She wiped her lips on her sleeve. "Anyone else for a second?"

It seemed the Armeahans caught Wyla's meaning and passed the *skog* barrel down the bench to where she sat. The cork came loose with a resonant pop, and she refilled her horn. Then Wyla sat back and swirled the *skog* in her drinking vessel. Though the barrel was passed back down the table, no one else joined her in refilling their own cup.

Azalweir was able to sip his drink without sputtering or coughing once the shock of the first mouthful was over. The *skog* had drained the nervous energy from his shoulders. With a slight glaze over his eyes, he waved his hand toward Torin and Wyla. "So, tell me, how does one kill a troll?"

Torin tilted his head to the side and looked down at the *skog* in his ale-horn. "The *skalds* say it best."

> *One hundred ways there are to kill*
> *A troll if you but have the skill*
> *And yet a thousand ways to die*
> *For those who have a mind to try*

Silence fell over the company, particularly the Greycloaks at the end of the table. They were familiar enough with the one hundred ways and all too aware of the thousand. Azalweir nodded and mouthed the words as if committing them to memory.

Wyla narrowed her gaze. "Have you ever seen a troll, Prince Azalweir?"

"Please, just call me Azal," said the prince, "I insist."

The old Lorekeeper rolled his eyes, then turned away to study the map.

"Well then, Azal," said Wyla. "Have you ever seen a troll?"

Azal shook his head. "We have no such things in Armeah. Wild cats are the most dangerous things to contend with there."

Torin nodded with a stern look in his eye. "Then you should count yourself lucky. Trolls are the most foul, wicked, and deadly creatures you'll ever meet."

"I've seen grown men stomped flat like toadstools," Wyla said, "And strong women snapped in two like kindling. I've seen bones piled up high outside the cracks and crevasses they call home. I've even witnessed a *trollting* where they flailed their bodies this way and that in some sort of gruesome dance around a roaring fire. Their garbled laughter was like a landslide of loose gravel and slime-ridden mud." Wyla shook her head and shivered. "I'll never forget the sound or the sight."

Azal wobbled as he nodded, no doubt an effect of the *skog*. "I've heard such stories. Terrible. But tell me, what do they look like? And how do you slay them?"

"That's just it," said Torin. "Trolls are nearly impossible to spot. Some have skin like the rugged bark of an oak tree, some like slick grey mud from a bog, and still others have irregular scales shaped like crusted fungus. As if that wasn't bad enough, one can hardly tell the clumps of moss on their heads from their hair."

"So how do you know it's a troll and not just a tree stump or mound of dirt?"

Wyla shrugged. "Easy. Tree stumps don't try to tear your arm out of its socket and eat it."

A voice called out from the other side of the hall in a low baritone boom. "And you can smell them!" Torin turned toward the sound to see that Grimsa had just stepped into Fjellhall.

"By the gods," said Torin, "How many times do we have to go over this? Trolls have no smell."

Grimsa waved his finger in the air as he walked toward them. "Maybe your nose is not as finely tuned as mine, but I can smell them from a great distance away."

Wyla picked up an empty goblet and tossed it at Grimsa. It hit him in the stomach with a thud then fell to the floor. "You're full of it, Grimsa," she said. "Come, sit with us! We are in the presence of royalty. This is Azal, prince of some far-off place."

Grimsa waved at the prince then knelt to pick up the cup at his feet. With a great grin on his face, he helped himself to a cup of *skog* and took particular care to fill it right to the brim. When he sat down the whole length of the timber bench creaked and groaned. The big man sniffed the strong spirits as if they were fresh-cut flowers then took a sip, smacked his lips, and sighed.

"You're just jealous," said Grimsa, "Of my keen senses."

Wyla smirked. "Keen is not a word I'd ever use to describe you."

Grimsa nodded at the prince. "See? Jealous."

Torin threw up his hands. "Then what do they smell like?"

Grimsa placed his goblet of *skog* down on the table and tugged at his great red beard. "Well, it's a rather peculiar smell."

"Like what?"

"Something like the smell of rotting fish, only the rotting fish have been eaten and excreted by a bear, then left to mold under a slimy rock." Grimsa took another sip and tilted his head to one side. "Or perhaps it is more like the smell of damp feet, but mixed with horse manure and rancid butter, then boiled up and distilled into a concentrated tonic." He thought for a moment more, then nodded. "Yes, that's it. Feet, manure, and rancid butter." Torin and Wyla shook their heads and Bari chuckled.

Azal looked a bit queasy. The prince pushed himself up off the bench with both arms and swayed from side to side as he steadied himself against the table. "I've had enough."

"Good," Aldrin said, "Trolls are an unseemly subject for a royal heir to the throne of Armeah anyway."

A flash of anger flickered in Azal's eyes. "No, not enough of the stories. Enough of this." He stretched his arms out and waved them up and down.

Aldrin scoffed. "What? Enough *skog*? Yes, I'd say you had quite a bit more than enough."

Azal shook his finger in front of Aldrin's face. "Incorrect again, wise Aldrin." The prince started to pace back and forth. From Azal's manner and the way Aldrin rolled his eyes, it seemed to be the prince's regular habit. "I am tired of these pompous clothes. I am weary of regal titles and all the nauseating ceremonies that go along with them. I am sick to death of the frivolous drivel of court life, the whispers and rumours, the nonsense and gossip, the petty grievances and the endless boot-licking."

The room was silent now except for the translator who whispered to the other Armeahans. By the way Aldrin rubbed his wrinkled forehead, Torin guessed the old Lorekeeper must have heard this speech before. However, the prince was just warming up his tirade. "And so you've all heard me say on countless occasions. So, manners be damned! I am my own person now and we are no longer in Armeah. Hear this: I'll no longer live in the shadow of my sister or my brother or my father!"

"Prince Azalweir," said Aldrin, "An heir to the throne should be more careful in his speech. It's the drink, no doubt. I think you've had more than your fill for today."

"Oh, I have had my fill indeed! I've had my fill of confinement, of restriction, of my sister's sheltering. I can't take another regal celebration or royal reception. And by the king's sword, if another pandering courtier tries to win my favour through presents or poems or more expensive bloody clothes, I swear I'll clobber them."

As the translation of these words reached the other Armeahans, Torin noticed a few of them discreetly shuffle further down the table.

Aldrin rolled his eyes again. "Then what will you do, royal son, you who are so terribly oppressed?"

The prince stood frozen, his mouth open and ready to unleash a storm of angry words. Then, like a candle extinguished, the anger was gone from his face. The flame that flickered in his narrow eyes was one of resolute certainty and of wicked mischief. Azal's right hand went to the clasp that secured his golden breastplate to his flowing scarlet cloak. He fumbled a moment to undo the clasp then slipped out of the armour. With quick, clumsy movements he wrapped the well-formed chest plate in the scarlet fabric and then hoisted it up above his head. "This is what I will do: I will be rid of these royal vestiges. Look around you, Aldrin! This mighty hall is no place for flimsy golden armour or long-flowing scarlet capes. I refuse to be draped in wall hangings any longer!"

Aldrin's face went as purple as beet juice, and he sputtered. "By the king's royal scepter, Prince Azalweir son of Ghezelweir, that armour was crafted by the finest smiths in Armeah. Its weight in gold alone could feed a whole town for a year!"

Azal wound up, more than tipsy from the *skog*, and flung the chest plate wrapped in scarlet cloth down the table. It knocked half-full vessels of the foul drink into the laps of some of the Armeahans along the table who all shouted and gasped as it skidded to a stop.

"Let it be sold then! I'll not insult this mighty hall any further by wearing it. And these!" He pointed to his fine leather boots bound together with gold-plated clasps. "Ridiculous! They wouldn't last a day in the woods." He kicked them off with such scorn that Torin thought the prince had been aiming for the fire. Each boot tumbled away then fell alongside the stone hearth.

Aldrin shouted in harsh, choppy syllables. "That is enough, you damned drunken fool!"

Azal tottered to the side then righted himself. "No, I've just started. This silken shirt reeks of royalty." He nearly toppled over again as he tugged the shirt up over his shoulders and off past his head. The prince's hair was a tangled mess and fell too much to one side of his head. "And these fine-threaded socks do not suit one who would sit in the company of troll hunters."

"Are you blind to your own stupidity?"

"No! I now see clearer than ever!"

Azal looked up toward the ceiling as if he could see the gods themselves. His chest heaved, and he breathed as one might after at last dropping a great weight carried over a long distance. The last thing the prince was wearing was a set of red trousers made of the same fine silk as his discarded shirt. Without looking down, he gripped the belt, his knuckles tense and white.

Torin was so caught up in the prince's rant that had not noticed Wyla laughing beside him with tears in her eyes. Both Grimsa and Bari wheezed while the Greycloaks down the table cheered the drunken prince on.

Aldrin shook his head and waved his arms. "No, Prince Azalweir, no you must not!"

And yet the prince did. With a roar he tore his trousers straight down the leg seam, a shrieking rip that lasted a full two seconds. Torin, still shocked at the spectacle, had not looked away before he could be spared the sight: Azalweir standing stark naked in the middle of Fjellhall.

Not a sound was heard as the shredded silk cloth that had been the prince's trousers floated softly to the floor. The Armeahans looked on with horror while a few of the Greycloaks fought down snickers. As for the prince, he seemed both relieved and content to stand in the middle of the room with nothing but a cozy draft over his skin.

Azalweir nodded resolutely. "Well, that's done." He looked down a moment then pursed his lips tight. "Is there anyone here who might lend me a cloak that is more worthy of this place? Not silk or gilded cloth but some damn honest fur or leather?"

One of the Greycloaks down the table chuckled and picked up a fur cloak that had been left at the table. "Not that I mind the view, but you'll catch a chill if you're used to warmer weather." She tossed it toward the prince who snatched it in mid-air, though the weight of it threw him off balance. Torin thought he saw tears gathering in the corners of the prince's eyes.

"Thank you," Azal said. "I will never forget this day."

Torin shook his head and laughed. "Nor will we. Though we'll wish we could!"

Wyla raised her cup of *skog* toward the prince as he wrapped the cloak around himself. "You've all heard of Beoric the Bear. Well, here's a toast to Azal the Bare!"

The others shouted in chorus. "To Azal the Bare!"

Azal stayed with them all afternoon, wrapped only in his cloak, asking about trolls, and demanding another story at the end of every tale. Torin told of his *bardagi* with the Troll-King, that duel of riddles, and how they escaped by the slightest chance with the help of Bari and his uncle Brok. Bari spoke of the deep tunnels, of the monstrous *skrimsli*, and their meeting with Mastersmith Ognir. Azal's eyes opened widest as Bari described the treasures forged by the Mastersmith and how each one in their company received a gift.

Wyla recounted the Battle of Gatewatch in great detail, how the walls crumbled, and the towers fell. She told of how her own father stood against the Troll-King, how he fell trampled beneath the *jotur's* steed. Torin took over the telling with the chase as they galloped after the Troll-King to the top of Shadowstone Pass.

Azal shuddered as Torin described the swirling cloud that gathered over the Troll-King's dark incantations, how it seethed with black fog and cracks of lightning. He told of his tumble down the mountain and of the spearhead *Skrar*, or 'Screamer', which the *nidavel* had given him. With hushed words, he described their desperate plan to defeat the ancient *jotur*.

At last, when Torin told of the Sunblaze arrows, his throat tightened. He spoke of Bryn, his childhood friend, who was pierced by the Troll-King's sword right before his eyes. He fought down the pain of that loss and described the blood rage that took him at the sight of a blade through his friend's chest, how he stormed ahead at the *jotur* and was nearly struck dead himself.

Grimsa, as if he was reliving the moment, leapt up to his feet and showed how he hurled *Skrar*, the mighty spear, at the vile Troll-King. It struck true, straight into the giant's heart, he said. Then Grimsa told of how Torin thrust the giant's sword into the Troll-King's belly and how, just a moment later, he swung it round to slice the tyrant's head clean off. Azal stood up and clapped as Grimsa took a bow.

At the end of the tale Keymaster Signy appeared in the doorway to the kitchens. Torin's stomach lurched, and he fought the urge to flee the hall. Signy put on a hostess' smile and opened her arms. "My soon-to-be son in law is quite the teller of tales. Some of them are even true!"

Grimsa rushed over and embraced the old woman then escorted her to the table. "This, Prince Azal, is Keymaster Signy, keeper of the key of Fjellhall, master of brews, and mother to the most beautiful woman in all the world."

Signy patted Grimsa on the arm. "Thank you, Grimsa. We've already met."

Wyla rubbed her forehead as if a headache had suddenly struck her temples. "Grimsa, your love-sick babble nauseates me. Whatever happened to gruff old stone-headed Grimsa?"

"I'm pretty sure his head is still made of stone," Torin said. "But a stone head doesn't mean a stone heart."

Wyla rolled her eyes. "You know what I mean."

Grimsa smiled a wide, toothy grin. "Aha! You're jealous again."

"No," Wyla said, "You'll have no contest from me over Signa."

Grimsa chuckled, his shoulders rumbling in time with the noise. "Well, she does have a brother."

Bari extended a hand toward Azal. "And here is a handsome prince."

Wyla swung her legs over the bench and stood up. "Gods, you're all hopeless. I'm off to the Cloaking Ceremony."

Grimsa called after her, a gleeful ring in his voice. "Troll hunters have hearts too, you know."

Wyla flashed an obscene gesture at them with her hand then slipped out the front doors. The others shook their heads as the laughter died down.

Bari looked around the hall and suddenly noticed the empty benches. "It seems everyone else has already left. Perhaps we should head over to Stonering Keep as well?"

"By the gods, I'm nervous," said Grimsa. "I can feel my stomach turning like a waterwheel."

Bari winced. "It could be nerves. Or it could be that foul drink."

"*Skog*," said Grimsa, "Is a wonderful drink."

Azal tilted his head and squinted. "I'm afraid I find myself agreeing with Master Bari at the moment. Though I am determined to gain an appreciation for the stuff before I leave."

Aldrin took care to roll the map, then stood and straightened his robe. "I give up. If you want to dress up in animal skins and drag an axe along the ground behind you, what is it to me? Can anyone in Armeah say that I didn't try? At least I can console myself in knowing that I guided your sister and brother along the road to royalty."

Azal winked at Torin and Grimsa. The prince shucked the last of the *skog*, coughed a bit, then rose from the table and started marching toward the door. A few steps later he stopped and paused a moment before turning back toward the others. "Um, where exactly is this ceremony taking place?"

"Stonering Keep," Grimsa said. "Here, I'll lead the way." He reached for the nearly empty barrel of *skog* as he stood up. "But perhaps I should take one more sip before I go, to calm my nerves."

Keymaster Signy smiled, a proud glow in her cheeks. "Go with the prince, Grimsa. I'm sure that Captain Gavring has a grey cloak waiting for you. First, I need to speak with Torin. We'll follow you soon."

As the others left, Torin kept his eyes fixed on the grain lines of the wooden table. Keymaster Signy sat beside him for a while in silence.

"Is there something you meant to ask me?" said Torin. "The cloaking is just about to start."

"I have no questions for you, Torin," Signy said, "But do you have questions for me? I at least owe you any answers I can give."

"Questions? I don't even know if you're telling the truth."

Signy's unwavering gaze locked with Torin's. "I think you know I am."

Torin shook his head and turned away for a moment. Then he swung back around with narrowed eyes. "If it was true then why would you tell me now instead of two years ago when I first arrived?"

"Part of it was practical. I didn't want to distract you from your duty as a troll hunter."

"And the other part?"

"Personal." She swallowed hard and motioned toward Torin's face with her hand. "Your father and I made an oath to wait until the day you could decide for yourself where to go. I regret it now, but a sworn oath must be kept."

Torin felt the stone-hard rage in his chest soften a bit and he let his shoulders down. He clenched his jaw and crossed his arms. "So now I am to choose between Ten-Tree Hall and Fjellhall with little more than a few hours to decide."

"Listen to the voice inside you," Signy said. "It will take you on the right path."

"I'm going back to Ten-Tree Hall. My father needs me."

"I think your father would want you to decide for yourself."

"You're trying to convince me to stay."

"No, I am urging you not to make the same mistake he did." Signy cast her eyes down and shook her head. "The mistake we both made."

Torin lingered a moment longer then ran his fingers through his hair. "I have to go."

Signy nodded, a smile tugging at the corners of her mouth. "I know. I am proud of the man you've become, Torin." She reached out her arms and embraced him, lightly at first, then with the full strength of a northern woman. Some part of Torin wanted to return her embrace, but a larger part resisted.

Torin pulled away. The anger that had burned inside him was now like melted wax, soft but still too hot to touch. He turned toward the oak doors without a word and did not look back.

4

◇ THE GREYRAVEN'S RING ◇

ALL THE FESTIVE BOOTHS and ale-wagons had been cleared from Stonering Keep to make way for the Cloaking Ceremony. Around the inner wall of the keep, between each decorative banner, hung braided evergreen boughs and wreaths of holly. The sky overhead was filled with swirls of grey cloud that had yet to decide whether to blow over or to spit down drizzle.

Torin weaved through the crowd of roving children, boisterous townsfolk, and anxious recruits. Along the top of the wall, the Greycloaks, those grizzled veterans of The Gatewatch, had already started gathering. Just below them, near the front of the assembly, Torin saw a low wooden barricade. It was roughly made and flimsy, not for keeping onlookers out, but meant to be lit with fire during the ceremony. Recruits who were offered a cloak would have to leap over the flame and scale the wall up to the other Greycloaks as a final test of their strength and determination.

Torin spotted Grimsa through the bustling host of onlookers. He nearly tripped on the loose edge of an old man's cloak then over an abandoned basket of wildflowers. He cursed and steadied himself as he squeezed in beside Grimsa, Signa, Wyla, and Bari near the front of the crowd.

"Good! You're here," said Grimsa. He bounced on his heels and shook out his hands. "Captain Gavring should be here any moment."

Torin slapped Grimsa on the back. "No need to worry, my friend. The captain has a cloak laid out for you, I'm sure. I'd bet my last piece of silver on it!"

"What if the cloak is too small to fit me? What if there is a mix up? What if they are short one cloak or Captain Gavring forgets to call my name?"

Signa squeezed Grimsa's arm and brushed his cheek. "The gods made you a troll hunter, Grimsa. You'll be a Greycloak by day's end."

Grimsa exhaled slowly, let his shoulders fall, then embraced Torin in a squeeze so tight it took him a moment to recover his breath. "You're right. You're right," Grimsa said. "Just nerves. Alright, let's get on with the ceremony already!"

Azal had sobered up by then, so he no longer wavered back and forth where he stood. With wide eyes the prince gazed up at the Greycloaks and spoke to Aldrin in his own tongue. The Lore-keeper intermittently gave compliant nods, his face scrunched into a grimace.

Torin leaned toward Azal and grabbed his shoulder. "Grow your beard out a bit more and you might fit in here. Perhaps you'll stay and hunt trolls a while when your errand is complete."

The prince laughed and shook his head. "It'll take a while to get used to that foul brew you call *skog*, but if I had my way, I would. Unfortunately, I think dear old Aldrin is already itching to leave Gatewatch."

Aldrin pulled his dark robe tight around his bony frame, the fabric shifting in colour between night black and crimson. The old man's wrinkled face was caught between a sneer and a shiver. "Curse this chill. What a foul place for a celebration."

Torin looked at the walls of evenly laid stone, at the fine wreaths of greenery, and the decorative banners. The sweet smell of evergreen sap floated through the crowd on a light gust of fresh, alpine air. High above them on either side of the valley jagged mountain ridges stood out against the clear sky. "Is it really that bad, Lorekeeper? If this seems foul, you must come from a fair land indeed."

Aldrin gave a bitter chuckle. "You don't see it, do you? I admit that I thought you troll hunters, stone-brained as you are, would have at least figured out what this really is."

Torin frowned. "This? You mean Stonering Keep?"

"A keep? That may be what you call it. It is no keep by my reckoning, at least not originally."

Azal rolled his eyes. "Forgive the old man, he always does this." The prince then turned to Aldrin and gave a mocking bow. "Enlighten us, Aldrin, with your bottomless knowledge and your bothersome wisdom."

Aldrin poked one hand out of his cloak and tapped his bald head. "I saw it when we made our way down the valley from Shadowstone Pass. Sometimes these things are easier to spot from a distance."

"Stonering Keep?"

"Not a keep, as I said before, but something else. Tell me young Master Ten-Trees, who was it that built Gatewatch?"

Torin narrowed his eyes. It was a simple question, but learned men rarely sought simple answers. "Beoric the Bear and his company. Don't you know of the Battle of Gatewatch? Haven't you heard the Lay of Beoric?"

"I have read it," said Aldrin, "And I know of Beoric's deeds. But this place seems rather strange, doesn't it? Where else in Noros have you ever seen a stone keep built in this circular fashion? You Norosi are more accustomed to building long halls of wood or turf, are you not?"

"By my father's royal sceptre, Aldrin," said Azal, "Get to the point!"

The scholar threw up his hands. "Think! Can't you see by the shape? It is not a keep but the remains of an ancient barrow, little more than the foundation as far as I can tell."

A shiver scuttled along Torin's spine. Behind Ten-Tree Hall where he grew up there was a wide field, less than half a day's walk, where his ancestors were buried. It was filled with low rolling hills, each one a circular grave mound with a tunneled entrance blocked up by boulders. His father told him tales of spirits that lingered over those barrows and sailed ghostly ships upon the mists that often covered the hills. As young boys, Torin, Grimsa, and Bryn would speak of sneaking out to those fields in search of treasure, but none had ever dared to risk rousing the barrow wights from their uneasy slumber.

Azal's voice broke the trance of Torin's eerie recollection. "Ha! That's unlikely, dear Aldrin. Look at the size! Not even the catacombs of the Armeahan kings are so large."

Aldrin smacked his wrinkled forehead. "My prince, will you never learn? Think again! Who could have built a barrow of such a size?" Aldrin turned to Torin, his crooked teeth bared.

Torin felt the blood drain from his face. "You mean giants? Ancient *jotur* of the far north?" Torin wanted to disagree but found that he could not reason otherwise. "By the gods, you might be right."

"Of course, I'm right," said Aldrin. "Long abandoned, obviously, and left to deteriorate, but of such a size that none other than the ancient giants could have been responsible for laying its foundation." For the first time since Aldrin arrived in Gatewatch, Torin saw a genuine smile stretched across the old man's face. "Perhaps you should spend some more time with this trollhunter, Prince Azalweir. It seems he's got a bit of the Greyraven in him after all."

Azal shrugged. "It's always like that with Aldrin. You get used to it."

The Lorekeeper patted Torin's shoulder. "Don't look so concerned, Master Ten-Trees. Every civilization is built upon the ruins of the last. For scholars of history, such as myself, it is no surprise that the sacred burial mound of an ancient northern giant should unknowingly become the festival grounds for barbarian troll hunters. It is simply the way of things."

That thought did not sit well with Torin, nor did the suggestion that Norosi were barbarians, but just then Captain Gavring appeared up on the wall.

Torin hardly recognized the captain. Gavring's frizzled hair, unruly strands of orange and white, had been pulled back and tied so that his great sloping forehead was fully exposed. His beard, trimmed and oiled, had been wrangled into a thick braid which hung straight down to the middle of his chest. Over his shoulders was laid a grey cloak made of tight-knit sheep's wool, waxed against foul weather, and lined inside with fur for warmth. At his belt hung a mighty sword which seemed nearly too big even for him; it was the blade wielded by Ur-Gezbrukter, the *jotur* that had amassed a troll army and attacked Gatewatch just two years before. In his hands, the captain held aloft three burning torches, two in his left hand and one in his right.

The crowd cheered, then fell silent a moment later. Wyla stretched her neck from side to side and Grimsa shook out his shoulders. Bari had to push through to the front of the crowd so that he could see; Azal and Aldrin shuffled in close behind him.

Torin felt his breath cut short as his chest tightened into a knot. Standing over what could be an ancient grave gave him an icy chill, as if frozen fingers were reaching inside to stroke his flesh and scrape his bones. A rushing sound like the swell of waves on the shore rose in his ears and he felt the world start to sway around him. As his balance gave way, he fell against something sturdy.

"By the gods, Torin," Grimsa said, "Don't try and spook me. I'm already tense enough!"

Torin gasped and clutched Grimsa's cloak just as his legs started to buckle. A rush of blood came to his head through his neck as he pulled himself up straight. Grimsa, his brows raised with concern, twisted around. "Torin? What's wrong?"

A moment later, Torin's breath came easier, and the rushing sound faded from his ears. "Sorry, Grimsa. It must be something I drank yesterday." Torin did his best to force a smile.

Gavring's voice rang out over the keep, the deep syllables like gusts from the bellows of a blacksmith's forge. "Greycloaks of Gatewatch, townsfolk and artisans, recruits, travelers and honoured guests, as Captain of the Gatewatch, I welcome you to the Cloaking Ceremony!"

The captain raised his arms up and held the torches high above his head. "I invoke Odd the One-Eyed, wise in war and keen in counsel. May he grant that each grey cloak falls upon shoulders fated for glory." Gavring threw one of the torches down onto the pile of tinder. He continued, louder then, so that his voice carried over the crackling flame. "I invoke Orr the Mighty, daring in deeds and fearless in the fray. May he grant that each grey cloak falls upon shoulders with the strength of steel and courage like iron." He tossed the second torch farther down so that it lit the kindling closer to the wall. The smoke rose to where Gavring stood and now swirled around his heels as if he stood upon a rise of fog. "And I invoke Fyr the Ever-Fair, beautiful of face and as fierce in love as the fiery forge. May she grant that each grey cloak falls upon shoulders whose hearts burn with pride for our kingdom and with fury against our enemies."

The dry kindling crackled with orange and yellow flame all along the base of the stone wall. Even from a dozen paces back, Torin felt the heat of it on his face. Grimsa, transfixed by the dancing tongues of fire, stopped fidgeting. Wyla crossed her arms and glared straight into the fire. Gavring cleared his throat and stretched his arms open wide with his palms raised to the sky.

"First, I call on Wyla White-Blaze, daughter of Calder Stone-Eye!" A cheer went up as Wyla stepped out from the crowd. Torin and Grimsa whooped, and Bari gave a shrill whistle that soared above the rest of the noise.

"As Captain of the Gatewatch I can attest to her strength and ferocity. Nine trolls have fallen under Wyla's axe! Would anyone speak against her?"

Wyla glared at the Greycloaks that stood in stoic silence then spun around to face the crowd. Her narrowed eyes dared any to speak. None did.

"Wyla White-Blaze," Gavring said, "You have been deemed worthy of wearing the grey cloak by those gathered here. Since none have spoken against you, will you swear an oath to defend Gatewatch with courage, to repel every harm, and to spare nothing to see it kept safe, not even your own life?"

Wyla nodded, her shoulders square and her stance proud.

"Then before this crowd declare, '*If my oath should fail, may I be as ash.*'"

"If my oath should fail, may I be as ash."

Gavring clapped his huge hands together. "Come! Brave the fire and claim your cloak!"

Wyla took a deep breath and stepped back. With a roar she charged forward and leapt high over the bright burning flames. She caught the wall halfway up and, despite a slip of her foot, managed to pull herself high enough to grasp the top ledge. A burly Greycloak grabbed her wrist and hauled her up to the top. When Wyla turned to face the crowd, a deafening cheer filled all of Stonering Keep.

Torin caught a glint in Wyla's eyes, tears of joy, as the cloak was laid on her back. He thought her body took to it as if she were a silver raven herself and the folds of the cloak were her wings.

With both hands, Wyla pulled the cloak tight around her then stepped back to stand among the other veteran troll hunters. Torin thought to himself that she had never looked so glad.

Gavring motioned for silence and then cleared his throat again. "Next I call on Grimsa Jarnskald, also called Grimspear, son of Gungnir Jarnskald and brother to Gunnar Grizzle-Beard."

At this, Grimsa threw his hands up in the air and rushed forward. "Here I am, Captain! I'm right here!"

Bari called out after him. "You're hard to miss, my friend!"

Those nearby applauded as Grimsa's face and ears flushed bright red. Despite any embarrassment, the smile that stretched wide across his face did not sag in the slightest.

"As Captain of The Gatewatch I can attest to Grimsa's deeds. It was he who threw *Skrar*, the spear that struck the Troll-King, and by his axe no less than seven trolls have fallen. Would anyone speak against him?"

Wyla stepped forward with a wicked grin on her face. "Well, he does eat a lot."

Another Greycloak nodded. "And he drinks a lot too."

Gavring's face fell into a stern frown. "Grimsa, would you deny these accusations?"

Grimsa paled. After a moment's hesitation he shook his head. "No, Captain, I would not."

With one hand held up to shade his eyes, Gavring searched the crowd. "Keymaster Signy, do the stores of Fjellhall have enough food and ale to keep this Jarnskald fed?"

Signy stepped forward and put her hands on her hips, a look of mock indignation on her face. "I've kept this one fed for the last two years, haven't I? My cellars are still fully stocked."

A wide smile broke on Gavring's face, and a deep chuckle rumbled in his chest. "Very well! Grimsa, you have been deemed worthy of wearing this cloak. Will you swear an oath to defend

Gatewatch with courage, to repel every harm, and to spare nothing, not even your own life, to see it kept safe?"

Grimsa let out the breath he had been holding in and nodded vigorously. "I do! If my oath should fail, may I be as ash."

"Then come claim your cloak! Dare to breach the wall of fire."

Grimsa barreled right through the burning sticks. Smoke and ash flew up where he trampled the barricade. He hopped from foot to foot to keep them from burning, then leapt as high as he could on the wall, just a hand's length below the top ledge. Wyla and another Greycloak each grabbed one of Grimsa's arms and helped haul him up onto the rampart.

As slid over the top, Grimsa looked down with wide eyes and cursed. His pant leg was smoking so he slapped the smoldering embers out with his hands. Once the embers were snuffed out, he held his fists high in the air and shouted, "Long live The Gatewatch!" The crowd echoed his response and then broke out into a swell of applause and laughter.

Torin suddenly felt the weight of the crowd's eyes fall on him. He did not look over his shoulder but could feel the force of their stares press into his back like pointed fingers prodding him to move ahead. Prickles of sweat ringed his neck and his face felt too hot.

Captain Gavring broke the silence. "Torin Ten-Trees! Come forward."

Torin's eardrums nearly split at the roar of the crowd. Like a sail caught in a gust of strong wind, his body lurched forward so that he stood apart from the crowd. He threw his shoulders back and steeled his gaze as his father had taught him long ago. Then the crowd, the noise, and the flickering flames all seemed far away. Torin was suddenly outside himself, as if someone else had been called forward and he was merely watching the spectacle.

"The deeds of Torin Ten-Trees have been sung in halls throughout every corner of Noros, as well as beyond the sea in cities whose names we do not even know. You have all heard of his duel of riddles with the Troll-King Ur-Gezbrukter, how he wagered his own head to rescue his company from certain death. It was he who took up Ur-Gezbrukter's sword to cleave the wicked *jotur's* head from his shoulders."

At this last line, the crowd's excitement overflowed into a chorus of cheers. Gavring paused until the noise began to fade. "And he has proven himself as a troll hunter. Ten trolls have fallen by his axe! One for each tree that stands around his father's hall." The noise of the crowd rose again, and the red-bearded Captain chuckled. "So, if anyone would dare speak against him, then let them speak now."

From where Torin stood, the Greycloaks atop the wall, Wyla and Grimsa included, were shrouded in a veil of smoke from the fire. Their forms appeared to fade in and out of the ash-grey swirls. He remembered his friend Bryn and how he had watched his body burn on the pyre. The thought nearly spurred him to dash straight through the flame and scramble up the wall to his friends. But then a dream he had dreamed long ago came to his mind in the glow of the pulsing embers, a vision of Ten-Tree Hall burning as an army of ghostly wights hovered around it. He knew at that moment what he had to do. He cleared his throat and raised his right hand.

"I must speak against myself."

If Torin thought that he had known silence before that moment, then he was mistaken. The emptiness around him was so vacuous that it seemed even the air itself had fled so that there was barely any left to breathe. His knees wavered. With his lips closed tight, he gritted his teeth and forced his body still.

Captain Gavring's shoulders drooped, and his rusty red eyebrows furled together. "Though your words are like arrows in my chest, I must hear you out. What would you say against yourself?"

"I am honoured to be considered worthy of wearing the grey cloak, but my father has felt the hand of time. I must take up his seat at Ten-Tree Hall when he joins my ancestors in the halls of the dead."

Through the smoke, Torin could see Gavring standing above him on the wall. He met the captain's gaze, not with hardened eyes but with the strain of grief. A puff of wind blew the smoke away where Gavring was standing and Torin saw him clearly. The captain's burly chest rose and fell with a sigh as he nodded.

"Then I declare before you all that Torin Ten-Trees, slayer of Ur-Gezbrukter and friend of the *nidavel*, has fulfilled his duty to the Greyraven and his service to The Gatewatch. As Captain, I release you from your oath of service to return to Ten-Tree Hall."

Silence surrounded Torin on every side and all was still. Until then he had not considered what he would do after his decision was made. Now he stood alone with nothing but the sound of crackling embers and the eerie sight of Greycloaks shrouded in swirling smoke above him. Grief strangled any words he might have spoken. He felt the crushing weight of the crowd's gaze. After a moment, he turned back toward town, dazed and numb. The crowd parted before him without a word.

Torin felt empty in his chest as he walked through the streets of Gatewatch toward the barracks to collect his belongings. In the distance, he heard the dull roar of the crowd at the announcement of the next name. That noise soon faded so that only the scuff of his own heavy footsteps could be heard in the empty streets. He had been angry before, like burning coals or red-hot iron, at Signy and his father for their secrets, at Wyla for her stubbornness, but perhaps most of all at himself for the decision he had to make. Now that fire had died, and he felt as cold as if the hollow in his chest where his heart was had become a cave of ice.

When he reached the barracks and shoved the door, a rusty creak screeched in his ears. He cursed and braced himself against the heavy timbers to dampen the piercing sound. The stone chamber was full of familiar smells: leather boots, fur blankets, rough-cut spruce bed frames, and lingering ash in the hearth. With them came a rush of memories which fluttered through Torin's mind like a flock of sparrows through a tree; he saw them all at once, as a whirling mass, so that he really did not see any one in particular but rather felt them wash over his mind.

Torin left the door open to let in enough light to gather his things. He picked up a dark blue cloak coated in wax and lined with grey fur, a gift from Bari's uncle Brok when he had been in Myrkheim, the city of Mastersmith Ognir. The spear, *Skrar*, or Screamer, stood propped up against the stone wall with a fitted leather pouch tied over its head. On his first patrol in the wilds, Torin had found a sturdy ash sapling and fashioned a fine shaft for his favourite weapon. Now, the shaft had been worn down where he usually held it, a grip formed perfectly to his hands. He used a wool blanket to wrap up some clothes and the rest of his belongings, then tied it into a neat bundle.

Last, from behind a loose stone in the wall, Torin drew out an arm ring made of three twisted strands of gold. It had been given to his childhood friend Bryn by Mastersmith Ognir. After Bryn had fallen against the Troll-King, the others said he should keep it. When Torin slipped it onto his wrist, he felt the enchantment tingle along his arm and up to his elbow. It doubled the strength of his arm, yet Torin wished then that it could have strengthened his spirit instead.

Torin crouched down and checked beneath the bed frame, then walked around it to make sure he had not left anything behind. Across from his own bare bed, he saw Grimsa's bed, a mess of wool blankets and furs piled on it with an axe shoved in behind the headboard. Torin grinned and shook his head. From his blue cloak, he unpinned a fine decorative clasp made of knotted silver branches, an emblem of Ten-Tree Hall given to him by his father on the day he left for Gatewatch. He polished it on his sleeve then hung it on the blade of Grimsa's axe.

With his cloak draped over one shoulder, his spear in his hand, and the bundle of extra clothes, he made for Fjellhall. He would attend the feast that evening to bid his friends farewell. Grimsa and Signa would exchange marriage oaths and that would be something to celebrate. Then Torin had it in mind to leave later that night, so he could ride up Shadowstone Pass and catch one last glimpse of Gatewatch at sunrise on his way home.

Home, of course, was Ten-Tree Hall. His father, Jarl Einar Ten-Trees, might already be watching for some sign of his son over the rolling green hills that tumbled down to the sea. Perhaps the old man had already started preparations for a feast when Torin returned.

Before Torin, Bryn, and Grimsa had departed for Gatewatch, his father had hosted such a feast as had never been seen in that hall. Rich red wine was served in smooth silver goblets along with platters heaped full of spiced lamb, salted beef, and full racks of pork ribs slathered in herbs and butter. Thorgrid, the head of Einar's household staff, had laboured all day baking as many of her far-famed honey biscuits as the hearth would hold. Torin caught himself smiling as he remembered Grimsa eating an entire batch himself while Thorgrid looked on with horror and amazement. There were round loaves of barley bread and wheels of white cheese coated in wax which his father had accepted in place of taxes from the farmers that year.

Even better than the food that night was his father's story on that occasion. The old man often entertained the guests who spent the winter with his tales, but at that feast he gave his greatest performance ever by Torin's reckoning. That night, Einar recited the Lay of Beoric, an epic skaldic poem about Torin's great-grand-father, who had founded Noros more than one hundred years before.

Einar began with how Beoric left his meager life as the son of a fisherman in the Grim Isles to sail north for riches and glory. He overturned tables as he told of the treacherous sea storm in which Beoric battled with the sea-beast Kolkrabba. Then, as if he were in the spring of his youth again, he hid behind his high carved seat to tell of Beoric's first sight of Fyra, the beautiful and mysterious maiden of the forest. The old man jumped up on the hearth and bellowed as he recalled Beoric's duel with the Troll-King. At last, Einar tottered and stumbled to the floor to re-enact Beoric's poisoning by the treachery of Fyra's cruel sister, Lysa. As soon as his father hit the floor, the whole hall erupted in applause. When Torin pictured the scene, the cold place in his chest seemed to warm as it had not in many days.

Torin approached Fjellhall with heightened spirits. He hoped for a few peaceful moments to himself in that mighty hall before the ceremony concluded and the crowd rushed in for the feast. Torin had already made and announced his difficult decision and so he now felt there was nothing else to worry about anyways.

Both doors were already propped open when Torin arrived. He stepped inside and filled his lungs with the scent of fresh baked bread, then exhaled with a long sigh. One of the hall hands tilted his head and greeted Torin with a cup of ale. Torin accepted it with a nod but gave no explanation of why he had returned without a grey cloak. For a little while, he could enjoy himself in the warmth of Fjellhall's hearth without having to defend his decision.

Though he tried to relax, Torin could not help but feel that something was not quite right. As he looked over the hall, loaves of bread lay like boulders on the table with chunks of cheese as big as Torin's head. The roasts sizzled on the spits all down the hearth and Keymaster Signy's gigantic cauldron, *Thaegindi*, simmered with the scent of boiling carrots, potatoes, and onions. Burly young men and women hauled up barrels of ale and stacked them

neatly at the end of each table. The banners had been straightened
and the floors were clean swept, so all was as it should have been.

Then Torin saw what was out of place. In the back corner of
the hall, seated at the far end of the long table, was a dark-cloaked
figure. The cloak was finely made but spattered with mud around
its edges. The hood was pulled up so that it obscured the face
beneath it. Torin was not accustomed to seeing strangers in the
hall, so he approached him slowly.

The figure looked up as Torin stepped closer and pulled back
his hood. It was Jarl Bor, the man who had led the Armeahan
delegation to Gatewatch. The old man waved and opened his hand
toward the seat across from him as an invitation to sit. Torin sat
down slowly then hailed him with a toast to the Greyraven. They
drank together but each kept his eye on the other all the while.

"So," said Jarl Bor. "You refused the grey cloak."

"My father needs me at Ten-Tree Hall."

Bor scratched at his beard and frowned, the deep wrinkles in
his forehead evidence of a lifetime of hard decisions. "Ah, if only
my sons had been so dutiful. But I worry you might come to regret
that choice when the years have passed and you're all alone."

"I've made my decision," said Torin. "Let the gods judge me
for it if they must."

"The gods, yes. Well, it seems they may have more in mind
than you expected."

Torin narrowed his gaze at the old man. He felt uneasy questions swirl into a torrent between his ears, each one buffeted by
the rising pulse of blood in his neck.

Jarl Bor reached inside his cloak and drew out a fine metal
chain. From it dangled a silver ring which was wondrously crafted
into the shape of a raven, its wings in the downward stroke of
flight so that they touched, wingtip to wingtip. The eyes of the
raven were two blood red rubies, cut so finely that they glimmered
with light at every angle. A runic inscription protruded from the

ring's back, distinctive strokes which Torin recognized as the Greyraven's sigil.

"Do you know what this is?"

Torin swallowed. "That can only be the signet ring of King Araldof Greyraven himself."

Bor nodded and reached over the table so that the silver ring hovered close to Torin's face. "It was given to me by Eramur the Elder, the head of the Grey Council and second only to King Araldof Greyraven himself. I was tasked with bringing this foreign delegation to Gatewatch with all possible haste. That has been done. Now I have the Greyraven's full authority to pass his ring to the one I think can complete the next task: to retrieve a healing draught from the Everspring." Bor lowered the ring down carefully to set it on the table then released the chain from his grip.

Torin's stomach felt like a sinkhole slipping down and falling in beneath itself. "And if I refuse?"

Jarl Bor smiled without warmth. "No one refuses the Greyraven."

5

◊ ODD COMPANY ◊

TORIN SAID NOTHING. He looked down at the silver raven ring with its inset ruby eyes. They stared back at him with an unblinking authority, as if Araldof Greyraven himself was glaring straight at him through those crimson stones. A chill ran up Torin's spine at the thought.

Bor chuckled and reached across the table to slap Torin's shoulder. "A quest to the ends of the earth is not an old man's task. If half the stories I've heard about you are true, then you are the one for the job." Then the old man stood, drained the last of his drink, and gave Torin a nod. "May the gods grant you luck, Ten-Trees."

Torin had hardly a minute to himself before the townsfolk started to trickle in through the door. He snatched up the delicate metal chain and slipped it over his head to conceal the ring beneath his tunic. Soon the quiet bustle of the hall hands' preparations became a clamorous chorus as the guests lined the benches.

Torin wanted to be angry for having such a thing thrust upon him, but instead he was surprised to feel a great rush of relief. Was it that he would not yet have to leave his friends? Or that he was not, as Wyla often said, about to trade a life of adventure to inherit a sleepy hall? Or was it, perhaps, that he was suddenly absolved of the guilt that he felt about whether or not to stay? As Jarl Bor had said, no one refuses the Greyraven.

Amid the noise, he shook his head. He thought about his father. After all, Einar was the reason Torin had refused the grey cloak in the first place. With a deep breath, he focused his mind on Ten-Tree Hall. But no matter how hard he tried to hold that image behind his closed eyes it faded and drifted to thoughts of the far north, to unseen places and to the legendary Everspring. What other fantastic things might the enchanted map lead them to? Still, Torin's heart strained again as he thought of his father waiting for him over the rolling green hills that led to Ten-Tree Hall.

Yet if the Greyraven commanded it then Einar Ten-Trees would have to wait for his son. Torin's shoulders relaxed and all the knots in his stomach unraveled. Perhaps the tale of his duel with the Troll-King would not be the last that he brought back with him to his father's hall.

His thoughts were interrupted by a whisper in his ear, as if someone had snuck up behind him so close that he should have felt their breath on his neck.

Torin.

Torin jumped in his seat and twisted around, but there was no one standing close to him. He looked down the length of the bench, but the nearest reveler sat a far way down, not nearly close enough to whisper. It was a woman's voice he had heard in his ear, a voice that he did not recognize. Torin closed his eyes as he tried to place it, but he could not. From down the hall he heard another voice, one he knew almost better than any other.

"Torin!"

Torin called back. "Grimsa! Wyla!"

Any thought he had for that strange voice vanished as he rose to greet his friends. He stepped up on the bench and then hopped right onto the table to cross over to the other side. "Look at you!

Greycloaks!" With his arms extended, Torin caught them both in an embrace.

Wyla was still elated from the ceremony. "I can hardly tell you how it felt climbing that wall. I remember launching myself up as high as I could. Before I caught hold of the top ledge, I looked down to see the flames licking my boots. It was as if every uncertainty and doubt fell away into the fire and was burned up within it. Then I was on top of the wall with a grey cloak wrapped around my shoulders." She straightened her cloak and threw back her shoulders. "When I looked down the valley, it felt as if I could have spread my arms and flown away."

"Not me," said Grimsa. "All I could think about when I reached the top were my trousers burning off in front of the whole crowd. I felt them catch fire as I hung there on the wall!"

Wyla turned to Torin and crossed her arms. "What's got you in such a good mood, Ten-Trees? Are you really so excited to leave? We haven't even feasted."

"No, it's not that," said Torin. "I've got a surprise for you both before I leave."

Grimsa grinned. "A surprise?"

Torin slapped them both on the back and sat down at the bench. "You'll find out soon enough. Now come on! Let's have a drink."

Bari joined them at the end of the table in the back corner of Fjellhall. Prince Azal, Lorekeeper Aldrin, and Jarl Bor sat at a small head table which had been set up at the back of the hall. It was laid full, with silver dishes, jeweled goblets, and flickering candles. After the rest of the Armeahan delegation squeezed in wherever they could among the common benches, there was hardly a spot left to sit in all Fjellhall. Finally, Captain Gavring and Keymaster Signy arrived and took the two high seats at the center of the head table.

Barrels of ale were cracked open and flowed over with honey-brown foam. A hall hand picked up one of the frothing casks then nimbly stepped up onto the middle of the long table. A second hall hand followed and did the same. With the barrel upside-down, they walked the length of the table at a practiced pace, slow enough so that the attendees could catch a cup-full when ale bearers passed but quick enough to reach the end before the barrel emptied. Soon everyone had a horn full of golden bubbling ale.

No one drank until Gavring and Signy stood up and lifted their goblets in a toast. The copper-haired captain cleared his throat. "To the newly initiated, I welcome you to Gatewatch again, this time as Greycloaks. There is a place for you beside every fire in this city."

Signy nodded. "And to Jarl Bor, Prince Azalweir, Lorekeeper Aldrin, and the delegation from Armeah, we welcome you most warmly."

"There is business to attend to," said Gavring, "But first we feast!"

All there hailed the Captain and the Keymaster with a cheer followed promptly by a deep draught of ale. Somewhere above the crowd, high up in the loft, musicians filled the air with notes which showered down into Torin's ears like little pattering drops of rain. Strings were plucked and strummed in time with the drums which beat a lively rhythm. Like the trill of birds in spring, flutes and pipes chased the melody from the verse into the chorus and echoed refrains or high soaring harmonies.

And so, the feast began. Hall hands cut enormous slices of meat off the roasts that sizzled on the iron spits and laid them upon copper platters to be served. Guests cut into the thick wheels of cheese and round crusted loaves of dark rye bread on the tables, while hall hands filled bowls with steaming stew. Another round of ale, a rich brown beer with hints of cedarwood, was opened and poured into any mug which was found empty.

Grimsa's face gleamed with a stuffed-cheeked smile, his mouth half full of bread dipped in stew. "By the gods, what a feast!"

Bari nodded and licked his fingers clean. "I have to admit that I've taken a liking to Norosi food, much more red meat than can be found in Myrkheim and fewer fish!" The *nidavel* laid a slice of salted beef roast onto a thick chunk of rye bread and took as large a bite as he could manage.

"And don't forget the beer," Torin said. "I swear I've never tasted a better brew than those found here in Fjellhall."

Wyla raised her cup. "I will toast to that!"

At last, when the meat left on the sizzling roasts became scarce, a sweet mead was served in place of ale. By then each loaf of bread and wheel of cheese had disappeared, every crumb eaten up by greedy hands. Sweet round honey cakes crusted with walnuts and lingonberry jam were sent out on trays. Once all the cakes had been served, a quiet contentment fell over the hall.

Gavring stood up from his raised seat and addressed the crowd. "Greycloaks and townsfolk of Gatewatch, guests and recruits, a cheer for Keymaster Signy for hosting this magnificent feast!" Everyone present whooped and whistled. Keymaster Signy stood up beside Gavring and gave a graceful bow.

"Now," Gavring said, "Since our stomachs are full, we can attend to business. First, it has been declared to me by Keymaster Signy, daughter of Sigrilinn, who was Keymaster before her, that her own daughter Signa should be matched with Grimsa Jarnskald in marriage."

All who were there cheered, and Grimsa blushed so deeply that Torin thought his friend's ears might burst. Torin and Wyla each grabbed one of Grimsa's arms and hauled him to his feet. Both, in turn, squeezed Grimsa with a hug. When Torin sat down, he saw that his friend's red-bearded grin was as wide as he had ever seen it.

Captain Gavring had a stern look as Grimsa approached the head table. "Grimsa Jarnskald, son of Gungnir and brother of Gunnar, is it your wish be pledged to Signa Signy's-daughter by an oath of marriage?"

Grimsa swallowed and nodded. There was a nervous flutter in his voice, his words spoken through a throat choked tight with emotion. "Nothing above or below the surface of the earth would bring me greater joy and happiness."

Gavring nodded. "Then call for Signa so I can hear her mind on this."

All turned away from the head table as the doors of Fjellhall opened. Both Torin and Wyla stood up on the bench so they could see over the crowd. So did Bari, but the *nidavel* could hardly see any better as, even when standing on the bench, he still only stood at eye-level with the rest of those seated there.

In through the doorway, lit by the red rays of sunset light, stepped Signa with all the radiance of the gods themselves. Her golden hair all tumbled over one shoulder in swirling braids and her dress was of a dark blue hue which Torin could only compare to the deep waters of the sea under a clear sky. At her shoulders were two magnificent oval clasps, finely made with knotted patterns of gold, which held her long flowing cape of light tan fur. In her hands, she grasped a bouquet of wildflowers and cedar branches, her emerald ring sparkling underneath it. That sparkle was dull, however, next to the glint in Signa's eye when she saw Grimsa across Fjellhall.

Torin glanced over at Grimsa and saw the great man's knees shaking. His friend had never looked so happy or so nervous in all the time Torin had known him. Then, in the corner of his vision, he saw Keymaster Signy. Her face glowed with joy as she looked at her daughter. For a moment, Torin imagined that face looking down at him as a small boy, the way a mother's gaze might have felt. He turned his eyes away.

Signa strode through the hall with slow, graceful steps. Wide-eyed children watched her pass and many of the townsfolk who had known her as a child looked on with joyful faces. At last, Signa stood in front of her groom and laid down her flowers so that she and Grimsa could grasp each other's hands.

"Signa Signy's-daughter," said Gavring, "Is it your wish to be pledged to Grimsa Jarnskald in marriage?"

Signa looked up at Captain Gavring then turned her eyes back toward Grimsa. "Yes, it is."

Captain Gavring opened his arms wide. "Then all those gathered here shall serve as witnesses. Grimsa and Signa have pledged their love to each other. Long may the sun and moon chase each other across the sky before old age or sickness or tragedy force them apart." He looked down at both of them. "You are to be each other's strength. You are to be each other's shelter. You are to be both blade and shield to the other, two parts of an inseparable whole, from this day onward incomplete without the other. And in all things, you must seek the health and happiness of the other so that the gods will grant you a long and joyous life together. Now, if it is your intention to live together in this manner until the end of your days then seal your oath to each other with a kiss."

Fjellhall rang with a chorus of cheers and applause as the couple kissed. Keymaster Signy stepped down from the head table and embraced Grimsa who lifted the old woman up off the floor. A bit of room was made for Grimsa at the head table, and he squeezed in between Signy and Signa.

Once everyone was seated again, Captain Gavring crossed his arms. "Now we must speak of darker matters, matters that involve King Araldof Greyraven himself."

Someone in the crowd shouted out in a drunken slur. "Long live the Greyraven!"

The captain shook his head and sighed. "You may have already heard rumours of the message brought by Jarl Bor, that King

Araldof Greyraven is gravely ill." Stifled gasps and muffled curses came from every corner of the room. Gavring spoke over the host of whispers. "And that is why King Ghezelweir of Armeah, a great kingdom far to the south of these lands, has sent a delegation to Gatewatch. This is Prince Azalweir, son of Ghezelweir, and his mentor, Lorekeeper Aldrin, who knows much of history, lore, and magic."

In the crowd, brows knotted with worry shot up in curiosity or sank deeper in mistrust of the dark-robed scholar.

"They have brought a map that shows the lands here and far to the north," Gavring said, "And the Grey Council has commanded that a healing draught should be retrieved to bring King Araldof Greyraven back to health. And so, we shall quest for the sacred waters of the Everspring."

By the time the captain had spoken that last word, the noise of the crowd rose above his own as the whole hall erupted into a chorus of voices. Cries of worry over the King's disease, cheers at the prospect of such a quest, and jeers at the Aldrin the Lorekeeper all rushed into Torin's ears. Who would lead the expedition? Who would join them? When would they leave? Aldrin narrowed his eyes and shrunk back into his seat. Azalweir sat stiffly, uneasy in his rigid chair.

Captain Gavring waited another moment for the barrage of questions to die down. Torin knew as well as Gavring that curiosity would douse the noise of the crowd faster than any shouting or arm waving.

As soon it was quiet again, Gavring cleared his throat. "Prince Azalweir and Lorekeeper Aldrin, forgive some of these stone-brained folk for their inhospitable words. They mistrust any who deal with magic, as is wise for most, but I assure you that you are welcome here in Gatewatch and stand under the Greyraven's protection."

Aldrin waved his hand and flashed a well-practiced smile toward the benches full of townspeople. "Thank you, Captain Gavring, but no need to explain. Indeed, it is prudent for all but the most rigorously educated to avoid any dealings with magic." He nodded toward a few of the most disgruntled near the head table and they let down their tense shoulders a bit.

One of the older men on the far side of the hall stood up. Torin recognized him as Rolof the Smith. "Captain Gavring, why do we speak of such foolishness? The Everspring is little more than a tale for children! And what is the use in sending brave young men and women to die for this foreigner's fantasies about what might lie at the edge of the world?"

At this Aldrin stood up and pointed a bony finger at the man. "You. Yes you. What is your name?"

"I am Rolof the Blacksmith," he said, "And I work honest metal into hardy tools and fine weapons. What is it to you, curse-caster?"

Aldrin chuckled at Rolof's attempt at an insult and bared his teeth in a smile. "And from where do you hail, Rolof the Black-smith?"

"I was born and raised in Gatewatch. It's here that I live and it's here that I'll die." Those around Rolof nodded and tapped the table with their mugs of ale.

"And can you read, Rolof?"

The blacksmith shrugged. "I've never needed to."

"And how many languages do you speak?"

Those around Rolof chuckled as he pretended to think. "Just one!"

"And how many kings have given you gifts in gratitude for your services?" Rolof opened his mouth to answer when Aldrin cut in again. "And how many souls have you wrenched back to life with your knowledge of healing herbs? How many king's sons have you tutored and how many troubled queens have you counselled? How many men have you sentenced to death in the name of the king's justice and in how many wars have you acted as a most trusted advisor? Have you sung for foreign courts or composed histories of ancient kings? Have you stood before the Grey Council or been paid a personal visit by King Araldof Greyraven?"

Rolof's face flushed as deep a hue of red as if he had been standing naked in front of the stone-still crowd. He swallowed and shook his head. Aldrin nodded with a tight-lipped grin. "Then I guess we will all be taking my advice on what lies at the end of the world and not yours." The old man turned to Captain Gavring and extended his arm toward him. "Captain, I believe you were about to tell us more about the expedition."

"Indeed, I was," said Gavring. "The Grey Council sent word to Armeah for aid. We have a map which the Greyraven himself entrusted to Lorekeeper Aldrin. Honour compels us to complete this task if it is in our power."

Another voice from the crowd called out. "And who will lead this expedition?"

Jarl Bor stood up and straightened his cloak. "I was tasked with leading the Armeahan delegation to Gatewatch and that is now done. The authority that was laid around my neck with the Greyraven's signet ring has been passed to another, one who is more suited than I to lead an expedition to the Everspring."

Torin scanned the room as hushed whispers scurried along the tables like many mice disturbed from their nest. Wyla and Bari both peered at Jarl Bor for any indication of who he might mean. Grimsa and Signa were too caught up with each other to notice much of what was happening, but Keymaster Signy stared straight at Torin. Though she held her face ceremoniously rigid, Torin could see creases of worry deepen around her eyes.

With a deep breath, Torin drew the ring out from under his cloak and stood up. Those seated around him gasped at the sight of those magnificent red rubies set in silver. For the only time that

Torin could remember, Wyla sat completely awestruck, her mouth hanging open and her gaze fixed on the silver ring.

"Jarl Bor has passed the ring of King Araldof Greyraven to me." Torin held the ring up high and walked down the hall slowly so all could see it. "Under his authority, I propose to lead a small company to the Everspring. If we are able, we will retrieve a draught for our beloved king and save all Noros from falling into wreck and ruin."

When he reached the far end of the hall, opposite the head table, Torin turned to face the crowd and raised his arms. "Jarl Bor has also generously offered, at his own expense, to supply and outfit this expedition with whatever we may need. For this, I am truly grateful." All cheered and turned their eyes toward Jarl Bor who stifled a cough, then forced a lordly smile. When the attention of those along the benches returned to Torin, the look of the old man's face darkened considerably.

"Torin Ten-Trees," Captain Gavring said, "You are full of surprises. Though my heart longs to join you on this journey, my oath as captain demands that I stay. However, if the Grey-cloaks can be of use to this quest for their king, then we are at your service." Through the crowd he could see the families seated around each Greycloak, spouses and children, lean closer and cling to them. Torin had seen that same worried look in Signy's eyes just a moment before.

"Gods keep you, Captain Gavring! I will need help in this quest and indeed there are no worthier warriors in all the world than the Greycloaks. However, there are only two Greycloaks that I would take with me and one that I would ask."

Many scratched their heads or tugged at their beards at that.

"I would ask, Captain, that you grant Wyla White-Blaze leave to join me. She is the fiercest soul I've ever met, and I trust her to the end of the world, which is exactly where I'm going."

Gavring turned to where Wyla was seated to ask her, but she had already sprung up from the bench and was racing toward

Torin. She nearly bowled Torin over as she locked her arms around him in an iron-brace grip. He squeezed her back, relieved to have her with him and glad to feel the warmth of their friendship rekindled. Wyla let go and slapped Torin on the shoulder, her smile wide and bright.

"Damn you and your secrets, Torin Ten-Trees," she said, "Of course I'm coming with you!"

Captain Gavring grinned. "Excellent. And would you have anyone else join you?"

"I would have Bari Wordsmith," said Torin, "If he is willing. He has proven his friendship to the Gatewatch, and he is a dear friend to me. Besides, the map we have is in *nidavellish* and he is best suited to read it."

All eyes fell on Bari, who stood on top of the bench at the end of the table. The *nidavel* furrowed his dark eyebrows and tugged at his beard. "I would not be speaking truthfully if I said I was not afraid of what might lie so far to the north. However, if I turned down such an opportunity, my curiosity might drive me to madness!" He pondered a minute more, then hopped down off the bench. "By the Mastersmith, I'd never forgive myself. Fate be damned! I will join you, Torin Ten-Trees."

The townsfolk clapped as Bari shuffled along the hearth to where Torin and Wyla were. Perhaps the loudest of all were the spouses and the children of the other Greycloaks because they would not have to watch their loved ones depart for such a treacherous journey. The Greycloaks themselves looked relieved as well, though a few had a fire in their eye for such an adventure.

Aldrin stood up at the head table and called out to Torin. "Master Ten-Trees, it was by the request of the Grey Council that I came this far, and it is no secret that they wish me to be a part of this expedition."

Torin crossed his arms. "It is a long journey, Master Aldrin, and you are not starved for years. We will move quickly and face countless dangers."

The old man sputtered and threw up his hands. "Danger? That's exactly why you need me along! Remember what I told you about Stonering Keep. You need a mind attuned the sensitivities of history and magic if you have any hope of reaching the Everspring."

A vein on Aldrin's forehead pulsed and he drew in a deep breath. "And I've travelled much farther in my time than all of you put together, so don't worry yourself about my keeping up. I am coming. There can be no argument."

Prince Azal stood up beside his mentor and squeezed the old man's shoulder. "And I am coming too!"

Aldrin shoved Azal's hand away. "By the royal sceptre, that will not be so! Your father was very clear: to Gatewatch and no further. To disobey his command could be considered treason!"

Azal shrugged. "Such an argument might sway me back home, but we're not in Armeah anymore. We are in Noros! So, his words hold no power over me here." The prince flashed a smile at Torin and opened his arms wide. "What do you say, Torin Ten-Trees?"

"I have no mind to anger a magic-wielder and a prince at the same time," Torin said. "The journey is open to you both." Each sighed, Aldrin with resignation and Azal with exhilaration, then sat back down at the head table.

Captain Gavring tugged at his beard. "And when will you leave?"

"Tomorrow," Torin said. "If the Greyraven is as ill as Jarl Bor reports, then we must waste no time."

Gavring nodded. "So be it. You'll have one last restful sleep before setting out into the wilds for the far north. We will outfit you with the best we can offer, including horses, provisions, and weapons." Gavring turned to Jarl Bor and nodded, with a knowing grin on his face. "In addition, of course, to whatever Jarl Bor has so generously offered to supply."

Torin opened his arms and bowed from the hip. "Gods keep you, Captain Gavring and Jarl Bor! You've given us every advantage. We will do our utmost to retrieve a draught from the Everspring." At this, the crowd hollered and cheered.

A heavy fist pounded the head table so hard that some of the empty ale vessels toppled over. Grimsa, his face full of hot red blood, stood up in a huff. "By thundering Orr and all the gods, what about me?"

Torin's eyes softened as he looked at Grimsa from across the hall. "Grimsa, you are my oldest friend. But how can I ask you to leave on a treacherous journey the very night of your wedding?"

Grimsa threw his hands up. "By simply speaking the words!"

Torin opened his mouth to speak but closed it again when he saw Signa stand up beside Grimsa. He thought she might calm him down, as she often did, but instead she picked up an empty mead horn and hurled it at Torin from across the room. It spun through the air and whizzed just over his head.

"Torin Ten-Trees, you don't stand a chance without my Grimsa," said Signa. "Look at the lot of you! Skinny as twigs. You need a bear of a man if you mean to contend with trolls and giants and who knows what else! Fyr's fire, get some sense into you."

Her words hit Torin like a spray of icy seawater and he stood speechless. Grimsa crossed his arms and grinned.

Signa waved her finger at Torin and narrowed her gaze. "Besides, you know him just as well as I do. If you and Wyla go trouncing off on some adventure without him, then he'll do nothing but mope. By the gods, your timing is awful, Torin Ten-Trees, but there is no way I'll let you leave my Grimsa behind."

Torin couldn't help but laugh. If he had ever doubted Grimsa's choice of spouse, he promised himself then that he never would again. "Well said, Signa! There is no arguing with you there." He turned his gaze back to Grimsa, who stood with his shoulders hunched and his arms crossed. "Grimsa, you're my dearest friend and the strongest man I've ever known. Will you join us?"

Grimsa tried to keep frowning, but a grin snuck up under his beard. He abandoned the act all at once and let his arms down. "Alright! You convinced me."

Captain Gavring clapped. "Then it is decided. Torin Ten-Trees, Wyla White-Blaze, Grimsa Jarnskald, Bari Wordsmith, Lore-keeper Aldrin, and Prince Azalweir have agreed to take up this quest. An odd company to say the least, but formidable, nonetheless. So, I raise this toast! To the Everspring Company!"

The ale flowed freely the rest of that night, round after round, until all had their fill and felt the weight of sleep fall heavy on their eyelids. Torin relished every minute of that evening with his closest friends at his side. And so, after much laughter had passed between them, he climbed up into the loft in Fjellhall and fell into one of the empty beds. His mind swirled with the mead, and he grinned as he lay thinking of the adventure before him.

As he lay there in the dark, he heard a voice, in the slightest whisper.

Torin.

Torin's eyes shot open, and a chill ran down his neck. He sat up and shook his head. The voice had been close, very close, as if someone had spoken the words right into his ear. He blinked and glanced around the dim loft but there was no one nearby.

Torin.

Torin felt a peculiar heat against the center of his chest, and he fumbled to draw the Greyraven's ring out from under his tunic. The raven's ruby eyes crackled with red light like the first sparks of a hungry fire. He held it close to his ear for a moment then whispered. "Who's there?"

Who I was and who I am matter only in that I possess what you need and what you truly desire.

Torin's heartbeat quickened. It was a woman's voice, one that he did not recognize. He knew the mead had loosened his senses and so held silent for fear of revealing too much to the strange speaker. "And what is it that you think I need?"

The same thing that everyone needs, though precious few ever truly achieve it.

Torin frowned. "And what's that?"

Power, Torin. Power is influence. Power is your wishes made tangible. It is what can reunite your parents. It is what can keep your friends close by. This power, in your hands, could even prevent those you care about from dying. Like Bryn did.

Torin's eyes widened with every word and his stomach roiled in a sick, swirling torrent. Sweat tingled at his neck beneath his collar and he clenched his jaw. It knew him. Whatever it was, it knew him. And it knew about him. Torin shivered. "No one should wield that kind of power."

He then heard a laugh unlike any he had heard before. It was hollow, devoid of light and mirth, a mocking shell of what such a sound should have been. Torin imagined the sound coming from the stale mouth of a long-rotted corpse or an empty-eyed skeleton.

Stop thinking like a child, Torin. This power exists and someone must wield it. Why not you?

Torin lay perfectly still as his heart pounded against his ribs. He waited for the voice to speak again, but the glow in the eyes of the silver raven ring faded and its warm metal cooled.

Eventually, Torin let out the breath he had been holding in his chest and slipped the ring back beneath his tunic. The sound of the woman's voice echoed through his mind as he lay there alone in the dark. However, the mead had made his limbs heavy, and it was already very late. Torin had hardly lain back down to wonder at what such a thing could mean when he fell into a deep, deep sleep.

6

◇ THE BELT & THE BLADE ◇

TORIN WOKE EARLY the next morning and stepped out of Fjellhall
to a glorious sight. The crisp golden dawn painted the mountain
ridges above Gatewatch with streaks of honeyed light so that their
peaks shone like jagged blades of rusted copper. The sky above
blushed pink at the horizon and he could already feel the warmth
of the sunlight on his face. He breathed in the morning air which
seemed, as his father had often described it, as if it had been
scrubbed clean by the stars and still faintly carried their scent. If
Torin had not declared his intention to travel with a company, he
might have simply commandeered a horse and galloped off into
the wild woods toward the Everspring right then.

The Greyraven's ring hung strange and heavy around his
neck. Though Jarl Bor did not mention anything about magic, it
certainly seemed to hum with energy, restless and reckless and
ravenous all at once. And then there was the voice he heard, or
thought he heard, last night in the loft. He wondered if someone,
or something, had actually spoken to him, or if it was simply an
effect of drinking too much mead.

A moment later his stomach groaned. Breakfast in Fjellhall
would be his last decent meal in a long while and he would regret
skipping it. He lingered for another moment in the brightening

light, its warmth washing over the exposed skin of his arms and face. Then the scent of fresh-baked bread wafted out from the hall. Torin stole one more glance at the golden-peaked mountains and took a blissful whiff of fresh morning air before slipping back inside that ancient hall.

When Torin had stepped outside, everyone was still fast asleep. Now a fire crackled in the hearth as hall hands rushed about in preparation for breakfast. He saw the whole Armeahan company gathered at the far end of one of the long timber tables. Each one had a cup of hot cider in their hand and listened closely to Aldrin and Prince Azal who were addressing them in their own language. Grimsa, Wyla, and Bari sat close by.

Wyla saw Torin and waved. "Ten-Trees! There you are. Let's get on with breakfast so we can get moving."

Torin bumped Grimsa on the shoulder as he sat down. "Shouldn't you still be cozied up to your bride in bed?"

Grimsa sighed. "Signy has something special planned, so Signa woke up early to help her."

One of the hall hands brought Torin a cup of steaming cider. He took a sip, the spiced apple flavour like a splash of sunlight on his tongue, then motioned to the group of Armeahans. "What are they talking about?"

Grimsa leaned toward him and whispered. "The old wizard wants to bring their men along."

Without the slightest pause, Aldrin turned to face them and waggled his finger at Grimsa. "I am not a wizard, Grimsa Jarnskald, I am a Lorekeeper. Let's be clear about that."

Wyla frowned. "What's the difference?"

Azal motioned to his left. "A wizard will set your cloak on fire with a magic spell." Then he motioned to his right. "A Lorekeeper will use the same spell, then proceed to write a book about it."

Torin motioned toward the Armeahan company with his mug of cider. "We can't bring them all along with us. We need to move quickly, and we can only carry so many supplies."

Azal threw up his hands. "That's what I've been telling him!"

"To be honest," Torin said, "I'm already worried enough about you two. The rest of us have fought trolls and giants before, but neither of you have ever even seen one."

Aldrin huffed. "I have read dozens of accounts of troll slayings and personally own enough books on the *jotur* to cover the entire floor of this hall. I think that knowledge shall suffice!"

"Reading and seeing are not the same thing, Lorekeeper."

Azal shuffled along the bench closer to Torin and the others. "I agree."

"Do you doubt the strength of your own men, Prince Azalweir?" said Aldrin. "They followed you all the way from the courtyard of King Ghezelweir's Palace to this wretched mountain outpost. Now you would leave them behind when we face the greatest danger?"

"I don't doubt them," Azal said, "I value their lives. What do you expect them to do against a troll? They are not troll hunters. Nor are they nameless pawns to be wagered and sacrificed whenever you please!"

Aldrin laughed; a humourless chuckle laced with a bitter edge. "Why do you ask what they will do? How about yourself? Is your life so cheap? What will you do when a troll attacks and your father's men are not there to defend you? And if a troll should stomp you flat, then what are your countrymen to do? Return home? I would not envy the one who brings King Ghezelweir news of his son's death."

"This is exactly what will happen: these men will stay here while we retrieve a draught from the Everspring. When we return, they will accompany us back to Armeah. It's as simple as that!" Azal breathed heavy, his words bouncing off Aldrin's ears like useless pebbles. The prince puffed out his chest and motioned toward Torin. "Besides, Torin Ten-Trees has been given the Greyraven's ring. He is in charge of this expedition and, like it or not, he agrees with me."

Torin held a stern look on his face as the Lorekeeper turned to him.

"Very well," said Aldrin. "But when we are short a dozen swords in two days' time, don't whine to me about it!" The Lorekeeper barked some orders in Armeahan, and the company dispersed with haste.

Feelings improved over breakfast. Each one stuffed themselves full with fresh-baked biscuits drizzled in blackberry jam, thick strips of smoked bacon, and golden-yolked boiled eggs. Even Aldrin took a second biscuit and reluctantly admitted that the jam was the sweetest he had ever tasted. They washed it all down with another cup of spiced cider, as sweet and crisp as an apple straight off the tree.

After breakfast, Aldrin pulled out the enchanted map. He used the sleeve of his tunic to brush away any stray crumbs. With a quick flick of his wrist, the map unrolled across the table.

Torin had been intensely interested in the map when he first saw it but had failed to study it closely. In viewing it a second time, he realized that the swirling strokes of blue ink around the border of the map were not the only sections of script. Every line on the page, from those that made up swaths of trees to those that outlined rigid mountains, was not made of simple ink strokes but of carefully shaped *nidavellish* text. He leaned in and squinted at the tiny letters.

Aldrin tapped a bony finger on the top left corner of the map. "This is our destination. The Everspring, according to legend, lies in the mountains far to the north, above a wide lake."

Wyla frowned. "Are you sure?"

Aldrin pulled out a piece of glass from another pocket in his cloak. It reminded Torin of a round river stone except that it was much smoother and ringed with a thin band of silver. The old Lorekeeper shoved it up against one eye and closed the other. He hunched over the map and traced the lines along the design he had pointed to just before.

> *The world mother spins her web*
> *From northern spring to ocean's ebb*
> *'Til all she 'twines in wat'ry strands*
> *To quench the thirst of distant lands*

Aldrin stuck out his chin and raised his eyebrows. The strange circular glass enlarged his eye so that he looked like a winking owl. "What do you make of that, Wyla White-Blaze? Does that satisfy your doubt?"

Wyla shuddered. "What does it mean by 'web'? I reckon that can only mean spiders."

Aldrin rolled the one eye he had open, which was greatly magnified by the round glass. "It is a *metaphor*, though I should hardly expect you stone-brained troll hunters to capture the nuance of such a thing." The old scholar sighed and rubbed his temples a moment before he continued. "Look, the spinning web is the swirling waters of the Everspring. It is called 'mother' because it gives birth to all rivers. And, if you look at the map, the rivers appear to create a web over the whole world in wandering strands like the webs that a spider makes. Is that so hard to comprehend? See? A metaphor."

Wyla shrugged. "I guess so."

Grimsa grinned. "Then we don't have very far to go. It looks about as far north and west as Ravensnest is east of here. You've already made half the journey, Lorekeeper!"

Aldrin shook his head again. "You've obviously never read a map before. The distances are meaningless. How would anyone measure them? It is the relative positions that are important and even those are only estimates. See, the more the mapmaker knows, the more they will include. Obviously, the illustrator of this map knew much about Noros and the lands surrounding it. Look at the detail, especially here in the forest around Gatewatch!"

The old man tapped on different areas around Gatewatch then worked all the way out to Ravensnest by the sea. "However, we should be wary of the fact that very little is written about the lands west and north of Gatewatch. According to the accounts I have read, the journey could take up to a full lunar cycle."

"How long?" said Bari. "We *nidavel* don't reckon time by the moon."

"About a twelfth-year," said Azal. "Twenty-eight days to be exact."

Torin frowned. "Is that one way or there and back?"

"We are headed to the edge of the earth, Master Ten-Trees," the Lorekeeper said, "Of course that is one way!"

Wyla crossed her arms. "If that's true, then winter will be well on its way by the time we return. The summers here are short; three moons at best."

"And that," said Aldrin, "is exactly why we came with such haste. We must leave as soon as possible."

Bari scratched his beard. "Where should we go first? North then west or the other way around?"

Torin leaned over the map to study it. After a moment, he pointed to one of the illustrations. "Here, just west of Gatewatch. I think I recognize that peak. It must be Troll's Tongue Mountain."

Wyla tilted her head then nodded. "I think you're right. And that must be the Vimur River there beside it."

Azal's eyes lit up. "Have you been there before?"

Torin shook his head. "No, but at the far end of one of our patrol routes, there is a bluff overlooking the Vimur River with a view to the west. The mountain looks like an enormous troll sticking its tongue out." Torin pointed again at the map. "Look, just like that."

Wyla traced the wandering line of the Vimur River with her finger. "According to this, it is connected to the River Noros a little way north of the mountain."

Torin grinned and continued to trace the route. "Then we follow the River Noros north and west, straight to the Everspring. With the spring thaw, it might be passable."

The company discussed a few alternatives, but no other route looked as promising. Other passages took them through bogs, dense patches of forest, or maze-like lake systems which might take months to traverse. Torin asked Bari whether any of the *nidavellish* roads, those deep underground tunnels, ran along their route. Bari pointed out areas to the west and south where the underground roads were secure and safe, but those would only lead the company away from their destination. For once, it seemed, the whole company agreed on something, and Torin thanked the gods for that.

One of the doors at the back end of the hall creaked open. Keymaster Signy emerged with Signa and Siggam following close behind her, each of the twins carrying a bundle wrapped in fine cloth.

"Keymaster Signy," said Bari, "Dinner last night and breakfast this morning make me wish that *nidavel* could be Greycloaks too!"

"You know," said Wyla, "It is not all just drinking and feasting in Fjellhall. There are actual trolls to slay."

"Better to be a guest," Torin said. "You get to eat all of the food without having to hunt any trolls. Besides, you know what the *skalds* say."

> *One day a guest is fair and fine*
> *For two a friend will share their wine*
> *For three might kinsfolk feast together*
> *But surely four brings stormy weather*

Grimsa raised a finger high in the air. "True. But to be clear, there is a lot of drinking and feasting."

Signy smiled and laid her hand on Grimsa's shoulders. Though the big man was sitting down, his shoulders were level with hers as she stood beside him. Signa squeezed in to sit beside Grimsa. Siggam, who was rarely one for words, stood silently beside his mother.

Keymaster Signy gave a long sigh and a tired smile. "I have something to declare, something that should have been declared long ago. Many years ago, I was a young woman, and my mother carried the key to Fjellhall around her waist. I had dreams of seeing the world, of travelling to far-off places and sailing upon the glistening sea far beyond these mountains. Yet here I am. Now that I am grey with age, I do not regret how the fate-threads of my life were spun. However, this may be the last time that all the family I have in the world is gathered together in one place and so I have some things to say."

The room fell silent as the last of the hall hands disappeared into the kitchen. Signy straightened her posture and cleared her throat. "First, I declare that I lost a child in my youth. The hole that this left in my heart was so savagely torn that I thought there would be little hope of ever healing and in truth it never has. Then a terrible tragedy led to something very special. Signa and Siggam's father fell against the trolls after their mother had died in childbirth. Adopting them was the spark that lit a blaze of hope in my soul, and it has burned ever brighter since."

Signa looked up at Signy with a smile and Siggam squeezed the old woman's shoulder. Torin clenched his teeth. He did not wish them unhappiness, but their happiness was a large portion of what should have been his. Somewhere inside the cage of his chest, a motherless child still wandered.

"And now, my dear Signa has married a fine young man." Signy looked at Grimsa with bright eyes. "I am so proud that you have been chosen as a Greycloak, even more that your duty to the Gatewatch and your friendship with Torin compels you to take up this momentous task. You are my son now and I will do all I can to equip you for the journey." Signy motioned toward the bundle that Signa had set on the table. "I have a gift for you."

Signa took the bundle from under her arm and laid it in front of Grimsa. As Grimsa unwrapped it, he found a belt made of silver clasps, each one interlocking with the next.

Signy beamed with pride. "This was a gift given to my father, Runolf the Old, by Araldof Greyraven himself. Its name is *Gingjord* and it is ripe with *nidavellish* magic. Try it on."

Grimsa stood and wrapped the belt around his waist. It fit, though only on the very last of the silver clasps. He looked down and gripped the buckle at his waist. "What sort of magic does it have?"

As Signa chuckled and blushed, Keymaster Signy raised an eyebrow. "Not that sort of magic." At that, Grimsa blushed red as cherry wine too.

"In his youth," Signy said, "My father, Runolf, fought alongside Beoric the Bear at the Battle of Gatewatch. When King Araldof Greyraven took up Beoric's throne, Runolf was already very old. His spirit was fierce, but his body had weakened with age. This gift was meant to help him regain the strength he possessed in his youth, so this belt should make someone like you as strong as a *jotur*. And I think you will need all the strength you can muster if you hope to return from such a far-off place alive."

Grimsa embraced the old woman with both of his burly arms. "Thank you, mother. I will wear *Gingjord* the whole way."

"Not too hard, Grimsa," said Wyla. "You already nearly crush those you hug with your natural strength. Breaking your own mother-in-law's ribs on the first day of your marriage is bad luck, I think."

Grimsa rolled his eyes then sat down beside Signa at the bench. Signy motioned to Siggam, and he laid his bundle on the table. "The other gift I have was also my father's and should be carried only by one with my own blood."

She drew aside the cloth to reveal a sword in its scabbard, the hilt finely forged, and the sheath made from black leather. All the way up, there were runes pressed into the dark material and etched into the metal hilt. The letters twisted and curved at cruel angles which wrapped their way around the scabbard like a shadowy serpent tied up with itself in knots.

"This blade is called *Tyrfang*. My mother, Sigrilinn, said she found it while wandering the wilds beyond Stonering Keep before the wall was built. She gave it to my father as a gift at their wedding. I do not know of its origins, but I do know this: the blade is blessed, and the blade is cursed. It is as light as a birch branch, as hard as granite, and sharper than an eagle's talon. However, once drawn it cannot be sheathed until it has tasted blood." She pointed to the letters along the sheathe. "That's what these runes say, or so I'm told. Whoever ignores the blade's warning will be betrayed by it. Sigrilinn gave it to Runolf on the night of their wedding. My father never transgressed the law of the blade, and he lived a long life. What's more, he was never once bested in battle with this sword in his hand."

"Who do you mean," Wyla said, "by one with your own blood?"

Signy closed her eyes. "I would not speak for him." Then she raised her head and looked straight at Torin. "But it is his if he would accept it."

Grimsa's eyes stretched wide and Wyla drew in a quick breath. Signa and Siggam looked back and forth between Torin, the sword, and their mother.

Torin felt his cheeks burn as hot blood pumped up through his neck. The whispers and shaking heads of the others blurred as he focused his eyes on Signy. Her steel-grey gaze met his and did not waver.

Torin forced a smirk. "How can I know until I hear it from my father? Besides, picking up a cursed blade without knowing for sure whether you're the heir is risky, isn't it?" He saw the sting of every word in Signy's expression and would have admitted then that he did not care.

Signy held firm and her voice only quavered a little. "Then what else am I to do to help?"

Torin shook his head. "I didn't ask for your help."

"Take the sword, Torin. Your grandfather's spirit is still in it."

"You said he died an old man. Did he die in bed?"

Signy shot a scalding look at him. "He died fighting trolls. You should know that he fell in battle. There were three of the beasts and only one escaped with its life. Despite his wounds he limped back to Gatewatch and died in the fields downhill from Stonering Keep. His blood ran down those hills and the grass there has ever grown greener for it." Signy fought to calm her breath but kept her gaze level. "He was seventy years and one."

"You are right," Torin said, "Your son should have been told such things. He should have known the story of his own grand-father's death and a great deal more." He turned to the rest of the company. "Ready yourselves. We will leave before midday. I'll be down at the stables." With a shallow bow toward Signy, he turned to leave.

Signy called after him. "Torin!"

But Torin did not stop or slow down. He did draw one last deep breath, the air rich with the scent of that place, before he passed through the door. With it came a rush of memories and the sting of tears that threatened to form in the corners of his eyes.

Down at the stables Captain Gavring and Jarl Bor had already seen to their provisions and their horses. Five sturdy mounts and a stalwart pony had been saddled. Two more ponies carried extra provisions. Stable hands tightened straps and checked harnesses, tying on gear, or double counting the canvas sacks. The whole place smelled like leather, rusted iron, and all the other scents that accompany horses.

"Ten-Trees," said Jarl Bor, "I thought it might have just been the drink talking last night, but here you are. So, you really mean to make a journey to the Everspring?"

Captain Gavring snorted. "Of course, he does."

Torin nodded. "And you should know, Jarl Bor, that even if you hadn't forced my hand, I would have gone at Gavring's request."

A smile spread across Jarl Bor's face beneath his grizzled grey beard. "I'm sure you would have. But would the captain have had the heart to ask you to undertake such a dangerous task?" The old jarl waited for Gavring's response, but he either didn't catch his words or he willfully ignored them. "I don't think so. But I chose the right man for the task. Besides, when you return, you'll gain even more fame than you did from slaying the Troll-King!"

"You say that as if you are doing me a favour," said Torin.

Bor shrugged. "Maybe I am. Only time will tell."

"Well thank you for so generously providing all these provisions," said Torin. "I promise I won't let my friend Grimsa drink up all the wine on the first night." Bor narrowed his gaze and Gavring grinned.

With that Torin left to inspect the horses. Each one had been freshly groomed with its girth done up tight and its saddle on straight and secure. He counted the provisions then counted them again. By his reckoning they would stretch about six weeks which was two short of Aldrin's estimate. However, with spring would come bushes full of berries, salmon running upriver, and plenty of wild game. If he and Wyla did a bit of hunting they could make it well into the fall.

Each horse also had a quiver full of finely fletched arrows strapped to its saddle. Torin recognized them at once as arrows made by Asa Grettir's-daughter. She had been a part of Torin's company when they were captured by trolls and then escaped to Myrkheim, but she had lost her leg in the battle against the Troll-King. The Greyraven's law decreed that the debt of service owed to him by any who lost a hand, a foot, an arm, or a leg was considered paid in full. As such, Asa was relieved of her duty and handed a bag of silver coins.

However, instead of returning home as most of the wounded do, she spent her silver on a small house in Gatewatch beside an old husband and wife who fletched arrows for the Greycloaks. She quickly learned the craft of fletching from them and had since made a name for herself as the finest maker of arrows in all of Noros. Several Greycloaks refused to use any arrows but those she crafted and some even bartered for goods with them down at the weekly market.

Soon the others arrived from Fjellhall with their essential belongings, mostly clothes and weapons, as well as a few loaves of fresh bread which Signy must have sent along.

"Look at this," said Grimsa, "I've never seen so many provisions on a horse!"

"It's a long journey," Torin said, "And we don't want you eating us."

With a grunt Grimsa hauled his bundle of belongings onto one of the ponies. "After a few days on the trail I wouldn't get within six paces of any of you. But hopefully the stench will keep the trolls away!"

Wyla tied her gear to her horse then tugged the straps to test them. "We'll be following a river, you know. If any of you start to stink, I'll just push you in."

Torin turned to Bari. "I know Grimsa, and I can swim, but can you?"

"Swim?" said Bari. "Of course not! Who would ever jump into a cold lake or river just to flail around like a fish?"

Wyla laughed. "Then I hope *nidavel* float!"

Azal inspected the various straps and knots that held his saddle in place. "I've never seen a design like this. It's so simple but seems effective."

Wyla grabbed the reins of her mount and stroked the steed's mane. "So, you spent a lot of time riding wherever you came from?"

"That's all he did," said Aldrin, "Nothing but the promise of meeting troll hunters could tear him away from his favourite hobby."

Azal groaned. "Riding is not a hobby! Not if you can win races. Last summer I won more than enough in prize money to feed and house a man for a year."

Wyla tilted her head. "Races?"

Azal gave a sweeping bow. "You are looking at last year's champion of the King's Race."

Aldrin chuckled and wheezed as he pulled himself up onto his horse. "Champion, yes. Well, some would say that no one dares to beat a prince at his own game."

"I know what they say," Azal said, "But no one has beat me yet! Not even the foreign princes, and *they* would relish a chance to knock me off the victor's pedestal." With a touch of his heels, Azal led his horse in a tight circle then trotted off toward Stonering Keep.

Grimsa stopped packing and stroked his beard. "I haven't quite decided whether I am fond of this Azal fellow or if I would rather just throw him into a river."

Aldrin sighed. "Of course, as a subject of the King of Armeah, I can't suggest that you throw him into a river, but I do admit that I have had the same thought myself."

"Hurry up, you louts," said Wyla. "I can hear the crowd gathering in Stonering Keep." She dug her heels into her mount and snapped the reins. With a whinny, the horse charged forward and disappeared around the corner down the street.

Bari and Aldrin followed Wyla, though at a much slower pace, while Torin and Grimsa checked over their gear. Torin tested the knots that held his belongings to the saddle as he checked it.

Grimsa moved close to Torin and kept his voice low. "Is Keymaster Signy really your mother?"

Torin stopped fiddling with the knots and clenched his fists. "So she says."

Grimsa's eyes went wide with disbelief. "After all these years. By the gods, I thought your mother was dead."

Torin shook his head. "So did I."

A wide grin broke over Grimsa's face. "I guess that makes us twice brothers! Once through fosterage and once through marriage. How about that?"

Torin turned toward Grimsa and gripped his friend's shoulder. "Grimsa, you are the only brother I have in the whole world. I'm sorry I didn't ask you to come along. I know you better than that."

"It doesn't make a difference," Grimsa said. "You never could have got away without me anyhow!"

Torin laughed and embraced his old friend. He thought again of Bryn, his other foster-brother, who fell against the Troll-King, and of his father who was waiting so far away. At that moment he missed them both fiercely, but there was a task ahead and answers lay at its end, if they made it back at all. Without another word each picked up the reins of his mount and led it out of the stables.

Stonering Keep was nearly as busy as it had been during the Spring Festival. A crowd of townsfolk waved cedar boughs and homespun raven banners. Above them, around the wall that encircled the courtyard, stoic Greycloaks stood proud and tall.

Torin and Grimsa led their horses to the center of the keep and Signa ran up to greet them. Meanwhile, Azal dazzled the crowd as he rode around the courtyard standing up on his saddle. A moment later, the prince spun mid-air in a perfect circle and landed back in his seat. Cheers erupted at this and every other trick he performed on horseback. With every round of applause, Azal's face beamed. At last, the company brought their horses into a line at the center of Stonering Keep.

"Torin Ten-Trees," Captain Gavring said. "Just yesterday you stood in that very spot and refused the grey cloak. Now here you are, ready to set out for the Everspring!" Greycloaks along the wall grinned and chuckled. "It is my deepest hope that the healing draught you bring back will free Araldof Greyraven of whatever ill magic holds his mind prisoner. Let it not be said that we equipped you poorly for the journey. Is there anything else you need?"

"No, Captain," Torin said. "We have all the equipment we need, and our horses' backs might break if we tried to load up any more provisions."

One of the Greycloaks pointed at Aldrin. "What about the wizard? He has no weapon. He can borrow my axe if there is enough strength in his arm to lift it."

Aldrin's wrinkled face flushed red. "For the last time, I am not a wizard! I am a Lorekeeper and yes, there is a difference."

The old Lorekeeper gripped his long wooden staff and whispered strange words in harsh, percussive syllables. Then, with a loud snap, the tip of the staff ignited into a swell of orange flame. Aldrin twirled it over his head with surprising dexterity and caught it again. The crowd gasped and then applauded him just as they had for Azal's stunts on horseback. Aldrin rolled his eyes and blew out the fire on the end of his staff. "I know well enough how to keep myself safe on the road. Keep your axe, trollhunter."

"Very well," said Gavring. "Then we wish you a swift journey! May the gods guide your way. We will eagerly await your return and will hope with every thought to see your faces again before the first snow of winter falls." The captain turned toward the gatehouse. "Open the West Gate! Make way for the Everspring Company! Long live the Greyraven! Long live The Gatewatch!"

A horn sounded as they passed under the West Gate, out of Stonering Keep, and down into the sloping fields beyond. Torin looked back and saw the ramparts packed full of Greycloaks, townsfolk, and Armeahans, all cheering and holding banners. Wyla and Bari both waved back at the crowd while Grimsa blew kisses to Signa. The Armeahans whooped with pride and shouted a chant in their own tongue. The roar of the crowd then spurred them on as they began the descent along the wide trail that led into the overgrown forest.

High above the others, up at the very top of the gate tower, Torin saw Signy's silhouette against the bright midday sky. He thought of her standing atop the East Gate tower on the other side of Gatewatch all those years ago, as she watched his father's men ride away with him in tow. That thought tugged at something in Torin's chest and his throat tightened. He kept his eyes fixed on her for a moment longer. Then, all at once, the path dropped steeply and all of Gatewatch disappeared behind a rise of rock and turf.

7

◇ SPELLFIRE ◇

THE WINDING TRAIL descended steeply over cold, trickling creeks and clumps of dewy turf, the air rich with an earthy aroma. During his years in Gatewatch, Torin had followed that rocky path down into the wild forest countless times and had grown fond of it despite the dangers it led to. Indeed, he thought that no one who had travelled west of Stonering Keep could deny the beauty of those flowering alpine meadows framed by towering slate-grey peaks.

Soon they left the open fields behind and entered the overgrown forest. Towering cedar and fir trees rose like the pillars of a giant's hall, its roof so large that it stretched across the entire valley. It was a little past noon, and the midday sun lit the uppermost branches while those further down cast a cool shade over the company. The forest floor was damp with moss and the sharp scent of evergreen sap tinged the air with acidic sweetness.

Those woods were full of life, wild and quick and untamed. Rabbits dashed through the dense ferns and birds of various colours, sizes, and songs nested high overhead. Between the enormous cedar trunks, Torin caught a glimpse of a nervous doe nibbling on fresh spring shoots. Its body was lean from the long winter, and it snapped up the foliage in quick, greedy bites. Torin's horse snorted, and the creature looked up. The doe froze for half a second then disappeared in a flash of tan fur.

As the trail continued to wind deeper into the valley, the trees stretched up ever higher. At first, the sunlight pierced the canopy to light the ferns, the ivy, and the moss far below, but now it came through in little more than a trickle. Bright greens dimmed to darker shades and the hollow spaces under dead tree trunks sank into shadow.

A branch snapped somewhere out in the forest and Azal gasped. "What was that?"

Wyla motioned for silence and Torin signaled the company to stop. There was a violent rustling in the brush about twenty paces up the trail.

Torin quickly untied the leather straps that held *Skrar*, his spear, to the saddle, as Grimsa dismounted and hefted his axe. Wyla and Bari reached for their bows and Azal drew out a curved sword with a thin blade. Aldrin whispered strange words and sheltered the tip of his staff like a candle flame. Torin saw a few small sparks fly out from the end of the Lorekeeper's staff, but another rustling sound drew his attention back to the trail.

A shrieking squeal erupted from the brambles, followed by a flash of bristling black fur. An enormous boar burst out of the bushes and charged at them, its tusks like rusty butcher's knives and its hooves tearing up the trail. Grimsa rushed forward with his long-neck axe overhead as Wyla and Bari's arrows whistled past him into the creature's shoulder.

Aldrin shouted a strange word. The ground beneath the boar erupted in an explosion of orange flame and brown dirt. With a stilted grunt, the creature was thrown off its feet and tumbled away down the trail. Grimsa, who had just started to swing his axe when the trail erupted with fire, lost hold of his weapon mid-swing and stumbled.

The flash of heat died down as quickly as it had appeared. Through a smoky haze, Torin saw the boar stand and shake itself off. The ends of the wiry hairs left along its back smoked like snuffed candle wicks and its right side had been scorched so it was completely hairless. Two broken arrow shafts protruded from its shoulder and the creature's eyes were bloodshot with rage. The boar snorted and wheeled around then let out a wretched squeal that nearly split Torin's ear drums.

Torin stood his ground with *Skrar* in hand as the creature charged at him. The beast's wounds hardly seemed to slow it down and Torin jumped aside just as its razor tusks flew by. With a quick lurch he thrust the spear into the boar's neck below its jaw. A spew of bright red blood splattered Torin's chest and face with a film of gore. Still, the boar kicked and thrashed, so Torin pressed his spear deeper and pinned it to the ground.

Wyla snatched up her axe, leapt off her horse, then swung the steel blade down. It sank deep into the boar's skull with a squelching crack. At that, the boar lay still and fought no more.

Everyone took a few more heavy breaths before Grimsa, red faced, threw up his hands. "Troll's blood! By thunderous Orr and all the gods, what sort of wizard magic was that?"

Aldrin pointed at Grimsa with his gnarled wooden staff. "That spell may have saved your life! Those tusks were coming straight at you."

"You nearly set me on fire with your damned trick! And by the way, I would have killed it with one quick stroke of my axe if you hadn't blown the thing ten paces down the trail. Now where's my axe? I lost my grip when your fireball exploded in my face."

"I was just trying to help," Aldrin said. "Besides, you all thought I couldn't defend myself. Well, now you know I can."

Grimsa huffed. "Well, the next time you get the urge to cast your curses, try not to singe my beard off in the process!" He scowled and peered off into the bushes. "Now where's my damn axe?"

"Never mind the old man, Grimsa Jarnskald. He's always like that. Here, I'll help you search." Azal hopped off his horse and followed Grimsa off into the woods.

Wyla yanked her axe out of the boar's head and looked at Torin with a wicked grin. "Were you really ready to give all this up?"

Torin wiped the boar blood off his face and spit out a bit that had dripped into his mouth. "You're right. What job could be more glamorous than this?"

"By the Mastersmith," Bari said, "I reckon you'd scare a troll off with that blood-smeared grin!"

Torin used the edge of his cloak to clean *Skrar* as best he could. Wyla wiped her axe on a patch of moss. Bari extracted the two arrowheads lodged in the boar's shoulder with his knife, then spit on each one to polish them up before slipping them into his pocket.

Through the trees, the sound of Grimsa's lumbering steps grew louder. "Found my axe," Grimsa said. "It was lodged in the trunk of a big cedar. Easy to spot."

"I tried to pull it out, but I couldn't," Azal said. "I even hung from it like a branch, but it wouldn't budge."

Grimsa slapped the prince on the back. "That's because you're too skinny, prince! But feasting with us for a while should cure that. And speaking of feasts, how will we carry our prize?"

"The boar?" Bari said. "It's bigger than me. And the horses are fully loaded with provisions."

Wyla gave the carcass a light kick. "A shame to waste it."

"It might save a few day's provisions," said Torin. "Besides, thanks to the Lorekeeper, it is already half cooked!" Everyone laughed, except Aldrin.

Grimsa slipped his thumbs behind *Gingjord's* silver buckle. "Well, I have a strengthening charm in this belt, or so Keymaster

Signy said. No time to hang the boar properly, but I'll carry the choice cuts on foot until we make camp. Then we'll have a proper roast for dinner!"

He made quick work of separating the shoulder, loin, and rump. He stuffed them into one of the extra canvas sacks, then heaved it over his shoulder. And so, the company continued down the trail.

Above the forest, a wind picked up and in their upper reaches the trees began to dance and sway. Through the small gaps between the lofty branches, Torin saw swells of grey cloud and the cool breeze carried the smell of rain. He reckoned it would fall before dinner.

And it did. Although they heard the patter of rain above them, only a sheer mist made it through the canopy. For the better part of the afternoon, it drizzled through the trees and dampened their clothing. Soon the trail was so slick with mud that even their horses, sure-footed as any, began to slip and stumble. Despite the rain, Torin and Wyla were in good spirits at the head of the party, with Bari and Azal close behind. Grimsa and Aldrin, both significantly more miserable than the others, brought up the rear.

Grimsa hefted the sack of boar meat which had slipped off his shoulder. "By Orr and all the gods, we'll be lucky to find any dry wood to make a roast in this weather."

Aldrin scoffed and pulled his cloak tighter around his chest. "Dry wood? We have enough provisions to last us for weeks. I am more concerned about finding a dry place to sleep. By the King's sceptre, the weather here! If the wind here is not biting my bones with cold, then the damp is soaking my cloak to try and freeze me to death."

Wyla turned around in her saddle. "How do you put up with all his griping, Azal?"

The prince shrugged. "You get used to it. For all his faults, the old man has his merits. Certainly no one in the kingdom of Armeah can match him for knowledge of history or languages."

"Language," Bari said. "Yes, that is his skill. I must say that he complains quite fluently."

Torin laughed. "Well, I suppose if I'm still riding out into the wilds at eighty winters, I'll have earned the right to complain."

Aldrin shouted at them from up the sloped trail. "Eighty winters? Do you think me a corpse? I'm barely past seventy-three!"

Torin craned his neck around toward the Lorekeeper. "I am amazed you can hear us! Most men as old as you can barely hear at all."

The prince leaned forward in his saddle and whispered. "He can't! The old man uses charms and spells to eavesdrop on conversations. Keep that in mind if you try to sneak out of your father's courtyard at night or plan to slip a tankard full of horse piss into the wine vats at the noble's feast."

Aldrin shouted back. "Horse piss in the wine vats? Ha! That's hardly the worst of it. Besides, your sister got away with far more outrageous things, despite my best efforts."

Azal jumped up and sat down backwards in his saddle. "My sister? Really?"

"Oh, yes!"

"Like what?"

Aldrin scrunched up his nose. "That will remain a secret to all but the king himself."

"But how? She is the most nauseatingly responsible person I know. And how did she get away with *anything* when a crowd of royal courtiers was watching her nearly every second of every day?"

"Because," said Aldrin, "she knew how to shut up and keep a secret, a skill that you seem practically incapable of acquiring."

The path widened and so Grimsa strode up beside the prince. "I know what it's like living in the shadow of an older sibling. My brother Gunnar was a mighty troll hunter, and everyone expected me to live up to his legend." Grimsa puffed up his chest and gave it a few hard knocks with his free hand. "But he was never offered a Greycloak! Now he's back at home fishing with my father. What's more, I have already managed to slay more trolls than him! When I go back one day, it will be him raising a glass to me. Won't your sister do the same when you return from the Everspring?"

"It's one thing to live in a sibling's shadow," said Azal, "and another to live under their royal thumb. Can you believe that my sister expects me to bow to her when she sits beside my father in court?"

Aldrin sighed, rubbing his forehead. "Prince Azalweir, everyone but the king must bow to her in court. It is protocol and it is proper."

A scowl swept across Azal's face. "That doesn't mean I have to like it. Or her."

"Your sister is the best thing to happen to the kingdom of Armeah since your father's coronation."

Azal rolled his eyes and spun in his saddle to face forward again. "Yes, yes. She's perfect. Everyone loves her and she never does anything wrong. Or at least she doesn't get caught."

"And in court life," said Aldrin, "those two can certainly be equated!"

Torin pointed down the trail. "We'll set up camp soon. I know of a place up ahead, a clearing beside the Vimur River. Then we can start a fire and get the roast going before sundown."

"Why not push on," Aldrin asked, "at least until dusk?"

"We need to cross the Vimur River," said Wyla. "Next to the clearing is a place where we can do that, but it's best we leave it until morning."

"Why wait?"

Wyla twisted in her saddle and narrowed her eyes. "I've seen things creeping around on the far side of the river at night and have no mind to meet them in the dark. Once we're on the other side, we can follow the Vimur up past Troll's Tongue Mountain to where it meets the River Noros."

Bari clapped. "And from there, onto the Everspring!"

Soon the trees spread thin. The sky above began to clear. The company heard the thunderous roar of the Vimur River close ahead and at last they came upon it. Azal and Aldrin's eyes stretched wide at the sight of the rugged boulders along the river-bed, some nearly the size of a house. A pale mist drifted off the foaming white waters and the flicker of bright fish scales flashed in the shallow pools along the river's edge.

"We can't cross here," Aldrin said. "This is a foaming mael-strom of death, not a river!"

Torin squinted through the haze of mist. "Well, in Noros we call this a river." He pointed upstream to a gorge cut from the rock through which the river flowed. White torrents surged forth from the narrow gap, then crashed down into a deep pool far below. "That up there is your maelstrom of death."

Wyla grinned. "And that is where we will cross."

Aldrin's face went pale, and it looked as if the old man might fall right off his horse. The Lorekeeper stuttered a moment before shouting above the noise of the falls. "By the King's sceptre! Do you mean to send us to a quick, icy death, Torin Ten-Trees? This is madness. There must be a calmer crossing!"

Torin shook his head. "Calm is not a word I would ever use to describe the Vimur River."

Wyla pointed up to the gorge. "Look, it's only about ten paces across. We will lay a bridge."

Aldrin threw up his hands. "A bridge? Out of what?"

Grimsa said nothing but pointed at the trees that towered high above them.

Bari nodded and hopped off his pony. "Of course! Well, if we can scavenge some dry wood then I will fashion a fire pit from these river stones, up the bank where it is a bit drier. Then perhaps the Lorekeeper could help speed dinner along with one of his magic flames?"

Grimsa dropped the sack of boar meat onto the bare rock beside the river. "Just be sure to warn me this time *before* you start slinging fireballs."

Despite rain and the mist, there was still a fair amount of dry kindling hidden beneath fallen trunks and rocky outcrops near the river's edge. Before long, they had each gathered a few armfuls of tinder and stacked it inside the neat ring of round stones that Bari had made.

When Aldrin approached the pile of kindling, all the others took a large step back. The old man cupped his hand over the tip of his staff and whispered words which Torin could not quite make out. Then, with a booming voice that seemed far too loud for his bony frame, the Lorekeeper shouted. "*Ahmahratha!*"

A white flame shot up from the wood in a swirling spiral that reached well above Torin's head. The rest of the company watched with wide eyes as it funneled down in between the dry sticks. At its base, the pile of wood crackled and smoked. Despite Torin's doubts, small tongues of orange flame appeared and soon the fire burned steadily.

A smug grin stretched across Aldrin's face as he sat down on a wide stone beside the fire. "Ah, that's more like it. Now, to warm my bones and dry my cloak."

Grimsa fashioned a spit from a few of the longer branches that he had found in the forest. Bari opened a satchel on his belt with a vial of salt and, with a few herbs that Wyla had plucked from the brush, soon had the boar meat salted and seasoned. Just as Grimsa lifted the spit into place, Azal drew out a flask of wine and passed it around. Then the whole company sat down and watched the dancing flames. It was not quite dusk, and the sky was still well lit above them. Each rested their saddle-sore legs as they listened to the crackle of fire and the rush of the river.

When the wine flask reached Grimsa, he took a sip and smacked his lips. "Ah, delicious! Now if only I had brought Drombir's magic cup, that bottomless vessel forged by the *nidavel*. We could have kept sipping this fine wine all night!"

"Yes, I remember it well," said Bari. "You didn't bring it?"

Grimsa shook his head. "No. Magic like that is far too rare to risk on a journey like this."

"Perhaps in Gatewatch," Bari said. "But you would not believe the incredible things that come out of the Mastersmith's forge in Myrkheim. Though I guess you *madur* are, for the most part, averse to dealings with magic."

"Well, not all of us," said Aldrin. "At least not those with a proper education."

Azal frowned and threw a small pebble into the center of the fire. "You know, Aldrin, education isn't all books and magic spells. Didn't you yourself once say that experience is the greatest teacher of all?"

The Lorekeeper gathered his cloak and pulled it tight around his bony frame. "Are you about to deliver a lecture on the subject of experience? Of everyone here, I think you may be the least qualified on that subject."

Azal sighed. "No, no. I have no mind for lectures tonight. But how about a story while we wait for the roast to cook? What do you say, Wyla? Another troll hunting tale, perhaps?"

Wyla motioned for the wine with one hand and pointed to Torin with the other. "Don't look at me. Torin is the one for stories." The others nodded and turned toward him.

Torin scratched his neck for a moment before he spoke. "Alright, let's see. Have you ever heard the tale of Beoric and Fyra? I always think of it when I travel through these woods."

Azal tilted his head. "Beoric? The first King of Noros?"

"Yes, that's him. He sailed north from the Grim Isles long ago. Then he and his company slew the sea-beast, Kolkrabba, before landing on shore where the River Noros meets the sea. The next part of the story happened in a forest not unlike this one. Here is the story as the *skalds* tell it."

> *So landed Beoric's band*
> *Fair timber halls they built*
> *Those dark woods held good game*
> *Thin backs and arms grew thick*
>
> *But night would bring wild things*
> *Which walked the woods and bogs*
> *Worse than the cursed wolves*
> *Trolls most foul and wicked*
>
> *Yet heart did bid him dare*
> *Ever deeper wandering*
> *Strange words he heard and songs*
> *Full of grief and sorrow*
>
> *"My sister were you mad*
> *To make so cruel a trade?*
> *To tear me from fair woods?*
> *Beast-bride of me you've made!"*
>
> *On her silver streaming*
> *Moonlight saw her suffer*
> *So also Beoric saw*
> *Sitting, hiding, listening*
>
> *"Hail pale stranger," said she,*
> *"Long I saw you coming.*
> *Now tell well – what are you:*
> *Wicked foe or hero?"*

Beoric grunted bluntly,
"Bear your own keen judgement.
My crew slew Kolkrabba
And many crafty trolls."

"Fortune fair this moon bears
For sister mine conspires
To dread Troll-King wed me
So she might take these woods."

Grave word he gave and blade
There onward her to guard
So, like a spell, love fell
Binding burning spirits

With Beoric she went quick
Through dark and guarded woods
Out of her sister's grip
And on to Beoric's hall

The company sat in silence for some time, each one reliving the scene in their minds. There, above them, was the moonlight slipping through the trees as Fyra wandered through the woods. Off in the distance, with whatever stealth a man of his size could manage, Beoric hid behind a gnarled tree trunk. Did the huge man stumble out of the bush with red-flushed cheeks, or did he try to remain hidden among the trees when she called to him? Most of all, Torin wondered what Fyra looked like, that woman of the forest whose beauty captured Beoric's heart at a mere glance.

The flames danced and flickered in a hypnotic rhythm. The whole sky faded from a rosy pink where the sun was setting to a murky deep-water blue on the far horizon. Along that dark edge, dim stars began to flicker, and the moon appeared from behind the clouds, a waxing ivory crescent. Despite the crash of the Vimur River behind them, Torin felt a deep peace settle over him.

After some time, Grimsa rubbed his hands together. "Well, it's getting dark. The roast must be done by now!" He stood up and pulled one of the skewers off the spit to take a bite. His grin vanished when his teeth sunk into the boar meat. His face contorted and he gagged. "By Orr! It's still completely raw!" Grimsa motioned for the last of the wine and set the spit back on its stand. With one swig he emptied the bottle and gurgled it.

Grimsa pointed his finger at Lorekeeper Aldrin. "So, you think you're funny with your damned wizard tricks?"

"Me?" Aldrin said. "By the King's sceptre, how is your undercooked roast my fault?"

"You set the fire with your spell and cursed it so it wouldn't cook the meat!"

"I did no such thing! Sure, I used a spell but there is nothing magical about that flame. Can't you feel its heat? Stick your hand in it if you don't believe me!"

The old man's face soured, and he muttered, mostly to himself. "Besides, what do you know about magic? You can't even read, you blundering oaf." Then the Lorekeeper stuck his arm out from under his cloak and pointed a crooked finger at Grimsa. "And for the last time, I am not a wizard!"

Silence followed the Lorekeeper's words. The others looked at each other with wide eyes. Torin stood up to poke one of the roasts with his finger. "Grimsa's right. Still raw."

Bari tugged at his beard. "It should be charred black after all this time. I fear that more than bad luck is to blame for this."

The old man sighed. "Well, I'm telling you for the last time, it was not me."

"Well, if not you," said Bari, "Then who?"

"Troll's blood," said Wyla. She snatched up her axe and peered into the dark forest. "Damn all this foul magic."

Azal drew his curved sword, though the blade quivered a bit in his grip. "You don't think it really was a troll, do you?"

Grimsa gave a grim chuckle and motioned toward the prince's gilded weapon. "If it is a troll then that flimsy thing won't be much use."

A shadow shot out of the upper reaches of the darkened forest. Like a host of candles snuffed out by a sudden wind, the stars above them went dark. A rush of cold air blasted the company and extinguished their fire in a sudden swirling gust. The inky form spread over them like a cloud, but far too quickly for smoke. Blind in the sudden darkness, Torin cursed and scrambled to pick up *Skrar*.

With his spear readied, Torin braced himself and squinted at the dark mass in front of them. As his eyes adjusted to the bleak moonlight it came into clearer view. It was not a cloud at all, but a creature covered in feathers. He shuffled back as he realized that what hovered over the company was an enormous eagle.

The giant eagle flapped its outstretched wings twice more then settled near the extinguished fire. It stood nearly as tall as Grimsa with a wingspan of what Torin reckoned must have been two or three full spear lengths. The whole company stood frozen in awe as the creature twisted its head to the side and fixed them with an enormous yellow eye. Its beak was ferociously curved, and its clawed talons scraped over the river stones, pinning the boar meat to the ground. In quick snaps, it tore long strips off the raw roast and swallowed them whole.

Grimsa waved his hands high over his head and roared. "Get away from my dinner, you mangy bird, or I'll roast you instead!" With a huff, he hefted a river stone and hurled it at the beast.

The eagle twisted to the side and watched the stone fly by with its keen eyes. Then it surged forward and slammed Grimsa square in the chest with its beak. The huge man tumbled backward onto the rocks as Torin and Wyla charged ahead.

Wyla was the first to get a decent swing at the eagle, but her stroke fell through a cluster of feathers. Before she could raise her axe again, an enormous wing swung out and sent her sprawling.

As the gigantic bird spread its wings wide, Torin dashed forward and thrust *Skrar* into the mass of feathers. The creature let out a piercing shriek as the spear struck flesh and bone. Torin planted his feet and drove *Skrar* deeper. At this, the eagle flapped with fury and pummeled him across the back with its wings.

The eagle's pointed beak came down on Torin's shoulder and his grip on *Skrar's* shaft slipped. The giant bird threw back its head to strike again. Right at that moment, Wyla struck a bludgeoning blow which Torin heard land with a thud. The eagle reared back and screeched in pain. Wyla jumped out of the creature's path as it flailed its mighty wings.

The eagle stumbled away toward the river and squawked furiously with *Skrar* lodged deep in its side. Torin scrambled over the smooth river stones as fast as he could. Bari's arrows zipped over his shoulder, each lost in the mass of feathers as Torin dove for the spear shaft.

One of Aldrin's spells ignited, resulting in a blast of flame that sent both Torin and the eagle tumbling toward the rushing river. The bird was hardly fazed by the blast and righted itself to make an escape. With a single stroke of its mighty wings, it lifted off the ground. Torin barely caught the end of *Skrar's* shaft before the eagle took flight. The bird crashed back down onto the stones under Torin's weight, but then beat its wings harder and took off a second time.

Torin grit his teeth. "By Odd, give me back my spear!"

Torin refused to let go of *Skrar* and the enormous eagle refused to give up its chance at escape. With the next beat of its wings Torin felt himself lifted off the ground. He dangled in the air; the spear shaft still lodged in a mass of feathers. Below him the round river stones became a blur.

Wyla shouted over the din. "Torin, let go! The river!"

Torin whipped his head around and saw the foaming white waters of the Vimur approaching fast. He hesitated for only a moment to tug again at the spear, but that moment proved too long. The misty froth soaked his legs and when he next looked down his feet splashed into the frigid current.

The eagle kept beating its wings harder and screeched as the spearhead started to come loose. The shaft wobbled as Torin tried to pull his feet up, but they splashed in the surging water, the numbing grasp of the current desperate to drag him in. Somewhere beyond the roar of the river, he heard the others shouting. The eagle rose again, this time dislodging the spear and sending Torin hurtling down to the ground.

Torin expected to splash into the freezing water, but instead he came crashing down on a bed of dry river stones. His knees and ribs smashed into the rocks and his head knocked against a stray log. Above him, the giant eagle shrieked and disappeared over the treetops into the gloom of night.

Torin let out a groan and lay still for another moment. In his right hand, he still had a white-knuckled grip on *Skrar's* wooden shaft which had splintered slightly, just below the spearhead. His ears rang from the knock on his head, and he could already feel bruises swelling up along his ribs, which he desperately hoped were not broken.

In the distance, he heard the others calling to him from across the river. Before he turned toward them, though, his eyes caught a flash of movement in the forest ahead. Torin's heart pounded in his chest. He peered into the dark and realized that the murky shape belonged not to a creature but to a woman in a dark green cloak.

She stared at him silently with an unwavering steel-grey gaze as fierce as a wildcat's. Her pale skin seemed to glow an eerie white under the moonlight and a swath of dark ink was smeared across her high-boned cheeks. Around her neck hung a fine silver neck-lace, each interlinked strand glimmering like drops of dew on a spider's web. Thick braids of dark hair, many of them interwo-ven with coloured lengths of leather, fell over her shoulders from beneath her wide hood.

The woman's hands, at first concealed beneath her green cloak, appeared like apparitions unveiled. Slowly, as if she were moving through water, she lifted them up and crossed them so that the tips of her long, slender fingers touched her shoulders. She did not blink or smile, but kept her eyes fixed on Torin with her pale lips drawn tight. At last, after what was only a moment but seemed to Torin like a long while, she opened her mouth as if to speak.

Torin blinked and she was gone.

8

◇ ACROSS THE VIMUR ◇

TORIN BLINKED AGAIN and rubbed his eyes. Not the quickest bird, the fleetest stag, or the slyest fox could have disappeared so quickly. There was not even a flash of green or a swish of her trailing cloak. She had simply disappeared.

Torin took a hesitant step back from the wood. "Who's there?"

His words rang out over the roar of the river, but no reply came from the empty space between the trees. The others were calling from the other side of the river.

"Torin! Can you hear us?"

"What happened?"

"Are you alright?"

Torin turned back toward the river with an uneasy tingle on his neck. After a few steps he glanced back to the forest but caught neither sight nor sign of the woman. He thought that perhaps he was seeing things after that knock on the head. Yet she had appeared in such detail that he doubted his mind could have conjured her up.

Grimsa shouted over the rush of water. "Torin, what's wrong?"

"In the forest," Torin said. "I saw someone!"

"A person?"

"Yes, a woman in a green cloak."

Grimsa paused a moment then called back with a scowl on his face. "No one lives over there. It sounds like the work of landspirits to me, or perhaps some mischievous faeries. We'd better get over to your side right away!"

Torin waved his arms. "No, crossing the river at night is too risky."

Wyla laughed and called back. "So, what? You'll just sleep under the stars by yourself on the far side of the Vimur? Forget it. Besides, we all have to cross sooner or later and there is no point in you coming back to this side. We're coming over."

The thought that the strange woman in the woods could still be watching him made Torin shudder. He glanced over his shoulder again then looked up at the narrow gorge where he had originally planned to cross over. "Meet me up there!" Grimsa nodded, then joined the others as they gathered up the gear and provisions that had been scattered in the fight.

Torin's legs were soaked with freezing river water and his ribs throbbed with swelling bruises. Despite the jabs of pain in his side, he scrambled up the rocky bank as quickly as he was able, eager to get away from the place where he had seen that fleeting figure. Beside him, the Vimur River thundered under the moon.

Yet a certain curiosity grew within him as he climbed. Who was that cloaked woman? Why was she there? She certainly was no commoner. Her cloak was richly sewn and the jewels around her neck sparkled like one hundred minnows in a moonlit pool. She possessed a beauty with force, the kind that could cut hearts open at a glance. Now, when he recalled her piercing gaze, he thought of a queen who might inspire *skalds* to compose epics or strong men to draw swords. Perhaps she was the ruler of the wood, he mused, but that thought left more questions than answers. Who were her subjects? Where did she dwell? And how could it be that the troll hunters of Gatewatch had never heard of her?

At last, Torin reached the top of the gorge. A narrow surge of white water shot over the precipice and dropped into a swirling pool far below. The rocks were slick with moisture but just rough enough for his feet to find a grip. When he peered down into the gap, his heart jumped up into his throat. One false step and he would be swept away, smashed against the rugged rocks, and then hurled over the cliff by the dark foaming torrent.

While the rest of the company picked their way up the opposite slope with the horses, Torin looked for deadfall that might span the gap between both sides of the river. Most of the fallen trunks that could have formed a suitable bridge were far too heavy for Torin to lift by himself. Nevertheless, he managed to drag half a dozen smaller trees out from the edge of the wood despite his throbbing head and his aching ribs. With a heave, he propped each one up and let it fall across the harrowing gap. A few of the thinner ones snapped clean in half as they dropped into the swirling river. By the time the rest of the company reached the top on the other side, Torin had laid a bridge just wide enough for someone to cross.

Grimsa grinned as he came up over the top of the ridge. "How convenient! A bridge built just for us. Could that be the work of faerie folk too?"

Torin leaned forward with his hands on his knees. "By the gods, you are the one with the belt of strength, not me! And don't look so smug. You are going to build another bridge for the horses."

Wyla hopped up onto one of the thicker logs and tested it with her weight. "Seems sturdy enough. Let me get over first before Grimsa breaks it." She grabbed her bow, a quiver full of arrows, and a loose bag of provisions, then darted across the gap. When Wyla reached the end, she hopped off the log next to Torin. "Damn you, Ten-Trees. I wanted to be the first one over."

Torin grinned. "Well, when we get to the Everspring I'll push you in. How about that?"

One of the horses whinnied and reared from the other side. A chill ran down Torin's spine. He squinted at the creature under the dim light of the moon, and he saw a rider on its back. It was the prince.

Azal kicked his heels into his steed's side and snapped the reins. Even from the far side, Torin could see the whites of the horse's eyes as it charged toward the shadowed gap. Then, in a surge of strength and power, it leapt across the gorge. Torin and Wyla stumbled back a few steps as it landed in front of them with the prince still seated comfortably in the saddle.

Azal's voice echoed down the canyon. "Ha! No need for bridges. At least not with a fine horse like this!"

Wyla chuckled. "Show off!"

"So," Azal said, "I've impressed the troll hunters?"

Wyla called back to the others. "Alright, you all saw the prince! Easy as honey-cakes. Now, you three do the same, then we'll all be over."

It seemed Aldrin had given up scolding the prince for such stunts and steadied himself on the far end of the log bridge. "By the King's sceptre, if I had the knees of my youth, I would be over this bridge in a flash. Someone hold the ends, so that the logs don't roll out from beneath my feet!" Bari and Grimsa steadied the logs on one side while Torin and Wyla held down the other.

A few steps in, Aldrin stumbled forward. It looked as if the old man had caught himself, but a second later Torin saw him slipping. Before any of the others could make a move, Grimsa, who was nearest the old man, lunged forward onto the log bridge to grab him. Grimsa's hands caught only a bunch of cloth and Aldrin continued to slide down toward the dark, icy current.

The old man flailed his arms in search of a hold. "Help!"

Grimsa took another step out onto the bridge and caught one of Aldrin's arms. When he did, there was a terrible crack which rattled through the logs so that Torin felt the shock of it in his wrists.

"The bridge," said Bari, "It's breaking!"

By that point, Grimsa was almost halfway across and, perhaps spooked by the cracking noise behind him, shuffled forward as fast as he could. Azal leapt off his horse to help Torin and Wyla as the logs ground over the rocks and slid slowly into the gorge.

"You're almost there," said Wyla, "Quick!"

Before another word could be said, the far side fell away and both Grimsa and Aldrin dipped down out of view, still clinging to the broken logs. Torin, Wyla, and Azal felt the full force of their weight and it nearly dragged them all down into the gorge. With grunts and curses, they fought to keep the logs from slipping any further.

Grimsa roared over the raging current. "My grip is slipping!"

Torin hauled on the logs with all his strength, but they would not budge. "Hold on!"

On the other side, he saw Bari looking on with wide eyes. Behind the *nidavel* stood the horses packed with provisions and supplies. "Bari! Where is the rope?"

Bari heard Torin from across the gap and dashed over to the horses. He yanked gear off the saddles, tossing it in every direction, until he found a length of rope. The *nidavel* took a deep breath then swung round and round. After two or three rotations he hurled the rope over the gorge.

Azal let go of the logs just in time to catch it. The prince fumbled with the knot for a moment before it unraveled then threw a loop around a thick tree stump a few paces back from the river. Torin saw Azal's fingers shake violently as he tied up the rope at a frantic speed.

"Azal," said Wyla. "Faster! The logs are starting to slip!"

The prince dashed back with the loose end of the secured rope. Torin was so close to the gap that the tips of his toes hung out over the edge. Only his heels felt the mist-soaked rocks beneath him, and he dug them in with all his might. Then he gave one final strain on the splintered tree trunks before his feet fell out from under him.

The remaining logs tumbled down into the raging river as Torin slowly slid down the edge of the cliff. He scrambled to find a grip as he skidded over the wet rocks, the churning mass of shadowy currents like a thousand silver snakes far below him. When it seemed that he might tumble down into the darkness, a violent tug choked him at his collar. Wyla had caught him just before he slid out of reach, and she dragged him back up over the top of the cliff's edge.

Azal breathed heavy. "Grimsa's got the rope, but he is too heavy to pull up!"

Grimsa groaned. "By thunderous Orr, I could pull myself up if I wasn't dragging this damned wizard along with me!"

Torin peered down, over to the edge where the rope hung taut. He stretched his hand toward Grimsa's white-knuckled fist, which was gripping the rope, but it was just out of reach. "Grimsa, can you pass Aldrin up to us?"

Grimsa's eyes shot open, and his wide nostrils flared. If he had not been dangling from a rope over that deadly torrent, Grimsa probably would have taken a swing at Torin for merely suggesting it. As it was, Grimsa clenched his jaw and bared his teeth. With a groan which grew into a roar, he gripped the rope with all his might in his right hand while raising Aldrin up in his left. Still, the Lorekeeper was just out of reach.

"Azal," said Wyla. "Lay flat on your stomach and stretch as far as you can down toward Aldrin. Torin and I will hold your feet, so you don't fall. When you've got him, we'll pull you back up."

Azal looked down at the gorge and hesitated.

"Quick," Wyla said. "Get down!"

Azal swallowed hard then dropped down onto his belly. Wyla and Torin each grabbed one of the prince's legs and dangled him into the gorge. Grimsa held the old man over his head and Azal, after a few grasping swipes, managed to catch the Lorekeeper's outstretched hand.

"Alright," said Azal. "I've got him!"

Torin and Wyla pulled with all their strength. All four of them tumbled backward, bruising ribs and bashing hips on the unforgiving stones. Aldrin was spared the worst of it as he landed on top of the heap. When they looked up, they saw Grimsa, red-faced and wheezing, hauling himself up over the edge.

Grimsa let go of the rope and fell flat on his back once he was safely away from the precipice. "Are the gods trying to smite us?"

Torin sat up and pulled his hair out of his face. "If not the gods, then who?"

Aldrin, though he was still trying to catch his breath, called out to the others. "The Greyraven's map! I felt it slipping out of my robe as you pulled me up! Where is it?"

Wyla's eyes shot open. "You lost the map? Fyr's fire! What are we supposed to do without it?"

The Lorekeeper stammered a bit as he desperately checked the many hidden pockets of his cloak. "Well, I didn't expect to be shaken and dangled upside down! It was tucked away, right here. I felt it slipping just as I came up over the top."

The others searched the ground in the dark, all except Bari who was still on the other side of the gorge with the rest of the horses. Though their eyes had adjusted to the dim light, they had to search by feel as each crawled over the rocks.

Torin's fingers felt a roll of soft leather near the edge of the gorge. A little further and it surely would have tumbled down into the river. "Here it is."

Aldrin threw up his hands. "Bless the King's royal ring!" The Lorekeeper rushed over to Torin and held out his hands.

Torin extended the map toward Aldrin but then retracted it. The old Lorekeeper frowned. "What?"

Torin stared at the Greyraven's map a moment longer before he spoke. "Perhaps it is better if I hold onto it."

Aldrin's face twisted into a scowl. "What? Why? It was entrusted to me by the Greyraven himself. Besides, you cannot even read it!"

Wyla pointed a stiff finger at the old man. "You almost dropped it in the river. What if we had lost it?"

Torin saw the corners of Aldrin's mouth twitch as the Lorekeeper tried to remain resolute. The old man took a deep breath and clenched his fists. "Of course, I didn't mean to drop it."

Grimsa, still winded, looked up with wide eyes. "Just like you didn't mean to slip on the bridge? Damn the map, we nearly died!"

Aldrin opened his mouth to reply then promptly closed it. "Fine then, for now. We can argue about this nonsense further once we have reached someplace safe to camp."

Across the river, the horses whinnied and stamped their feet. Grimsa had opened his mouth to say something else but closed it when he heard the disturbance. Torin stepped toward the gorge and squinted at the dark forest.

Wyla's face darkened. "Something spooked the horses."

Then Torin saw them, a pair of sickly yellow orbs hovering between the shadowed trees. His heart jumped in his chest as they disappeared and reappeared; a monster blinking. Out from the woods stepped a towering troll, its pale-yellow eyes flickering in the silver moonlight.

"Bari! Troll!"

Bari spun around and squeaked with fright. The noise spooked the horses and they reared in terror at the sight of the monstrous troll. Each one yanked free and galloped away in a fit of panic as the towering creature took a step out from the woods.

Grimsa stumbled toward the forest. "I'll grab another log!"

"No time," Wyla said. "Use the rope!"

Wyla snatched the rope that Grimsa had used to climb out of the gorge. Though she flung it as far as she could, the rope fell again by its own weight about halfway across.

The troll stepped out of the forest's shadow into the moonlight. Torin saw its skin, rough like bark but grey like stone, with moss and twigs strewn about its head like hair. It took another heavy step toward Bari, a leathery smile stretched across its wrinkled face.

Torin called out across the gorge. "Bari! You have to jump!"

Bari's eyes were wide and his whole body trembled. The *nidavel* nodded, though not with the greatest confidence, then took a step back from the gap to get a running start.

Wyla shouted over the roar of the river. "Now or never!"

Hardly a second before the troll swiped its hooked claws, Bari launched himself into the gaping gorge. Wyla threw the rope. Torin felt his chest constrict as, for a moment, both Bari and the loose end of the rope hung in midair over the raging water. At the last moment, just when it looked as if the *nidavel* might go plummeting down into the void, he caught the rope.

Bari gripped it with all the strength he could muster and squeezed his eyes shut. He came hurtling downward at great speed and smashed into the rock face below. Bari's grip slipped and he plunged into the foaming current. The surging river swallowed him up with little more than a splash.

Torin's stomach twisted into a knot, and he thought he might heave up what little was left within it right then and there. However, in the next instant, Wyla lurched forward as the rope went taught in her hands.

"He's got the rope!" she said.

Grimsa shoved Wyla aside and hauled on the rope with his doubled strength. Bari came flying up out of the water like a great bearded fish. Grimsa hauled him up, hand over hand, until the *nidavel* lay coughing and sputtering at the top of the cliff.

Across the gorge, the troll shrieked, a terrible noise like creaking hinges and twisting metal. Its pale eyes were fixed on Torin as it pointed a jagged claw and called out in a deep throaty gurgle. "Mindthorn!"

Torin felt the blood drain from his face. That was the name given to him by the Troll-King after their duel of riddles. How could the troll have known it was him? Did it recognize Torin, or had it somehow learned of their quest? The creature hacked and coughed as if it had nearly choked on the word, then it uttered a vile curse.

> *May snakes enwrap your throat and fill your eyes with venom tears*
> *Let maggots feast upon your tongue while ravens peck your ears*
> *May rats infest your rotting corpse and lice consume your hair*
> *As wolf-cubs gnaw your scattered bones in some forgotten lair*

Wyla raced back to where she left her bow. She drew an arrow, quick as the flutter of a falcon's wing. "Sunlight take you!"

The arrow struck the troll in the shoulder and sunk into its flesh down to the feather fletching. A sound like a hiss came from the troll's open mouth as yellow-green spittle ran down its chin. It stooped down to pick up a rock nearly the size of Torin's head and hurled it across the river in a fit of rage. The stone flew straight at Wyla and would have struck her dead if she hadn't thrown herself out of its path.

"Into the trees!" said Torin. "Quickly!"

Azal and Aldrin had already made their way into the shadowed forest with the prince's horse. Grimsa scooped up Bari and hurried away from the river's edge. Wyla fired one more arrow before retreating to the woods.

The company heard the troll continue to hurl stones into the trees. Deep enough to be out of sight and range, each sat on a stump or leaned against a gnarled tree trunk to catch their breath.

"Damn that troll," Wyla said. "It's like we've been cursed."

Grimsa scowled at Aldrin. "It's the wizard! I'm sure of it. Wizards attract the worst of luck. I should have let you plunge into the river!"

The Lorekeeper glared at Grimsa and pointed a bony finger at him. "Perhaps I should have let that boar cut your fat belly open! And by the King's sceptre, Grimsa Jarnskald, if you call me a wizard one more time, I really will scorch your beard off!"

As Grimsa opened his mouth to respond, a horn sounded in the distance. Torin did not recognize it, nor did Grimsa, Wyla, or Bari by the look on their faces. However, Azal went pale as an egg white. The prince's hands shook as he raised them to his mouth. Torin was just about to ask Azal why he looked so grim when the Lorekeeper spoke.

"Just in time," said Aldrin. "I was beginning to think they might have lost our trail."

Azal buried his hands in his hair and pulled it hard. He stumbled back against a tree. "Aldrin! What have you done?"

A smug grin rested on the Lorekeeper's wrinkled face. "Shouldn't you be glad, young prince? Your father's men are here to defend us, and just in time too!"

Torin felt his heart drop inside his chest. "By the gods, what do you mean?"

Aldrin's grin twisted into a sneer. "Well, don't thank me all at once! It seems I was the only one with enough sense to know that we would need more men. I bribed one of the hall hands in Fjell-hall to sneak them over the wall at night and gave your father's men orders to come find us. It seems they found us just in time!"

Torin dashed out of the forest and into the clearing beside the gorge. There was no sign of the troll. Just a little way down the hill, he saw the Armeahan soldiers picking their way up the slope. Their leader caught sight of Torin and blew the horn again.

Torin cupped his hands to his mouth and shouted as loud as he could. "Run!"

The leader waved and motioned for the rest of them to hurry forward.

As Wyla and Azal ran up beside him, Torin cursed. "Troll's blood! Azal, how do you say 'run' in Armeahan?"

The Armeahans cheered as they came up over the crest and caught sight of the prince. Azal started shouting in his mother tongue but, by their reaction, it seemed his words were lost under the roar of the river. Torin, Grimsa, Wyla, and Bari made wild hand gestures to signal that grave danger lurked in the woods behind them, but still the troupe rushed forward as if their frantic flailing was a sign of welcome.

The Armeahan company was nearly at the river's edge when the troll stepped out from the shadowed fringe of the forest. Its pallid yellow eyes glared down at the unsuspecting soldiers like a wolf eyeing a handful of mice. Though Torin jumped and shouted and pointed, the foreigners did not understand his meaning.

The troll's slimy grey lips curled into a smile. Its back arched as if to pounce. In the clutch of the troll's clawed fingers, it gripped half a tree, either ripped from its roots or scavenged from the deadfall.

At last, the Armeahans came close enough to hear what Azal was shouting. They spun around to see the monstrous troll nearly upon them. As their leader drew his sword, the troll swung its mighty tree trunk club.

With a sickening crack, the log struck the group of Armeahan soldiers and sent them flying like a cluster of empty mugs swept aside by an angry drunk. Some tumbled down into the river while others desperately grasped for a hold as they slipped into the gorge. The Vimur River far below devoured each one in its watery grasp as they fell. The cries of those still alive when they hit the water lasted only until the surging current flung their bodies over the falls.

Only one Armeahan remained at the top of the cliff's edge. The lone soldier struggled to his feet and clutched his arm. The troll stepped closer with a ravenous gleam in its bulbous eyes. Even from across the river, they could hear all the creature's awful chuckle, phlegmy gargling spasms which jiggled its grey jowls.

Wyla picked up the rope again. "The rope! Azal, tell him to jump just like Bari did!"

Azal shouted in Armeahan as loud as he could over the rush of the river and the deep rumbling noise of the chuckling troll. The Armeahan heard him and stumbled forward, still clutching his arm with his free hand. There was a desperation in the man's eyes that made Torin confident he would actually jump. However, just when it seemed he might make a narrow escape, the soldier's foot caught a stone. He tumbled forward over the rocks and the troll's clawed foot came down on his ankle.

The troll grunted with glee as it leaned forward to press its weight down. Torin's heart seared with fury as the man cried out in pain. But the cry was not so loud as to drown out the crunch of the bones in his foot as they snapped under the cruel creature's weight.

Torin's eyes darted back and forth along the bank looking for any way of reaching the far side. As he looked up stream, his eye caught Wyla pulling an arrow tight against her bow string. There was a dark look in her eye and her jaw was clenched tight.

Azal jumped up and down as he cried out. "Yes, yes! Shoot the troll! Stop it as quick as you can!"

The arrow flew through the night air, silent amid the chaos. It struck its mark with deadly accuracy, the shaft sinking deep into the soldier's throat. The man's hands went to the feather fletching as blood gushed from his neck onto the stones, not red but black beneath the moon's silver light. A moment later, his arms went limp, and he moved no more. Torin's gut clenched tight with anger, though he knew it was a kinder fate than being left to the cruelty of a troll. Between Torin and Wyla stood Azal, frozen in place and as pale as the moon above them.

The troll's eyes bulged out in anger as it watched its prey die quickly. It bellowed with such rage that birds all around them fled from their nests high up in the trees. In a fit of frenzy, the troll snatched up anything it could get its grey leathery hands on, rocks, tree trunks, or stray provisions that had fallen off the horses, and hurled them across the river at Torin and his company.

Azal stood there speechless as he stared at his lifeless country-man on the far side of the gorge. One of the troll's rocks whizzed so close to his head that it nearly took it off, but Azal hardly flinched.

Torin called back as the others fled into the forest. "Azal, run!"

Still, the prince stood frozen. Torin ran back and grabbed Azal by the arm, then dragged him into the dark shadows of the wild forest, the prince stumbling along in silence.

9

◇ THE STONE BARROW ◇

THROUGH THE WOODS, just deep enough to avoid the stones hurled by the troll, they picked their way upriver. Going was slow, as they clambered in the dark over the swollen roots of untamed trees, but an unspoken consensus pushed them on. It seemed best to put as much distance between themselves and the angry troll as they could.

By then, night had truly fallen. Hardly a sliver of moonlight slipped down to the forest floor. As the roar of the river and the bellowing of the troll faded behind a wall of trees, the quieter sounds of the forest came through. Bird calls rang out in the thick canopy, haunting hoots and eerie whistles. There was the soft rustling of leaves among the branches, and occasionally the older trees creaked under their load. Every few steps, Torin heard the scuttle and scurry of small creatures dashing off into the dark. Deep in the shadows, he felt eyes watching him again.

Wyla and Bari led the company through the winding wood, with Grimsa leading Azal's horse close behind. Aldrin did his best to keep up and, besides a few half-hearted requests for the others to slow down, he stayed silent. Azal trailed the old Lorekeeper and Torin brought up the rear. Between the dim shadows cast by the cragged branches, Torin caught sight of the prince's face, pale and streaked with tears.

After some time, they came to a clearing. The towering trunks gave way to an open field with rolling slopes that stretched on in either direction. The grass was wild and the fresh spring shoots stretched up to Torin's waist. As for Bari, the stalks stood just above the *nidavel's* eyes, and he muttered curses in *nidavellish* as he shoved them aside.

Ahead of them lay a hill, almost perfectly round and well above the rest of the field. Wyla motioned toward the mound and Torin nodded. From the top, he thought, they could at least catch sight of whatever else might spring out from the woods before it tried to kill them. The ground was even and easy to walk over, a particular relief to Torin's feet after trekking through the forest with all its sharp rocks and uneven roots.

The sky had cleared to reveal a thousand flickering stars overhead. The jagged line of treetops etched an irregular pattern across the lowest edge of the sky, a thin barrier between the realm of light above and the realm of darkness below. Soon the company reached the crest of the hill and gave up their weary march.

"Not a bad place to camp," said Grimsa. "From here we'll see anything large enough to do any harm before it gets to us."

Bari grunted. "Maybe you can! I can hardly see anything over all this tall grass. But I'd rather spend the night here than anywhere near that cursed forest."

Wyla yawned. "Agreed. I don't think we will find a better place to camp tonight."

"I don't suppose anyone is keen to take the first watch?" said Torin.

Azal shrugged and raised his hand. "I'll take it."

There was no lively flicker left in the prince's eye, no easy manner or devilish grin. He seemed heavy, his arms, shoulders, and head drooping like wilted branches under winter snow. His eyes were red and swollen and his face looked drained of colour.

"You don't look well, Azal," Torin said. "You should rest."

Azal shook his head. "I won't sleep. Not tonight."

"Fine by me," said Wyla, "Though I reckon the sun will be up soon anyways."

Grimsa grinned. "Well, at least we won't have to worry about trolls then!"

Bari patted down a section of grass, then ripped some up for a pillow of sorts. Aldrin had done the same, only a bit further away from the others. After tying the horse up to a large stone, Grimsa fell over on his side and began to snore right away. Wyla leaned back against that same stone and dozed off almost as soon as she sat down.

Torin laid down in the tall grass and let his weary limbs fall limp against the ground. Though the night sky was ablaze with stars and a cool breeze floated over the field, he felt a knot of dread in his stomach. Alongside the terrible fate of the Armeahan company, they had lost all their provisions. He knew, despite his frustration, that they would have to return to Gatewatch the next day. It would have been just a little more than a day's journey back, if not for the angry troll blocking their way. Now they would be forced to return through unfamiliar territory, which would take time, and they were already short enough on that.

Some part of him wondered if they could press on, but he saw little hope of reaching the Everspring with a single horse and so few of the supplies they had set out with. Of course, they could hunt, trap, and fish as they went, but that would slow their progress considerably and winter would not spare them the time. From his two years in Gatewatch, Torin knew that if smoke from the fire of Fjellhall was not in sight when the first flakes of snow started to fall, they might never be heard from again.

Despite the worries crowding his mind, Torin was tired. He closed his eyes and took in a deep breath then exhaled slowly. As the shadow of sleep began to slip over him, he heard the whispering voice.

Torin.

Torin drew in a sharp breath and froze.

I saw you. At the river. And you saw me.

Torin's heart thumped hard in his chest. With a trembling hand, he drew out the Greyraven's ring from beneath his tunic. The eyes glowed the colour of bright red blood and the metal was warm to the touch. Torin held his breath another moment, then whispered back. "Who are you? What do you want?"

I once ruled this wood. One day I will again. What I want is a willing champion to prepare the way for my return.

"King Araldof Greyraven rules these woods, no one else."

The Greyraven is old and weak. Soon, he will die.

Torin clenched his teeth. "Not if we can reach the Everspring."

Again, the hollow sound of her terrible laughter rang in Torin's ears. It was almost a shriek, nearly deafening, and yet none of the others stirred. Torin knew then that she spoke to him and to him alone.

And how will you do that, Torin? You have no horses. You have no supplies. You barely made it across the river with your lives. If only you knew what kind of power you could wield with my guidance.

Torin thought again of the lost provisions, the scattered horses, and the cries of the Armeahan soldiers as they tumbled into the river. Quietly, cautiously, he whispered. "This power, could it be used to save the Greyraven?"

Of course, it could. But I would not allow it.

Torin frowned. "Why not?"

Because I am using it to destroy the Greyraven's mind.

Torin sat up and glared into the crimson glow of the raven's eyes. As he opened his mouth to speak, the light flickered and vanished. For a long while he sat there, her final words stinging like a knife in his gut. He wanted to hurl the ring far off into the woods. Could he do that, he wondered, to the King's own signet ring? Perhaps it would be wiser to consult with the others in the morning. That is, if they did not think he had lost his mind.

In any case, the haunting echo of her laughter had chased away any chance of Torin sleeping that night. He tucked the ring back inside his cloak. With a few mumbled curses, he rose to his feet and trudged toward the prince. Azal stood watch wrapped in the cloak he'd been given in Fjellhall.

Torin scanned the tree line. "I can't sleep either."

The prince did not speak and kept his arms crossed. He fixed his eyes on the rippling grass below them.

"I'm sorry about your countrymen," said Torin. "What a terrible way to die."

Azal swallowed hard. "The man who almost escaped, the one Wyla shot, I can't stop thinking about him."

"It was an act of mercy. Death in the clutches of that troll would have been far worse."

"Of course," said Azal, "I know that. It's just that he gave his life to defend mine and I don't know what his name was." The prince paused a moment, then looked Torin directly in the eyes. "I guess I just wish I did."

For some time, they stood on the crest of the hill and listened to the soft sounds of the night drift over the dell. Many times, it seemed that the shadows stirred between the trees, but the only creature to emerge was an owl that swooped down silently over the field. In his head, Torin passed the time as he often did on watch during patrols, by finding constellations. First, he found Erik the Wanderer, then Vili's longship, Grimnir's ravens, and finally Thorunn's goats, which heralded the arrival of spring.

Before long, a faint swell of colour warmed the edge of the horizon, a prelude to the rising sun. Torin thought of a story his father had told him when he was just a young boy, the tale of a beautiful woman with flaming red hair being chased by a pair of giant wolves. That woman was the sun and, though she raced across the sky on her fiery steed, she was doomed to one day be devoured. On that day, when the wolves finally caught up with her, the sun would shine no more, and the world would fall into a wintry night to last a thousand years. The thought of wolves brought to mind their present situation, and he surveyed the tree line again for any sign of movement.

The prince jumped up and startled Torin.

"What?"

"I just remembered something," Azal said. "By my father's crown, I'm glad we did not lose my horse."

Torin felt a twinge in his stomach. Besides the loss of the provisions, their horses were some of the best mounts that side of Shadowstone Pass. Most were born and bred in Gatewatch and would eventually find their way back to Stonering Keep, but a bear or a pack of wolves was bound to catch one or two along their way.

Torin rubbed his temples. "Right, the horses. Thanks for reminding me."

Azal walked over to his saddle and untied his woolen blanket which had been packed up in a roll. "It's just that we would have lost this along with everything else."

"Your blanket?" Torin said. "By the gods, are you really concerned about a bloody blanket when we are stuck out in the middle of these cursed woods without food?"

Azal shook his head. "No, no, not the blanket. This!"

From the folds of the blanket fell a long narrow object which at first Torin did not recognize. Azal caught it before it hit the ground and held it up in the moonlight. In the prince's hands, Torin saw a dark scabbard etched with runes.

Torin's face flushed red hot at the sight. Before he had taken care to speak quietly and not wake the others, but at the sight of

Tyrfang, Signy's family sword, he took no heed of them. "By thunderous Orr! What in Fyr's name are you doing with that sword?"

Azal stumbled back a step. "I, well, but, Keymaster Signy said you would need it!"

Torin kicked at nothing and threw up his hands. "You idiot! If that really is her family's sword, we could have lost it. You risked jumping across the river with that heirloom strapped to your horse?"

"I thought—"

"No. You didn't think. Maybe you really are as stone-brained as Aldrin says you are!"

The shouting woke Wyla. She groaned as she stood up. "What's all the racket about?"

Torin was about to snap back when he saw Grimsa's arms flailing. At first, he thought his friend might have woken from a bad dream, but Grimsa kept wriggling in a strange way among the tall grasses.

Grimsa grunted then called out in a muffled voice. "Help! I'm sinking!"

Torin and Wyla rushed over to find Grimsa half sunken in the dewy earth of the mound. "I tried to stand just a moment ago," said Grimsa, "And the ground gave out below my feet. Help pull me out before I slip any further!"

Torin and Wyla each grabbed one of Grimsa's arms and tried to haul him up. At first, Torin thought they were succeeding with quite a bit more ease than he expected. However, he soon realized that it was not Grimsa rising, but he and Wyla that were sinking into the damp soil. A great crumbling crack came from somewhere far below them. Then the loosening turf gave way.

Torin's heart jumped up into his throat as all three fell, a knot of flailing limbs, into the dark interior of the hill. Along with them fell clumps of turf and a heap of muddy soil. Then, just as the rush of air rose in his ears, it all stopped with an enormous thump as they hit solid ground.

Torin's heel bashed against the stone floor beneath them, but the rest of his body was cushioned somewhat by the sod and dirt. He laid on his back for a moment and heard Grimsa and Wyla's aching groans nearby. Through the opening above them he could see a small patch of sky, the stars doing little to light the dark cavern inside the hill.

Grimsa rolled over and brushed himself off, kicking and sputtering as he did. "By Odd's one and only eye, if it isn't eagles and rivers and trolls, it's hollow bloody hills! We really are cursed!"

Grimsa's words echoed through the darkness for a moment then faded into silence. It seemed to Torin that they had not fallen into a muddy hole but rather a large rocky cavern. With his hands, he felt the stone floor below him to find it was flat and made of well-cut slabs. Though he could not see much, there was a strong scent of must and rot, like in a long-abandoned cellar full of moldy stores.

There was a scuttling noise in the dark. Torin heard Grimsa scramble to his feet.

"Troll's blood," Grimsa said, "What was that?"

Wyla pushed herself up off the floor. "Rats? Or worse."

Torin brushed off his cloak. Grimsa bumped up against him in the dark and offered his hand. Torin took it and pulled himself up to his feet.

"Plenty of room to stand up straight," said Torin, "What is this place?"

Above them the silhouette of a head appeared in the hole they had fallen through. Torin recognized the outline; it was Azal. A second dark form, Bari by the looks of it, appeared a moment later.

"Torin? Wyla? Are you alright?"

"Just bruised," said Wyla. "Don't get too close to the edge."

"Thank the Mastersmith!" Bari said. "Let me get some rope and then we'll pull you out."

Wyla waved her hands and called back. "No, that won't work. We fell in because the turf was too loose. There is no way you'd be able to pull us back up without bringing the roof down on our heads."

Torin peered into the shadows around them, but it was no use. The darkness was so complete that he could not even guess how large the room was or if there was anything else in it. However, as he looked up at Azal he saw a glow, like a star grown too bright. Torin blinked and squinted in the dark, but the light remained.

"Azal," Torin said, "What is that in your hand?"

"What?"

"That there, in your hand. It's glowing."

Outlined in silhouette above them, they saw Azal look down at this hand then jump with a start. "Royal blood! It's the sword."

Torin shuddered. So, the sword held some magic after all, he thought. He cursed the prince under his breath for bringing it along, as if their troubles were not enough already.

Wyla's voice came from somewhere nearby. "Sword? Which sword?"

"*Tyrfang*," said Torin. "Signy's family sword. Our beloved prince brought it along on Keymaster Signy's orders."

Grimsa chuckled. "Gods keep her! We may need it, after all."

"I'll draw it out," said Azal, "Then you can see what is down there."

The prince's hand was already on the hilt when Torin, Grimsa, and Wyla all shouted all at once. "No!"

"Don't draw it," Wyla said. "Remember the curse!"

"The curse?"

Torin felt another blaze of heat rush over his face, and he clenched his jaw. "By the gods, didn't Keymaster Signy tell you when she gave it to you?"

Azal shook his head. "Well, she told me not to unsheathe it, but she didn't tell me anything about a curse!"

Wyla scoffed. "So, you took a magic sword without knowing anything about it?"

Azal spoke with an edge as he shook the sword. "Well, I would have asked if I knew it was a magic sword!"

"Fine, fine," said Torin. "Just don't draw the blade. Whoever unsheathes it must draw blood or else they will be cursed."

Torin rubbed his head for a moment then looked around. The cavern was still veiled in coal-black shadows, and he bumped into Grimsa as he stepped directly below the hole in the ceiling. "Here, toss it to me. First, tie the belt around the hilt, so that the blade doesn't fall out by accident."

As *Tyrfang* fell, Torin followed the glint that shone from where the hilt met the sheath. When it landed in his hands, he was surprised by how light it was, hardly weighing more than if it had been made of wood. In the small sphere of light it cast, he could see Wyla and Grimsa, but little more beyond that. His friends looked rather ghostly, their pale muddied faces floating in the darkness. He suspected that his own was in a similar state.

Grimsa fixed his wide eyes on the eerie glow then swallowed. "More damned magic."

"What do you see?" said Bari.

Wyla wrinkled her nose. "Not much. The darkness is too thick, almost like a fog. And the smell is horrid."

"Aldrin says he could cast a small flame to illuminate the cavern." said Azal.

"No," said Grimsa, "No, no, no! I've had enough witch-fire slung at me today by that book-brained sorcerer. Azal, tell Aldrin that he better not utter a single word!"

Wyla grimaced. "What then? It's too damp down here to light a torch."

"Maybe so," said Grimsa, "But this little bit of light is better than whatever disaster will come of that wizard setting the whole place on fire. He'd probably even say it was an accident!"

Wyla leaned in toward *Tyrfang*. "I guess pulling the blade out just a little wouldn't really count as drawing it. Then we could see what we've fallen into."

Torin hesitated for a moment, then exhaled as he gripped the hilt and the sheathe, one in each hand. "Alright, I guess we'll try the sword."

Tyrfang's glowing blade slid out with ease, like an adder slithering out from its nest. The wispy glow intensified as if the steel edge was a sharp tongue thirsty for blood. Torin took care to stop once a quarter of the blade was exposed but found he had to hold it in place to keep it from sliding further. His heart skipped as he felt some invisible force continue to push the blade out of its scabbard, not strong but certainly insistent.

Grimsa and Wyla each drew in a sharp breath which startled Torin. He looked up from *Tyrfang's* glow to a ghastly sight. The three companions were standing near the center of an empty stone hall that was almost as large as the hill itself. Around its edge, amid sickly swirls of musty fog, there were tables and benches set for a feast long past. All manner of dust and rot had taken whatever the cobwebbed bowls and goblets had once held. Rigid, shadowy figures loomed behind these furnishings, but were too far from the center of the room for Torin to make out exactly what they were. Everything was perfectly still.

Torin felt a cold drip of sweat slip down his back. The moisture of the cavern and the perspiration on his palms caused the etched leather to slip in his grip. A flash of light illuminated the cavern as the scabbard slipped more than halfway down the blade. In *Tyrfang's* light, the faces of the stone-still figures were revealed, gaping jaws half hinged to empty skulls with ragged strands of unkempt hair falling down upon hollow rib cages. Torin thrust the blade into its sheath and the room plunged back into darkness.

Grimsa grabbed Torin's arm in the dark and shook him. "By the gods, bring back the light!"

Torin wiped his hands on his cloak then drew *Tyrfang* part way, with as firm a grip as he could manage. He noticed a tremor in his arms and knees as he tried to hold the light up and steady. Again, the darkened figures seated around the tables emerged from the shadow, their forms shrouded by the mist.

Grimsa crouched down low. Wyla narrowed her gaze and pointed toward the edge of the hall. "Look there," she said. "A gap between the tables. Perhaps a door to the outside?"

Torin called up to Azal and Bari. "We may have found a door. We're going to take a closer look."

Azal repeated the message for Aldrin. "They found a door!" The prince turned his head and then called back again. "Wait, Torin! Aldrin says don't go yet."

Torin frowned. "Why?"

"Aldrin and Bari just read the Greyraven's map. It says something about the hill."

"But I have the map," said Torin. "It's right here."

Torin sheathed *Tyrfang* and cursed under his breath. To make sure the blade would not come loose he wrapped the leather belt around the hilt. He fumbled to feel for the map where he had tucked it away but found his pocket empty. "By one-eyed Odd, I've lost the map!"

"No," said Azal, "Aldrin has it! It's right here."

Torin pulled *Tyrfang* out a little way for light and leaned in toward Grimsa and Wyla. He spoke harshly, but in a tone low enough so those up above could not hear. "That damned wizard must have plucked it right out of my cloak."

Wyla grinned. "Your pocket got picked by that old goat?"

"What have I been saying all along?" said Grimsa. "Never trust a wizard."

Torin shouted out to Azal. "What does the map say?"

Azal drew away from the opening for a moment then returned. "Bari translated it. It is some kind of riddling verse."

> *Beneath the stones, the restless dead*
> *Beneath the crown, a royal head*
> *Beneath the brow, two watchful eyes*
> *None here that tread are counted wise*

A shiver ran up and down Torin's body at the mention of restless dead and watchful eyes. He suspected that any talk of crowns and royalty could only mean more trouble. After repeating the riddle to himself a few times, he began to move ahead slowly through the dimly lit room.

Azal called out again. "Wait!"

"What?" said Wyla.

"Well, what should we do?"

Grimsa chuckled and called back up to the prince. "Try not to get eaten by trolls!"

The light from *Tyrfang's* blade lit their way as Torin, Wyla, and Grimsa shuffled ahead. Strewn across their path were the droppings of vermin and a few rat bones which had long been picked clean. Between the trailing wisps of milky mist, the floor was damp with grime. Scuttling noises came from the dark corners of the room where the light could not reach. And above it all was the musty smell of foul rot.

They came to the end of the long, curved table where a carved step rose above the rest of the floor.

"Stairs," said Grimsa. "That's a good sign! Perhaps they lead to a door."

A chill swept through the room as Grimsa's words echoed in the darkness. Torin felt his shoulders tense and he raised *Tyrfang* above his head. The fog around them swirled up before settling where it had been a moment earlier.

Torin stepped closer to his companions. "Best not to speak, I think, unless it's important." Grimsa and Wyla nodded.

Each stone step was wide and took three paces for Torin to cross, though for Grimsa it was only two. The edges were round and well cut, certainly the work of a skilled mason from some age long gone by. Between the edge of each step and the next, small tiles had been laid in an intricate pattern depicting monsters and serpents in knots and curves. Torin stepped up again and again, nine times by his count, before he came to what seemed to be the end of the stairway.

What they found at the top was not the threshold of a door, as Torin had hoped, but a pedestal which supported an enormous throne. It was carved entirely of ice-white quartz and glowed in *Tyrfang's* light. Each armrest flared out at a wide angle, emblazoned with vines as if clinging to an ancient tree. The milky white back of the throne furled out at its edges into carved branches, and its feet were gnarled roots sprawled out before it like grasping claws. As they drew closer, Torin saw that the bark was etched with strange runes. However, what disturbed him more than the markings or the throne's enormous size was the fact that it was empty.

Grimsa leaned in and spoke in a harsh whisper. "There's the throne. Now where's the king?"

Wyla raised an eyebrow. "Why not a queen?"

Torin thought of the voice that had spoken to him through the Greyraven's ring and shuddered. As he opened his mouth to respond, a chill draft blew through the room. It rattled the debris scattered along the floor and sent an empty goblet tumbling off the table. The metal cup fell with a metallic clang that rang loud through the empty cavern. The companions froze in place, but nothing stirred once the sound died out.

Torin punched Grimsa in the arm. "Damn your big mouth, Grimsa. Keep it shut!"

The draft rose again, this time twice as strong and with a horrible rasp that scraped at Torin's ear drums. Long-settled dust flew up in whirling clouds and made the companions cough. Torin lifted his arm to cover his mouth and in doing so shoved *Tyrfang* back into its sheath. All at once the light was gone and the three companions were left in darkness. Somewhere among the shadows there came a familiar sound, one that Torin now recognized had come with each rising gust and had grown louder every time.

It was the sound of breathing.

10

◇ RESTLESS DEAD ◇

Grimsa grabbed Torin's shoulder in the dark and shook him. "The sword! The sword!"

Torin was already fumbling to pull *Tyrfang* from its sheath to shed some light on the dim cavern. Again, the raspy scrape of a breath being sucked into long-dry lungs echoed in horrid drawn-out gasps. Before he could draw the sword, the humidity of the dank cavern and the slick sweat on his hands caused him to slip and drop it to the floor with a clang. The next rasp came with a blast of cold air and a string of wheezing coughs which sounded very, very close. Torin cursed as he knelt and searched for the sword on his hands and knees, the dark dust swirling up into his mouth and nose.

After a second of scrambling, his hand found the hilt. Torin picked *Tyrfang* up and noticed that the scabbard felt unnaturally warm. The rasping breaths ceased, and the cold breeze fell still. Torin froze in place, crouched low to the ground. The silence loomed long and dark. Then, from out of the black shadows, there came a deep, rumbling voice.

> *Who alive would dare to tread*
> *Within the hall of those long dead?*

> *Who would speak and break the spell*
> *That kept me sleeping 'neath the dell?*

Torin's heart pounded against his ribs at the booming words, low and loud like the rumble of a mighty river.

> *Long since ears heard sparrows call*
> *Long since cheeks felt raindrops fall*
> *Longer still since time of death*
> *When last I drew a living breath*
>
> *Who alive would dare to tread*
> *Within the hall of those long dead?*

Torin forced himself to his feet though his knees shook terribly. He fought to keep his voice firm as he shouted with as much confidence as he could muster. "I am Torin Ten-Trees, son of Jarl Einar Ten-Trees! Show yourself, wight!"

> *Ten-Trees…*

Torin's name echoed through the darkness before dying out in the dim shadow. He felt a chill ripple over his skin and the hairs on the back of his neck stood on end. The sensation was suddenly so palpable that Torin felt as if some vermin had crawled in beneath his tunic. He frantically patted his cloak to find the icy fingers that he had felt stroking his skin, but there was nothing there. After a moment, he stood still to calm his breath. "Who's there?"

> *Your father's name, I know it not*
> *Unknown to me or long forgot*
> *But one alone no child can bear*
> *So speak the name of mother fair*

Torin stepped back and swallowed. "My mother?"

The memory of Keymaster Signy sitting beside the low-burning hearth of Fjellhall flashed through his mind. He shook his head then cleared his throat. "I grew up without a mother. I don't know who she is."

> *Though lies might fool a living ear*
> *The dead have counsel you can't hear*
> *That sword I know, Tyrfang its name*
> *For countless deaths it's held to blame*

Torin stayed silent for another moment. The sound of his own heartbeat thumped hard against his eardrums, and he felt beads of sweat trickling down his forehead. "There is a certain woman who claims to be my mother." He paused to take a quick breath. "Her name is Signy, Keymaster of Fjellhall in Gatewatch and daughter of one she called Sigrilinn."

Torin waited in the dark for a response but there was no reply. He thought to draw *Tyrfang* again but saw a dim green luminescence spread around the edge of the cavern. The light seemed to have no source. Perhaps it even came from the murky mist that clung to the floor. Its eerie glow lit Wyla and Grimsa's pale faces, their eyes wide and their cheeks speckled with grimy dust.

Grimsa pulled Wyla and Torin closer to him and whispered. "We have to find a way out!"

"Either that," said Wyla, "or we get the others to start digging from outside."

Torin frowned. "I doubt this wight will take kindly to us digging more holes in the barrow."

Torin felt Grimsa yank on his cloak. "Did you feel that?" Grimsa said. "There is a chill creeping over my skin, like the ghost of an ice serpent."

"Or corpse-cold fingers reaching out to grab us," said Wyla. "I felt it too."

Grimsa shuddered. "What does it want?"

Torin waited another moment, but all was silent. He took a deep breath. "I guess there is only one way to find out." Torin stood up straight and planted his feet firmly on the stone floor. "I have answered you, wight! Now, answer me. Who are you?"

Again, the breeze picked up, this time swirling back and forth across the room so that the curls of fog lilted like rising waves in a brewing storm. A few more copper vessels fell off the cobwebbed tables and one of the skeletal corpses collapsed in the dark, its bones clattering as they hit the floor. From somewhere within the slow pulsing glow, which by then had grown even brighter, the voice boomed with pride.

> *Of father Thrudnir have you heard?*
> *High in hall and wise in word*
> *High in hall and proud of mind*
> *With reddest gold and sweetest wine*
>
> *Mother mine was Skathi bright*
> *Swift on skis o'er hills of white*
> *Huntress wielding fiercest bow*
> *Who fell in wars fought long ago*

The companions waited for the creature to keep speaking but it did not. Wyla narrowed her eyes and tilted her head. "Whatever it is, I don't think it means to harm us."

Grimsa's eyes were still wide with fright. "And how can you say that?"

Torin spoke in a low voice and kept a wary eye on the shifting green fog. "Because if it wanted to kill us, I think it already would have." He cleared his throat and called out to the swirling mass. "Hail, son of Thrudnir! Hail, son of Skathi! Hail, Lord of the Barrow! By what name are you called?"

Again, silence lingered over the darkness. A moment later, with a shuddering ripple, the glowing fog began to spin into cruel curls. From somewhere within the murky mass came a groan like those of one picking up a heavy load or feeling the twinge of an old wound. It grew in volume until Torin had to cover his ears, then the voice fell silent all at once. The light was gone, or so they thought, until Torin saw a wispy green form step through the wall from the far end of the cavern.

The lordly figure stood twice Torin's height, and his robes flowed out to either side like a gushing waterfall. His face was stern with broad cheeks and a proud nose. Wild curls of translucent hair tumbled down over his shoulders and his beard was tied up in braids decorated with jewel-studded rings. Upon his head he wore a crown made not of metal but of lush foliage and pale wildflowers. Indeed, Torin would have found him altogether magnificent if it had not been for the blank stare of his white colourless eyes.

> *When this wood was full of light*
> *The huldur called me Ballur Bright*
> *Long it rang with joyous verse*
> *Before the shadow and the curse*
>
> *Now the wood is dark and dim*
> *Now its paths are scarce and grim*
> *Now the trolls, like rot, have spread*
> *And huldur-folk have long-since fled*

Torin took a cautious step toward the towering spectre. "What do you mean about a curse? And a shadow over the forest?"

Wyla stepped up beside Torin, keeping a wary eye on the glowing ghost. She grabbed Torin's shoulder and whispered into his ear. "Speaking of curses, why not ask about the sword? Didn't it say it knows something of *Tyrfang*?"

Grimsa squeezed in between Torin and Wyla. "By the gods, forget about the forest and the sword! Ask it about the quickest way out of this rot-ridden barrow!"

Torin motioned for quiet then opened his arms toward the towering figure. "Hail, Ballur Bright, son of Thrudnir! Will you tell us the way out?"

Again, Ballur groaned as if an old wound had been torn open and he threw his head back. The wight spoke as his centerless, unblinking eyes twitched and shivered.

> *The way out…*
>
> *Hear me, son, with with'ring ears*
> *Beyond this realm of dwindling years*
> *An Ash there stands, a timeless tree*
> *Its boughs stretched wider than the sea*
>
> *When Ash leaves quake then time is nigh*
> *As wolves rend sun and moon from sky*
> *Then you'll rise from cold, dank tomb*
> *And proud asyr will face their doom*

The ghostly figure hovered in place and continued to stare at some point far beyond the three companions. Something in Torin's chest urged him to run but there was no place to go. They waited for the apparition to speak more plainly but it offered no explanation.

Grimsa pulled at his hair. "What kind of answer is that?"

"It's a damned riddle," said Wyla, "that's what it is."

"Well, that's your game, Torin." Grimsa said. "Be quick about it too! I've no mind to die in this mold-ridden cave."

"No, I don't think it is a riddle," said Torin. "Perhaps it is some sort of prophecy?"

Grimsa threw up his hands. "It has to be a riddle because it doesn't make any sense!" He crossed his heavy arms and narrowed his eyes. "Something about a tree and a wolf?"

Wyla grabbed Grimsa by the shoulder and pulled him back. "By the gods, Grimsa. Give him a minute to think."

The green glow of the wight flared, in a flash of emerald light. With this burst came a squealing hiss, like the cooling of red-hot iron in ice-cold water. All three companions crouched down and covered their ears as the towering figure writhed and roared. Ballur clutched his ears and shrunk down as he appeared to melt into the floor. From every direction the fog pulled at the edges of his robe until the figure was nothing but a formless, whirling cloud. The floor rumbled below them. Bits of the ceiling crumbled and fell a storm of stones and dust. The light in the fog flickered and wavered, like the flame of a candle fighting a rush of wind, then disappeared in one final splash of curling wisps.

All at once, as if the whole scene had been a dream, the screeching ceased and the air stood still. At first, Torin breathed a sigh of relief but then a familiar tingle prickled his neck. He spun around and froze. The enormous quartz-carved throne was no longer empty.

There, on its wide seat, sat a robed figure with a dark green hood pulled over her face. Below the hood's shadow lay a necklace of silver which glimmered like drops of dew on her moon-pale chest. Torin recognized her at once: it was the woman from the forest at the Vimur River, the one who spoke through the Grey-raven's ring. In the dim light, her sharp chin and thin pale lips emerged from under her hood, a slight but mocking smile.

"Hail, Torin Ten-Trees. Our paths cross once again."

Wyla moved closer to Torin. "Who is that?"

Torin kept his eyes fixed on the cloaked figure and whispered. "That was the woman I saw in the woods on the far bank of the Vimur River."

"Do not act as if we are strangers, Torin," said the regal figure sitting on the throne. She grinned at Wyla, with the white glow of her teeth just visible beneath the shadowed hood. "We have spoken on several occasions already."

Wyla sneered, then glanced back at Torin. "Do you know her?"

Torin gave a slow nod.

"How?"

Torin swallowed and pulled the ring out from his cloak. Its ruby eyes danced with red flames and the silver was nearly too hot to touch. "The Greyraven's ring. The ruby eyes lit up and I heard a voice, a whisper. At first I thought I was hearing things." As he spoke, Wyla and Grimsa stared at the glimmering rubies with wide eyes and gaping mouths.

Torin took one cautious step toward the throne. "Who are you, really?"

"I am the rightful ruler of these woods in which you are all trespassing. Once, I was the queen of a fair race known as the *huldur*, and the echoing refrains of our joyous songs stretched to every distant corner of this wood. Now, the forest is silent in its death."

Wyla narrowed her eyes. "Well, I've never heard of you."

The queenly figure chuckled in that same hollow tone that Torin had heard before. "You have not earned the right to my name yet," she said, "and so you may simply call me your Queen."

Wyla spat on the ground. "We've already got a king, Araldof Greyraven. I suppose you've heard of him?"

The queen gripped the arms of the quartz throne with her thin white hands, her fingers spread like the gossamer strands of a spider's web. She leaned forward and spoke very slowly. "You three have a very important decision to make and I am only going to offer you this choice once. Will you be my subjects, or will you be my slaves?"

Grimsa scoffed. "A Greycloak stops fighting for the Greyraven only when his heart stops beating."

The queen grinned and leaned against the back of the throne. "Such a loyal puppy," she said. "You remind me of a mongrel dog cowering under its master's table barking for scraps."

Grimsa's face flushed red hot, but she spoke again before he could respond. "However, Torin Ten-Trees refused the Grey-cloak. I suppose he is the only one who is truly free to choose his own destiny, the only one of you who hasn't enslaved himself to a weaker master."

Torin shook his head. "Not with you. You are the one poisoning the Greyraven. You said it yourself." Grimsa and Wyla both shot a nervous glance at Torin.

The queen shrugged. "All mortals die."

"And," said Torin. "you sent that eagle to kill us at the Vimur River. Why kill us if you had any intention of asking for our help?"

The queen laughed again, a shrill sound that made Torin's spine shiver. "Hraesvelgir, the eagle? That overgrown mass of feathers is Thrudnir's favourite pet. He's not my creature. His master is a *jotur* who fancies himself a king and calls himself Thrudnir the Wise. But I suppose you've heard of him already, since you were clumsy enough to disturb the spirit of his late son, Ballur. I doubt that Thrudnir will be pleased to hear that."

"Enough talk," Wyla said. "Either tell us the way out or get out of our way."

The queen leaned back in the rune-carved seat. "You three need not worry yourselves about escaping Ballur's tomb. None of you will be leaving alive." Two bright flickers of red flame ignited beneath the queen's green hood in exactly the place where her eyes should have been.

Wyla crouched down and snatched up one of the stray goblets. "Damn your magic, twig-witch! We'll answer your petty charms with steel!"

Again, a thin-lipped smile spread across the regal figure's face. "How brave," she said. "How stupid."

Wyla hurled the goblet straight at the queen's head. In less than a blink, the throne was empty, the mocking grin and the folds of green cloth nowhere to be seen. The vessel struck the throne with an ear-piercing clang which echoed through every corner of the cavern.

Wyla snatched the cup back up off the floor and held it over her head. "Show yourself, coward!"

Her challenge was met with a faint creaking sound from the far end of the cavern. The companions whirled around but saw nothing through the shadow. With slow, cautious steps each turned so that they stood back-to-back, preparing for whatever might spring out of the dark.

"Ballur?" said Torin. "Is that you?"

A louder creak came from somewhere nearby. The musty air stirred with a chorus of raspy scrapes that filled the dim corners of the cavern.

Torin swallowed and he gripped *Tyrfang* by the hilt. "We need to find a way out, and we need to find it quick."

Grimsa rolled his eyes. "Haven't I been saying that since the moment we fell into this cursed hole?"

Torin peered into the dark. He could not see anything but knew from the noises that something lurked amongst the misty shadows around the edge of the room.

Soft rain pattered down onto the stone floor from the hole where they had fallen into the barrow. Faint hints of sunrise filtered in so that it fell through a column of pale-yellow light. Emboldened by these signs, Torin stepped away from the mass of churning shadow and into the small ring of sunlight.

From everywhere and nowhere, the queen's voice echoed through the cavern, reverberating in every direction. "How long have you slept, you who mourned Ballur at his death? Certainly, you loved him best, you *huldur* folk who danced under the light of the stars and sang sweet songs of spring when this *jotur* prince still drew breath. How were you to know that his funeral draught would send you down to the slumber that never ends? But now I call you back, you disloyal subjects. I awaken you from a life which you thought had passed as does a dream."

The creaking noise was getting louder and Torin thought he saw slow, shifting figures in the misty shadows.

Wyla took a quick step back. "They're moving."

Grimsa did the same. "Moving? Who's moving?"

Wyla cursed. "By the gods, does it matter who? Grab something to bludgeon them with."

Torin shouted up to the opening above them. "Bari! Azal! Did you find a way out?" No response came from the surface.

The queen's voice softened with surprising gentleness. "But look at you! How bare your bones! How foul your flesh! Once you *huldur* folk were so beautiful, the fairest of all who dwelled within the wood. Now step closer to the light and see for yourselves what you have become. You are hideous. Wretched. Loathsome."

What Torin witnessed next would haunt him for as long as he would live. Out from the swirling mist emerged countless faces, rotting, empty, monstrous faces. The look in their eyes, or that which was left of them, shifted from wide mournful stares to glares of absolute horror as the soft sphere of light illuminated their wretched forms. All at once, the withered creatures wailed. One grasped her hair with bony fingers and shrieked when it came off in knotted clumps. Another held his hands up to the light and roared through a half-rotted throat. But worst of all was the smell, a putrid stench of freshly disturbed rot.

The tone of the queen's voice turned knife-sharp in an instant. "But these three here have hearts which still pump warm red blood. Tear the flesh from their bodies and I will clothe your naked bones with it. Rip their sinewed muscles from their joints. Peel back their youthful skin and I will make you beautiful again!"

Torin counted the host of horrid eyes before him. He did not like the odds. The creatures did not rush ahead but leaned in slowly as a starving man might lean toward a steaming loaf of bread.

Wyla's voice cut through the silence. "Damn you, wights!" She hurled the goblet at one of the creatures with all her strength. The iron vessel shattered its skull and the creature fell back into the darkness.

All at once the host descended on them, a wild flurry of despair and rage. Torin saw a dozen bony hands stretch out toward him, each trying desperately to grab hold of the exposed skin of his forearms. He pushed them back with *Tyrfang*, still in its scabbard, and kicked away fingers that grasped at his ankles. The wailing of the horde was awful. Every time Torin struck a blow another shrill shriek rose above the din.

Grimsa roared. He was angry, and that filled him with no place left for fear. Again and again, Grimsa pummeled the creatures with his fists and sent them tumbling backwards. He picked up one of the larger creatures and twirled it around before hurling it far off into the veil of shadow. As soon as he did so, three more barrow creatures rushed up to grapple him, while still others rose to renew the charge.

Torin kept himself planted in the ring of light underneath the opening at the center of the cavern, but he could feel the desperation of the corpse creatures to pull him out into the inky darkness. Some had bony fingers with little but pale skin covering them while others had cruel, curled nails that had grown long over countless years. All of them tore and scraped at his body and soon he saw trickles of red running down his forearms.

Torin cursed and shouted up toward the sky. "Azal, tell Aldrin to send every blazing ball of fire he can summon down here!" Still, Azal's form did not appear in the ring of light above their heads and no scorching bolts came to their aid. "Azal! Aldrin? Bari?"

Torin heard Grimsa call out behind him. "Torin, they have Wyla!"

He turned to see Wyla kicking and flailing as a mob of corpses dragged her toward the shadow. Blood ran down her face where the creatures had clawed it. No matter how many she hit with her fists and kicked with her feet, the writhing mob kept pulling her further into the darkness.

Grimsa had just turned to take a step toward Wyla when half a dozen creatures pounced on his exposed back. He tottered from side to side before tumbling over in a mass of twisted arms and legs, all slick with sweat and rot and gore.

Then Torin felt time slow down, as if the chaos around him had stopped and he was standing still inside a frozen moment. The only sound he heard beyond the ring in his ears was the pounding of his heart which thundered like the rumble of approaching horses. The sting of the cuts on his neck and forearms faded into numb tingles as the dim scene in front of him came into sharp focus.

There was Wyla being dragged away by the monstrous creatures. There was Grimsa under a pile of writhing corpses. And there was Torin's own hand on *Tyrfang's* hilt, his fingers wrapped tight around the warm leather grip. The queen's voice, soft but audible, slipped through the chaos around him.

Let Tyrfang taste their tainted flesh.

In that moment, Torin knew there was no other choice. He lifted *Tyrfang* over his head and drew the ancient blade out of the rune-carved scabbard. The flash from the blade blinded the creatures around him and, in that light, Torin saw their awful eyes stretch wide with terror.

All at once, the world rushed back to Torin. He tightened his grip as the battle-fire surged in his chest. With a roar of fury, he brought *Tyrfang's* bright blazing edge down upon the creature grasping his arm.

Torin hacked and hewed, he severed and skewered, he kicked and bludgeoned and sliced his way through the crowd of corpses. With neither grace nor form, he committed his full weight to every slash and thrust, showing no regard for his exposed arms and face. There was no chance of retreat, no thought given to his own defence, just the reckless push forward, doubly fueled by rage and fear.

When the creatures around Torin had fled, he rushed over to Wyla. Grabbing her arm with his free hand, he cut away with sweeping strokes at the corpses that gripped her arms and legs. The severed hands still clutched Wyla's ankles and wrists, even after being separated from their body. She yanked them off like loosened shackles and scrambled to her feet.

Torin and Wyla sprinted across the cavern toward Grimsa, who was hardly visible under the pile of clawing corpses on top of him. Wyla dragged the creatures away from his head while Torin hacked at those who had climbed on Grimsa's back. Soon they had cleared a ring around their battered friend, and he stood up. The companions shuffled, back-to-back, toward the center of the cavern where the column of light was growing in intensity.

The barrow corpses circled around them, some missing limbs and others limping because of broken bones. Nevertheless, they drove forward in wild desperation. Though Torin slashed *Tyrfang* at any who dared to step too close, he knew the creatures would soon overtake them.

Torin shouted up toward the sky. "Azal! Bari! We need to get out!"

This time a response came, not from the opening overhead but from the far end of the cavern near Ballur's throne. The roof caved in above the stone chair and light spilled over the finely carved quartz through a cloud of dust and debris. As the white stone became illuminated, the runes carved into it shone a bright green, like light through fresh-budded leaves in springtime.

"There," Grimsa said, "they've made an opening!"

Wyla kicked away another creature as it swung at her. "If we climb onto the top of the throne, we might be able to get out."

"To the throne," Torin said, "Together. Wait. Now!"

The three companions barreled toward the high carved seat, Grimsa at the center with Torin and Wyla on either side. They trampled a row of corpses, slipping and nearly tripping on the slick grease of their decrepit bodies. Torin and Wyla helped Grimsa up onto the throne's seat, then Grimsa turned around and pulled them both up at the same time, one with each hand.

From their elevated position, Torin kept the creatures from scaling the front of the throne, though others had started up the sides and the back using the carved branches as holds. The ceiling over the throne was lower than at the center of the domed cavern and the light was more intense. The grey skin of the corpses sizzled and burned as they climbed up closer to the sunlit sky at which they shrieked in agony.

"Wyla first," Torin said, "She's the quickest!"

She shook her head. "Grimsa first. He'll never make it up otherwise!"

Both Torin and Wyla crouched down on the flat seat of the throne as Grimsa stepped up onto their backs. His heels dug into them, and both cursed under his weight. Grimsa wobbled, his foot nearly slipping off, before his hands found a grip firm enough to steady himself.

"Damn it, Grimsa," Wyla said, "You're going to break my back!"

Grimsa grunted and pulled himself up onto the top of the throne. When Torin stood up, he saw only Grimsa's feet as they disappeared over the top of the opening into the realm of sunlight.

Torin slashed at the creatures clambering up the sides. "Go! I'll follow."

Wyla nodded and scaled the throne using the bark-like runes carved into the stone. One creature popped up from behind the throne, but she struck it with her fist, sending it tumbling back into the darkness. Torin hacked again at the creatures who had climbed onto the seat, and when he glanced back, Wyla had climbed over the top to safety.

Then Torin saw *Tyrfang* in the light, slick with grease and gore but without a drop of blood on it. He felt his stomach drop like a stone. He hesitated a moment then shoved the sword back into the scabbard. A hand grasped at his ankle, and he stomped on the fingers. With the black leather sheath in hand, he scrambled up onto the back of the throne.

By the time he had reached the top, a few of the barrow corpses had managed to climb onto the throne's seat. He kicked away another grasping corpse then forced himself up so that he could kneel on top of the throne. With a sickening lurch, Torin nearly tumbled back down into the swarm of seething corpses but managed to catch himself before toppling over.

Above him, from outside, a hand stretched toward him. As he squinted, it seemed that the hand was so large that it could only be Grimsa's. Torin strained to reach it but could not. As he looked up, the light blinded him, so he simply closed his eyes and stretched out his arm as high as he could. A large hand caught hold of his and, with one strong pull, Torin rose out of the barrow into the realm of light above.

11

◇ IN THE HALL OF THE MOUNTAIN KING ◇

THE HAND THAT HELPED Torin out of the barrow yanked him up much faster than he expected. As soon as his feet felt the dewy turf, he lost his balance and tumbled down the grassy slope. At the bottom of the hill, perhaps twenty strides from where he had emerged, he rolled to a stop and lay flat on his back.

Far above Torin, misty grey clouds let enough sunlight through the drizzle to blind him momentarily. As his eyes adjusted, he heard the thump of heavy footsteps approaching, far heavier than Grimsa's could have been. A surge of panic shot through his chest as the ground rumbled beneath him. Through squinted eyes, Torin saw a blurred form approaching. When he opened his mouth to speak, the figure swung its foot and kicked him in the ribs, sending him sprawling over the turf. Before he could scramble to his feet, an enormous boot came down on his back and pinned him to the ground.

A low, coarse voice spoke over him. "Lay still where you are, *madur.*"

Up the hill, a few of the corpse creatures scrambled out from the hole in the barrow. Torin craned his neck up and saw them crawling toward him. His breath caught in both relief and horror as their rotted flesh fell away into heaps of dust in the sunlight. Soon they were nothing but piles of windblown ash upon the hill.

Torin felt the foot press down on his back so hard that for a moment he could hardly breathe. With his face squished into the wet grass, Torin coughed. "By the gods, get off me!"

The pressure released. Torin sucked in a full breath of air. As he tried to stand, he was caught by a lazy kick to the ribs which knocked him onto his back.

"Damn the gods," said the booming voice. "The *asyr* can burn in the fiery realm of Muspell for all I care."

Torin gazed up at the gigantic figure standing over him. The giant's stern glare seemed to shimmer like ice. His hair and beard were neatly braided, the colour a mix of snowy white and iron-rust red. The skin of his burly arms, which were folded across his wide chest, was pale with the slightest tinge of blue. A scarlet cloak hung over his shoulder and a coat of well-polished chain-mail hung down to just above his knees. His dark leather trousers were pressed with an intricate pattern and the jeweled scabbard of an enormous sword hung at his waist. Torin had seen such a creature before; it was a *jotur*, one of the ancient immortal giants from the distant North.

"Who are you that dares disturb the tomb of Ballur the Bright, late son of the mighty Lord Thrudnir?"

"Thrudnir?"

The giant kicked Torin again. "Are you deaf?"

"No, I —" said Torin, "I am Torin Ten-Trees. My company is from Gatewatch. We are travelling north to the Everspring by the order of King Araldof Greyraven himself."

Another voice, not as deep but still loud and bellowing, came from behind the giant. "Same nonsense as the others."

Torin's hands shook but he managed to pull out Araldof's silver raven ring from his cloak. "No, I am telling the truth. Look! This is the signet ring of King Araldof Greyraven himself!"

The giant narrowed his eyes and crouched down, his braided beard dangling just above the ground. When the two inset rubies caught the sunlight, the *jotur's* bushy brow shot up. "A fine trinket indeed. So, it is as I suspected."

Torin frowned. "What? That we are telling the truth?"

The giant groaned as he stood back up to his full height. "No, that you are grave robbers! Treasure mongers and barrow thieves, all of you. And none too bright by my reckoning."

Torin sat up and rubbed his sore ribs. A short distance away, he saw the rest of the company: Grimsa and Wyla, Azal and Bari, even old Aldrin, were tied up with thick rope and gagged with scraps of cloth. Another *jotur*, a giantess with wild curls of copper-red hair, stood over them with her hands on her hips. She also wore a crimson cloak over a polished coat of finely crafted mail.

"What? Wait. No," said Torin, "We are on our way to the Everspring."

The *jotur* chuckled as he caught a length of rope tossed to him by the giantess. "The Everspring? Well then you've still got a long way to go." He loosened a coil of rope and began to tie a knot as he stepped toward Torin.

Torin shuffled back. "With the authority of the royal signet ring from King Araldof Greyraven himself, I demand to speak with Lord Thrudnir!"

"Lord Thrudnir," the giant said, "Is not one of whom you can demand anything, no matter what name you utter. The Mountain King is lord alone over this ancient realm." He finished tying a knot in the rope and pulled it tight. "But you shall certainly have an audience with him to explain why you injured his most beloved eagle, Hraesvelgir, and then proceeded to desecrate his beloved son's tomb. I cannot speak for Lord Thrudnir, but I expect that he will not be pleased in either case."

Torin thought of dashing into the forest, but the *jotur* was towering over him and he was not keen on getting kicked in the ribs again by those enormous feet. "No need to tie me up. I'll come along if it means I can speak with him. Who are you?"

The giant gave an exasperated sigh. "I am Jolvar, cousin to Lord Thrudnir and, apparently, runner of petty errands such as this. Now, hold still while I tie you up or I really will break your ribs the next time I kick you."

Torin realized that he was still gripping *Tyrfang*, sheathed. He held it up to Jolvar and the giant jumped back with wide eyes.

"So," Torin said. "You recognize this trinket?"

The *jotur* furled his brow. "From what foul pit did you pluck that wicked weapon, grave robber?"

Torin ignored Jolvar's question. "Take me to Lord Thrudnir. I will have answers for him, if he agrees to help us."

The second giant picked something up off the ground. Torin put his hand on the hilt of the blade, ready to draw it, but then he hesitated as he remembered the curse. Had its thirst for blood been satisfied as it cut through the barrow corpses? Or had the curse already been laid on him because there was no blood in those creatures? Would the blade turn on him if he dared to draw it again?

But it was too late. The second *jotur* flung a net, much like those used by village fishermen, and tangled Torin in a hopeless mire of knotted rope. With a single tug the giantess pulled it tight. Both Torin's arms were squeezed so close to his body that he could barely move them, much less draw the sword that was caught up with him in the net.

"Good throw, Ulfrun," said Jolvar. "Now back to Thrudnir's hall. If we ride hard, we might still make it in time for the feast!"

Torin felt red hot blood surge through his veins as he struggled to free himself from the net. "By thundering Orr and all the gods! Let me out!"

"The gods can wait," Jolvar said, "but Lord Thrudnir cannot."

The giantess, the one whom Jolvar had called Ulfrun, led two huge horses out from the edge of the forest. Torin would have marveled at the size of the creatures and praised their saddles of finely worked leather had he not been unceremoniously strapped to one of them like an extra saddle bag. The rest of the company fared no better. One by one, they were tied onto the horses like spare bed rolls.

Everyone except Torin was gagged with a strip of cloth, so he made up for the rest of them in both vehemence and volume. He cursed the giants and shouted threats of violence against one, then the other, then both at the same time. It was no use. The net had him bound so tightly that he could barely move, and the more he struggled the tighter it became. He did succeed in being loud enough that Ulfrun tried to gag him. However, she could not easily reach him through the knotted mesh and so left him to shout his lungs raw.

After testing the knots that secured the prisoners to the saddles, Jolvar and Ulfrun each claimed a horse and rode north. They picked their way through a treacherous path obscured by evergreen branches with sharp needles that whipped Torin's face as they rushed by. At first, the scrapes from the corpse creatures in the barrow flared with pain every time a branch struck, but after a while they grew numb from the cold, and he was better able to ignore them.

By midday, the forest grew thin and gave way to an open field where nothing but tufts of hardy grass clung to the dry, crusted earth. A plume of dust rose behind the galloping horses, and Torin's eyes watered in the wind that whistled across the rugged plain.

In Gatewatch, rocky ridges cluttered the skyline and made the world feel close. But here, the sky seemed to stretch off to the edges of the earth, if such a place existed. Billowing patterns of grey clouds covered the blue sky in ragged patches like a beggar's cloak pulled tight at the edges. How long had it been, Torin thought, since he had seen the open sky stretched so wide over a flat horizon? Certainly not since he had left for Gatewatch two years ago. Not even the fields around Ten-Tree Hall stretched so far or so wide. The only comparison Torin could make was to a childhood memory he had of looking out over the northern sea on a clear day from the very top of the Shrieking Cliffs.

As the field widened, Jolvar and Ulfrun spurred their horses on to a much quicker pace. At the crest of each gallop, Torin floated away from the horse's body only to fall back down against its rock-hard flank, a steady pounding on his side which he reckoned would significantly worsen his existing bruises. However, he soon fell into a rhythm and, despite the discomfort of his situation, felt his eyelids weigh heavy with sleepiness.

A sudden burst of heat on Torin's chest startled him awake. Though he could not move his arms, he could crane his neck down just enough to see a flicker of red light from where the Greyraven's ring was tucked into his shirt.

I am disappointed. You do not want to disappoint someone like me.

"What?" said Torin. "Disappointed that we are still alive?"

No. Disappointed because you made the wrong decision. The weak decision. But I see strength in you yet and so I have decided to give you one last chance.

"Do you think I am out of my mind? You tried to kill us!"

Let us consider that a test. You passed.

Torin opened his mouth to speak again, but suddenly the ring erupted into small crackling flames. He hissed through clenched teeth as the hot metal seared his chest. The scent of burnt flesh and singed fabric stung in Torin's nose.

One last chance, Torin Ten-Trees. We will speak again soon.

Torin cursed as the fiery silver ring blew out in the whipping wind. The icy breeze rushing past him cooled it quickly, but the metal still rubbed against the burn. With his eyes squeezed shut he listened for any trace of the queen's voice. A long while passed without a sound and eventually he surrendered to an uneasy sleep.

Torin woke when the rhythm of galloping hooves broke into an easy canter. He shivered, his nose runny and his ears numb with cold. The sun had not yet set but was low enough in the sky that it singed the horizon ahead of them with orange.

"By Ym's beard," said Jolvar, "These horses are slow with all this extra weight. It's a miracle that we made it back before sundown."

"Just in time," said Ulfrun. "I would have blamed you if I missed dinner."

Torin strained to look ahead and see what kind of place they had come to. Before them stood an enormous mountain which towered high over the plain. A leaning column of steam rose from its peak and veins of ash-black coal ran down its slopes. The dark ridges were bare and lean with glaciers of sea-green ice cast over them like armoured plates. Directly in front of them stood a sheer cliff face, carved out of the mountain side which seemed as tall as any of the peaks that surrounded Gatewatch.

Torin cleared his throat. "Where are we? Back in the mountains?"

"Back in the mountains?" said Jolvar. "Those were not mountains *madur*, merely hills. These are mountains!"

"Well then, where?"

Jolvar reached behind his cloak and grabbed the netting, grasping some of Torin's tangled hair in the process. Torin gulped down a shout as the *jotur* yanked him up for a better view.

"This," Jolvar said, "is the Hall of the Mountain King."

Torin winced. "By the gods, you're ripping my hair out!"

"Quiet, *madur*! Watch."

Torin's eyes widened as he saw the base of the precipitous cliff ahead of them flicker. At first, he thought it was just a trick of the late afternoon light, but then it happened again. A vision of towering crystal pillars rising on either side of an impossibly large door that appeared and disappeared in as much time as it took to blink. As the horses thundered over the plain toward the mountain, it flickered again, more clearly and for a moment longer. Then, all at once, it appeared and did not disappear. High above them, reflecting the warm glow of evening light on the horizon far to the west, stood a magnificent wall of quartz pillars which rose in a sweeping inverted arch to a narrow-pointed spire.

Torin gazed up at the otherworldly gate. Jolvar laughed, a jolly rumbling sound that rang out over the pounding of the horse's hooves. The orange and red in the sky set the shining gate ablaze with colour, the milky-white crystal columns swirling with sunset hues. The ash-black mountainside rose up behind it, consuming the grey clouds high overhead until it seemed that the mountain itself was the sky. Without warning, the *jotur* released Torin's tangled hair and he fell back alongside the horse's flank.

Given the direction of the setting sun, Torin reckoned they were then travelling nearly due north. He had never even heard any stories about the desolate plain beyond the wild woods or this range of towering ash-black mountains on its far side. He closed his eyes and summoned whatever memories he had of the Greyraven's map. He strained to recall what lay at the furthest edge of those blue-inked swirling strokes, but his mind was too dull from the miserable journey.

The sun fell out of view as they entered a canyon between two of the mountain's sprawling arms. They rode up the winding path toward the gate for what seemed to Torin like a very long time. A whistling wind picked up overhead. Soon the clouds cleared, and the first stars peeked through the darkening sky. Their twinkling glow far overhead did little to light the path as the shadow of the mountain swallowed them up.

At last, Jolvar yanked on the reins and his horse came to an abrupt stop. A moment later, a ringing tone blared above Torin's head, a pure note so loud and so clear that it made his skull rattle.

Out of the corner of his eye, Torin saw Jolvar holding a long spiraled horn. The *jotur* took a deep breath then raised the horn to sound a second blast which echoed through the canyon.

A moment later, Ulfrun cursed. "Damn that Gerd. By Ym, that blast should have roused the dead."

Jolvar sighed. "If she is not asleep on her watch, then she must have snuck down to the feast."

"Well, that is going to make for a long night. These stinking little *madur* will be little more than frozen lumps of ice by then."

Jolvar sounded the horn again, this time so loud that Torin's ears rang. Once the ringing faded, he heard a few loose rocks tumble down the mountainside somewhere down the canyon. Then there came a strange rumble, a vibration through the stones that hummed a single tone in reply.

Jolvar laughed. "So old Gerd is not entirely deaf after all!"

"Not completely," said Ulfrun. "Thank Ym!"

From somewhere behind the cliff face, there came a grinding groan, the coarse scrape of quartz on stone. Torin arched his back to catch a glimpse of the opening gate. From the ground to a point far higher than he could see, a rich red glow lit the widening crack between two central pillars. A rush of warm air blew past his face and carried with it the savory smell of roasting meat. His empty stomach ached and grumbled.

Jolvar reached back and patted Torin on the head, which knocked his skull against the horse's stone-hard, muscular flank. "Well, grave robber! It seems you will have your audience with Lord Thrudnir after all."

Torin thought it wise to stay silent and so stifled the crude response that nearly slipped from his mouth. He was jostled against the horse as it moved through the enormous crystal gate. Ulfrun whistled a lively tune as they passed under the high arch, the notes echoing off the smooth stone walls of a tunnel that led down into the belly of the mountain. Once they passed through, the gap in the gigantic crystal pillars shrunk until the chill of the frigid northern night was shut out behind them.

Torin realized then how frozen his hands, fingers, and ears were. The stifling heat that rose through the giant's tunnel brought feeling back to his limbs, an agonizing pain like a thousand tiny pins. The cuts on his face and arms throbbed. Even worse were the blistering burns where the rope had rubbed against his arms and neck.

Jolvar dismounted and tossed his cloak over the saddle. "Gerd! Come see to these thieving *madur*. Clean them up then bring them down to the main hall when they are in a more presentable state."

Ulfrun stepped up to Torin where he hung from the saddle and grimaced. "By Yg! These creatures smell awful, nearly as bad as the inside of the barrow. Do all *madur* reek like this?"

"I would assume so," said Jolvar, "Wretched creatures that they are."

The two *jotur* turned away and continued down the tunnel, leaving Torin and the others strapped tight to the horses. Torin tried twisting in every direction but could not get a hold of *Tyrfang's* hilt. No matter how he craned and strained, the netting held him tight.

When he looked up, Torin found himself staring straight into the eyes of the ugliest creature he had ever seen. It had wild hair of wispy white strands that fell too far to one side and a pointed chin that had sprouted a forest of curly hairs. Its wrinkled cheeks sagged under two sunken eyes and the loose translucent skin of its ancient forehead slumped down over two bushy eyebrows. It grinned to unveil two rows of crooked yellow teeth, some of which came to sharp points and others that had been worn down into little more flattened stumps.

The creature leaned in toward Torin and chuckled. "Now, you're a handsome one!" Its acrid breath nearly made him gag.

Torin coughed before he caught his breath. "Who are you?"

"I have been known as Ancient-Root, Withered-Bough, Brown-Leaf, and Wrinkled-Bark, but most who dwell here in the Hall of the Mountain King call me Gerd the Old."

Torin fought down another coughing fit and forced a smile. "Greetings, Gerd the Old. I am Torin Ten-Trees, son of Jarl Einar Ten-Trees."

"Two in Tentys? Two of who? And what, by Ym, is a Tentys?" The old *jotur* frowned a moment then shrugged. "You mortals live such short lives it is hardly worth keeping track of your names anyways. You spring out from the womb one day, then the next you're old and shriveled like me!"

Torin looked down at the creature's catastrophic smile, like the planks of a collapsed house all piled in a heap. He tried not to stare. "Are you going to free me? As you said, my life is short, and I don't mean to squander it tied to this damned horse."

"Ah yes," said Gerd. "We can't keep Lord Thrudnir waiting now, can we?" She reached down to her belt and drew out a rusty sword, its crooked blade bent and twisted. However, in her large, wrinkled hands it looked like little more than a paring knife from the kitchen. "Hold still now."

Torin held his breath as the elderly giant raised the weapon up to his face. It shook in her unsteady grip, the rusted edge sliding dangerously close to his neck. He arched his back to pull his head away, but the ropes held him in place.

Gerd stuck out her tongue and squinted. "My sight is not all that it used to be. Stop squirming and hold very still now or this might end badly."

Torin squeezed his eyes shut. Gerd grunted as the first rope snapped, then a second. At last, she managed to cut through a third rope and Torin broke free. He dropped down from where he had been strapped to the saddle and hit the stone floor with a dull thud. He groaned and rolled over onto his back. Under his breath, he cursed his bruised bones while also thanking the gods that Gerd had not accidentally sliced his head clean off.

"Now help an old giantess with the rest of these *madur*. My joints are stiff from opening the gate and my fingers are no good with tiny knots anyways."

Torin's knees shook in an awful dizziness as he stood but he steadied himself against the horse's leg. He stretched his stiff arms out wide and flexed the fingers that had gripped *Tyrfang's* hilt throughout the long journey. He took extra care to tie the blade into its sheath as he secured it to his belt.

Torin saw that Bari and Aldrin had also been tied to Jolvar's horse, while Grimsa, Wyla, and Azal still dangled from Ulfrun's. He hobbled over to Wyla and stretched up toward the knot that held her in place but could not reach it from the ground. Though he strained on his tiptoes, it was still too far above where he stood. So Torin climbed up onto the horse using the giant stirrup on the saddle and hoped it would not bolt or kick. To his relief, it hardly seemed to notice him climbing up onto its back.

Torin loosened the scrap cloth that gagged Wyla and slipped it off her head. She coughed a moment then spat a few times to clear her mouth.

"By thundering Orr and all the gods, untie me already!"

Torin fumbled a bit with the knot but managed to pry the rope loose. Wyla dropped down to the floor with more grace than Torin had managed. She groaned and stretched out on the stones a moment before she rose to her feet.

"Well," said Gerd. "Another one survived the journey! Surprising, as you *madur* are so frail."

Wyla's nostrils flared. "Frail? I'll show you frail!" With that she charged at the old giantess, her fists clenched tight, and her teeth bared. She crashed into the old giantess and Torin expected the ancient creature to topple over. Instead, Gerd began to giggle as Wyla's blows fell upon her.

"A feisty one, that's for sure!"

Wyla roared and redoubled her assault, this time striking Gerd's nobbled knees with all the fury she could muster. The giantess grinned and reached down toward Wyla with her crooked, wrinkled hand. As one might nab a mouse by the tail, Gerd pinched Wyla's hair with two fingers and pulled her up. Wyla kicked and cursed in midair as the old giantess inspected her more closely.

Gerd squinted at Wyla for a moment then raised her eyebrows. "Ah, it's a she!"

Torin slipped off the horse and rushed over to help Wyla but could not get close as her legs flailed in every direction. Wyla managed to grab hold of Gerd's wrist and pulled herself up high enough to bite one of her wrinkled fingers. The old *jotur* gave a shrill yelp and dropped Wyla back down to the ground.

Gerd shook out her hand. "Nasty creature, that one."

Torin caught Wyla by the shoulders before she could charge ahead again. "Stop! What's the use?"

Wyla tried to pull away one more time then quit struggling and slumped down. "Fyr's fire. What are we going to do?" Torin helped her up to her feet. Wyla pulled him close in an embrace. "By the gods, I thought we were going to die in that barrow."

Torin squeezed her back. "We nearly did."

Wyla looked down at Torin's chest and frowned. She raised her hand to the scorched fabric. "What happened?"

Torin pulled his damp shirt away from the scalded mark. "It's the Greyraven's ring. Whenever that cloaked woman from the barrow speaks, I can feel heat in the metal."

Wyla's eyes went wide. "She speaks to you through the ring?"

Torin nodded. "I was strapped to Jolvar's horse. She got angry and the ring burned right through my shirt."

Wyla winced as she inspected the burn. "Why wear it then? Why not throw it away?"

Torin pulled out the ring, so it hung down over his chest in full view. He shrugged. "It's the Greyraven's signet ring. I don't think that it is a thing I can just toss away."

Wyla rolled her eyes. "You and your sense of duty. It is going to get you killed one day."

Torin grinned. "Perhaps. Let's get the others untied."

Gerd coughed, shaking her finger at the others, who were still tied to the horses. "No more nasty business from the rest of you or I will sit on you one by one until you are all squished flat."

Torin and Wyla helped Grimsa down from Ulfrun's horse, then all three worked together to free the rest. Grimsa caught Bari as he came loose and Wyla helped Azal down. Aldrin was the last to be freed, partly so the others could catch him, and partly because they were still cross over what had happened at the Vimur River.

Aldrin slid down the side of the horse and steadied himself on Grimsa's arm. The old man's face and arms were badly bruised, and he could not walk without help. The company huddled close together and spoke in whispers.

"What a fine mess we're in," said Grimsa. "A whole mountain full of these damned *jotur*. How are we going to get out?"

"As for me," said Wyla, "I'd like to give those two oafs who tied us up a taste of my axe before we leave."

Aldrin shook his head and opened his bruised eyes as wide as he could. "Nonsense! We must do no such thing. This Lord Thrudnir might be able to help us!"

Bari shivered. "Trust the *jotur*? They may be wise, but I would not trust them with a single ounce of copper."

Wyla pointed at *Tyrfang* which Torin still clutched tightly in his hand. "That blade might end the jabbering of this old hag. The horses are still here. We could take those!"

Torin's heart jumped in his chest as he remembered *Tyrfang's* curse. He was about to speak when Aldrin cut in.

"And what about the gate?"

"Damn the gate," Wyla said. "We can find another way out."

"Another way large enough for horses?" Aldrin said. "Seems unlikely to me. And it took us a full day riding at break-neck pace to reach this mountain fortress. If we can't take the horses, then how long will it take to trek back, even if we can find a way out?"

Gerd clapped her wrinkled old hands and motioned for the company to follow her. "What are you all whispering about? No time to waste. Come, come! We must not leave Lord Thrudnir waiting."

Grimsa sighed. "Do you think this Lord Thrudnir will at least feed us before we are stomped flat or cut in half or roasted over the fire?"

Wyla pressed her hands into her temples. "Really? You're thinking about food right now?"

Bari shrugged and grinned. "Well, I wouldn't argue with a bowl full of steaming stew at this point."

Grimsa gave a half-smile and patted the *nidavel's* shoulder. "Bari, sometimes I feel that you are the only one who understands me."

"Quickly now," said Gerd, "or I'll have to tie you all up again."

That got the company moving right away. They shuffled along behind the old giantess down a small corridor off the main tunnel-way. The floor of polished marble felt warm under Torin's feet, and the sweet smell of fresh baked bread and savory meat drifted through the air.

Soon they turned another corner and entered a large room with a stone hearth sunk into the wall and a wide wooden table. Torin's eyes stretched open at the sight of knives dangling off hooks and pots stacked on a tall shelf. Scraps lay all over the floor, especially under the table: large potato peels, gigantic onion ends, enormous carrot tops, skull-sized garlic cloves, and the odd bone.

Gerd hobbled over to the table and reached up to the shelf above it. She felt around with her fingers and knocked over a few pots which came tumbling down to the marble floor with a crash. At last, her fingers found a large round cauldron and she stretched up onto her toes to haul it down. With a grunt, she yanked it free. Gerd held it above her head and swayed from side to side for a moment. She nearly lost her balance but managed to guide the cauldron to the floor without falling over or crushing any of the wide-eyed *madur* below.

Gerd leaned over the black rim of the cauldron and panted. "By Yg, I really should not be hauling such things around at my age." She squinted at the company and pointed to each one as she counted. "Should be big enough. It is hard to tell sometimes with my poor sight."

Azal gripped Torin's shoulder with a shaky hand. "What do you think she means by 'big enough'?"

"Why else would she have brought us to the kitchen?" said Bari.

Torin tightened his grip on Tyrfang's hilt. "*Tyrfang* will taste her blood before she sips ours."

"Wait," Azal said. "In Armeah we have a famous folktale about a young prince who escapes this very situation. I think we could do the same."

Torin motioned to Grimsa, Wyla, and Bari to move closer, then Azal whispered as quietly as he could. When the prince had finished, the others looked at each other.

"It could work," said Torin.

"By the gods, let's just use the sword and be done with it," said Wyla.

"At least give it a try," said Azal. "If we attack head-on then one or two of us are sure to get stomped!"

Torin looked back at Wyla. She sighed. "Ok," she said. "Let's try it."

Azal straightened his posture, smoothed back his hair, and put on a well-practiced smile. His eyes were lit with that same mischievous twinkle that Torin remembered from when he had first met the prince in Fjellhall.

Azal summoned all his princely charm and cleared his throat. "I have been wondering, Gerd the Old, just how old are you?"

The old giantess chuckled and shook her head. "You *madur* count time in years but that is far too small a span to measure my age. I can remember a time in my youth when Yg, the tree which holds up the world, was still a green-leafed sapling. At that time, the reign of Ym, first of all giants, had not yet ended. That was long before the war with the *asyr*, when Ym was torn to pieces and cast upon Yg's boughs."

"Oh, really?"

"Yes," Gerd said. "His salty blood became the ocean, his wide skull the sky, his soft brains the clouds, his jagged teeth the mountains, his thick arms the hills, and his broad chest the green fields. Indeed, the first trees that sprouted from the ground were the hairs upon his chest!"

Lorekeeper Aldrin leaned against the prince and raised one hand to his forehead. "Damn this miserable northern weather! If only I had some dry parchment, I could capture a small sample of your elegant words."

Bari stepped up beside the old scholar and clapped enthusiastically. "Oh, I must agree! Even within the halls of the *nidavel* the eloquence of your speech would silence the clanging of hammers. Why ever do they call you Gerd the Old and not Gerd the Flower-Tongued?"

Meanwhile, Torin, Grimsa, and Wyla sidled out of Gerd's sight and under the table.

12

◇ JOKULHEIM ◇

GERD LEANED ON THE CAULDRON and sighed. "Yes, I suppose I do
have a way with words. You know, at one time I was an enviable
beauty as well. This grey hair once tumbled down my shoulders in
golden ringlets and these shriveled lips used to be as red and crisp
as a ripe apple. I was courted by lordly giants and shining *asyr*. To
think, you *madur* call them gods! Why, Odd himself even begged
a place in my bed! Three blissful nights we spent in each other's
company."

Torin saw Azal's princely smile twitch. The thought of loving
one such as Gerd was too much for even a king's son to main-
tain his composure. The prince swallowed hard and forced a polite
smile. And, as this exchange continued, Torin, Grimsa, and Wyla
went on crawling beneath the table and creeping around to the
rear of the old giantess.

"Little did I know that Odd, the scheming trickster, was using
me to steal away one of my father's dearest treasures! Not that I
cared much for my father. He may have been among the first of
the giants, but he never did much other than drink from his vat of
mead or threaten to marry me off to a troll if I didn't keep up with
all the chores. Still, I like to think that Odd still dreams of me
sometimes. It is as if I can relive those wondrous nights by simply

closing my eyes, every detail so perfectly clear even after all these years. Oh, how we indulged in the warmth of each other's arms! How broad his shoulders! How sweet his kiss! How wonderful the feeling of his strong hands upon my—"

Azal coughed and held up his hands. "Please, tell us more about, um, well, how about Lord Thrudnir?"

"Lord Thrudnir? Ha! My face was already full of wrinkles by the time he was born. He certainly has made something of himself. Look at the size of this place! And not a soul goes hungry in the Hall of the Mountain King. Of course, there was the death of his wife in the wars with the *asyr* and the tragic affair of his son Ballur. But I suppose all that is passed and done now."

Torin gave a silent countdown on his fingers. Along with Wyla and Grimsa, he rushed out from under the table. Before Gerd noticed them, they had their arms around her ankles, Torin and Wyla on one and Grimsa on the other. They all held their breath to block the acrid smell of her aged skin and tightened their grip.

"Now lift!"

The three companions strained to lift Gerd up off her feet. At first, the giantess did not budge. A second later, with strained groans, they managed to raise her feet a little way off the floor. Gerd squawked and flailed as she fell backward into the cauldron. Torin let go just as the *jotur's* putrid feet flung up toward the ceiling.

Torin shouted over the ringing clang of Gerd's fists from inside the iron vessel. "Steady the cauldron!"

Grimsa and Wyla circled around each side and braced themselves against the rusted metal pot before it could tilt over.

"Grab scraps, bones, anything," said Wyla, "Jam them underneath so it can't tip over!"

Azal and Bari did just that and soon the cauldron was secured. Though Gerd kicked and flailed her feet in the air she could not tip the vessel. Torin, Grimsa, and Wyla stepped back to catch their breath.

Azal clapped his hands. "It worked!" The prince paused a moment then frowned. "Now what?"

Wyla rolled her eyes. "Isn't it obvious? Kill the *jotur* then find a way out."

The rest of the company turned to Torin. He stared down at the rune-etched scabbard. "If I draw *Tyrfang*, I think it will turn on me."

Azal tilted his head. "What do you mean?"

"I drew it to fight off the corpse creatures in the barrow."

"So?" Wyla said. "Didn't you hack a good dozen of them into pieces?"

Torin frowned. "I did. But they didn't bleed. *'Once drawn it cannot be sheathed until it has tasted blood.'* Isn't that what Keymaster Signy said?"

Grimsa crossed his arms. "Odd's Eye, if only you had given Jolvar a taste of *Tyrfang's* edge before you sheathed it." He leaned to one side and winced. "I nearly broke a rib bouncing off the hindquarters of that *jotur's* horse all day."

Bari looked up at Gerd's flailing legs and shrugged. "What difference does it make? She is not likely to run us down, even if she can right herself. But we can't just stand here. One of the other *jotur* is sure to come by sooner or later."

Wyla glanced out of the kitchen and into the tunnelway. "Every *nidavel* has a good head for tunnels, right, Bari? How do you reckon we escape from this marble dungeon?"

Aldrin coughed, and a scowl was drawn across his bruised face. The old Lorekeeper steadied himself against Azal's shoulder. "Escape? What is the use in that? We have the map, but we have no supplies and no horses. It will take us weeks to cross over those desolate plains on foot. And we will most likely freeze before we starve."

Torin crossed his arms. "Speaking of the map: how, by thundering Orr, did you steal it out of my cloak?"

Aldrin grinned, a bit of blood on his teeth where his bruised lip had split open. "A man does not grow old in the court of the Armeahan king without learning a few tricks."

Azal shook his head. "Damn you and your tricks, Aldrin. My father's men were massacred because of you. I am through with listening to any of your advice."

Aldrin narrowed his gaze at the prince. "I've got much more blood on my hands than a petty detachment of guards, young prince." The old man's eyes softened. "But if you are really so upset, I suppose I at least owe you an explanation."

"Explanation?" said Azal. "How could you justify sending men to their death like that?"

Aldrin sighed. "Why do you think I let you come along on this journey, Prince Azalweir? Why do you think I would risk the life of the Ghezelweir's heir on a quest for a foreign king? Why are you here when you could be safe behind the stone walls of Gatewatch with your father's men?"

Azal scoffed. "You didn't risk anything. It was my choice to come on this quest."

"Certainly, you wished to come along to the Everspring, but I never would have allowed it if I did not suspect treachery from the band of soldiers that accompanied us."

"Treachery?"

"Yes," Aldrin said. "I suppose there is no harm now in telling you the truth. Another day's ride upon a *jotur's* horse would be the end of me, and then you'd be blind to the whole affair. You see, prince, as we speak, your brother is attempting to murder your father and usurp his crown."

"What?"

Aldrin held up a finger and continued. "And, by your sister's cunning, he will be caught in the act before it can be done, and the

King will come to no harm. Then your brother, Zalaweir, will be tried for treason. By the time you return home, your power-hungry brother will be locked away in the dungeon, safe from himself and others until such time as he can see reason."

Azal shook his head. "That can't be true."

"Think," Aldrin said, "Think, young prince. Why else would I have brought you along? How else could I have convinced your father to let me take you to the edges of the known world? By what other means could we have ferried you away from your brother's impending insurrection without raising his suspicions? This was for your own protection, even though I fear we now find ourselves in even greater danger."

Azal took a step back. "Why wasn't I told about this?"

"You did not need to know. What's more, you are terrible at keeping secrets." Aldrin narrowed his eyes and pursed his lips. "But I guessed that your brother was suspicious enough of our departure to infiltrate our company with a few men loyal to him. On our way to Gatewatch, I kept a close ear on the company. I overheard a conversation late one night. A few of them were whispering about how they might quietly dispose of you once I had departed for the Everspring, though I could not discern which ones were speaking. Therefore, I had to bring the whole company along, in case I met my end on this journey. You might have returned to them unaware."

Azal's face was pale, and his mouth hung open for a moment. Then the prince hung his head. "I suppose I should thank you for saving my life. Again."

Aldrin squeezed Azal's shoulder. "I have sworn my life in service to the crown and, to my dying breath, serving it is exactly what I will do. But now is not the time for reflection, prince. It is the time for action." The old man looked up at Torin. "So, do you want my advice or not?"

"What are you suggesting, Lorekeeper?"

Aldrin frowned, focusing his gaze on the floor in front of him. "Escaping would be difficult. Not only that, but it would also be useless. We would either starve or freeze to death out on that frigid plain. Worse, we will fail in our quest to reach the Everspring. Our only chance for success is to present ourselves to Lord Thrudnir and ask for his assistance."

Torin bit his tongue. Wyla did not.

"Fyr's blazing fire," she said. "Were you asleep just now? This Thrudnir is waiting for us to be served up to him as some sort of stew! And your advice is to ask him for help?"

"I am afraid I have to agree," said Grimsa. "I would rather risk freezing to death than ending up in the belly of some *jotur* lord."

Aldrin shrugged. "If you are so keen to die for no reason, then go right ahead. But at least with Thrudnir there is a chance. If we could convince him to help us, we might make it to the Everspring after all. Besides, did you not best a *jotur* once before, Torin Ten-Trees? I would guess that news of that affair has reached his ear."

Wyla closed her eyes. "Tell me you are not suggesting what I think you are."

Grimsa waved his arms. "No, no, no! I will not risk my head in another one of Torin's damn riddle contests!"

"We are not playing politics in the Armeahan court," said Torin, "We are in the Hall of the Mountain King."

Aldrin grinned and raised a crooked finger. "Ah, but one learns certain things about the rich and powerful when one spends their life in foreign courts. If I had to bet my last ounce of silver on anything, it would be on the vanity of a powerful lord." The others looked at each other, but no one spoke. Aldrin smiled at Torin. "Challenge Thrudnir. There is no other way."

The company stood in silence for a moment longer before Torin shook his head. "Are you always like this, Aldrin?"

The Lorekeeper raised his eyebrows. "Am I always what? Right? Yes, I suppose."

Bari crossed his arms. "I hate to agree with the old Lorekeeper, but he is right. Approaching Thrudnir is our best chance."

Grimsa groaned. "Gods spare us."

"But," Bari said, "we must be sly about it. If we all go marching into Thrudnir's Hall unannounced, they may just try to squish us as if we are cellar rats."

"Of course," said Torin. "I'll go in by myself. Then, if the plan fails the rest of you can still attempt an escape."

Bari shook his head. "That's not what I meant. I am saying that we have to work together to make an entrance." The *nidavel* fumbled in his pocket for a moment and then pulled out a shiny silver ring. "Look! This is *Havaerari*, a gift given to me by the Mastersmith himself. Do you remember it?"

Grimsa's eyes opened wide. "It is hard to forget a gift as fine as that! It has some sort of magic, doesn't it?"

Bari nodded. "It amplifies my voice tenfold so that I can speak over the largest crowds. I will announce your arrival, as if you are some great lord making a long-expected appearance."

Azal leaned in toward the ring to get a better view. He snapped his fingers then pointed at the old Lorekeeper. "Aldrin! You could surround him with swirling mist, just like you did for me at my tenth birthday party."

"Yes, I remember that," said Aldrin. "Perhaps I could also conjure up some sparks. That would really make an impression!"

Grimsa snorted. "Then I guess Wyla and I will just sit outside in the hall and twiddle our thumbs."

"No," said Azal. "No, I know exactly what you can do! Keymaster Signy gave you the belt, *Gingjord*, to double your strength, didn't she?" Grimsa nodded but continued to pout. "You can hold Torin up on your shoulders. If the fog around you is thick enough, it will look like Torin is floating above the ground like some sort of powerful sorcerer."

A grin tugged at the edge of Grimsa's mouth, and he raised his thick red eyebrows. "Well, that would certainly catch their attention. Though I hardly need *Gingjord* to carry Torin on my shoulders, skinny as he is."

Bari stroked his beard. "Yes, I doubt that even the Mountain King could ignore a floating sorcerer in his hall."

Torin felt dry and his heart raced. It was a chance, but a truly desperate one. He strained to think of a better plan, but nothing surfaced.

Azal gripped Torin's shoulder. "It could work."

"It has to work," said Bari.

Wyla crossed her arms. "So, I guess everyone has a part to play except for me."

"No," Torin said. "You have the most important job of all."

Wyla glared at Torin. "Are you mocking me, Ten-Trees? Just because I can't sling some stupid spell? And what if something goes wrong? Am I just supposed to just stand by as Thrudnir devours each of you one by one?"

Torin held out *Tyrfang*. Wyla looked down at the rune-pressed leather sheath with wide eyes. "Take the sword," Torin said. "Sneak around the rest of the giants while we hold their attention. If things go foul, you have to kill Thrudnir."

Wyla slowly stretched her hand out toward the black scabbard, then quickly drew it back. "But it's your family's sword, Torin. Keymaster Signy gave it to you. You should be the one to use it."

"If I charge at Thrudnir, he will see me coming," Torin said. "What chance do I have against a single *jotur*, never mind a room full of them? Besides, I fear that I've already been cursed. It may just as quickly end my life as his if I dare to draw it."

Wyla hesitated a moment more then looked Torin in the eye. Her jaw was set and her steel-grey eyes gleamed. "If that *jotur* dares to lay a hand on you, I will plunge *Tyrfang* straight into his heart." Torin nodded then placed the sword into her hands.

"Then we are set," said Bari. "No time to lose!"

The companions shoved a few extra scraps under the cauldron that held Gerd to make sure she could not alert the other giants. Though he could not be certain, Torin thought he heard the old giantess snoring.

Torin was so hungry that he considered scavenging some scraps off the kitchen floor, perhaps a half-rotted carrot or a shred of dried potato peel. He decided against it despite the hunger that rumbled at the bottom of his empty stomach. If their plan worked, they might get a taste of Lord Thrudnir's feast after all. If it failed, he would be dead.

Bari led the company back up the way they had come. Where the smaller hallway met the main tunnelway, the *nidavel* sniffed the air and strained his ears. Faintly, from somewhere deep down inside the mountain, there came a chorus of booming voices and the rhythm of music which fell strange upon their ears. Bari motioned silently for the others to follow as he moved quickly down the slope toward the giant's feast.

As they descended, the main tunnel continued to curve down and to the left. Though this seemed better than a straight tunnel, where a *jotur* might spot them from one hundred paces away, Torin worried they might stumble upon some unfortunate guard that had not been invited to join in the festivities.

Torin also noticed that all the passages leading away from the main tunnel, like the one to the kitchen, were on the right. As the road spiraled down, not a single passage led off to the left. However, after the company had walked for what seemed to be a very long time without interruption, he noticed a thin crack in the wall on the left-hand side of the tunnel. Torin stopped and stepped up to the opening. A dim light came through it which flickered like a flame. Grimsa, who had been walking behind him, bumped into Torin, and nearly knocked him over.

Grimsa steadied himself then whispered. "What is it?"

"Look! There's a bit of light coming through."

Torin leaned against the stone wall and pressed his eye to the narrow gap. Through it, he saw an enormous circular cavern that stretched so high that the top could not be seen. However, he could see the bottom. There was an immense round feasting hall, ringed with large wooden tables around a circular stone hearth. A great fire blazed and crackled at its center. The light of its flames danced up the walls and illuminated figures of tremendous size who sat feasting at the tables.

"By the gods," Torin said. "All this time, we have been circling around the upper reaches of Thrudnir's feasting hall. This winding path must lead down to the hall's entrance."

Grimsa shoved his way in and pressed his face to the wall. "By Orr, I think you're right!"

Bari snuck underneath Grimsa to look and gasped. "There must be two or three dozen of them!"

Wyla pushed Grimsa out of the way and Azal crouched down where Bari had been. Torin thought that both Grimsa and Bari looked a little pale as they stepped back from the crack in the wall, and he imagined that he probably did too.

Grimsa tugged at his beard. "Are you still sure this is a good plan?"

"I never said it was a good plan," said Aldrin. "I said it was our only plan."

From down the tunnel there came the distant trudge of heavy feet. The slurred syllables of mumbled words echoed up the marble stairway and through the far reaches of the passage.

Bari motioned frantically for the others to follow him, then scurried off into one of the smaller openings that led away from the main tunnelway. The companions had barely slipped into the shadows of the side room as a towering *jotur* stumbled into view. The giant mumbled a tune as he tottered from side to side. His heavy steps rumbled through the floor, and he had to brace himself against the curved inner wall to stay upright. As he passed, the giant swerved across the hall and nearly tumbled right into quivering company. However, the *jotur* caught himself on the corner of the entryway and pushed past without any sign of having noticed them.

Torin let out a sigh of relief as the drunken giant passed out of sight, his song fading into dull echoes up the spiral tunnelway. Bari poked his head into the main passage and signaled that all was clear. The company hurried after him in silence for fear of another close encounter.

At last, they stood before the grand entryway to Thrudnir's feasting hall. Two doors, each crafted of finely carved wood and hung on decorative iron hinges, stood wide open. Torin shuffled in behind the door and peered into the giant's hall through the gap between the stone doorframe and the heavy timbers. The *jotur* had seemed large when he looked down on them from above, and now they looked even bigger. Whereas Jolvar and Ulfrun were about twice Torin's height, there were some giants within the hall that reached just as high while seated. One of the *jotur* cast a glance toward the door and Torin jumped back.

Azal grabbed his arm. "Did they see you?"

Torin's stomach fluttered and thought he might be ill. "No, I don't think so."

Aldrin nodded. "Alright, let's not waste any more time."

Torin wished then that there was some other way to escape. He had been thinking all the way down the spiral tunnelway, but nothing had come to him. He exhaled slowly, closed his eyes, and pictured Ten-Tree Hall in his mind. There it was, at the top of a rolling hill nestled within a grove of ancient, gnarled oaks. His heartbeat slowed as he imagined it in winter with a soft coat of snow covering its arched wooden roof. An inviting trail of swirling grey smoke signaled that a warm fire had been kindled in the main hall, a fire that would melt the ice from travelers' boots and warm their frost-numb fingers. His stomach ached to think of a roast upon the fire, a stew in the old, blackened cauldron, and spiced cider in wide-brimmed horns.

He remembered, as a boy, wrapping himself in the thick furs that lay on the benches and pretending to be a wolf, only to quickly drift off into sleep under their warmth. How he craved that warmth now, the soft feel of fur under his fingers and the heat of a savory stew filling his empty stomach.

The memory of Ten-Tree Hall suddenly came alive in such a way as Torin had never experienced, as if he was really there. He felt the path beneath his feet as he moved down the hill. A figure emerged from that high-gabled hall. He thought it was his father at first, but then realized it was not. Instead, he saw a grey-haired woman with her hair pulled into a long braid. She stood proud with a heavy set of keys dangling from her belt, smiling at Torin from a distance. Torin recognized her: it was Keymaster Signy. The scene swirled before his eyes and suddenly she was no longer standing in front of Ten-Tree Hall but in the doorway to Fjellhall.

Then, all at once, it was winter in Gatewatch and the howling winds churned up a blinding billow of icy snow. Signy extended her hand toward Torin, her form illuminated only by the warm glow of the fire through the open door. His heart raced as he sprinted toward her. No matter how fast he ran, the soft ring of orange light grew more distant, as if the snowstorm had claws and was dragging him away into the darkness.

From close behind, there came a sound that chilled him to the center of his chest. The queen's voice slipped into his ear with a soft, seductive whisper. Torin could almost feel the winter wind whipping around him and he held his breath.

You are headed toward your own death, Torin. You know that as well as I do. Don't be a fool.

Torin squinted in the storm and said nothing.

You have the sword. You felt its power in the barrow. It is thirsty for blood.

Torin whispered through a clenched jaw. "You tricked me into drawing it once. I know about the curse. I won't draw it again."

That curse was laid on the blade by the one who made it. But in the hands of another, someone with a stronger will, perhaps the curse's magic could be tamed.

"And even if I could overcome the curse, what good is a single sword against a mountain full of giants?"

How little do you know of that ancient blade? Did you not see the jotur quiver in fright when you revealed it outside the barrow? Draw the sword, Torin. Force it to submit to your will. Claim it. Conquer it. Then let Tyrfang's black steel drink its fill of jotur blood. It has waited so long to taste living flesh again.

Torin felt his heart pounding in his chest. He blinked, and the winter storm was gone. In his mind, he saw himself, as if in a mirror, cutting a swath through the *jotur* hall. He saw blood and fire. He felt mighty giants tumbling to the floor with a crash. Then he was sinking, almost as if he was slipping out of a dream.

Grimsa slapped Torin's shoulder and startled him awake. "Torin? Are you alright?"

Torin jolted upright and drew in a quick gasp. "What?" He looked at Grimsa and shook his head. "Yes, I'm fine."

"Well, then let's get on with it," said Aldrin. "Either we will soon be joining these *jotur* in the feast or we will all be dead." The strange vision flashed before his eyes again, but Torin shook his head free of it. He clambered up onto Grimsa's shoulders with the queen's words still echoing in his ears.

Grimsa twisted his torso as Torin settled into place. "By Odd, you've lost weight. You are hardly heavier than a bundle of twigs!"

The queen's words faded now as Torin gripped Grimsa's shoulder. "I guess I should be glad that there isn't much left of me for Thrudnir to chew on. Perhaps I'll look less appealing to a hungry giant?"

"By thundering Orr," Grimsa said, "I hope so. If this doesn't work and we all end up as dinner, then Signa is going to march down to the realm of the dead herself just to kill me all over again."

Bari held *Havaerari* up to his finger and prepared to slip it on. The *nidavel* gave Torin a firm nod. "Alright, Mindthorn, it's time to best another giant."

Torin exhaled slowly. "Just like last time, right?"

Bari grinned. "Except this time, it won't be in a hall packed with yowling trolls."

"I think I would take a room full of trolls over these towering *jotur*."

Bari pursed his lips, a gleam in his eye. "Good luck, Torin." Then he slipped the ring onto his finger and ducked into the feasting hall.

Torin looked at Wyla. Her jaw was clenched tight, but she held her gaze steady. "Odd grant you wisdom," she said. "Either we will feast today here in Thrudnir's hall or tomorrow in Valhol with the gods."

"Now that is a comforting thought," said Grimsa.

Torin swallowed. "I bet Bryn has been saving us a place by the fire all this time." He straightened his back and cleared his throat. "Long live The Gatewatch."

Wyla nodded. "Long live The Gatewatch."

Grimsa patted Torin's legs and turned toward Aldrin. "Alright, wizard! Turn me into a cloud of smoke. And do mind the beard!"

Aldrin cleared his throat and pulled back his sleeves. In a harsh whisper, he began to chant. "*Niebla, Niebla, Niebla Espesa!*" Then, with a slow sweeping motion, the old Lorekeeper moved his hands from side to side. Torin felt a breeze swish back and forth across his face.

Aldrin pulled both hands in toward his chest and spun them around like a swirling funnel. An icy chill fell over Torin, and he shivered. Below him there appeared a thick cloud of milky-white fog. It hung in the air for a moment then started to swirl around his legs. It grew and grew until Grimsa was wholly enveloped in swirling white tendrils.

Grimsa sneezed. "By the gods, it is damp and frigid as a troll cave in this cursed cloud."

"Move ahead," said Torin. "The sooner we go, the sooner we get to feasting."

Grimsa took a step forward then stopped. "Which way? I can't see a single thing through this damnable fog."

Torin nudged him in the ribs with his left heel. "Here, I'll guide you like this."

Grimsa stifled a groan. "Not so hard! By the gods, I really think that rib might actually be broken from our miserable journey here."

"Alright, I'll try," said Torin. "Two heels mean forward. One heel means left or right."

Grimsa sneezed again then started forward. A few steps later, they had left the shadows along the side of the hall and stood squarely in the middle of the open doorway. Torin nudged Grimsa to turn so that he faced the feasting hall head on. There, in a room that could have housed Fjellhall three times over, Torin saw a great many *jotur* feasting and drinking.

Bari's voice boomed over the noise of the crowd from wherever he was hiding. "Hail, Lord Thrudnir," said the *nidavel*, "Hail to the Mountain King! High may your gold-hoard grow! Feast-Maker, Ring-Giver, Wise-One, I hail thee! Long be your beard and tall be your crown! Father of Ballur and Lord of the North, I hail thee! May the silver rim of your royal cup be always wet with wine!"

There was a mighty commotion among the giants as they jumped up from the benches and searched for the source of the sound. Soon all eyes fell on Torin and the whole hall went silent.

Bari continued. "It is my honour, oh great and mighty King, to introduce a visitor of great importance. Far-Traveler, they call him; Troll-Slayer and Riddle-Maker. He is of kin with Araldof the Greyraven who rules a realm called Noros which lies beside the glistening sea. So, too, is he a friend of the mighty Master-smith Ognir whose forge in Myrkheim never cools."

Torin felt the ground rumble beneath him as an enormous figure on the far side of the room slid his house-sized chair back and rose to his feet. A crown of finely forged silver inset with enormous gems of azurite blue and white crystal shards sat upon his head of long, frost-white hair. His proud cheeks glinted with specks of silver in the firelight and his eyes, as clear and sharp as sea ice, glared down at Torin. A patterned patchwork of large furs, each as white as fresh-fallen snow, hung over his shoulders and were clasped across his wide chest with a golden latch. The *jotur* crossed his arms and frowned. "Who is this tiny traveler that dares to disturb my feast?"

Bari called out again, his voice still echoing through the whole hall so that none could tell where he stood. "Has no word reached your ear, oh mighty Lord Thrudnir, of the *madur* who slew the Troll-King? This is he, the one who was named Mindthorn."

Torin kept his gaze fixed on the towering giant and fought the nausea welling up in his stomach. Thrudnir narrowed his eyes then called out in a baritone voice that rumbled like an earthquake. "Do you think I am ignorant of that which happens in the fringes of my own realm?"

Bari called out again. "Far-famed is your wisdom, oh mighty Thrudnir! What I meant to convey is that the one who stands before you has never experienced the majesty of your glorious hall and so his face will likely be unknown. Therefore, I shall introduce him. He is renowned among the Greycloaks of Gatewatch and is far-famed as a slayer of trolls. Both *jotur* and *nidavel* have known him as Mindthorn!"

Thrudnir pounded his fist on the table. "Silence, speaker!" A deadly quiet fell over the feasting hall and nothing but the crackling fire dared to make a sound. "Step forward, Mindthorn, and account for this unwelcome disturbance."

Torin clenched his fists and guided Grimsa very carefully toward the stone hearth. All around the room, giants leaned forward over the tables to catch a glimpse of the strange sight, a young *madur* floating on a swirling cloud. Heat radiated from the hearthfire and Torin did his best to steer Grimsa in a wide path around it for the sake of maintaining the cold swirl of fog. Whispered words flitted between the *jotur* men and women, all adorned in flowing robes and fine jewelry, as they beheld the spectacle.

When he was nearly half-way across the room, Torin noticed movement under one of the tables. Bari had made his way around the giants' feet and now waved to Torin from behind an enormous empty mead horn. Torin frowned then looked away so as not to draw attention to the *nidavel*. A moment later, he looked back and saw the glimmer of a silver ring flying toward him. He flinched and leaned back just in time to snatch the shining object out of the air. There, in his hand, was *Havaerari*, the ring that Bari had used to amplify his voice. Torin, as well as a few of the giants in front of him, looked down to where Bari had been but the *nidavel* had already slipped away.

Grimsa yanked on Torin's leg. "Fyr's fire, stop twisting around! I nearly fell over."

"Alright," said Torin. "Just about there." He managed to shove the *nidavellish* ring onto his smallest finger as he guided Grimsa forward with his heels.

At last, Torin stood directly before Lord Thrudnir's table. Though it was a strain, he was able to crane his neck back and look at the *jotur* in the eye. Torin cleared his throat and stretched his arms out wide.

"Forgive me, oh wise and benevolent King, for the intrusion. We did not mean to disrupt your feast. However, when your kinsfolk, Jolvar and Ulfrun, snatched us up we had little choice. They carried us far across your realm against our will, through wooded hills and over barren plains, here to your magnificent hall."

Thrudnir drew his eyes into a narrow glare and lowered his head. "Ah, yes. The grave robbers! I remember now. You also attacked my prized eagle, Hraesvelgir!"

Torin opened his mouth to speak but Thrudnir raised his hand for silence. The *jotur* drew in a deep breath then exhaled slowly. The blue tinge of his bulging cheeks darkened as a frigid breeze rushed out of his mouth. The gust grew into a shrieking wind, its whistle echoing in the upper reaches of the chamber. Empty cups tumbled off the wide wooden tables and the giants scrambled to hold down the heaping platters of fine food that lay in front of them.

Torin felt the cold sting of icy snow on his cheeks as flecks flew past his face. Grimsa wavered below him for a moment and Torin worried they might topple over, but Grimsa found his footing and braced against the force of the wind.

Just as the howling wind reached a deafening volume, it suddenly ceased. All the contents it had thrown around the room fell to the floor in a chorus of clashes and clangs. Torin coughed as the icy flakes settled, only to find that both he and Grimsa, with frost in their hair and icicles in their beards, stood plain sight of the entire host of *jotur*. The cloak of fog was gone.

Thrudnir grinned as he settled back into his gigantic throne. "Welcome, Mindthorn, to Jokulheim, the Hall of the Mountain King."

13

◇ A DESPERATE WAGER ◇

GRIMSA WHISPERED through the icicles in his beard. "So much for the plan."

All eyes in the room were fixed on the awkward pair. Torin's face flushed red hot, melting the frost on his hair and his eyebrows into trickling drips. He held still for another moment then cursed. "By Odd, let me down."

Grimsa crouched down and Torin hopped off his shoulders onto the smooth marble floor. A few of the giants snickered as he straightened his cloak. Thrudnir said nothing more than the smug grin on his face revealed.

A familiar and unfriendly voice called out from the other side of the room. "Here are two others. I found them hiding just outside the door." Torin turned and saw Jolvar in the doorway with Azal and Aldrin, one dangling in each hand.

Ulfrun crawled out from under one of the tables. "And here is the *nidavel*." She held up Bari by the scruff of his cloak, which she had pinched between two fingers. He kicked and wriggled furiously, but it was no use.

Jolvar frowned. "There were six of them. Where is the last one?"

Torin caught a glimpse of Wyla as she dove under one of the large, discarded cloaks scattered around the edge of the hall. He cleared his throat to distract the crowd and then shook his fist high over his head. "She was eaten! Swallowed up in a single gulp by that awful creature Gerd who guards your gate. And it is for her death that I am seeking reparation, Lord Thrudnir. I might have considered forgiving our mistaken abduction. But, on account of my companion's unfortunate demise, I cannot. Therefore, I must demand *weregild* from you, full reparation made through gifts of reddest gold!"

At this, the guests in Thrudnir's hall broke into howling laughter. *Jotur* stomped their gigantic feet and pounded their massive fists on the wooden table, making a thunderous clamour that rattled Torin's skull. He kept his gaze fixed on Thrudnir.

Lord Thrudnir nearly choked on his wine. "Do I hear your words correctly? Do you demand gold from the Mountain King?" Great dimples bulged out from Thrudnir's bluish cheeks as the old king nearly giggled with glee. "You must imagine yourself to be very brave, tiny *madur*, to make such a claim. If there was any brain between your little ears you would know not to challenge a *jotur*, especially in his own hall."

"Do you dare call me a fool?"

Thrudnir smacked his own forehead. "By Ym! I need not speak the words, young *madur*. Your own actions speak loud enough!"

Torin shouted back but his words were drowned in a chorus of laughter. After a moment the noise of the crowd died down and all the *jotur* leaned in to see what preposterous thing Torin might say next. At least they were entertained, Torin thought, and that meant he had their attention. "Have you not heard the name 'Mindthorn'? It was given to me by one of your own!"

Thrudnir looked around the room with an exaggerated sweep of his arms. "Now, I know that you are truly delusional! No one here has ever seen your face."

Torin thrust out his chest with all the confidence he could muster. "Then it is up to me to make it known! And if I succeed in making a name for myself here, perhaps you will repay me for the many ills committed against my company." He turned around slowly so that all the *jotur* there could see his face. Then, once all had seen him, he pointed up at the Mountain King. "Let everyone in Jokulheim hear this: to prove the fame and worth of my company, I challenge Lord Thrudnir to a duel of riddles!"

The uproar was deafening, with *jotur* on every side doubling over and wiping tears away from their blue-blushed cheeks.

"Riddles?" said Thrudnir. "Of all things, you would challenge Thrudnir the Wise to riddles? Your chances of pinning me down in a wrestling match would be better, little *madur*!" At these words, the other giants fell into another round of laughter.

Torin shifted his weight as he waited for the crowd to settle. There was a tremor in his knees, but he forced them still. At last, he called out over the last snickering whispers. "So, Lord Thrudnir, do you accept my challenge?"

Thrudnir wiped tears of mirth from his eyes. "Do I accept?" The *jotur* nearly fell into another giggling fit but managed to straighten his face. "Tell me, tiny *madur*, what would the terms of this challenge be?" All around the room, giants leaned in to hear Torin speak.

"These are my terms," said Torin. "First, if I best you in this challenge you must pay *weregild* for that companion who was devoured by Gerd. It should be no less than her weight in gold."

Ulfrun chuckled. "The *madur's* weight or Gerd's? There is a significant difference!"

Torin raised his hand for silence, then held up two fingers. "Second, I demand that my company be given horses and supplies, enough to take us wherever we wish to go."

The laughter rose so that Torin's voice was drowned out again. Thrudnir slammed his goblet on the table and waved his hand. "Silence! Silence! Let Mindprick speak!"

Grimsa waved his fist. "Mindthorn! His name is Mindthorn!" Torin motioned for his friend to step back. Grimsa stuffed his pride, crossing his arms and glaring at the mountain king.

Thrudnir grinned, his teeth gleaming in the flickering firelight. "And what if I best you?"

"Simple," Torin said, "We will forget your injustices against us and leave you to your feast without any further disturbance."

Thrudnir blew his nose on a silk cloth so large that Torin could have used it for a bedsheet, then settled back into his throne. "I cannot recall the last time my stomach ached from so much laughter. For simply that, tiny *madur*, I will forgive your company's intrusion on my springtime feast. Why, I was in the prime of my youth the last time someone dared to challenge me to a duel of riddles!"

The *jotur* took a sip of wine then held up his hand in mock protest. "But I am afraid I cannot agree to your terms. When we *jotur* take part in *bardagi*, a duel of wits, there is only one set of terms to follow: the traditional ones."

Torin crossed his arms. "And what are those?"

"Your opponent's head, cut clean from his body and brought to you upon a plate of gold. Though, as I doubt you brought a plate large enough for my head, I will lend you one if you should win." Wicked grins spread across the faces of the other *jotur* around the room as they fought to stifle another outburst of laughter.

Torin's stomach twisted like a wet rag being squeezed dry. He drew in a sharp breath and nodded. "Then you accept my challenge?"

"Only if you agree to the traditional terms of *bardagi*."

Torin swallowed, an itch tingling the back of his neck, then narrowed his gaze. "I agree."

Thrudnir clapped. "By Ym! This will be some fine entertainment for my guests. So, it will be *bardagi* between us, on traditional terms, myself against this strange young *madur* who calls himself Mindprick."

Grimsa waved his fist again and called back. "That is Mindthorn to you, you brazen, bellowing, blue-faced brute!"

However, the bustle about the hall drowned Grimsa's words as attendants rushed to fill every goblet full of rich red wine. The finely adorned *jotur* guests swept the tables clean to get a better view of the contest. Those who were seated near the hall's entrance shuffled over to join those who were closer to the Mountain King's throne.

Thrudnir reached forward over the table and grabbed one of the *jotur* attendants by the arm as she rushed by. "A thimble," said Thrudnir, "For the challenger. Let no one say that we neglected the ancient traditions of *bardagi*!"

The giantess fumbled around in the pockets of her apron for a moment then produced a small iron thimble. *Jotur* all around her laughed as she struggled to pour the tiniest drop of wine into it from an enormous silver pitcher. Very carefully, she crouched down and passed it to Torin. He ignored the jeers and nodded to her before hailing Thrudnir with a toast.

"May the sharpest mind prevail," Torin said.

The sweet liquid ran over Torin's parched tongue like the first fall of rain soaking the dry ground after a summer fire. It was sweeter than fruit plucked straight off the vine and its headiness made his whole body feel impossibly light. By the second mouthful, a warm sensation filled his chest, the sweet juice stoking a fire beneath his ribs that warmed his body all the way out to his fingertips. By the third sip, he felt as fresh as he had been on the day that the company departed from Gatewatch.

Thrudnir stroked his beard. "How long has it been since riddles were heard in Jokulheim? By Ym, let us not squander this opportunity with a verse that is too difficult. For the sake of the crowd, I will begin with something easy." The *jotur* cleared his throat then spoke, his deep-toned voice echoing high up into the mountain chamber.

> *A river flows both up and down*
> *To ferry men from town to town*

A trickle 'neath the moon at night
Yet flows again at touch of light

"Answer, listener, if you can."

All eyes fell upon Torin. His heart pumped furiously inside his chest, as mention of a river conjured up the memory of the Armea-han company falling into the Vimur. He pushed the thought from his mind then paced back and forth in front of the fire as casually as he could.

"You are long in responding, little *madur*," Thrudnir said. "Do not tell me this simple verse has stumped you already!"

Torin stopped and held up his hand. "Not at all! Everyone knows that a river can only run one way and that its flow does not rise and fall with the sun. However, I know of something that runs between towns and upon which men ride; not the river, but the road! Yes, it is a road that slows to a trickle once night falls, only to fill with travelers once light breaks over the sky."

Applause filled the room as Thrudnir raised his glass to Torin. "Well spoken, *madur*! You have guessed my first riddle correctly. Now speak yours for all to hear!"

Torin let the room fall silent as the crowd of *jotur* leaned in to hear his words. He slowed his breath and tried to imagine himself back in Gatewatch, perhaps in Fjellhall or Stonering Keep, but his heart kept racing. "Prepare yourself, Lord Thrudnir!"

A sleeping serpent, scaly grey
Encircles kings in troubled days
No man may cross its rugged hide
Unless its jaws are open wide

"Answer, listener, if you can."

Thrudnir's snow-white eyebrows shot up. "Not a bad verse, tiny *madur*, for a mortal mind at least. Lesser minds would think of

dragons or perhaps a creature like mighty *Storkrabba* who haunts
the deepest depths of the sea. But how would a man cross its hide
and why would he try to enter through the mouth? No, it is not
a beast that you speak of, but a castle wall! Kings will hide within
their castles in times of trouble. The wall, rugged like a serpent's
hide, can only be crossed when its mouth, the gate, is open to
them."

Torin hailed the Mountain King with a toast. "You have
answered correctly, Lord Thrudnir!" The *jotur* crowd cheered and
reveled in another round of toasts.

Thrudnir tugged at his beard for a moment then lifted a finger.
"Ah, yes! This riddle once won me the head of a jewel-hungry
nidavel. Let us see if it claims yours as well!"

> *A dragon that devours men*
> *Then spews them out at journey's end*
> *With one great wing on wind it soars*
> *To seek the wealth of distant shores*

"Answer, listener, if you can."

Torin's heart jumped into his throat as the answer came to his
mind. Under his breath he thanked the gods for such luck. He
knew, though, how to humour a crowd and so pretended to delib-
erate for a moment longer before he spoke.

"My travels have taken me to Myrkheim, so I know that the
wisdom and skill of that race is great," said Torin. "However, I
think I can see why such a riddle might prove difficult for them.
The *nidavel* are far-famed for their love of treasure and it was this
distraction that I would guess led your opponent to his doom.
Besides, what knowledge of distant shores would a *nidavel* have?
They spend little time enough above the surface of the earth to
guess that. But I have no such love of treasure and I grew up not

far from the howling winds that haunt the Shrieking Cliffs on Noros' southern border."

"Do you have a guess, tiny *madur*," said Thrudnir, "or are you stalling for time?"

Torin smirked. "You underestimate me, Lord Thrudnir. It is known to all who dwell beside the sea that sailors will imagine their long-planked ship to be a dragon, its sails the wings and its prow the monstrous head. So, the answer to your riddle is a long-ship, one of those vessels that carry men who seek gold from shore to shore in their wooden bellies."

Thrudnir raised his goblet again. "Well spoken, tiny *madur*. Now that three riddles have been answered we have reason to drink. Bring more wine for all! Not this common stuff either. Crack open an ancient cask brewed from the fruit of Yg, the world tree, when its boughs could still be measured!" Thrudnir motioned toward the rest of Torin's companions. "And search your cloaks for more thimbles so that these other miserable mortals can taste a sip of wine to rival that which is served in the halls of the *asyr*!"

Jolvar released Aldrin and Azal then motioned to Ulfrun to do the same with Bari. All three rushed across the wide hall to where Torin and Grimsa stood.

"By the King's royal crown," Azal said. "I was holding my breath the whole time."

Torin passed the thimble cup to Grimsa and yanked *Havaerari* off his finger. "By the gods! This is absolute madness. He's simply toying with me to entertain his guests. Soon he'll start riddling in earnest and that will be the end of us. We have to find a way to escape."

"There is no escaping," Aldrin said. "Best to press on with the duel. Besides, Thrudnir's guests seem thoroughly entertained, and that has got to count for something."

Torin spoke through clenched teeth. "As much as I would love to keep at this all day, I can only answer so many of this *jotur's* riddles before I lose my head."

The old Lorekeeper winked. "No, you do not see my point. The curse of an immortal life is that food loses its flavour, wine fades in its sweetness, and laughter comes with far more difficulty as the endless years drift by. I would suppose that it is hard for even one as grand as the Mountain King to entertain a court of immortals for eternity."

"Aldrin is right," Bari said. "We are better off trying to win Lord Thrudnir's favour. Even if we could slip out of the hall unnoticed, how long would it take us to climb all the way up to the gate? Thrudnir's servants would catch up to us before we reached the top and I doubt they would fail to cook us a second time."

"What if we ran down instead of up," said Torin. "Surely there must be a *nidavel* tunnel somewhere in this damned mountain."

The *nidavel* shook his head. "There is strong magic about this place. I can feel it in the stone floor. I doubt that even the sharpest *nidavel* pick could cut the slightest crack either in or out of this giant's fortress."

One of the attendants crouched down to offer them thimbles full of a sweet-smelling pink liquid which shimmered like a thousand tiny crystals. The wine startled Torin as soon as it hit his lips. The honey-sweet liquor fizzed and bubbled in his mouth, a strange tingling sensation like numbness, but without losing feeling. His limbs loosened so that his shoulders no longer slouched and in his mind, he felt brighter somehow, like a shaded grove that passes from the earliest twinkling of dawn-light to the full strength of day.

Grimsa stared into his thimble cup and raised his eyebrows. "By the gods, this is a rarified drink! This is by far the sweetest and most satisfying thing I have ever tasted!" He took another gulp and nodded toward Torin. "By Odd, if any man alive can match this giant riddle for riddle, it's you, Torin. Long live The Gate-watch!" The others raised their thimble cups and drank deep.

"Now," said Thrudnir. "We have drenched our throats and whetted our minds, so let us begin this *bardagi* in earnest. Unleash your word-horde and assail the towering battlements of my intel-lect!"

Torin slipped *Havaerari* onto his finger and called out. "Listen, *jotur* of Jokulheim, to my next riddle!"

> *I've seen a bird that wingless flies*
> *Without a song across the skies*
> *No feathered breast, no taloned feet*
> *It always hunts but never eats*

"Answer, listener, if you can."

Thrudnir leaned back in this throne and clapped three times. "Now that is a worthy verse! I must admit that I once again expected to be disappointed, but you have produced a fine riddle."

Torin took another draught of the sparkling wine, its sweet-ness loosening his tongue. "Is that to say that you do not know the answer?"

"Ha," Thrudnir said, "Not in the least. It is only that it took me a moment to ponder, which is more than most who have crossed wits with me can boast."

"Then what is your reply, Thrudnir the Wise?"

"At first it came to my mind that a shadow flies without a song, yet it cannot be a shadow for how can a shadow travel across the sky? No, a shadow only slips along the ground or slides over the rippled surface of the water." Murmurs and nods came from the *jotur* crowd clustered around the tables. "So, what else flies? A bird? Certainly not, for a bird has a feathered breast. Nor can it be a great and ancient dragon with fuming nostrils, for such devours all that it hunts."

With a slight sway, no doubt because of the strength of the wine and his empty stomach, Torin nodded. He steadied himself then raised his iron-thimble goblet toward the Mountain King. "Your insight is unrivaled, but you still have not produced the answer."

Thrudnir frowned for a moment, then let out a gleeful roar. "Ah! The answer is clear. What flies and hunts but has no wings? And why would anything hunt if not to eat what it catches? Nothing but the huntsman's arrow, unleashed from a tight-strung bow, could be the answer."

Torin felt his stomach drop as the giant spoke. Had he convinced himself that he could somehow outwit the ancient giant? He forced a smile and raised his drink to Thrudnir as applause filled the towering chamber. The clink of silver vessels came from every direction as all there toasted the Mountain King's reply.

The *jotur* chuckled and took another gulp of wine. "And now it is my turn to fire an arrow at you, tiny *madur*. Here is a riddle that has never been unleashed on mortal ears. See if the shield of your mind is thick enough to deflect its bite."

> *Arms that have never known an embrace*
> *Feet that have never moved out of place*
> *A heart that is hard, no face to be seen*
> *Ever asleep and yet never a dream*

"Answer, listener, if you can."

The giant's hall seemed to shrink around Torin as he pondered the riddle. Sweat gathered on the back of his neck and slipped along his spine beneath his tunic. Everywhere he turned, the *jotur* stared down at him, their eager gazes pressing him for the answer.

Torin's mind felt like a torn sail vainly flapping against an approaching gale. He wished then that he had never challenged

Thrudnir, that he had never set out to find the Everspring, and more than anything that he had left Gatewatch to make for Ten-Tree Hall. If he had slipped out the night before the feast, he would now be only a few days' journey from his father's high-gabled house. He pictured Ten-Tree Hall again, with great clarity, and felt, as he did so, that he could almost smell its cedar rafters.

He let himself linger there for a moment and released the present moment only to be yanked back to reality by the *jotur's* booming voice. "Has the wine dissolved your tongue, *madur*?

Torin shook his head. "Ever asleep and yet never a dream. And arms that do not embrace?" It was right there, hovering at the edge of his mind but just out of reach.

Thrudnir sipped his wine and smacked his lips. "Come now, tiny *madur*. Do not let this be the riddle to claim your head. I am just beginning to enjoy myself!"

All at once it came to Torin just as a wave crashes upon a rocky shore. "What type of thing could have a heart but no face? What purpose could feet have, if not to move, or arms, if not to embrace?" He saw a host of wide *jotur* eyes fixed on him and a smile spread wide across his face. "A tree."

All eyes turned to Thrudnir and the giant nodded, a glow of approval in his sea-green eyes. "Correct! You live to speak another verse."

Torin felt dizzy for a moment and the ground beneath his feet suddenly felt unsteady. He swore off the wine, as fine as it was, until the *bardagi* was over. "It seems the shield of my mind was thick enough after all. On the topic of weapons, I offer this verse."

> *Lighter than a gust of air*
> *Thinner than a strand of hair*
> *Easy to wield and cheaply made*
> *Yet draws more blood than any blade*

"Answer, listener, if you can."

The great grin of the *jotur* lord began to fade. He shifted in his high-backed throne and tugged at the white braids of his beard. "The best blades are light indeed, but to say that they are cheaply made is certainly not true. And what weapon could draw more blood than a well-forged sword? Not the curved axe or the pointed spear or the bludgeoning hammer."

Torin felt a swell of hope in his chest. "Ha! So perhaps my mind is less of a prick and more of a thorn, after all. Or has your side simply grown tender after all these years?"

A flush of blue came to the *jotur's* face, and the Mountain King slammed both fists down on the table. "Do you dare, lowly *madur*, to insult a king within his own hall?"

As soon as the giant spoke, Torin felt the blood drain from his face. Though he tried to hide his fear, Torin could tell from Thrudnir's smile that the *jotur* had seen him flinch. Not for fear of offending the Mountain King, but fear of hinting at the answer.

"Ah," said Thrudnir, "I see. A clever turn of phrase! What could be more cheaply made than words spoken? Even a ragged beggar could summon such things! And one might ask how words could draw more blood than any steel-forged edge? In my countless years I have seen insults spur mighty *jotur* kings to war and send proud *asyr* into flurries of bloody vengeance. No weapon ever held in the hands of either *jotur* or *asyr* can claim to have spilled so much blood. So then, an insult must be the answer to your riddle."

Torin cursed himself for giving the *jotur* a hint. If only he had waited a little longer, he thought, he might have had a chance. He felt nauseous as he raised his glass to the Mountain King.

Thrudnir basked another moment in the applause of his guests, who hollered and cheered his response. At last, he held up his enormous hands and addressed the crowd. "You have patiently watched our *bardagi* play out. Though your cups are full, your bellies must be grumbling by now. As tradition dictates, food must be served after six riddles. So, let food be brought forth from the kitchen!"

"On silver platters carry in the finest fillets of arctic char," said Thrudnir, "All basted in butter and rubbed with savory herbs. Take steaming loaves of dark-grained bread to each table and set a rich wheel of soft white cheese between each one. Bring in copper bowls filled to the brim with herring and cod fish pickled in brine. Haul up heaps of chilled oysters and boil all the shellfish in my saltwater cellars."

"Once all that is rich and savory has been brought up from Jokulheim's stores, fix dessert! Fetch the last of the previous year's berry preserves, those jams and jellies made sweet with all the woodland's bounty. Prepare apple cakes crusted with cinnamon and honey-drizzled pastries stuffed with gold-ripe pears. Then, to wash it all down, bring cloudberry mead and strawberry wine, strong scented spirits, and dark, frothy beer. Pour until every bottle lays empty! And let not a single cup remain empty while wheat-golden ale remains in barrels!"

At every detail of the Mountain King's description, Torin's stomach cramped tighter with hunger. Grimsa's eyes wide and watering. Both Azal and Aldrin looked pale, and Bari's lip quivered at the thought of such a magnificent feast.

"By the gods," Grimsa said, "Could such a feast really exist?"

Even as Grimsa spoke these words, attendants came streaming in from the hall, carrying out Thrudnir's order down to the last detail. Torin and his companions shuffled closer to the fire to avoid being trampled by the *jotur* servants that rushed from table to table.

Thrudnir pointed to Torin and his companions. "Come now, do not leave our guests unattended. Give them a loaf of bread and a bit of cheese. Be careful, little *madur*, not to let it crush you!"

The crowd of giants chuckled at the Mountain King's words, though the sound was muffled by all the food they had stuffed in their mouths. Meanwhile, the same giantess that had served them wine knelt to place a gigantic loaf of bread and a round block of warm white cheese down beside them.

The company rushed to take a bite of the loaf but found that the crust was too thick to break through. Torin pounded the crust with his fist along with the others but could not break through to the soft airy dough inside. Of course, the company of giants broke into an uproar at this and pointed long blue-knuckled fingers at them.

Grimsa's nostrils flared and the blood vessels in his face nearly burst with rage. He stepped back, raised both fists, then threw himself at the hardened crust with all his might. With a dull crack the crust broke open and he fell straight down into the loaf. Torin and Azal had to grab hold of Grimsa's flailing legs and drag him out. Even as they pulled him along the floor, Grimsa was stuffing handfuls of bread into his mouth.

Hunger dulled their ears to the howling laughter of the *jotur* crowd as they tore into the loaf. By the time Torin slowed enough to think clearly, he had eaten more bread than would have been in a whole loaf back in Fjellhall. The dull cramping ache of hunger gave way to the pleasure of feeling his stomach full for the first time since they had left Gatewatch.

All in all, they had hardly eaten more than a few *jotur* bites, but each of them could barely stuff any more into their stomachs. As Torin slowed, he saw movement beneath one of the tables. He peered closer and saw Wyla's head peeking out from beneath a giant's cloak. He gave a quick nod in her direction and ran back to the loaf. With both hands he ripped off as much bread as he could hold. He pretended to totter back and forth as if the wine had made him dizzy then threw himself headlong onto the floor. The bread flew through the air and rolled under the table.

All around them giants roared with glee as Torin picked himself up off the ground. When he looked up to where he had tossed the bread there was nothing there, just a cast-off cloak with an irregular lump beneath it. With all eyes fixed on him, he grinned, pushed himself up off the ground, and steeled himself for the next round of riddles.

14

◇ THE WISDOM OF GIANTS ◇

AFTER DINNER, Thrudnir pounded his fist three times upon the table and the crowd fell silent. Torin thought he noticed the old giant trying to suppress a smile but could not be sure. When the *jotur* spoke, his words were low and grave. "A *bardagi* must come and go, as must all mortal things. Therefore, the time has come for me to end this contest between us. I have little doubt that this will be the last riddle your ears will ever hear, Mindthorn. Yet, for the sake of your own legacy, you must try your best to answer it."

> *A teller of tales that seldom is heard*
> *As wide as the sea yet as small as a bird*
> *As quick as a sparrow yet still as a stone*
> *Constantly wand'ring yet ever at home*

"Answer, listener, if you can."

Now that Torin had stuffed himself full at the giant's feast, he wanted nothing more than to lie down and let sleep carry him off into the realm of dreams. Worse, now that his stomach no longer ached with hunger, he felt the sting of each cut and scrape that the barrow creatures had given him, the pain in his joints from days of travel, and the stiffness in his neck from their rough journey to Jokulheim. He shook his head and took a swig of wine.

Over and over, he repeated the riddle to himself. The reference to birds and sparrows made him think of the trilling melodies of springtime, but he suspected that was just a distraction. What could wander yet remain at home? How could it be as wide as the sea and yet so small as to be compared to a bird? And why would a teller of tales rarely be heard? His heartbeat quickened as the answer seemed to slip farther and farther away from him.

A twisted smile spread across Thrudnir's face. The giant straightened his crown and cleared his throat. "Do you concede defeat, young *madur*? This is your own head's only chance to save itself."

Torin felt a tingling at his neck at the thought of losing his head. He closed his eyes and forced his tense shoulders down. With every breath, he tried to push himself away from the giant's hall and to some place more peaceful, some place he could really think. In his mind, he imagined that he was home, either under the towering rafters of Fjellhall or along the warm cedar benches of Ten-Tree Hall. If only he could fly like a bird back to some friendlier place. Perhaps then the key to unlocking the *jotur's* verse would land in front of him.

Thrudnir chuckled. "Come now, Mindthorn, give us your answer! We *jotur* may be immortal but we will not spend the rest of eternity waiting for your reply."

An image of Fjellhall flashed through Torin's mind and he opened his eyes wide. There it was. He had just travelled back to Fjellhall faster than any bird could have. How far could he go in his mind? Was there any limit to what he could conjure up? His heart pounded in his chest as he considered the thought.

Thrudnir took another sip of wine. "Has the *madur* gone mute? Or deaf? Perhaps I should just call an attendant to fetch a golden plate right now? I wonder if we have one small enough?" The *jotur* crowd grinned and chuckled.

Torin looked up and saw a dark shape stir behind the Mountain King's crown, a flash of grey and black. It was Wyla. She had somehow scaled the back of Thrudnir's throne and now hovered over the Mountain King, just above the *jotur's* jewel-studded crown, with the sheathed sword clutched tightly in her hand.

Torin's heart skipped a beat. He threw up his hands and shouted. "Stop!" Everyone in the room froze and fixed their eyes on him. Wyla lowered herself back behind the throne and out of sight. Torin let out a sigh of relief. "I have my answer."

Thrudnir rubbed his hands together. "Alright, young *madur*. Speak your final word before my good cousin, Jolvar, claims my prize."

Jolvar put a hand to the hilt of his enormous sword and stepped toward Torin.

"Wait," said Torin. "Wait until I have given my answer."

He held up one hand and cleared his throat. "What travels as swiftly as a sparrow yet never needs to leave its place? What can be so wide as to be compared to the ocean yet is little larger than a bird? What constantly speaks but is rarely heard? The answer can only be one's own imagination, all that happens inside the mind."

A trail of silence followed Torin's words. Jolvar froze mid-step as all the attendants stopped their tasks and turned toward the center of the room. Every set of eyes slowly shifted from Torin to Lord Thrudnir. The old giant sat with a stiff spine and a slack jaw. Torin thanked the gods that Wyla had hidden herself behind the throne before the crowd's attention fell on the Mountain King.

A flush of blue rushed over the Mountain King's cheeks and his wide nostrils flared. With whatever kingly grace he could muster, Thrudnir forced a polite smile. "Correct, young *madur*! Your mind is sharp indeed." Thrudnir's words hung in the air a moment before the giant raised his goblet.

Torin raised his own in response and took another deep draught to calm his nerves. His head spun and his hands shook. For a moment, he thought he might topple right over in front of the crowd of giants, but he managed to steady himself against Grimsa before he lost his balance.

Grimsa gripped Torin's shoulder with one hand and slapped his back with the other. "By the gods, Torin, you had me nervous for a moment. Please tell me you have a riddle to sink this *jotur's* ship."

Torin shook out his arms then planted himself in front of the Mountain King. "Lord Thrudnir, our *bardagi* has been lively and it seems that all your guests have enjoyed our exchange." The crowd of *jotur* applauded his words and raised their goblets. "But as you said, every *bardagi* must come to an end. Further, I have an urgent task that requires me to depart from Jokulheim as soon as possible. If I have proven the worth of our company through this exchange, perhaps we could agree to conclude this affair?"

Thrudnir grunted and stuck out his chin. "By Yg! Are you asking if I concede? Certainly not! Let no one say a mere *madur* youngling matched Thrudnir the Wise in a duel of riddles. Never! Indeed, my next riddle will claim your head for sure. But you speak another now, so that no one can say I neglected the ancient protocols!"

"So," said Torin, "The original terms stand unchanged? You will not deviate from tradition?"

"One of our heads on a golden platter," Thrudnir said. The *jotur* chuckled deep in his chest and a wicked grin tugged at the corner of his mouth. "You have my word."

Torin nodded. He closed his eyes and breathed deep. "Alright, then here is a riddle of my own making. See if you can unlock its meaning."

> *Rarely kept but often made*
> *Freely given, costly paid*

Once it's placed, forever sticks
Once it's broken, can't be fixed

"Answer, listener, if you can."

Thrudnir laughed at first, a hearty bellow that filled the hall from the stone floor to its cavernous ceiling. Though at first it sounded genuine, it soon faded into forced chuckles. The *jotur* fell silent. He shifted in his chair and tugged at his beard.

"Not a difficult riddle," said Thrudnir. "Not difficult at all."

Hope flickered in Torin's chest as he saw the Mountain King's dwindling expression. "Does the ruler of Jokulheim have an answer to offer?"

Thrudnir's face contorted into a wrinkled frown. "Silence! You can demand nothing of me. I am lord of this hall! Besides, you had plenty of time to respond. Now, let me think."

Whispers rippled through the crowd of *jotur*. The Mountain King slammed both fists on the table. "I said silence!"

Torin's heart beat so hard in his chest that he could hear its rhythm pound against his eardrums.

The Mountain King mumbled to himself. "Once it's broken, can't be fixed. Always sticks. Damn this confounded verse." Though the crowd said nothing, their eyes grew wider with every minute that passed.

Torin looked back at Grimsa, who grinned wide. Bari rubbed his hands and Azal bit down on his fist. The old Lorekeeper leaned on the prince's arm with his eyes squeezed shut.

Suddenly Thrudnir broke the silence with a thunderous call. "Ha! Yes, I see now. A very clever verse, but not too clever for me."

Torin's stomach sank like a pebble in the center of a deep lake as he turned to face the Mountain King again. He cleared his throat and forced his shoulders straight as he felt the last wispy threads of hope slipping out of his grip. "What is your answer, Lord Thrudnir?"

The giant chuckled to himself and shook his head. "It is so simple once you see it. What is made often but rarely kept? What is free to give but can cost you dearly? And what cannot be fixed once it is broken? Nothing but a promise. Of course! Once you make a promise it cannot be taken back."

Torin's vision blurred a bit and he thought he might be sick. He hardly remembered raising his cup or hearing the thunderous applause of the *jotur* crowd that rumbled through the floor as if the earth itself was shaking. All the chaos around him seemed dull and a sudden numbness tingled in his chest. As the room began to swirl, Torin felt himself tottering over.

Two strong arms caught his shoulders. Grimsa held him upright until Torin found his feet again. "Keep at it, Torin," Grimsa said. "You are our only chance! If the gods mean to spite this damned *jotur* through you, then you cannot fail them."

Torin breathed slowly and felt the world come back to him. Grimsa was right, he thought. If it was his fate to die in a duel of riddles with the Mountain King, then there was no avoiding it. All Torin could do was hope that the gods had enough use for him to lend him some bit of luck against the immortal king.

"Mindthorn," Thrudnir said. "I must confess that I have enjoyed this *bardagi*. Not since my youth have I set the blade of my mind against another mind so sharp! But now I must end our duel with one final riddle." A cruel smirk spread across the *jotur's* wrinkled face, and his ice-green eyes darkened. "Let us see just how wise you really are, grave robber. Answer, listener, if you can: What were the words that I whispered to my son Ballur as he burned on the pyre?"

Torin stood at the center of the hall in silence as a chorus of gasps came from every direction. The guests looked at each other and whispered back and forth about the *jotur's* devious question.

Grimsa threw his hands up in the air. "You cheating scum! What sort of question is that? That is not a riddle!"

Jolvar and Ulfun stepped forward and took Grimsa by the arms. Though he flailed and kicked, the giants held him back. Azal and Bari looked ready to fight but neither had weapons, so their anger was of little use.

Torin should have been outraged. He should have shouted and cursed and decried such a preposterous question. But in that moment, he heard the echo of a noble voice, a memory of something once said. The words were those spoken by the apparition of the *jotur* prince, Ballur, who had appeared to them in the barrow. The words flowed from his mouth as if it were not a memory but Thrudnir's long-mourned son himself speaking to the crowd.

> *Hear me, son, with with'ring ears*
> *Beyond this realm of dwindling years*
> *An Ash there stands, a timeless tree*
> *Its boughs stretched wider than the sea*
>
> *When Ash leaves quake then time is nigh*
> *As wolves rend sun and moon from sky*
> *Then you'll rise from cold, dank tomb*
> *And proud asyr will face their doom*

Thrudnir pushed himself back against his throne, speechless. Many of the *jotur* crowded around the tables drew back from Torin, a flurry of hushed whispers filling the room.

The Mountain King's eyes stretched wide with fright. "By mighty Yg and blessed Ym! What sort of dark magic do you possess?" Before Torin could respond, Thrudnir pointed at him and shouted to the *jotur* warriors around the edge of the room. "Seize him! Seize the *madur* wizard before he lays some bitter curse on us!"

Before they could make a move, Wyla appeared atop the back of the throne. She stood over Thrudnir's shoulder with a look in her eye that Torin knew well. She was out for blood. A giantess near the Mountain King shrieked and pointed at Wyla. The *jotur* lord twisted in his seat and to see what had clambered up behind him.

Wyla stood atop the throne and roared. "Orr's thunder strike you!"

With one hand on the sheath and the other on the hilt, Wyla raised *Tyrfang* high over her head to draw the blade. However, when she pulled, it would not budge. She strained harder, then again a third time. Though her face flushed red with exertion, she could not free its black steel edge.

Thrudnir stretched back and snatched Wyla up by the cloak. She bludgeoned his hand with the exposed hilt, but the Mountain King held his grip. As she raised the sheath to strike a second time, he caught her by the leg and she lost her balance. With two fingers pinching her by the ankle, he dangled her upside down.

Wyla flailed and thrashed, her hair and arms swinging madly from side to side. "Release me you wrinkled, ice-brained brute!" She caught the *jotur* by surprise with a blow to the nose, as she swung *Tyrfang*, still stuck in its scabbard, with all her might.

Thrudnir winced and plucked the sword from her grip with his free hand. The giant's white eyebrows furled together like two snowdrifts sliding into a ravine. "Wait! I know this blade."

A few of the giants seated near the king pulled away with frozen, pale expressions. The panic that had taken the room faded as the Mountain King let down his shoulders and settled back into his throne. He inspected the dark blade closely, as if relieving a rush of memories.

"Ah, yes," said Thrudnir. "Now I understand." The giant raised his eyes and glared at Torin. "I suppose I should have seen the resemblance."

Torin frowned. "Resemblance? What resemblance?"

Thrudnir exhaled and dropped Wyla onto the table. She sprawled on all fours then jumped to her feet to redouble her assault. Before she could charge forward, Thrudnir emptied a bowl and trapped her beneath its filigreed dome. Muffled curses and threats came from beneath the metal vessel, but it did not budge.

Thrudnir set *Tyrfang* on the table and stroked his beard. "I should have suspected that she had a part in all this. But why would she send you?"

"She?" said Torin. "Do you mean the queen of the wood?"

The *jotur* narrowed his gaze. "So, you do know of her! Enough of your games, you slithering spy. Speak the truth or I will roast you alive over the fire!"

"By my oath to The Gatewatch," Torin said. "I do not know who she is. She appeared to us in Ballur's Barrow and tried to kill us. I don't know what she wants exactly, other than to claim the throne of Noros. But I do know that she is the one poisoning our king. That is the reason we are here, not in her service, but to draw a healing draught from the Everspring for Araldof the Greyraven."

Thrudnir paused and studied Torin's face. The *jotur* glanced down at the blade and then nodded. "Ah, yes, Araldof, the *madur* king. He is the descendant of that troublesome fellow, Beoric, who slew my cousin, Gezbrukter."

Torin felt the blood drain from his face and his stomach lurched. Before he could think of something to say in response, the giant continued.

"And good riddance, I say. That weasel, Gezbrukter, was in league with her as well. Indeed, Beoric swore a solemn oath to me that his kin would never conspire with her against me, yet here you are." Thrudnir gave a long sigh. "Of course, what constancy can one expect from mortals? And still, the news that this Araldof has fallen prey to her magic falls ill upon my ears."

Torin swallowed hard and wondered whether he should press his luck. "In that case, it may also please you to know that this present company defeated Gezbrukter's son, Ur-Gezbrukter, who tried to reclaim his father's kingdom in Gatewatch two years ago."

A flash of anger lit Thrudnir's eyes. "That traitor! Do not speak his name in my presence. I took him in after his father's demise and still he betrayed my trust."

The giant sneered as he looked past Torin to the flickering fire at the center of the room. "Yet another one of my kin that foul woman turned against me. Besides, Gezbrukter was lord of nothing but a ragged horde of trolls, a master of little more than oversized maggots. Yet even he was not the first that she lured into such delusions!"

Though his hand trembled, Torin pulled Araldof Greyraven's silver ring from beneath his shirt and held it up for all the *jotur* to see. "I do not know who this queen is, but I can assure you, by the authority of Araldof Greyraven's own signet ring, that Noros has no alliance with any friends of Ur-Gezbrukter."

Thrudnir sunk deeper into his throne. "I fear that the seeds of her deception have grown roots far deeper than I had imagined they could. Tell me, *madur*, who is your father?" When Torin did not answer immediately, the giant slammed his fist on the arms of his throne. "Speak, mortal! The Mountain King demands it!"

Torin cleared his throat and squared his shoulders to the *jotur* lord. "My father is Einar Ten-Trees, kin to King Araldof Greyraven."

"Ah, then there is *huldur* blood in you after all. I thought I saw it in your face!"

Torin opened his mouth to speak then closed it again. What was it that Thrudnir had said? When he looked at his companions, Grimsa shrugged. Torin narrowed his eyes and tilted his head. "What do you mean by *huldur* blood?"

"How little of the history of this land do you know?" Thrudnir said. "Do you think that Beoric was the first to lay claim to the mountains that tumble down toward the sea? The *huldur* danced through the shadowed paths of the ancient forest long before Beoric clumsily stumbled into it. Surely, you know your own history well enough to know that Beoric the Bear met a woman as he explored the darkened forest. Did you really think it was a *madur* woman that Beoric saw there in the moonlight?"

Torin thought again of the tale of Beoric and Fyra, of that strange meeting under the light of the moon. His stomach churned with an uneasy feeling. "What is a *huldur*, exactly?"

Thrudnir eyed Torin a moment longer before he spoke. "They are little different than yourself in appearance except that their faces are fairer, and they live one hundred mortal lifetimes. Most telling of all are their tails, which twist and flicker as they dance beneath the green boughs of the forest. Long ago, they ruled over the ancient wood through the strong magic of their enchanted songs. So rich were their woodland burrows with gold that even the *nidavel* of the mountain looked on with envy!"

"I have no tail," said Torin. "What sort of creature do you think I am?"

Thrudnir rolled his eyes. "Of course, you don't. How ignorant are you? Do you not know that when a *huldur* commits their heart to a mortal soul, their tail falls off, and they are doomed to live but the span of a single lifetime? Their face remains fair, but whatever immortal energy the forest graced them with is lost forever." Thrudnir squinted at Torin for any sign of familiarity with such things and found none. The *jotur* threw up his hands and shook his head. "By Ym! Brainless mortals."

Torin shifted his feet and crossed his arms. "So, Fyra was one of these *huldur*?"

"She was, until she was betrothed to Beoric. Fyra chose a mortal life when she bound herself to him, but the blood of her descendants will always carry some trace of the *huldur* magic. That, I suppose, accounts for your exceptional skill in riddling verse."

Thrudnir sat in silence a moment longer and tugged at his great white beard. Every eye in the hall shifted from Torin to the old giant, and no one dared to utter a word. At last, the *jotur's* frown broke and his blue lips spread into a wide grin. "So perhaps for once the weavers at the Well of Fate, the ancient *nornir*, have tied a lucky knot into the long length of my thread."

"What do you mean by that?" said Torin.

"If you truly are a descendent of Beoric and Fyra then you have *huldur* blood in you, there is no doubt about that. That means you can also trace a family line back to her sister, Lysa. Surely even you know of the quarrel between these two sisters!"

Verses and images swirled around together in Torin's mind as he recalled the Lay of Beoric. Fyra's sister Lysa tried to force her into marriage with the Troll-King, and Lysa had ended Beoric's life with a poisoned draught. "Do you mean the same Lysa spoken of in the Lay of Beoric? Fyra's sister and Beoric's doom?"

"Perhaps that is what you *madur* call her," Thrudnir said, "But here in my hall, I have named her the Green Witch, the Ivy Queen, and Nettles-Daughter."

The Mountain King sat silent in his own thoughts for a moment then sighed. "This complicates our *bardagi*, Mindthorn. You see, red-headed Fyra was once married to my son, Ballur the Bright. They swore their love to each other in a secret grove deep within the wood, not far from where his barrow lies today. And since she was at one time a daughter-in-law to me, that makes you a relative of my relation. A distant link, to be sure, but a link all the same. By the ancient traditions of *bardagi*, it is strictly forbidden to challenge one's own kin. Therefore, our *bardagi* is nullified and the contest must be ended."

Torin's fingers felt numb as the Mountain King's words fell on his tingling ears. A rush of relief swelled up inside his chest and his knees felt dangerously unsteady. He inspected the giant's face for signs of treachery.

Thrudnir called out in a bellowing voice. "Hear me, you ancient *jotur* of Jokulheim! My estimation of these visitors is greatly changed. Bring thick furs and blankets of dyed wool! Fetch a dish of steaming water with sweet-scented oils so that they may wash their road-weary faces! Show them the full hospitality of the giants. Then, once all have settled, I feel I must recount the tragic tale of the *huldur* and the death of my own son. More than one hundred winters have passed since his death and, though it pains me to speak of it, it must not be forgotten! I forget how quickly such knowledge fades among mortals. If any from this strange company survive their journey north, they will carry a fuller understanding of the Green Witch's treachery back to their own people in the land beyond the mountains that tumble down into the sea."

Wyla was released from under the giant's bowl and the others were brought to the center of the room. A place was set for them right beside the fire.

Grimsa grabbed Torin by the shoulders and lifted him up off the ground. "By Orr and Odd and Fyr and all three of them together. You did it!"

Torin stumbled back when Grimsa let him go and Wyla caught him in a tight embrace. "Damn you and your riddles, Torin Ten-Trees," she said. "And damn your cursed sword too."

Azal's hands trembled. "By the king's sceptre, I think I still might be sick."

"If I have another brush with death today," said Bari, "I think my heart might give out."

Aldrin squeezed Torin's shoulder. "Well done, Torin Ten-Trees. It seems this day might not be our last after all!"

The *jotur* servants hauled in a copper basin full of steaming water. The steam was scented with pine and cedar, the richest smells of the forest. The whole company laughed as they splashed their faces in the soothing water. Then the giants brought furs and enormous woolen blankets which were set on the floor for the company to sit on. Cups of wine were refilled and the *jotur* crowd settled into their seats in anticipation of Thrudnir's tale. The servants made sure that the thimbles of the mortal company were filled with wine and then, when everything else was set, poured drinks for themselves too.

Once every vessel had been filled, the Mountain King stood up and cleared his throat. The old *jotur* opened his arms wide then spoke in a loud voice that echoed all the way through the hall up to the top of the domed ceiling. "Here begins the story of the fall of the *huldur*, the rise of the Green Witch, and the death of Ballur, my own son."

15

◇ THE FALL OF THE HULDUR ◇

"LONG AGO, at least by the reckoning of mortal minds, the *huldur* ruled the wood. They were a strange folk, each keen for wine and song, with little care for the vast stores of treasure hidden away in their winter burrows. Indeed, any *nidavel* who stumbled onto their troves in those days would have writhed with envy. Where the *huldur* got that rich treasure even I cannot say for certain, though I have heard rumours that their songs could draw out the earth's treasures, both gold and silver, up through the roots of trees until it leaked out like sap. Others say that the *huldur* could converse with the trees to ask them where the richest veins of ore lay so they could dig it up with ease. However, the black smoke of the smelting fire was never seen in those woods. By whatever means they got it, it was there, and they heeded it little. Crowns spun of gold twine or arm-rings made of braided silver were often left strewn about the wide green meadows where the *huldur* sang to celebrate the changing of seasons."

"Year after year, they sang to the trees and danced under the swaying boughs of the forest. They hailed the spring and rang in autumn with lavish feasts of plumpest fruit and sweetest wine. Throughout the winter, they would warm the roots of the trees in their cozy burrows and sing of great tales, all in full chorus and harmony. Hidden away from the rest of the world, from the mighty wars of the *jotur* against the *asyr* in the north or the countless squabbles between petty *madur* kings to the south, the *huldur* enjoyed the seemingly endless bounty and enduring peace of the forest."

"After countless cycles of freeze and thaw, there arose a poet of such renown that no one among them could match him for verse. And at the same time, a singing voice rang out above the others, so sweet and clear that even the birds fell silent to listen whenever she opened her mouth. Skaldi and Synga were their names, and they were two bright shining stars amid a sky of twinkling lights."

"Skaldi's tales inspired Synga's songs, and the purity of her voice provoked his spirit to draw ever deeper from its well of words. It seemed that fate had drawn them together, the poet and the singer. All *huldur* folk reveled in their music and soon hailed them as king and queen of the wood. Long they reigned, the harmony of their union more perfect than the rustling of leaves, the trickle of rain, or the clearest trill of birdsong."

"After many such seasons, Synga's belly grew moon-round with twins. The king and queen of the wood were so overcome with joy that they ignored the dark omen of a twin birth. For three full seasons, they celebrated with dance and song."

"Twin daughters were born to them. The king and queen of the wood named the sisters Lysa and Fyra. These two were twin moons in the night sky of their mother's eyes, two golden suns hovering over the horizon of their father's proud cheeks."

"And yet, though they were twins, Lysa and Fyra were as distinct from one another as the sun from the moon. Lysa had her father's complexion, his quick grey eyes, and his night-black hair. Fyra was a reflection of her mother, with eyes as green and bright as the sea, and hair that tumbled down her head in rust-red curls. And so, the twins grew up under a gold-twined bower, in an age immersed in song and ripe with joy."

"Lysa, the oldest by only a moment, had snatched up all the talents of her celebrated parents. Her voice rang loud and pure through the woodland meadows and along the winding paths of the forest. She could recite every verse she had ever heard from memory, and all stopped to listen in awe whenever she opened her mouth to sing."

"Fyra, the second, inherited the kind spirit of her parents but little more than that. Though she loved the trees and the wandering creeks within the wood, she never had a keen ear for song or much interest in the *huldur* verses. However, Fyra happily trailed along behind Lysa, free of cares, though she was unpossessed by the celebrated gifts which had been bestowed upon her sister."

"The *huldur*, though long-lived, are not immortal. The long years carved deep wrinkles into Skaldi and Sygna's fair faces. Over time, Skaldi's memory began to waver and Sygna's strong voice thinned to little more than a whisper. I have heard it said that when Skaldi and Synga passed into the realm beyond the earth, they passed together, hand in hand with fingers entwined as roots grow between trees. The *huldur* folk mourned them in their own custom, with verses of praise and solemn songs which stretched throughout the whole winter."

"It fell then to Lysa and Fyra to lead the songs of spring, to stir the chorus in summer, and to sing the hymns of autumn. The highest and most noble blood flowed through them, though only Lysa truly possessed the skill to match the performances of Skaldi and Sygna. So, season after season, they led the *huldur* through the ceremonies that they held sacred."

"But then the dark omen began to spread its shadow over the twins. It began with a festering wound, an ache in Lysa's heart at the loss of her parents, the only two voices that had been strong enough to match her own. Long hours she would spend reciting her father's verses and singing Synga's songs. *Huldur* folk marveled at the beauty of her music, and the sadness of it only enhanced its entrancing effect. The fame of her voice spread so that news of her songs reached even the ears of the *jotur* and *asyr*."

"So possessed by grief was Lysa that she began to neglect the seasonal chants, the melodies of spring and the refrains of autumn. Though Fyra begged her sister to sing the incantations, as only she could, Lysa refused to perform anything but the songs of her late parents. In a span of seasons shorter than a mortal lifetime, Lysa abandoned the old verses entirely. She decreed that only the songs of Skaldi and Synga should be heard within the wood."

"Yet Skaldi and Sygna had been named king and queen of the wood for a good reason, for few *huldur* could manage their magnificent melodies. In sorrow and anger, Lysa silenced every stuttered word and untuned note until only those who could master the intricate verses remained. Before long, the only voice to be heard in the entire wood was hers. Even Fyra, her sister and only living kin, was shamed into silence because of the slightest imperfections in her voice."

"And so, an ancient evil began to seep into the forest. For countless years the *huldur* songs had cleansed the shadowed bogs and the mounds of rotting wood, but under Lysa's rule the long-held traditions ceased. Strange and vile creatures that had slumbered deep underground in decay and slime rose to the surface of the silent wood. Tame creatures turned feral, tree leaves turned black with rot, and wicked trolls began to creep forth from the dark caves that fell in the mountains' shadows"

"Perhaps the beauty and power of Skaldi and Sygna's verses could have held that evil back if all the *huldur* were united in song. But Lysa never strayed far from her home at the heart of the wood, and so the rest of the forest remained sorely neglected."

"It was during this same time that my son, Ballur the Bright, set forth to hear the legendary songs of the *huldur* for himself. I admit that I thought him soft, especially as he grew up in an age of peace after the terrible wars of the *jotur* and *asyr* when an uneasy truce held the powers in balance. He had no love of blades or bows, of mighty steeds or hardened steel, or even of hunting as the son of a mighty lord should. But he reveled in the music of *huldur* folk, and they admired his gentle way of moving about the world."

"Indeed, they loved him so dearly that they taught him to sing in their manner, a strange mingling of voices that produces a wash of beautiful sound as the notes blend together. Ballur the Bright, they called him. So gifted was Ballur in their craft that he even took to their custom of conversing in rhyming verses. Many moons passed overhead before he returned home from the wood. From then on, he spent more days wandering through the forest than under the roof of my mighty northern abode, Hjartahall, of which more shall be said later in this tale."

"It became evident that Ballur found more than just songs in his time with the *huldur*. My son's eyes fell on Fyra, that red-haired daughter of the *huldur* king and queen. No sooner had Ballur seen Fyra than was his heart lost to her forever. And she too, seeing his handsome form and his gentle way, was similarly stricken."

"They vowed their love to each other in secret, deep in the wood, where none but the trees and the breeze could hear. In time, it came to pass that Fyra's belly became round with child so that their love could no longer be kept hidden. Ballur and Fyra approached Lysa and declared their intent to marry."

"Lysa, enraged by their secret betrothal, would not have it. Lysa told her sister of visions she had seen as she slept in the deep, dark heart of the wood. In those visions, she saw a great host of *huldur* children that she and Fyra would bear, each one full of their parent's royal blood and blessed with all their skill in craft. A child born of a *jotur* and a *huldur*, she argued, would be the undoing of such a vision. And so Lysa drove Ballur from the *huldur* wood. Then she trapped Fyra in a cage of tree roots which were bent and twisted into Lysa's wicked service by the powerful magic of her own voice."

"Ballur's heart burned with fury, and he refused to leave the wood. Therefore, on Lysa's order, the *huldur* folk hid away from him. From spring until fall, Ballur wandered the forest alone in search of Fyra. By then he had become nearly witless, his hair in disheveled knots and his eyes red from the salt of all his tears. At last, when perhaps Ballur thought he had only ever dreamed of his meeting Fyra and the rest of the *huldur* folk, one *huldur* had the courage to betray his queen. This *huldur* sought out Ballur in secret and described to him a most terrible thing."

"Fyra had given birth to their child in the tree-root cage that her sister Lysa had wrought. As Fyra cried out with the pains of labour Lysa would still not let her free and forbade any of the *huldur* from approaching the cage. Fyra suffered through the night alone and, in the morning, cradled her newborn son in her arms."

"The *huldur* queen returned to the place where her sister was held captive and sang back the gnarled root cage. A great host accompanied Lysa as she cursed and spat on Fyra for bringing such a child into the world. Lysa began a chant of shame and ordered the crowd of *huldur* to join in. Soon a chorus of twisted words surrounded Fyra like thrashing waves assailing a sinking vessel. As the noise reached the peak of its deafening crescendo, Lysa drew out a pouch from her cloak and flung a cloud of grey spores at Fyra and the child. The infant cried and coughed then breathed no more."

"No sooner had Ballur heard the gruesome tale than did he tear across the northern plain toward my seat in Hjartahall, which sits beside the roaring Everspring. Not even quick-winged Hraesvelgir could have outpaced him that day. Never had I seen him so full of grief and anguish."

"Ballur knocked over benches and overturned tables as he came crashing through the doors of Hjartahall. He shoved aside guards and smashed mead barrels, careening toward my throne. I called for wine, for warm furs, and for steaming stew, but he refused them all. All there in the hall stood silent among the wreckage and beheld my son, the *jotur* prince, with fearful eyes."

"And so, I listened to the story. Yet even as Ballur told of Lysa's horrendous act, the beams of Hjartahall began to rumble with distant, groaning thunder. Dark clouds spun over the horizon, and the crackle of lightning tingled through the air. Then thunder boomed overhead and all the roof tiles rattled. A deluge of rain hammered the roof and quickly turned to pellets of icy hail. I knew then that the *asyr* were on their way."

"Just as Ballur finished his story, the doors of Hjartahall flew open and Orr, that self-proclaimed Lord of Thunder, stepped in from the storm. His terrible form filled the doorway, an awful silhouette against each flash of lightning. His limbs were monstrous, great burly arms with hair of ember-bright red, a thicket of twisted strands, which he calls a beard, around his face, and two horrible eyes like hot coals, blazing forth in anger."

"According to the truce that had put a stop to centuries of violence between the *jotur* and the *asyr*, I was honour-bound to offer him drink. This I did. The one that you *madur* call Orr the Thunderer drank a dozen barrels of my best wine before he agreed to state his purpose. Never has he repaid me a single coin or kindness for the hospitality shown to him!"

"Of course, the rage of the *asyr* had been ignited by the abominable evil committed by Lysa. That *huldur* queen had grieved them much by letting the forest fall into shadow, but to kill one's own kin, an infant no less, was a transgression of the most ancient and sacred laws. I speak not of the lesser laws of the *asyr*, but those set down by the ageless *nornir* when the seed of the world tree, Yg, first sprouted a tender green shoot. The *asyr* were but children when those sacred words were spoken! Indeed, I had never once agreed with the *asyr* about anything until that day. I could not ignore such treachery at the border of my own realm and continue to call myself wise."

"After consuming six whole cows, Orr bellowed in monstrous grunts that he would flush out Lysa and all the *huldur* of the forest to smite them with *Mjol*, his gruesome hammer. Ballur, with great courage, challenged the red-haired *asyr* to reconsider. If Orr loved justice, Ballur argued, he should then hate injustice in equal measure. My son knew, as well as I did, that if the Thunderer let loose his anger, the entire forest would burn to ash-black coal, that mountains would tumble over, and the land would lay in waste for a thousand years to follow. No trace of the *huldur*, Fyra included, would ever be seen under Yg's boughs again."

"And so, it was decided, for the sake of all those who had no part in Lysa's crime, that we *jotur* would see justice served in our own realm. Orr agreed that the *asyr*, once they received word that the sentence had been carried out, would not loose their wrath upon the land as they had in the old warring days."

"Ballur demanded to ride alone into that wood to confront Lysa, so that the rest of the *huldur* might not suffer. But I knew that the *huldur* were a proud and loyal folk. Even in light of her most heinous act, I knew that some among them would stop at nothing to preserve the celebrated songs of their beloved Skaldi and Synga as kept alive by Lysa, that doom-struck queen. Ballur wandered the woods for an age, as the *huldur* hid away in their secret burrows. In my own mind, the *huldur* folk had stood by while such a thing happened and so the blood of my own grandchild stained them all."

"Though we could have assembled a great host, a few of my own rubble-brained kin sided against me. Gezbrukter, my cousin, was foremost among them. They argued that the *asyr* should hold no sway in the land of the *jotur* and that we should spite them whatever their demands. But I knew better. It was not the law of the *asyr* that had been broken, but a law much more ancient and sacred. Still, my son Ballur had a deep love of the *huldur* and for that reason I could not openly raise my hand against them."

"So, I found an ally for the task from the *nidavellish* city of Myrkheim a host of blades eager to exchange blood for gold. It was Mastersmith Thrain who ruled Myrkheim when I sent a messenger in secret. My swift rider enthralled the *nidavel* with tales of the wondrous plunder that lay just beneath the forest floor in the *huldur* burrows, mounds of red gold and moon-bright silver. Soon, every *nidavel* in his court was salivating at the thought of the unguarded treasure of the *huldur* folk in the realm of light and stars far above them."

"Even before my messenger returned, news of Thrain's campaign to claim such treasures reached Hjartahall. The *huldur* knew little of the ways of war, and the magic which guarded them had dwindled along with their songs. I saw the blaze in Ballur's chest as our scouts told of *huldur* being cut down left and right. It did my heart good to see my son's blood boil with fury. The forest floor, they said, was strewn with fair-faced *huldur*, now lifeless and silent."

"I confess that I was proud when my son roared in his anger. How the shields along the mead benches clamoured in tune with the ring of his voice! He cursed the *nidavel* as the son of a *jotur* lord should curse his enemies, and he demanded a sword from me. Never before had he asked me to search my treasure hoard for a blade to fit his hand, not even the smallest rune-carved dagger had he ever requested. How long had I waited for that moment? My chest swelled with pride as I ordered his birthright be brought in from my armoury, a magnificent blade forged during the old wars. He brandished it in the presence of all there and with stern words rallied the hall troops."

"What a sight he was! Ballur thundered over the plain toward the *huldur* wood. Great curved war-horns blasted battle-notes and bright banners fluttered in the wake of his charge. I watched him ride forth from Hjartahall under a crisp northern sky, the wind tugging at his crimson cloak as the pounding hooves of his steed kicked up a trail of dust and snow. A host of *jotur* followed behind him on war-ready mounts, each racing to catch up with my son, the Prince of Hjartahall, Ballur the Bright."

"He arrived with little time to spare. Thrain's forces had cornered the last of the *huldur* on a rocky bluff overlooking the forest. Only a few dozen remained to stand by Lysa and Fyra, sticks and stones in hand, as the greed-driven *nidavel* scaled the slope. In mighty bounds, Ballur's steed galloped over the invaders and up to the top of the rugged hill."

"With a radiant flash of silver steel, Ballur leapt from his horse and cut down *nidavel* on every side. He rallied the remaining *huldur* behind him along the bluff and faced the host of rune-etched *nidavellish* blades. By the time I arrived with my retainers, they were at a standstill. Dozens upon dozens of *nidavel* lay slain at Ballur's feet, his face speckled with blood and his blade slick with gore. Thrain demanded that Lysa and Fyra, as well as the treasure of the *huldur*, be surrendered, but Ballur refused to give ground."

"For the first time I looked upon my son, Ballur the Bright, and saw a full-grown prince, not the dreamy-eyed youngling who had tumbled about my hall and frolicked in the forest. How handsome he was in that scarlet cloak with my runic sigil gleaming on his breastplate, how brave and bold with his enemies slain at his feet."

"After brief consideration, I proposed that Lysa be handed over to the Mastersmith as a prisoner along with half the treasure, for I could see the lust in Thrain's eyes not only for gold but also for the *huldur* queen. Fyra and the remaining *huldur* would live under the protection of the *jotur* with the other half of the *huldur's* treasure being given as blood money for the slain child."

"Thrain was furious at my proposal, as he had lost many kinsmen to Ballur's blade. But the fires of lust burned bright beneath the fury in his eyes, so he agreed. Indeed, to the end of his lengthened days, that *nidavel* bore a grudge against the *jotur* for the other half of the *huldur* treasure. And so Fyra and those last few *huldur* were spared. As for the rest of the treasure, I took it into my own keeping to protect it from the greedy hands of the *nidavel*."

"That winter was one of woe. In all my years I could not recall a heavier snow, more bitter days of biting wind, or heavier sheets of blue-green ice. Despite winter's clawing grasp, the love between Fyra and Ballur grew each day as they feasted under the rafters of Hjartahall. Meanwhile, Lysa languished beneath the surface of the earth somewhere in the *nidavellish* city of Myrkheim."

"Then came the spring, a time for rebirth, renewal, and the speaking of vows. All the remaining *huldur* folk gathered in the forest to celebrate the marriage of Ballur and Fyra, their eyes lit with hope at this new beginning. There in the forest, amid the first flowers of spring, the *jotur* prince and the *huldur* daughter tied their hands with white cloth and spoke solemn vows."

"At the end of the ceremony came the exchange of swords. Of course, the *huldur* rarely had need of such things, and so Fyra had no weapon to offer. But, at that moment, a cloaked figure appeared. All the guests gasped as she pulled back a green velvet hood to reveal her face: it was none other than Lysa."

"Lysa was thin and pale from a winter spent under the ground, her cheeks both gaunt and hollow. From beneath her cloak, she drew out a finely crafted *nidavellish* sword in a black leather sheath etched with swirling runes. All my finest warriors drew their weapons, but Lysa called for calm. She said that the sword was a gift on behalf of the Mastersmith and an offering of peace following a season of strife.

"I counselled against accepting such a gift, but headstrong Ballur would not heed my advice. Both he and Fyra were lovers of peace and vainly wished the wood to return to such harmony as had been known before. And so, the wedding feast began, and all drank to their health, though some, as we shall see, not so deeply."

"As the last of the wedding wine was served and the couple prepared to depart to their marriage bed, the glint of the rune-etched hilt caught Ballur's eye. He drew it out to view the blade in the light of the fire then sheathed it again. It was a fine blade, Ballur said, and though small for him, it certainly was a weapon worthy of a prince. Little did he heed the runes that Mastersmith Thrain had carved into that darkened steel! Indeed, how could he have read them under the dim light of the stars and under the influence of so much wine? Yet so fine was the sword that his misguided curiosity urged him to draw it a second time. When he did, the blade slipped in his hand and plunged deep into his belly."

"Guests screamed at the sight of the sword blade piercing that fair groom straight through. I leapt up from my bench and ran to my son, but the dark magic of that blade had already done its work. Only then did I read the runes, a terrible curse, that any who drew the sword must satisfy its steel edge with blood or else suffer its wrath. I could feel the tingle of its magic as I drew the blade from his stomach, a strange humming power which seemed to me to surpass even the skill of the *nidavel*. I think it must have been affected by some twisted *huldur* melody that Lysa had sung over the steel in its making. Look closely at the runes carved upon that sword and one will find its name: *Tyrfang*."

"In the chaos that followed, Lysa and a band of dark-cloaked *nidavel* dragged Fyra away. Down to the city of Myrkheim, Lysa fled with her sister as her prisoner. Ballur died there in my arms, and to this day I have never known such pain. Just to speak of it shreds the sinews of my heart!"

"I later learned that Lysa had fanned the flame of Thrain's discontent at losing the *huldur* treasure. She had convinced the *nidavellish* Mastersmith to help her regain her woodland throne, a seat which she alone would sit on. It was for this reason that Thrain and Lysa had wrought *Tyrfang*, the darkest steel ever forged by mortal hands."

"Lysa formed an alliance with my troublesome cousin, Gezbrukter, with a false promise of betrothal to Fyra. Though angered, I was hardly surprised, as my cousin had been jealous of my seat in Hjartahall for one thousand mortal lifetimes. They had no army, save the foul trolls that had crept out of the dark places in the *huldur* wood after the ancient songs had been silenced. So, with curses and dark runes, they coerced those foul creatures into their service."

"Yet the *huldur* knew none of this. All they saw was their new-crowned lord, Ballur the Bright, lying dead beneath a silver moon. Their hopes of reclaiming the wood with light and song had been utterly dashed. How torn their hearts, how sorrowful the melody of their songs! All hoped for the return of Fyra, fair and full of grace, while for Lysa they felt only spite."

"The *huldur* raised a barrow for Ballur there in the wood where he had most often been found singing with them. I commissioned a throne of white quartz, quarried right here in Jokulheim, to be placed there, a royal seat that would stand forever empty in waiting for a prince who would never come. Then, after the barrow was complete, his body was burned on the pyre. In his ear I whispered, against all hope, across the shadowy veil of death, a prophecy of the final doom of the *asyr*, when the *jotur* would rise in vengeance and bathe the world in fire."

"So great was my grief that I could not linger after the *huldur* carried his remains into the barrow. I set off for Hjartahall far in the North as smoke still rose from the ashes of Ballur's pyre. Of course, for those who are mortal and doomed to die, the sting of death is sharp. But how much sharper it is when an immortal soul crosses that darkened threshold!"

"The *huldur* remained at the barrow and continued to mourn, as was their custom, with songs and deep draughts of red wine. Yet, one final tragedy was sprung upon them. Under the shroud of night, moving silently and wrapped in a dark green cloak, Lysa slipped a powdered poison into the funeral wine. There, as they toasted Ballur in his royal barrow, each one fell into a sleep from which they would never wake."

"Fyra, still a prisoner in Myrkheim, rallied her courage and used what magic she had to escape her prison cell deep underground. She knew of her sister's scheme to marry her to Gezbrukter, my cousin, in exchange for his support. How Fyra managed to navigate the *nidavellish* tunnels and find the surface I can only guess."

"It was in that wood, as Fyra wandered, bereft, that she encountered Beoric. Such things you know well from your own tales, yet it seems to me that the manner in which these things came about was previously beyond your knowing."

"As for Lysa, she met nothing but ill fortune. Fair payment, I would say, for her evil deeds! Yet, her evil was not yet finished. Gezbrukter fell against Beoric, and all hope of reclaiming the wood was ruined. Lysa felt betrayal brewing among the *nidavel* and so fled Myrkheim to a place much deeper and darker than that"

"From there, I can only guess what happened. Somehow, in the twisted tunnels that burrow deep down into the earth, Lysa found a secret path to Nilfhel, the realm of the dead. From there she lay dormant for the length of a mortal lifetime until one day she rose and appeared in the middle of Hjartahall."

"Lysa unleashed some terrible creature from the realm of the dead, an unspeakable monstrosity that we have named the Shadowstalker. Never should that beast have been freed from its chains! Yet, Lysa tore the barrier between worlds just enough to let it slip through."

"It ravaged Hjartahall and slew my kinsman left and right. Every wall was splattered with *jotur* blood as we raced to escape. So many of those loyal to me were lost on that terrible night that I can hardly name them all."

"We retreated here to Jokulheim, my fortress in the old days of war with the *asyr*, and here I have remained ever since. The Shadowstalker still haunts Hjartahall, my beloved abode, beside the thundering Everspring. And somewhere below us, in shadowy Nilfhel, Lysa bides her time as she plots her next assault."

16

◇ A<ROSS THE NORTHERN PLAIN ◇

THE LAST OF THE WAX CANDLES flickered and went out at the final word of Thrudnir's tale. Only the last crackling embers of the fire still lit the feasting hall of Jokulheim. With the warm fur blanket below him and half a cup of warm cider in his hand, Torin could hardly stay awake a moment longer. He finished the last of his drink, then lay down beside his companions. As he stared up at the towering reaches of the cavern ceiling, images swirled through his mind, scenes from Thrudnir's tale cycling through his head over and over. Around the edge of the room, he sensed large forms move quietly away. Torin thought to himself that he should stay awake to keep guard, but his whole body was sinking into the warmth of the furs beneath him. His eyes shuddered and his limbs were like heavy stones. With that, he drifted off into an uneasy sleep, and a dream full of monstrous shadows moving through a darkened wood.

Torin woke up in a room he did not recognize. He scrambled up to his feet from the pile of white furs beneath him and glanced around with squinted eyes. It was not Thrudnir's feasting hall, but a smaller room with no light except for the glow of torches which came in from a hallway through a doorless arch.

Torin saw Wyla, Bari, Azal, Aldrin, and Grimsa sprawled out on heaps of white furs which had been piled at the center of the circular room. He shuddered to think that the *jotur* must have moved them as they slept. Every muscle in his body ached as the drowsiness wore off and his stomach groaned with hunger.

The room itself was large and rose in a cylindrical shape far beyond Torin's height. As he craned his head back, he could see a domed ceiling high above, its contours shrouded in shadow. Along the wall hung intricate tapestries suspended from the top of the curved walls and falling all the way down to the floor. Each woven piece depicted all manner of ancient things. He recognized Orr, the Lord of Thunder, battling an army of *jotur*. Another panel depicted a giant stealing a basket full of golden fruit from the *asyr* and yet another showed a *jotur* making off with Orr's legendary hammer. He walked about the room for some time, admiring the intricately woven silk.

At last, Torin came to a tapestry near the back of the room where the torchlight from the hall was strongest. Strange characters with thin tails danced in a leafy green wood. Certainly, those were the *huldur*, he thought. The dancing figures encircled two particularly regal figures at the center, perhaps Ballur and Fyra. In the shadowed corners of the tapestry, he saw a dark-haired *huldur* peering out from behind a tree with menacing eyes: Lysa, the Green Witch. A tingle rippled down his spine as he inspected the picture more closely. Could he have really been descended from such creatures? Torin rubbed his lower back where a tail might have protruded if he had been a *huldur*, and he shuddered.

The next panel was full of bright red silk spilling down from the *huldur* as they fled from dark embroidered blades. In intricate knots, the crimson strands ran down between the trees to the bottom of the tapestry where they hung off the edge in ragged, unfinished ends. Halfway up the hill, amid the gory scene, was a small figure with dark blue tattoos swirling up both arms. Torin had seen such patterns before when he met Mastersmith Ognir in Myrkheim. That figure at the center of the tapestry could only be Mastersmith Thrain leading his army of gold-hungry *nidavel* in a hunt for the *huldur* treasure. At the very top he saw Lysa and Fyra against the rocky bluff, protected by a figure outlined in golden silk, surely Ballur the Bright.

Torin was lost in his own thoughts when a voice startled him.

"Do you believe any of it?"

Torin jolted and turned to see Wyla standing beside him with a white fur blanket wrapped around her shoulders. She stared up at the shining silk figure of Ballur at the top of the woven scene. Behind her, the rest of the company was still asleep, each one lost to their own dreams.

Torin shook his head. "I don't know what to believe. Less than a week ago, I thought my mother was dead. Now it seems she has been alive all this time and that I am also connected to some long-lost kingdom that I have never heard of."

"If you really are some part *huldur* that would explain why you are so damn good with riddles," Wyla said. "But it's a pity you didn't inherit their skill in singing. Every fair creature of the wood would flee at the sound of your grunting voice."

Torin grinned. "Honestly, I was more disappointed about the tail. Think of the title that would have earned me!"

Wyla gave a long bow as she spoke. "Torin Longtail, Lord of Rats and Cats and Squirrels."

"Sounds fine to me. Better than settling squabbles between farmers and fishermen."

Wyla frowned. "I don't understand you, Torin. Whenever you talk about returning to Ten-Tree Hall you look like a wolf trapped in a cage, but there is no cage except the one you have created in your mind. You are free, not some animal locked into a prison."

Torin said nothing, staring at the blood-red crimson threads of the tapestry.

"Maybe," said Wyla, "you are miserable because you are fighting your fate? Before you felt the only path for you to walk was your father's, but now you know who your mother is. And if your ancestors really were these *huldur* folk, then your blood ties you to the wild woods west of the mountains."

Torin glanced at Wyla, then looked back up at Lysa and Fyra. "I feel like my whole life has been a lie. My mother has always been alive. Worse, my father knew about it and never told me. And if what Thrudnir says is true, then I have even stranger blood in my veins. It's like I've become a stranger in my own body."

"Not a stranger," Wyla said. "You've always been there. It's like you're waking up from a dream you've been in your whole life. Now you are awakened to who you really are."

"And who is that?"

Wyla stepped toward Torin and gripped his arm. "You know I can't answer that. Only you can."

Wyla's gaze, so close and direct, stirred Torin's blood. When she looked at him like that her eyes gained such depth that he wished he could dive into them, to shed his every defence and bare his soul. She waited a moment more for him to speak but his words all stuck in his throat. Wyla stepped back and turned her eyes to the tapestry.

"The sword," she said, "It wouldn't budge for me. But when you drew it in Ballur's barrow it nearly jumped out of the scabbard. Why do you think that was?"

Torin shook his head, clearing it of whatever he had meant to say before the moment had passed. "I think I've been cursed by the blade. There was not any blood in those creatures."

He looked down at the doomed figures being cut down by sharp *nidavel* blades all the way up the rocky slope toward the precipitous outcrop. "I think Lysa tricked me into drawing *Tyrfang* so that it would be my end. Now the blade has a grudge and refuses to be drawn until my hand pulls it out."

"You really believe in the curse?"

Torin pointed to the next banner. "Look what it did to him."

Further along the wall, dim in the grey shadows where the torch light hardly reached, was Ballur the Bright. He lay in the middle of a green meadow with *Tyrfang* stuck deep in his belly. Fyra, adorned with gold and silver in her bridal dress, knelt in anguish beside the fair-faced *jotur*. All around them, the *huldur* wailed and cried. In the bottom corners of the tapestry, one on each side, lurked Lysa and Thrain, the two that had hated Ballur the most and so conspired to curse the blade. Around each villain's head was a series of foreboding runes in knotted threads of red and black.

A moment later, a large silhouette appeared in the doorway. A heavy-set *jotur* servant cleared his throat. "Thrudnir the Wise, Lord of Jokulheim and King of the Mountain, demands your presence in his feasting hall."

The others stirred from where they lay at the center of the room. Aldrin sat up and stretched, his movements stiff and slow. "Well, if Lord Thrudnir demands it, then we had better come quickly. Tell me, is his mood any better than yesterday when he tried to cook us?"

The giant stiffened his lip. "The Mountain King does as he will."

The *jotur* moved aside as three more servants came into the room, one with a flickering torch on a stand and the others with a long copper basin full of steaming water, much shorter than the one in Thrudnir's hall the night before and far wider. Torin's stomach lurched as he recalled how Gerd had tried to cook them in the giant's kitchen. But this basin seemed much too decorative to be a cooking dish, and water in a free-standing tub could hardly be hot enough to scald them. The first servant set the torch at the center of the room while the other two shuffled along to place the basin right beside it. It was waist deep and stood on four clawed feet that looked like the paws of a wolf or a bear. The whole company fit into the basin with plenty of room to spare, though Bari needed a hand to get up over its smooth polished edge.

Scented steam rose from the warm water, scented with cinnamon and cloves. Boughs of cedar had been tied to the far end and hung down into the bath. Torin felt the warm tingle of the winter spices all over his aching body. There were a few small, dark stones in the bottom of the tub which sent up streams of bubbles so that the bath churned in a sweet-scented swirl.

Once they were all settled in the bath, the *jotur* servant sniffed. "Be sure to wash well. I could smell your lot from all the way down the hall."

Grimsa's eyes lit up. "Will there be breakfast?"

"Only for those that hurry, you sluggish oaf," said Wyla. "Those who come late *are* breakfast."

Torin pulled his fingers through his greasy hair until it was fresh and clean. Little by little, the dirt and grime on his arms and chest washed away. Long scratches from the barrow creatures stood out in bright reds along his arms and a cluster of purple bruises ran over his ribs. Every cut stung as it sunk into the water but once soaked, faded into little more than a dull ache.

"This is more like it," Bari said. "A bit of a frosty reception yesterday but I guess the *jotur* this far north are not used to having guests."

Azal slid down to his neck in the swirling water. "Well said, Bari. By the king's sceptre, I'll have quite the book to write when we return."

Aldrin winced as he stretched his neck then scoffed. "You? Write a book? Shouldn't you first learn to read?"

The prince sighed. "You're right. Writing a whole book sounds rather bothersome. Perhaps I'll simply orate my travels to one of the scribes in my father's court."

Bari chuckled. "You seem rather confident that we will come out of all this alive."

"This Lord Thrudnir reminds me of my father and my sister," Azal said. "If he wanted us dead, we already would be."

Bari splashed his face with steaming water and let it trickle down his cheeks. "I would bet my beard that we will have more trouble from the Mountain King before we ever make it home."

Another one of the *jotur* servants, a giantess with round cheeks and wide hips, came in from the hall.

"Still lounging in the baths?" she said. "Come now, you cannot keep the Mountain King waiting."

She set a folded pile of new clothes beside the bath for each one of them: a blue wool tunic with dark leather pants and a white fur cloak. "Lord Thrudnir will not suffer the sight or the smell of your travel-worn garments again, so I have sewn you all something more suitable. You are all rather small, and I had to guess your sizes. It wasn't easy sewing the stitches so tight together! Certainly not my best work, but it will have to do. Hurry up now!"

Torin stepped out of the warm basin and shook off as best he could. He picked up the trousers first and found they were lined with soft fur on the inside. It was nearly a perfect fit as he pulled them up and tied them at the waist. The tunic was made of tightly knit fabric dyed a brilliant blue that ran soft against his skin. As he pulled the garment up over his shoulders, it fell down just a bit past his waist. Torin thought that he had never worn anything so finely tailored to his form. Around the collar was a border of intricate stitching, gold and silver threads that crisscrossed in an intricate knotwork pattern. Last, he wrapped the white fur cloak around his shoulders. It fit snugly as he closed the silver clasp together across his chest. Torin then felt a warmth in his chest such as he had not felt since he had departed from Gatewatch.

The others, equally arrayed in such fine garments, exclaimed with delight, all except for Wyla. She pulled on her tunic only to find it was a full-length dress sewn diagonally across the front so that it pulled tight across her hips. The neckline was richly embroidered with elaborate gold and silver stitching and the hem along the bottom was slanted.

"By thundering Orr, what is this?" she said. "Am I really expected to go waltzing around in this ridiculous piece of pageantry?"

The giantess' eyebrows shot up and she huffed. "It is a dress. You may have come from an uncivilized hovel where women go tromping around in men's clothing, but in Jokulheim the women must wear dresses."

Wyla sneered as she looked down at the delicate stitches. "How am I supposed to fight trolls in this?"

The giantess flushed blue in her cheeks, and she stuck up her nose. "I can assure you with utmost certainty that there are no trolls here in Lord Thrudnir's hall."

"Who's got a knife?" said Wyla, "I'll fix this up quick."

"Don't you dare! That hemline took me nearly an hour!"

Wyla glanced over at Torin with a sour look on her face. He grinned. She clenched her fists and stomped out the door after the others. Torin saw the giantess roll her eyes as he strode by her to join Wyla and the rest of the company out in the wide-open tunnelway.

Down they went, round and round, until the spiraling walkway came to an end at the towering arched door into Thrudnir's feasting hall. Both doors were wide open and all the candles that had burned through the last of their wicks the night before had been replaced with fresh ones. The flicker of the flames danced against the walls as busy servants hurried between the tables to satisfy the crowd of *jotur* guests.

"Ah," said Lord Thrudnir. The giant's voice boomed through the hall and Torin's heart pounded at the rumbling sound. "The strange mortal company has arrived!"

Grimsa leaned toward Torin. "So, we've gone from dinner, to prisoners, to guests. If we stick around much longer, we'll all be sitting on Thrudnir's lap like pets."

Aldrin motioned for him to hush. "Tie your loose tongue, Grimsa Jarnskald, before it gets us in trouble!"

As Grimsa opened his mouth to respond, Lord Thrudnir's voice rang out again. "Come! Sit by the fire. You must be well rested by now. My servants are bringing out breakfast: wild-berry cakes, roasted hazelnuts, crisp strips of bacon, and warm-spiced cider."

Aldrin bowed before the Mountain King and called out. "Far and wide we will tell of your generosity and hospitality, oh Lord of the Mountain."

Thrudnir popped a whole cake in his mouth. "Do not baste me with compliments, as you would your petty *madur* kings. Even an immortal lord like me scarcely has time for that kind of drivel. Besides, there is no need. I have already set my mind on helping you."

Torin took a step toward the Mountain King. "You are going to help us reach the Everspring?"

"Yes," Thrudnir said, "in a manner of speaking. Though perhaps it is more accurate to say that I will be helping you to help me."

None of the companions liked the sound of that, Torin least of all.

"Hjartahall," said Thrudnir, "lays far to the North beside the surging Everspring. The mighty hunting lodge where I spent my happiest years chasing reindeer, grey elk, and the great white bear, has stood abandoned since that dreadful day when Lysa unleashed the Shadowstalker. Guarded by that vile spawn from a realm far below, not a soul that has crossed Hjartahall's wide threshold has ever returned. Many brave *jotur* that have attempted to win fame and to gain my favour by unseating the nightmare-creature, but none have succeeded."

Thrudnir gave a tired sigh. "So here I sit, year after year, in my stuffy wartime fortress of Jokulheim. I long to feel the fresh northern air blowing in through the open door. My heart yearns to see the frothing waters of the Everspring through my window at dawn, and to gaze at the sun rising over the distant sea. My ears ache to hear the hunting horn blown to the chorus of barking hounds!"

Torin narrowed his eyes. "So, you want us to face the Shadowstalker?"

Thrudnir shrugged. "Of course, I wish there was another way, but you will never pull a draught from the ancient spring unless the Shadowstalker is slain. It jealously guards its blood-stained seat and it will not suffer visitors to pass by with their lives. So perhaps it is you, more than me, that needs the Shadowstalker dead and gone."

Thrudnir paused to nibble another golden-crusted cake, then continued. "See, you may have repaid your debt of intrusion by entertaining my guests with your riddles, but the crime of breaking into Ballur's tomb still stands unaccounted for. However, in my great benevolence, I would consider the liberation of Hjartahall as fair payment for your grievous error."

Torin raised one eyebrow. "And if we refuse?"

The Mountain King snorted. "Refuse? Well, I suppose I would accept a white bear hide, stripped, cleaned, and dried, covered down to the last hair in gleaming red gold." The giant waited a moment in mocking silence. "But should you not be able to produce such a treasure, then I guess I will have to settle for having your heads boiled up in a soup instead. What do you say, Torin Ten-Trees?"

The giant's offer was like being handed a knife, blade-first, when one desperately needed a weapon; Torin saw no choice but to take it. He looked at the others. Grimsa shrugged and Wyla grinned. Bari and Azal both looked a bit pale, and Aldrin had a grimace drawn over his face.

"We accept, Lord Thrudnir," Torin said. "If it is our fate to slay that foul creature, then so be it. If not, then we take the advice of the skalds."

> *The faint may flee both sword and spear*
> *And run when battle's roar draws near*
> *Yet still the swiftest Time shall slay*
> *So grasp at glory while you may*

Thrudnir clapped his hands. "Well spoken! May Ym's strength fill your sword arm, and may your courage be as firm as Yg's towering boughs." The giant raised his cup to the company and toasted them. "This strange fellowship of mortals is increasing my opinion of your kind. You are proof enough that not all are feeble and cowardly! Now bring in breakfast so that our guests may leave with a fire in their hearts and a warm meal in their bellies!"

The company sat near the fire at the center of the feasting hall, as they had the previous night, except this time the servants laid the furs over lengths of firewood as makeshift benches. Every companion was given an enormous pastry of light-flaked dough. Of course, to the *jotur* these were hardly bite-sized morsels but to Torin and the others they were nearly as big as their heads. At the center of the pastry was a thick cream mixed with sweet purple berries and nutmeg. Bowls of savory nuts were served, each roasted brown and rolled in flakes of sea salt. Then came sizzling strips of bacon which were so large that Torin could only manage to finish one. Grimsa somehow managed three. To wash it all down, each companion drank a thimble filled to the brim with warm-spiced cider. None of them managed to empty their cup, because it was constantly filled up again by the *jotur* servants who attended them.

Breakfast was over too soon, at least as far as Torin and the rest of the company were concerned. The servants cleared away the food and the mortal company rose to their feet as the Mountain King gave them an official send off.

"Hjartahall, which stands beside the Everspring, lays a half day's ride to the North," said Thrudnir. "You would be wise to wear the wool tunics and white cloaks that I commissioned last night instead of the road-stained garments you came in. Those grey rags, lined with fur and waxed against the rain, might fare well in the damp forest, but here in the north there is little need to worry about getting wet. These white fur cloaks will keep you warm against the blustering wind and will hide you from sight if you need to take cover behind a bank of snow."

Thrudnir lifted something off the table and held it up. Torin recognized it as *Tyrfang*, still sheathed in its scabbard. "As for this foul weapon, I am glad to see it leave my hall. Jolvar's riders will cast bones to decide who must carry the wretched thing. It would make me glad to know that Lysa's cursed sword was used against the Shadowstalker, an abomination that she herself summoned! Though if you were to leave it where it lies when my riders toss it in the dirt, I think that may be the wiser. What but harm can come from a blade cursed by both the *nidavel* and the *huldur*?"

As Torin pondered the *jotur's* words, Aldrin shuffled forward and took a deep bow. The old man's swollen bruises were like a dark purple shadow under his eyes and his stiff posture was a sure sign of many other less visible injuries.

"Lord Thrudnir," Aldrin said. "If it were in my power to aid this company in liberating your beloved Hjartahall, I surely would. However, this difficult journey has nearly broken my body and I fear another day of hard riding might be the end of me. With the utmost humility, I request an extension of the hospitality you have shown for a few days more, so that I can recover my strength."

Aldrin coughed and then cleared his throat. "I have sworn an oath to serve my king until my dying breath and if that breath should be drawn today, then so be it. But if there is more that I can do in the service of yourself, Lord Thrudnir, and that of my beloved king, I should wish to be of as much use as possible before

I meet my end." The Lorekeeper turned to Torin. "That is, if the leader of our able company would grant it."

Torin and the rest of the company looked at Aldrin with wide eyes. For the first time Torin noticed that only a shadow remained of the proud scholar who had blustered into Fjellhall a few days before. Without his thick cloak, the company could see how frail the old Lorekeeper really was and how deep his eyes had sunk beneath the wrinkles of his wispy white brow.

"Of course," said Torin. "Most your age would never have even made it to Gatewatch."

Thrudnir nodded slowly. "Very well. No one in my hall goes hungry! You shall wait here until this company has cleansed the hall of the darkness which now inhabits it."

Torin frowned. "And if we don't return?"

Thrudnir shrugged. "Then this old *madur* will be waiting here for a very long time."

Before Torin could reply, Aldrin bowed again then raised his arms toward the Mountain King. "I shall never forget your grace and benevolence, Lord Thrudnir. With deepest admiration, I thank you for your generosity."

Azal stepped up to Aldrin and grasped the old man's shoulder. "I've never seen you like this," said Azal. "Why didn't you tell us how serious your injuries were?"

"Prince Azalweir," Aldrin said, "I am not the kind of man who is well acquainted with reaching his own limits, yet I am also not so foolish as to push myself any further beyond them."

Azal shook his head. "Perhaps we should wait a day or two so you can recover your strength. Then, perhaps, we can all go together?"

The Lorekeeper waved his arms. "Nonsense! I will not be the cause of such a significant delay." The old man paused for a moment as he looked the prince in the eye. "This is the time for strength, son of Ghezelweir, and to apply all that I have taught you over these past few years. I suspect the success or failure of this final task depends upon it."

Aldrin reached inside his cloak and drew out both the Greyraven's map and a translucent flask made of green glass. "Take these. I am entrusting them to you, my prince. You must reach the Everspring and complete the task which we were sent out to accomplish."

Azal's eyes grew wider as the Lorekeeper placed both the map and the flask into his hands. The prince opened his mouth to speak but then shut it. Then, as he closed his fingers around the two objects, a devilish grin tugged at the corner of his mouth. "Aren't you going to try to stop me from going? Aren't you going to tell me that this is all much too dangerous for a king's son?"

Aldrin shrugged. "Has my telling you that ever stopped you before?"

Azal embraced the old Lorekeeper. "I will make you proud, Aldrin, I promise."

Aldrin's wrinkled face tightened as he returned the Azal's embrace. "May the grace of your royal blood guide you, young Azalweir." He stepped back and turned to the others. "To you, Torin Ten-Trees, Wyla Wightbane, and Grimsa Jarnskald: may your arms be filled with the strength of Orr in every strike against that shadowy beast. And to Bari Wordsmith: bring greetings to Mastersmith Ognir on behalf of King Ghezelweir of Armeah if this should be our last meeting before you journey home to Myrkheim. Now, delay no longer on my account!"

After saying their goodbyes, the company left Aldrin in the feasting hall and followed Jolvar and Ulfrun up the spiraling hall to the main entryway. At the top of the stairwell, six horses had already been saddled and equipped with all they would need for the day's journey.

Five of the riders would bear a companion, while the last would carry *Tyrfang*. After a second round of laying bones to decide who had to carry Grimsa, the others were each assigned to a rider. Ulfrun, the giantess that had dragged them to Jokulheim in the first place, was assigned to take Torin. However, this time he did not have to ride tied up like a saddle bag, but instead sat in a small notch in the saddle in front of her.

When the riders were ready to depart, Jolvar called for the gate to be opened. In the shadowy room that held the gate winch, Torin thought he saw a set of ancient *jotur* eyes glaring at them. No doubt, if it was Gerd the Old, she would shed no tears over their departure.

Torin braced himself against the icy wind that blew in through the widening gate. Ulfrun kicked her heels into the horse's hindquarters. As her mount lurched forward, Torin was flung back, and would have fallen off to one side if he had not gripped to the leather saddle with white knuckles. The horse's hoofbeats fell into a pounding rhythm as the stony trail flew by beneath its feet.

The sun was rising over the wide plain in cloudy plumes of brilliant orange as they raced away from Jokulheim's crystal-pillared gate. Torin thought it might have been the second morning after their descent into the giant's fortress, though he could not be sure as there was no such thing as day and night down below. The rush of air, fresh and crisp against his cheeks, made his eyes water, and he was glad to breathe it deep.

Since Ulfrun and Jolvar rode at the head of the column, Torin's view of the landscape was not obstructed by the clouds of dust kicked up by the other horses. Behind them rose a strange mountain range, towering ash-black hills capped in ice of which Jokulheim was merely the first. Ahead lay an open plain with little more than drifts of snow, tufts of wild grass, and the occasional weathered knoll which stood in defiance of the whistling wind.

Once they had passed out of the long reach of Jokulheim's rugged arms, they veered to the west, with the rising wind gusting up against their backs. If Torin recalled correctly, a half day's ride southeast would have taken them back to Ballur's barrow on the way to Gatewatch. Instead, they pressed on westward, gaining ground at incredible speed. For the rest of the morning, they rode alongside the range of mountains to the north which seemed to grow ever taller.

When the sun reached its peak in the sky, they came across a wide creek, but so shallow that even Torin could have waded through it if the water had not been so icy cold.

Jolvar stopped and dismounted. "That was the easy part of our journey. Let the horses drink before we climb up the gorge."

Ulfrun hopped down from the saddle and led her horse to the stream. She pointed at the horizon far to the west. "Look! The reindeer are on the move. There must be a few hundred of them."

Off in the distance, Torin saw a cluster of brown and grey specks. "Reindeer?"

Jolvar held his hand up to block the midday sun. "One of the few creatures that can scrape a living from this frozen tundra. Those and the white wolves that hunt them." The *jotur* shook his head and let his arm fall to his side. "These plains used to be covered in trees, much like the *huldur* wood around Ballur's tomb. That was before the wars with the *asyr*, and before the endless assaults of crackling lightning bolts that seared the land with fire."

Ulfrun gazed off at the herd of reindeer in the distance a moment longer, then she squeezed Jolvar's shoulder. "Trees will grow here again one day."

Jolvar stood silent in his own thoughts a moment more, then turned back toward his horse. "Alright, back on your mounts. We have a long ride home after we deliver this strange company to their doom."

After crossing the stream, they turned due north and rode with the wind coming side on. The jagged peaks over the horizon looked like the crooked teeth of a broken jawbone, ever growing in size so that they nearly devoured the sky. They followed a winding trail up a narrow valley between two of the peaks. Its towering walls were stark and treeless with silver-blue sheets of glacial ice along the top of both ridges. Trickling water leaked from the frozen plates and flowed together at the center of the gorge to create a bright gleaming stream. Hardy mountain flowers and slimy green moss along the bank cut the grey landscape with a thin streak of colour.

Along one of the ridges, Torin saw a flash of white. A moment later another appeared and then a third. Against the coal-black mountain, he could make out the shape of long muzzles and pairs of pointed ears. Each creature fixed the band of horses with an unblinking glare and watched them pass by from an outcrop just below the top of the ridge. Torin shivered. Never had he seen a northern wolf, with its hunched shoulders and its grim snarl. And when the wolves had passed out of sight, Torin felt the hairs at the back of his neck stand on end he recalled their ghostly forms.

As they reached the northern end of the gorge, a gust of cold, damp air rushed by. Torin pulled his white fur cloak tighter around his chest. There, at the valley's head, stood a sheer rock face split in two by a sunlit column of water. Billowing clouds of mist floated off the surging falls and refracted the afternoon light into a brilliant splay of colours, red and yellow and green and blue. It was thin, no wider than a few paces across at the top, but fell from such a dizzying height that Torin's stomach clenched just from looking at it.

Ulfrun pointed up to the top of the waterfall and shouted over the freezing wind. "That is where we will leave you. From there, your fate is in the hands of the *nornir*."

Torin's heart pounded as they approached the bottom of the cliff. He wondered if anyone in Gatewatch would learn of their demise if this dreaded Shadowstalker tore them to pieces. More likely, all those back home would continue to wait for a reunion that would never come. First, he thought of Signa looking out over the wilds every day in hopes of seeing Grimsa. Then he thought of the glimpse he had caught of Keymaster Signy where she stood atop the Western Gate as they rode away. Torin closed his eyes and imagined her watching his father's men take him away when he was just a child. After all those years, he had returned to her in Gatewatch. And, if the gods would grant it, Torin was determined to return again.

17

◇ SHADOWSTALKER ◇

AT THE END OF THE VALLEY, they started up a long series of grueling switchbacks that snaked up toward the top of the falls. The column of thundering water sent sheets of chilled mist tumbling over the rocky trail. The gusts of moist air blown about by the freezing wind would have been deadly if not for their white fur cloaks and the leather trousers that kept the damp off their skin.

The higher they climbed, the farther the view stretched out behind them. In the distance, Torin caught sight of the reindeer herd as they trekked across the empty plain, a shifting mass of browns and greys against the black soil and white drifts of snow. Beyond that, on the very edge of the horizon, ran a thin band of green, the wild forests around Gatewatch. Torin had once thought that the wood was endless. He had picked his way through its gnarled paths for weeks at a time while hunting trolls and had never once come close to the edge. Now, he was so far away that the wood could hardly be seen. Had they reached the end of the world, he wondered, or were they simply crossing its border into the next?

The roar of the falls fell to a dull rumble as they came over the crest of the cliffside trail. The road leveled out onto a wide open plain. Across the alpine plateau was an enormous lake of turquoise blue which fed the thundering falls. The rippling water of its surface gleamed a strangely luminescent colour that seemed almost otherworldly. Far across the lake, another set of dark jagged mountains rose even higher than the ones they had just passed through.

Jolvar and Ulfrun urged their horses on, and the others did their best to keep up. Torin felt the lean shoulders of Ulfrun's mount tense. He wondered if the steed recognized this place and knew what terrible danger loomed ahead.

They followed the lake's edge around its eastern shore as the sun tilted past its zenith and began its descent down toward the western horizon. There they came to an old stone bridge made of finely cut slabs of granite. Over the years, the wind had worn down its sharp corners, and orange lichens crusted most of its surface. Still, not even a strand of hair could have slipped between the carefully chiseled blocks. Beneath the bridge ran a rushing river which spilled out from the lake at its eastern edge and flowed over the gentle slope of the plateau.

Jolvar pulled the reins of his horse and held up one arm. "This is as far as we take you. From here, the trail leads straight to Hjartahall on the north end of the lake. Behind it you will find the Everspring, if you can slay the Shadowstalker." The other riders gave a grim chuckle. "Drop the cursed blade and the other supplies then let us be off."

Ulfrun grabbed Torin by the scruff of his cloak, then hoisted him over the saddle and down to the ground. The giantess looked at him and grinned. "I like you, Torin Ten-Trees. You *madur* are troublesome, but your mischief is a welcome break from the endless cycle of passing seasons. Thrudnir's eagle Hraesvelgir will fly over the lake tomorrow to bring us news of your death. When that happens, I will drink to the memory of you and your company."

Torin was not sure if Ulfrun expected him to thank her for the gesture, so he simply nodded. The other companions were unceremoniously dumped onto the rocky trail before the giant bearing *Tyrfang* cast it down onto the rugged stones. That same *jotur* also dropped Grimsa and Wyla's axes, which had been confiscated at Ballur's barrow, along with Bari's bow and Azal's sword. Torin's spearhead *Skrar*, repaired by the *jotur* and fitted with a rune-etched shaft, was added to the pile as well. Last of all, the rider left a canvas sack, with enough provisions for what was expected to be their final meal.

Ulfrun wheeled around on her mount as the others started down the trail. Before she sped away, she waved at Torin. "Farewell, Torin Ten-Trees! Ym's strength to you, heir of both *huldur* and *madur* blood. May Yg's wisdom find you in your final hour, Mindthorn. Look to gain glory! Your ancestors await you at the feasting table in Valhol!"

With that, she dug her heels into her horse's flanks and raced to catch the others. Unburdened by their companions, the *jotur* riders went swiftly south on the road from which they had come. Torin stood at the foot of the bridge and watched them shrink into the distance. He had little doubt that the horses were as eager as the *jotur* to be rushing away from Hjartahall instead of toward it.

Torin trudged over to where *Tyrfang* lay and picked it up. As he looked down at the rune-sketched scabbard, he felt as if the sword was sneering at him. His fingers were cold, and he fumbled a bit as he tied it to his belt.

"Damn those maggot-bellied *jotur*," Torin said. "They could have at least taken us within bowshot of Hjartahall."

Grimsa grunted as he hefted the provisions over his shoulder and snatched up his axe. "Immortals, maybe, but yellow-livered, blue-nosed, milk-slurpers all the same."

Azal rubbed his arms beneath his white fur cloak. He squinted at the steep hill ahead of them as a chill breeze rose from across the lake. "I am beginning to think that this was not a very good idea, after all."

"Well," said Wyla, "I guess we could just take a two week stroll back to Gatewatch on nothing but a single meal." Wyla picked up an axe and used the sharp edge to cut her dress so that the fabric fell away from the waist down. Along with her brown leather pants, the well sewn top almost looked like a tunic. She smiled at her handiwork, then tied the axe to her belt. "I would rather take my chances battling the beast that has these *jotur* scared stiff."

Bari shivered. "Besides, Thrudnir would send the same riders that brought us here to hunt us down if we broke our agreement. We would stand a better chance outrunning those ghastly wolves that leered at us all the way up the gorge."

Torin tightened his belt and started for the bridge. "We left Gatewatch in search of the Everspring and here we are. There is no road back now." The others said nothing and followed close behind.

No birds flew down to rest on the surface of the lake and no trees sprouted up along its rocky shore. Beyond the wide stone bridge, the path trailed away from the lake shore and turned north up a steep hill. For the better part of the afternoon, they followed the trail as it rose sharply above the north end of the lake. By Thrudnir's account, the path had not been used for almost one hundred years, and yet it was not overgrown. Torin heard a distant rumble as they continued to climb, a dull roar which came from some place high above the lake. Though Torin could not see its source, he reckoned that such a thunderous noise could only be one thing: the Everspring.

Torin caught his first glimpse of Hjartahall as the sun sank to the west. The hall stood on a rocky outcrop above a wide set of steps cut into the mountain's southern edge, the only approach. All the way up the stone stairway were pillars carved with monstrous faces etched in runes. These steps led to a spectacular door with four gilded pillars to either side, each connected by rounded arches.

Above Hjartahall's glinting pillars there rose a steep pitched roof with black slate tiles, some of which had come loose over long years of weathering the northern winds. On either end of the roof, two enormous wooden beams met in the center at a sharp angle, each carved with knotted beasts and swirling foliage. When the company reached the base of the stone steps that led up to the entrance, they stopped and set down their supplies.

"Perhaps we should eat here," said Torin. He recalled then that their flint and steel had been lost back at the Vimur when their horses were spooked. "Can you make a fire, Azal?"

Azal rubbed his hands together and blew into them to warm them up. "By the king's sceptre, I wish Aldrin was here now."

"Well, he isn't," said Wyla. "Can you make a fire or not?"

Azal swallowed then nodded. "It will be easier with something to burn. I am not sure if some twigs pulled from this low brush will be dry enough, but I can try."

The rest of the company spread out to collect whatever kindling they could scavenge, though each was careful not to wander out of sight of the others. After a few false starts, a lot of smoke, and a great many curses, Azal managed to spark one of the smaller twigs. The others crouched around the prince to protect the flame from the wind, and soon after they had a small fire to warm themselves.

From the canvas sack, Grimsa pulled strips of smoked cod, a loaf of bread baked with herbs and garlic, and a wheel of hard white cheese. There was also a wineskin which they quickly emptied into a set of silver cups. There they sat around the fire in silence as they ate and warmed their hands. An evening breeze picked up, so they huddled closer to protect the flame. Torin felt the chill of it down to his soul. As he looked around the fire at the others nibbling what would likely be their last meal, his heart ached.

Torin raised his vessel toward the others. "Whatever happens tonight, I am glad to have called you all friends. It was never my intention to put you in such a dire position, but it seems our fate is to face this creature and there is no other company that I'd have by my side for the task ahead."

Wyla looked up at Torin. She thought for a moment, then straightened her back and raised her cup to Torin's. "Long live The Gatewatch."

Grimsa raised his cup as well. "And the Greyraven."

Bari stood up and held his wine out. "Long live the Mastersmith!"

Azal was the last to raise his cup. It shook in his hands as he shivered from the cold, but the prince's eyes were as hard. "And long live the King!"

With hope kindled, the company began to plan their approach. The only way up, besides scaling a sheer face of rugged rock, was to ascend the huge stone steps. At the top stood Hjartahall with its towering iron-bound doors facing south over the lake. From the bottom of the hill, they could see that one door was slightly ajar, a sliver of an interior shrouded in dark shadows.

After deliberating for some time, they decided to consult the Greyraven's map for any clues about what might await them inside. Azal pulled the map from his cloak and unrolled it over the cold stones. Torin held two of the corners while Azal held the others. Then, together, they let the last of the tiny flames flicker up from their campfire and brush the bottom of the map. The azure ink lit up with a blue glow and burned brightly right beside the illustration of the Everspring. Bari leaned over the map and squinted at the cold-burning script.

> *Hjartahall, the empty throne*
> *Drip of blood and clack of bone*
> *Swirl of dust 'neath gallows grim*
> *As moonlight stirs the dread within*

Grimsa shuddered. "By the gods, I'm also starting to think we should have stayed in Gatewatch."

"Swirl of dust? Clack of bone?" said Wyla. "Damn all these cursed riddles!"

Bari tugged at his beard. "The clues may become clearer when we enter the hall, but it seems to me that the creature only emerges at night. Perhaps in the last bit of daylight, we should explore the hall?"

The others nodded and prepared to ascend the enormous stone steps. By then the fire was smoldering, soon to be extinguished by the wind. They abandoned the empty canvas sack and the wineskins, then started the climb with weapons in hand. Between the gusts of whistling wind, Torin heard Lysa's voice whisper to him through the Greyraven's silver ring as it dangled from his neck.

I promised you power. Now look at you.

Torin clenched his jaw but said nothing as he continued to clamber up the giant stairway.

I gave you a second chance. It was a chance to redeem yourself and avenge your humiliation at the hands of the jotur. Instead, you groveled before Thrudnir and now serve him like a reeking thrall.

Torin spoke under his breath, and he pushed himself up the next step. "Well, I'd rather serve a giant than a kin-killer and infant slayer."

That thing that crawled out of my sister's womb was an abomination. It never would have been worthy of the songs of the huldur.

Torin hissed. "He was your nephew, your own blood."

If it had been my own child, I would have thrown it from the highest cliff. To put it to sleep with poison spores was a mercy.

Torin's stomach clenched tight, and he stomped ahead toward the next enormous stone step. He hated to admit that, for the briefest moment, he imagined Signy throwing him away as a child. Had she not thrown him away, though? Perhaps not thrown away, but sent him away to grow up without her, motherless. The image stung him deep in his chest. Rage burned so hot in his chest that he did not feel the northern cold.

I forget that you've never heard the songs of the huldur. The ancient melodies of our people would stir your blood in ways that you could never imagine. They would spur you to do things you thought you could never do, to achieve things you could only dream of.

"I doubt it," said Torin. "Speaking of songs, why don't you speak in verse or sing like Thrudnir said you once did? Whatever became of your far-famed voice?"

A silence followed, an empty, hateful pause.

Power always has its price.

"As does evil," Torin said. "And if the gods have willed that I am the one to pay you back for your crimes, then so be it."

You will serve me, Torin Ten-Trees. In fact, in a way you already have.

"Enough of your lies."

You will learn the truth soon enough. Your will is strong Torin, but not strong enough. Once I break you, I can mold you to whatever form I please. You'll wish you had bent your knee to me earlier. They all do.

"You've underestimated me before."

You've disappointed me before. But now I have you exactly where I want you.

Torin smirked. "Now I know you are lying. Once we have a draught from the Everspring, we'll return to Noros and heal the king. What will become of your schemes then?"

Who do you think crafted the map that your witless Lorekeeper carried to Gatewatch? They were right when they said that no nidavel could have made such a thing. The map is an ancient huldur treasure that once belonged to my father. I led Araldof Greyraven to it. Indeed, I led him to many such treasures, but in the end, he failed me. He is too old and weak to fulfill my vision. Mortals expire so quickly, you see.

Torin stopped where he stood on the second last step and stared up at the mighty hall that rose before him. A shiver ran over his body as he gazed at its doors.

You thought you were escaping me all this time. No, Torin, you are about to step beneath the dreaded rafters of this cursed hall and into the blood-thirsty maw of the Shadowstalker, my favourite pet. The next time we speak, you will be begging for mercy.

Torin gripped the Greyraven's ring, the red rubies scalding hot in his hand, and tore it from its chain. Then, with all his strength, he hurled it over the precipitous edge toward the lake.

Wyla watched the glint of silver fall down and out of sight between the rocks far below them. "By the gods," said Wyla. "Was that the Greyraven's ring?"

"Damn the ring."

"It was Lysa, wasn't it? Is she whispering to you again?"

Torin turned to face Hjartahall. "Not anymore."

The whole company stood on the broad porch in front of the towering doors. The mountain peaks had punctured the sun's glowing sphere to the west, so that a wash of red and purple light spilled out over the horizon. The lake was ablaze with reflections of those reds and purples. Soon the sun would be swallowed up, and night would fall over the desolate plateau.

Once the others had made it over the final step, Torin gripped *Skrar* by its rune-etched shaft and approached the threshold. Wyla and Grimsa followed close behind him with axes in hand. A huge copper torc hung from each carved door panel. One of the doors had been left slightly ajar. Torin took a cautious step into the opening and peered within.

A few streaks of light streamed into the high-raftered hall through the open door, and others from the gaps in the ceiling wherever the stone roof tiles were missing. But nothing stirred inside Hjartahall, and it stood in terrible disarray. Benches were overturned and bright silken banners that once displayed Thrudnir's runic sigil hung off the walls in shreds. Cutlery and drinking vessels lay scattered around the room alongside a smattering of rusted weapons. Worst were the streaks of crusted blood that trailed along the floor and the reddish splatters behind the throne that stood empty across the hall.

Torin slipped through the open door. The bottoms of his boots were sticky against the floor as he stepped over the debris, dust, and scattered bones. Dark cobwebs had gathered in all the corners and wispy threads of silk hung down from the shadowy rafters above them. Torin motioned silently for the others to follow. Wyla, Azal, and Bari managed to enter Hjartahall in silence, but the gap was too small for Grimsa. A terrible grinding screech echoed through the empty hall as he squeezed through.

Wyla raised her axe and spoke in a low, harsh voice. "By the gods, you might as well blow a bloody horn to announce our arrival."

Bari held his finger up and the others stopped. The *nidavel* strained his ears then whispered. The last echoes of the creaking hinges died out a moment later. "Can you hear that?"

Torin listened but could not hear anything. "Hear what?"

"The way that creak echoed through the room," said Bari, "There must be a tunnel somewhere." The *nidavel* pointed toward the east end of the hall. "Yes, I would bet my beard that there is a tunnel somewhere down there."

Azal's eyes went wide as he stared into the dark. "How could you possibly know that from a sound?"

Bari shrugged. "One of the useful things that comes from living your life underground, I guess."

The company crept along the edge of the room to the east end of the hall. As their eyes adjusted to the dim light, they saw that several of the broad wooden planks in the floor had been pulled up. At the center of the gap in the floor there was a large hole ringed with grime. Torin stepped toward the edge of the hole and peered down into it. It fell into darkness with no bottom in sight.

Azal jumped back. "What type of monster might live in such a wretched hole?"

Grimsa grimaced. "I think we'll find out sooner than we'd wish to."

The light was already turning from orange to red and it cast long shadows along the wall. Torin looked over the wreckage. It seemed that most of it had been pushed away from the gaping hole, whereas all the streaks of blood seemed to lead toward it. He pointed at the grim markings. "If the creature drags its prey back into the hole, then I would reckon it emerges from it as well."

Azal inspected the gory streaks and swallowed hard. "I can see the sense in that, but how does that help us?"

"We could set a trap," said Torin. "Look, these floorboards near the opening are loose. One of us could hide beneath one and strike at the creature from below while the others draw it out." He crouched down and shoved one of the loose boards aside. "It might even be wide enough for you to lie in, Grimsa."

Grimsa's eyes opened wide. "In there? It would be like lying in your own grave, waiting for that monster to appear! And what if you got stuck?"

"If the rest of you stood at the far end of the hall," said Torin, "I could shove the board aside and strike its underside with *Skrar* while it's distracted."

Bari leaned toward the gap in the floorboards and shuddered. "Does this Shadowstalker even have an underside?"

"No more time for questions," Wyla said. "Look, the last of the sunlight is fading."

At the far end of the hall, the red sunset streak that ran across the room from the main door was hardly visible. Above them, the faint glow of the moon and the stars came through the gaps in the tiled roof, a cold silver light.

Torin shoved the wooden planks aside and lay down in the gap between the floorboards. "Quickly! Cover me up."

Grimsa knelt beside him and gripped his hand. "May the gods guide *Skrar's* sharpened edge straight into that creature's heart. We will distract this Shadowstalker as best we can."

Wyla opened her mouth as if to say something, then closed it. Torin looked back at her with a hard gaze. "Unleash Fyr's fury on that creature," said Torin. "Now close this up, quick!"

Wyla looked at him a moment longer, her steel-grey eyes pale in the darkness, then nodded and helped Grimsa conceal him under the loose floorboard.

As the board slid into place, Torin gripped *Skrar*. He could feel its flat edge against his chest as they pressed the wood plank down flush with the rest of the floor. Already, the air was uncomfortably warm and carried the scent of must. He breathed in slowly through his nose which was less than a finger's width from the broad plank above him. He held the smell of dust and aged cedar in his chest for as long as he could, then slowly exhaled. The sound of his own breathing seemed too loud in such a cramped space. He heard the others above him dragging benches across the hall into a barricade. Then the noise ceased and Hjartahall fell silent.

Torin thought he felt a strange heat radiating from *Tyrfang*. He recalled how the blade had glowed in Ballur's barrow and he suddenly felt an urge to draw it. But he was too tightly packed beneath the floor to move his arms. Again, he breathed deep and tried to relax. The heat of the sword in that cramped space soon became stifling.

A noise startled him, and his chest clenched tight. It was a dull clack, a familiar sound that Torin was surprised to recognize though he could not quite place it. Again, the same noise rattled through the air. Then he knew exactly what it was. As boys, Torin, Bryn, and Grimsa had picked up stray bones from cattle or sheep and imagined they were swords. The sound he heard was the same noise they had made by swinging bone swords against the wide wooden pillars of Ten-Tree Hall, the empty clack of bone on wood.

Another clack came from somewhere nearby, followed by two or three more in quick succession. Then, in a strange undulating pattern, there came a rising chorus of these sharp sounds, as if it were a whole gang of children beating the floor with dried bones in rhythm.

The sound was close, dangerously close, and Torin felt a terrible weight press down on him. The board above him creaked and bowed so that Torin had to twist his head to the side to avoid scraping his nose against the rough underside of the plank. At its lowest point, it pressed on his chest and slowly forced the air out of his lungs in a quiet hiss.

From the far end of the hall came Grimsa's booming voice. "Curse you, Shadowstalker! Odd's ravens greet you! Orr's thunder strike you! Fyr's fire take you!" He heard Wyla roar and Bari shout as the sound of rattling bones shook the floorboard above him.

The instant the creature moved forward, the board covering Torin sprung back into shape and he burst out from his hiding place. Above him, he saw nothing but a grey shadow. He blindly thrust *Skrar* upward with all his might. It cut into something hard, and a bit of greasy black blood came trickling down the shaft onto Torin's hands. He felt a terrible shudder through his forearms as the creature let out a chittering squeal. He held *Skrar* for as long as he could, though it was only a brief second. The thunder of clacking bones rang in Torin's ears from all sides, and the creature wrenched itself away with *Skrar* still lodged in its underside.

The shaft slipped in Torin's blood-slicked grip as the creature lurched forward. He sat up just in time to see a moon-white mass of broad, spiny bones jump up onto the wall and skitter straight up into the ink-black shadows above them. *Skrar* came hurtling down and stuck into the floor. Shreds of silken banners fluttered down where the creature had disappeared, and all fell silent.

The others rushed over from the far side of the hall. Grimsa extended his hand and yanked Torin up to his feet. Wyla pulled *Skrar* from where it had lodged in the floor and passed it back to Torin.

Bari's face was sickly pale. "By the Mastersmith, not in the deepest, most foul reaches of the underground caverns have I ever seen such a thing."

Wyla drew in a sharp breath and held up her axe. "It must have had a dozen legs, all white and hard like bone with wicked spines that curled out like fangs."

Azal's voice trembled in the dim grey dark. "Did anyone see its face?"

"It had no face," said Grimsa, "No eyes at all or at least none that I could see." He stared up and scanned the ceiling with wide eyes.

The clatter of the Shadowstalker's bones echoed through the hall from its highest reaches. The light in one of the small gaps between roof tiles disappeared, then reappeared in the time it would take to blink. Torin's heart thrashed inside his chest, and he searched the shadows above for any sign of movement.

From the center of the hall, there came a noise like an old dry hide being cut open or a cracked wine skin being torn in two. Torin's shoulders tensed and the whole company braced themselves, back-to-back, for whatever might emerge from the shadows. They waited a moment but heard nothing more.

Grimsa pointed toward the center of the hall and the others turned to see. In a low, hoarse voice he whispered to the others. "Look! It must be there."

At the center of the room, a fine yellow powder floated down through the faint rays of silver starlight. In a swirling cloud, like dust being blown off a long-forgotten surface, the delicate particles came to settle on the debris-littered floor.

Torin saw something else descend through the cloud of dust, a dark form suspended by a slick, wet thread. At first, he thought it might have been the creature, but it was far too small. The dripping thread was covered in a slime that shimmered like liquid silver wherever it caught the light. The dark form that hung from it swung back and forth with a sickening creak.

Wyla held the others back. "It must be some sort of trap. Don't move toward it."

The slimy thread stopped slithering out from the empty shadows, dropping into place with a jolt. Its formless shape hung at the center of the hall, halfway between the floor and the ceiling. A trace yellow dust fell around it, some which stuck to the slick thread. For a moment, it hung in silence, save for the sickly creak as it slowly swung from side to side.

The creature scuttled overhead. Between the click of the creature's bone legs against the rafters, came more quick ripping and puncturing sounds, like a room full of canvas bags being ransacked by knife-wielding thieves.

Torin saw a swirl of yellow powder above him. He jumped back only to see that puffs of dust were sprinkling down over the whole hall. A strange tingling came over his nose and he sneezed.

"The yellow dust," said Bari. "It is everywhere!"

Torin pulled the neck of his tunic up over his mouth with one arm and waved *Skrar* with the other. "Don't breathe it! Quick, toward the door."

The whole company rushed over to where they had entered the hall. High above them, the rumble of spiny legs thundered through the walls just a short distance ahead of them.

A stone roof tile slipped and fell through one of the gaps. It hit the floor just behind them with a deafening crash and shattered into splintered shards. Azal stumbled and cried out, trailing the others. Torin turned and saw the prince clutching his hand, a trickle of red blood running down his forearm. He darted back and seized Azal by the shoulders to drag him along.

The mighty doors of Hjartahall slammed shut. Grimsa threw himself against them a second later and pushed with all his might but could not move the towering iron-bound timbers. The others lined up against the door, but it was no use. The doors refused to budge. With wide eyes, the company backed up against the door and scanned the ceiling for any sign of movement.

The bitter taste of the yellow dust seeped into Torin's mouth. He spat and coughed. When he tried to wipe his mouth with the sleeve of his cloak, he found that it had also been covered in powder and so only tasted it more strongly. He cursed under his breath. His mind raced.

Wyla coughed. "What is it? A poison?"

Bari sputtered and spat. "A paralytic perhaps?"

Torin lifted his tunic to his mouth again and did his best to keep his breath shallow. The others clutched at their cloaks as well and huddled together against the wide beams of the locked door. Torin looked to the west end of the hall through the shroud of yellow dust for any sign of an opening to escape through.

But by now, the hall had fallen into darkness and every corner faded into an abyss of black shadow. The only light that leaked in came from the patchwork of holes in the ceiling. Torin stared up at the nearest gap and cursed; it must have been at least a dozen spear lengths above them.

Bari called to Azal, his voice muffled by his cloak. "Light! We need light! Azal, can you light a fire?"

Wyla coughed and shook her head. "By Orr, don't set off a fire. We're trapped in here! We'll all burn alive along with everything else in the hall."

Grimsa nodded but kept his eyes fixed on the dark ceiling above them for any sign of movement. "Wyla's right. More damned magic will only make this worse!"

"If we can't see this cursed creature, then how are we supposed to fight it?" said Bari.

As Torin turned to face Bari, he caught the look of Grimsa's face in the dim light. The huge man looked toward the center of the room with wide eyes, his jaw hung slack as if he were in a trance. Grimsa let go of his cloak as his arms fell limp at his sides.

"Grimsa?"

Grimsa mumbled a moment before his words trailed off into a whimper. His lip began to quiver, and two tears slipped out from the corners of his eyes. He stretched both hands toward the center of the room and lifted them up as if he was reaching for something, for someone.

Torin felt his heart pound in his chest, and he turned around slowly. There, at the center of the room, hung the dark mass they had seen descend a short while before. It creaked as it turned. Vaguely at first, then in painful detail, the form of a man strung up by his neck emerged from the shadow. The sound of Torin's heartbeat hammered against his ear drums as the mass turned and the figure's face fell into a sliver of moonlight.

The corpse's mouth hung open with its neck twisted at a cruel angle. It stared with a cold and hollow gaze into the dim upper reaches of the hall. All at once Torin recognized the figure's face. His eyes shot open wide, and his stomach lurched. It was the face of his father, Einar Ten-Trees.

18

◇ TYRFANG'S CURSE ◇

TORIN'S CHEST WENT COLD. A chill swept across his skin as blood drained from his face. At first, he did not believe it. How, he thought, how could it be? Torin tried to deny what he saw, in the hope of convincing himself that this was some other person. He could not tear his eyes away from the terrible sight. The proud forehead, the high-set cheeks, the angle of the nose, the thick chestnut beard, even the wrinkles around the corpse's eyes all suffocated any doubt that might have lingered in Torin's mind.

Einar Ten-Trees, Torin's father and longtime Lord of Ten-Tree Hall, hung as if on the gallows from a high beam at the center of the hall. There was no light in his eyes, his gaze as fixed and as cold as the glossy stare of a severed fish head. His face was pale and tinged with yellow from the powder that had fallen from the ceiling. The skin was an awful hue of purple where the blood pooled in his calloused hands and swollen feet, like a terrible bruise all over his limbs. Torin knew as he watched the body sway that the physical vessel that carried the warmth of his father's spirit was now empty and cold.

A storm of nausea swirled in the pit of Torin's stomach. He took one step away from the horrid sight, but his knees shook so terribly that he stumbled into the heavy wooden door behind him.

He braced himself against it as a high-pitched ring deafened him to all other sounds. Hot tears spilled out from the corners of his bleary eyes, and he struggled to draw in each ragged breath.

Though his vision was blurred, and the light was dim he could see Grimsa stumbling toward the hanging corpse. The huge man's shoulders shook as he reached for the figure. Einar had been Grimsa's foster father, Torin thought, and seeing his friend wail tore the wound in his heart even wider. Grimsa was only a few paces ahead of Torin, but the bellowing cry of his oldest friend seemed to come from far away.

A moment before Torin surrendered to the grief that was taking hold of his body, before his knees buckled and he crumpled to the floor, something struck him in the face with such force that it set his vision swirling with bright, flashing stars. He tumbled over sideways and onto his back. As he coughed and clutched his face, a heavy weight landed on his chest.

Torin struggled but the weight pressing down on his stomach had him firmly pinned. He tried to pull his chest up off the floor, but something grabbed both his shoulders and slammed them back against the wooden floorboards.

"Torin, wake up!"

Torin thought he recognized the voice but the ache in his heart flared, and he felt nothing but the pain of grief, like a knife thrust into his stomach, again and again. Hjartahall spun in dizzy circles, and he began to sink into the twirling chaos.

"Torin! By Orr, I will punch you again if I have to!"

Torin blinked and squinted. Wyla's face hovered just above his own, the cold light from the night sky illuminating only one side of it. Torin coughed and groaned. He could barely form the words as he raised his limp hand toward the center of the hall. "My father, he's there. He is hanging right there."

A sudden rage flared up in his belly and he grabbed both of Wyla's wrists. The bitter taste of the yellow powder stung at the back of his throat and the edge of his vision blurred red.

"You! You wanted me to stay in Gatewatch. I would have been home to protect my father if you had let me go. This is your fault!"

Wyla broke free of his grip and slammed him into the floor again. "Torin! Listen!"

The knock on the back of Torin's head was so sharp that the pain of it dragged him back into the moment. He shook his head, then caught the words that Grimsa cried, his friend's voice hoarse with ragged sobs.

"Signa! How? How could I let this happen?"

Torin quickly wiped his eyes on his sleeve and sat up after Wyla rolled off his chest. There was Azal curled up on the floor, the prince bawling and calling out in Armeahan. And there was Bari, crawling toward the center of the room, his beard dragging along the floor.

"Uncle Brok," Bari said. "Curse my beard! No, it cannot be. Uncle!"

Torin looked back to the corpse at the center of the hall and once again saw a perfect image of his father. A stab of pain pierced his heart, and he could hardly tear his eyes away from that horror. He forced his eyes down, then spat as a bitter taste rose in his mouth again. "By the gods," he said. "This cursed dust must be making us see a corpse!"

Wyla's face twisted into a grimace. She nodded. "Whichever face would cause us the most pain."

Torin frowned and shook his head as his mind began to clear. "How did you know?"

Wyla swallowed then shook her head. "No time now. The Shadowstalker must be close."

Torin coughed to clear the phlegm and salty tears from his throat then pushed himself up to his feet. A wave of relief was quickly followed by a surge of rage at the creature's deception. He thought his ears might burst from the rush of blood.

As he turned toward Wyla, Torin caught a glimpse of a mass of bone-white limbs. There, behind her, spiny legs were stretching out over Azal who was curled up on the floor. Torin shoved past Wyla and charged at the creature.

The Shadowstalker retracted its limbs, each as long as Torin was tall, but could not reposition itself before he came crashing into its bony arms. The curled spines on its thick armoured appendages cut into Torin's cloak and tunic as the two clashed. Long, spindly legs flailed and scraped against the wooden floorboards as it tried to scurry away, but Torin refused to let go.

The Shadowstalker caught Torin's chest between two of its barbed bone plates. It squeezed hard and Torin felt its cruel spines cutting into the flesh of his chest and back. He gripped the arm in front of him, trying to push it away. But as he did so, the spines pressed deeper into his back.

The steel edge of a trollhunter's axe flashed in the dim light and Torin heard a dull crack. The whole body of the bone-clad beast shuddered, and its chittering shriek pierced his ears. Torin slipped from its grip as the creature writhed. He watched with wide eyes as it retracted all its armoured limbs toward its hard-shelled body.

Wyla's axe had not pierced the plate but had broken one leg at the joint so that it hung limp. The Shadowstalker scuttled backward, hissing as black blood trickled down from the wound.

"I won't let it get away," said Wyla. "Get the others!"

Torin took a cautious step back, then ran to where Grimsa lay on the floor. He knelt down and shook his friend's shoulders.

"Grimsa, it's not real!"

Grimsa sucked in a lung full of air then let out a terrible wail that echoed up to the darkened rafters. "She's gone, Torin! She's gone!"

"It's the dust, Grimsa, that yellow powder. It is making all of us see things!"

Grimsa stopped mid-sob and glared at Torin. His eyes were glassy, and his face was swollen red. "You! You dragged me along on this cursed journey! If I had been back in Gatewatch I could have stopped this. I could have saved her!"

Grimsa threw a clumsy punch that caught Torin on the chin and knocked him over. Torin rolled to right himself, but Grimsa caught his ankle.

"Grimsa, wake up! Let go!"

Grimsa looked up at the hanging corpse again and began to wail and cry. Torin yanked his ankle free as Grimsa crumpled to the floor.

Torin gripped his friend's shoulder with one hand and wound up to strike him with the other. His open palm flew across Grimsa's face. Grimsa's eyes snapped wide open in shock, as if he had just been roused from the deepest sleep and had not yet felt the sting of the blow.

"I saw my father," Torin said, "and Bari saw his uncle! It's some sort of terrible illusion caused by that yellow powder."

Behind him, Torin heard a metallic clank followed by a violent scuffle. Wyla shouted a muffled curse. He turned to see the creature looming over her with one of its spiny limbs drawn back to strike. With a flash of white bone, it pinned her to the floor then leaned forward, sinking its dagger-sharp claw deep into her shoulder. Wyla let out a cry of agony and writhed beneath the Shadowstalker's terrible form.

Torin leapt up and snatched Wyla's axe from where it had clattered to the ground. He raised it to strike the beast at the center of its body, but the Shadowstalker lashed out with terrible speed. It caught him in the shin and tripped him so that he tumbled forward. Before he could scramble to his feet, the same limb shot out and struck the axe from his hands, sending it skittering across the floor.

Blood surged through his veins as he lurched forward to catch the Shadowstalker's spiny leg just before it plunged into his stomach. Pain shot through his hands and wrists as the wicked spines tore into his palms, but he gritted his teeth and gripped the leg even tighter. Through the puffs of yellow smoke kicked up by the tussle he could see the reddened tip of its claw, the same sharp point that had sunk into Wyla's shoulder. He watched it press down slowly until it was less than a hand's width away from his stomach.

At the very moment that Torin thought his grip would give out, another set of hands appeared beside his. The palms were wide, and the calloused fingers were thick. With a grumbling heave, they pulled the claw away from him.

There stood Grimsa, his blood shot eyes lit with fury as he grappled the Shadowstalker. Moonlight flashed off his silver belt, *Gingjord*, as he braced himself against the floor. With a groan that turned into a roar, he bent the creature's arm back toward its body. The Shadowstalker shrieked as the bone limb creaked and, after a moment of struggle, snapped clean off.

The cracking sound echoed through the hall like a clap of thunder and the creature's piercing screech felt like sharp pins puncturing Torin's ears. The Shadowstalker flailed and thrashed then clambered up into the shadowy rafters, the grinding scrape of its claws pounding against the walls.

Grimsa stood above Torin with one of the creature's long jagged limbs in his arms. The sharp end of it twitched with lifeless spasms for a moment more before falling still. From the other end, a trickle of oily black blood leaked out onto the floor.

Torin and Grimsa breathed heavy in the silence that followed. Above them nothing stirred except a midnight breeze that whistled through the patchwork of holes in the ceiling. Then, from the corner where the creature had disappeared, Wyla groaned.

Torin rushed over to her, a plume of yellow powder rising in the wake of his footsteps. Wyla clutched her right shoulder, and both her hands were slick with blood. Torin's stomach twisted at the sight of the deep gash, the dark liquid like a well of black ink in the shadowy gloom. Wyla bared her teeth and squeezed her eyes shut tight.

"That thing," she said. "Is it dead?"

"Not yet."

Wyla winced. "Then what are you waiting for? I'm fine. Go!"

"Wyla, you're—"

"Go! If we don't kill this thing soon, we'll all be dead!"

Torin snatched up the axe that she had dropped and searched the shadows for any sign of movement.

Azal and Bari still writhed on the ground, sobbing and whimpering. Grimsa stomped toward the center of the hall until he stood just below the hanging corpse. With the bony leg in hand, he spun around and tossed it upward. The sharp spines cut clean through the slick thread that held up the creaking weight. The shadowy mass, which had looked so much like Torin's father, fell into the stone-ringed hearth at the center of the room with an echoing crash. The creature's dismembered leg smashed into the wall off in the darkness and clattered to the floor.

At once the powder's spell broke. Azal and Bari jolted upright as if startled from a terrible dream. They looked at the other companions with wide, frightened eyes. There in the center of the hearth was not a human figure but a mass of sticky threads roughly shaped like a body.

"Look," Grimsa said. "Nothing but slimy webs."

Bari's hands quivered and his knees wobbled as he stood up. "By the Mastersmith, I could have sworn an oath that I saw my Uncle Brok hanging there!"

"And I saw Signa," said Grimsa. The huge man grimaced and shook his head. "I doubt I will ever be able to purge that awful image from my mind." Grimsa grabbed Azal by the shoulders and lifted the prince to his feet.

Azal wiped his eyes. "I saw Aldrin. I saw him as clearly as I see you now."

"No time to talk," said Torin. "Wyla's badly hurt, and that creature is still lurking around up there."

Azal went pale as he gazed at the black oily blood on Grimsa's hands and clothing, some of which had smeared onto the prince's tunic when the huge man hauled him up. "By the king's sceptre, what happened?"

Grimsa flexed his shoulders. "I cracked one of its spiny legs off, though I would say that damned monster still has too many limbs."

Bari squinted up at the shadowy ceiling. "How are we supposed to get at it when it's all the way up there?"

"We climb if we have to," Torin said. "But first, we need some light."

Azal hesitated for a moment then nodded. He moved toward the huge stone hearth at the center of Hjartahall. In among the ashes, there were charred remnants of logs burned long ago, and enough dry wood to at least get a few sparks going. The knot of slimy webs that had been hanging from the ceiling sat in a pile at the hearth's edge.

Azal extended his hands over the wood and ash. "*Ahmahratha.*"

A light breeze whisked through the hall, but not even the faintest glow of light came from the hearth. The prince squeezed his eyes shut, shook out his hands, and straightened himself.

"*Ahmahratha.*" A swirling wind blew around him, but no flames crackled under his outstretched fingers.

Azal inhaled deeply, his brows furled and both arms stretched out wide as if he was about to summon a storm at the center of

Hjartahall. The prince's voice rang clear as he cried out the third time. "*Ahmahratha!*"

A hot gust of wind whipped through the hall, dust swirling everywhere. A few loose roof tiles slid out of place and came crashing to the floor. A column of yellow dust rose over the hearth. There was a crackle of light, a few sparks, and a puff of ash-grey cloud, but soon the wind died, and nothing but a wisp of smoke rose off the logs.

Azal slumped to his knees. "I can't do it."

Bari ran up to Azal and grabbed him by the collar of his tunic. There was a wild look in the *nidavel's* eyes, and he shouted every word so that they rang up to Hjartahall's rafters. "Azalweir, son of Ghezelweir, I hail you! Apprentice of Lorekeeper Aldrin and Victor of the King's Race, I hail you!"

Torin knew then that Bari had slipped *Havaerari* onto his finger, for his words rumbled through the floorboards and rattled the roof tiles. In a bellowing voice, Bari continued to shout. "You who leapt over the Vimur River and galloped across the Northern plain! You who sipped *skog* with troll hunters and drank the wine of giants! Son of the King, Prince of Armeah, remember who you are and rise now to help your companions!"

Azal's eyes opened wider at Bari's every description and his shoulders stretched back with pride. Then, at the *nidavel's* last word, he rose to his feet and threw both hands forward with a roaring cry. "*Ahmahratha!*"

An orange flare exploded from the log at the center of the hearth, and the aged wood burst into flames. Heat swept over the hall and stirred swirls of yellow dust in every corner. The light of the fire illuminated the whole hall, causing the crossbeams high above the companions to cast flickering shadows onto the ceiling.

Every corner of the hall was lined with silky grey sacks, many of which had been torn open and still leaked thin streams of yellow powder. Above the companions, the wounded creature skittered toward the shadows, its white bone limbs appearing and disappearing as it searched for a dark place to hide. Wherever it went, a trail of oily black blood dripped down onto the dust-covered floor.

"There it is," said Azal, "up behind the throne!"

Grimsa retrieved the spiny arm and hurled it toward the ceiling. The creature chittered and scuttled away before the dismembered limb struck the place it had been a second earlier.

"Throwing things is no use," said Torin. "It's too quick."

"Then how else are we supposed to get at it?" asked Grimsa.

Bari tugged at his beard a moment then looked up at Grimsa with stern eyes. "Either it comes down," the *nidavel* said, "or one of us goes up."

"Up?"

Bari nodded. "You've got your belt of strength, and I am the lightest among us. Toss me up as high as you can, and perhaps I can grab a hold of one of those tattered banners." The *nidavel* gazed up at the ceiling a moment longer then nodded. "Yes, and from there I could climb onto the rafters!"

Grimsa looked up at the enormous crossbeams that ran across the upper reaches of the hall, then stammered for a moment. "But what if you fall?"

"Then, by the Mastersmith, you had better catch me! Come on now, Wyla is injured and there is no time to waste!"

Torin looked up at the shifting shadows lit by the hearthfire. Between the swaths of darkness, the spiny limbs of the Shadowstalker appeared and then vanished as quick as the flicker of the flames. He retrieved *Skrar* from where it lay on the floor, then followed Bari and Grimsa to the throne at the back of Hjartahall.

"Here," Torin said. "Once you're up, I'll pass *Skrar* to you. Best to keep as much distance between yourself and that vile creature as you can."

Bari nodded. "By the Mastersmith, I can still see the pale-white image of my uncle's corpse-like face. I'll repay this creature tenfold for that horror! Now quick, throw me up as high as you can!"

Grimsa squatted down low and gripped Bari at the hips. With a grunt, he sprung up, flinging the *nidavel* straight up into the air. Bari flailed as he soared up toward the ceiling and barely caught hold of one of the long-tattered banners. A terrible rip echoed through the room as Bari gripped it tight, but the tear in the fabric stopped when it met a section of elaborate stitching. He swung for a moment before his other hand caught a fistful of the silky fabric. Then, with his feet flat against the vertical timbers, Bari climbed up, hand over hand.

Somewhere far above them came the rumble of the Shadow-stalker's legs. It hissed as it raced out of hiding across the broad wooden timbers. Bari had hardly steadied himself on the cross-beam when the creature came charging at him.

"Bari! Here!" Torin hurled *Skrar* upward. It stuck into the wood right where the wall met the ceiling.

Torin saw a flash of bone-white limbs above him. Bari yanked at the spear shaft as the monster rumbled toward him, but it held fast. Bari pulled again with all his strength and nearly lost his balance as it came loose.

The Shadowstalker swiped at Bari and its claw came within an arm's length of his head. Bari cursed and shuffled back against the wall. With a roar, the *nidavel* thrust *Skrar* at its monstrous, spiny shell. The steel spearhead scraped against the rugged bone and the creature recoiled.

Torin caught the first sight of the Shadowstalker's mouth from below, jagged mandibles clicking over a grey orifice slathered in spittle. Some of the viscous fluid dripped down from the creature's mouth and splattered onto the floor at Torin's feet.

The Shadowstalker clawed at Bari again, but the *nidavel* drove it back with angry jabs. The creature swung its heavy limbs, strik-ing at the shaft, and Bari nearly lost his balance. Torin felt sick in the pit of his stomach as he watched the *nidavel* totter and flap his arms at such a dizzying height. Bari caught his balance just in time to fend off the next strike.

Bari surged forward, thrusting *Skrar* at the thick bone plating of the Shadowstalker's spiny limbs. This time the blade stuck, and its steel edge wedged into one of the creature's sinewy joints. It shrieked and pulled away so that Bari lost his grip on the spear. The *nidavel* tumbled forward, barely catching the smooth wooden beam as he started to slip off the edge.

"Grimsa!" called Bari. "Grimsa, I'm slipping!"

The Shadowstalker writhed and shook with all the force it could muster. It managed to loosen the steel edge as it flung its wounded limb back and forth. *Skrar* tumbled down onto the floor with a ringing clatter. But the force of the movement set the monster off balance. Though it clawed at the wooden rafter, its weight was too far gone. It fell and crashed down to the floor just a few paces from where Torin stood.

Torin hurled himself at the creature. Behind him, he heard Bari cry as the *nidavel's* grip gave out. Grimsa caught Bari as he fell. Then both rushed over to grab hold of another one of the creature's spiny limbs.

Azal called out as he ran toward the others from where he was standing by the roaring hearthfire. "Over here! Drag it into the flames!"

The spikes of the Shadowstalker's limbs scraped their arms as it twitched and writhed. With its free limbs, it clawed the floorboards, the sharp bone digging into the wood.

Torin groaned. "It's too heavy! We'll all be cut to pieces before we can drag it that far."

Grimsa growled, his hands bloody and torn. "Then I will break off every last one of your legs, you cursed spiny-legged scum!"

As Grimsa leaned his full weight on the beast, a spurt of black blood squirted into his eyes. He let go of the creature with a roar of pain and stumbled back, clutching his hands to his face.

The Shadowstalker shoved Azal back, nearly right into the fire, and hurled Bari into the dark corner of the room. As it rose on its many legs, Torin refused to let go and was pulled along with it.

The creature scuttled in an awkward arhythmic stumble to where Wyla lay on the floor. It stuck one of its hooked claws into the gaping wound in her shoulder and began to drag her along the floor toward the cavernous hole from which it had emerged. Its claw tearing into Wyla's shoulder shocked her back to full consciousness and she cried out in pain. Her legs and arms flailed as she slid along the floor.

Torin rushed forward and took hold of the arm that pinned Wyla to the ground. With all his might, he braced himself against the floor to lift it up. The creature hissed and threw its full weight on top of Wyla, its slavering mandibles dripping with toxic spittle. Torin pushed back with every last ounce of strength he had but was sorely outmatched for weight.

The Shadowstalker tilted forward until its grey gaping throat hovered over Wyla's face, which had gone deathly pale. Still, Wyla still grit her teeth and pounded the creature's legs with her fists. The Shadowstalker thrust its weight forward a second time. She caught one of its mandibles with her hand and pushed it away from her face. With white knuckles, she gripped the creature's pincers. The jagged edges, slick with slime, strained toward her.

Torin's stomach dropped when he saw the Shadowstalker's slimy mandibles close on Wyla's hand. It squeezed like a vice. Her fingers twisted at a terrible angle just before the bones within them cracked, snapping as if they had been a handful of dry kindling. Wyla let out a scream such as Torin's ears had never heard, a steel-sharp shriek that seemed cut right through his chest. The flailing mass of spiny limbs pulled back and took Wyla's mangled hand with it. She yanked the bloody stump to her chest and wailed.

Torin's heart seemed to beat in his throat, and his body felt numb. A bright glow caught his eye; the runes on *Tyrfang's* scabbard were blazing bright with piercing streaks of blue fire. Torin glanced again at Wyla, at her blood-stained tunic and the red streaks across her white fur cloak, then grasped the cursed blade as the creature leaned in toward her.

Tyrfang's edge rang with a bright metallic tone when Torin drew it out from its scabbard. Streaks of blinding light shot out from the runes along its black-steel edge, and the heat of its fury was sweltering. Torin gripped the blade with both hands and thrust it into the mass of spiny bones with all his weight.

Tyrfang's tip sliced through the Shadowstalker's bone shell and sunk down to the hilt. Black blood leaked out from the wound and sizzled on the hot metal blade. Torin drew *Tyrfang* out to strike again and a gush of gore flooded out from the wound.

As Torin braced himself to strike the final blow, he skidded on the greasy black liquid and tumbled back on his heels. Torin felt the sword, slick with oily blood, slip out of his grip. The light flickered as the blade spun upward, then all at once the blue glow was extinguished, the hall falling dark to Torin's eyes.

The back of Torin's head slammed against the wooden floor and set his ears ringing. A sharp pain cut through his stomach. He gasped and clutched at it only to feel a hot steel blade and a well of warm gurgling blood. As his eyes adjusted to the dim light, he saw that *Tyrfang* was run clean through him and stuck fast into the wooden floor below.

As if from another room or from a place very far away, he heard Grimsa's voice, not as words but a as blur of garbled noise. Torin's limbs all went ice cold in an instant and a frigid sweat broke out over his brow. The edges of his vision blurred with searing hot tears. The only thing he could bring his eyes to focus on clearly were the jagged runes etched on the steel blade that ran through his stomach. Torin thought he was going to be sick and then he thought he was going to scream. He did neither, but instead watched the shadowy rafters above him start to spin and sink into a pool of shadow.

19

◇ DARKEST DEPTHS ◇

TORIN FELT HIMSELF sinking down as if he were in a deep pool. Everything around him was as dark as the deepest cave and no sound reached his ears except for the slow thump of his beating heart. He would have guessed that he was floating in water except that he could still draw slow, shallow breaths into his lungs. When Torin tried to raise his hand to his face, sharp needle pricks tingled up his arm as if it had completely numbed. And so, he floated, aimless and immobile, a dreadful chill gripping him right to his bones.

There was an ache in his stomach, though it seemed dull like pressure applied through many layers of fabric. His head swirled with thoughts that seemed too slow, each one congealing out of a mass of unformed shapes. Once a thought became clear, it would slowly melt and dissolve before the next could start to form.

Quite some time passed before it occurred to Torin that he might be dead. He strained his mind to recall how he had come to that dark place, but he could not conjure any memory of it. Through the fog in his mind, he glimpsed Grimsa's tear-streaked face staring up at the corpse, the flare of Azal's conjured fire rising up in the hearth, and the sound of snapping bone as Wyla's hand was crushed. The memories stopped there. Any events that followed were lost to him.

After a time by which Torin had nothing to reckon, a small light appeared above him. It came in glimmering ripples, the distinctive shimmer of light through water. Perhaps he was in an underground pool, he thought, or at the bottom of a deep lake.

The first thing Torin saw was his own hair, the dark strands floating over his face. Next, he glimpsed the outline of his arms and legs. Torin began to suspect that he might really be dead because he felt no burning suffocation in his lungs and only the dead can float through the water without a breath.

Slowly, the light began to strengthen. Torin tried to kick his legs and move his arms to swim upward but his limbs ignored every command. No matter how he urged them to move they hung limp and lifeless. The light grew brighter, and the rippling rays stretched further into the watery void below him. Either the light was moving toward him, or he was rising upward toward the surface.

A pale hand broke the slow rippling stillness of the water in a swirl of silver bubbles. Torin watched the fingers grip the front of his tunic. As the hand pulled, he could not feel the fabric against his skin, but he knew by the way his hair swirled over his face and by how the light shimmered around him that he was being drawn up. It tugged again and pulled him so close to the light that he felt the warmth of it on his face. With every bit of determination that he still possessed, Torin commanded his limbs to struggle and kick, but they would still not obey. The silhouette of a dim figure appeared above him, the lines of its outline blurred by the rippling water.

As Torin broke through the water's surface, he felt warm air rush him, and his frigid skin tingled with pain. His eyes adjusted to the light, and he realized its source. White-blue flames flickered from nine burning torches hanging over the circular pool that he floated in. Behind him rose a flat surface, rough and gnarled like tree bark. If it was a tree, it must have been enormous because Torin could not see even the lowest branches. He strained to look down past his feet, but saw only the night sky, dark and deep and full of shimmering stars, as if the far edge of the pool stood near some impossibly steep precipice.

The torches flared up all at once as the strange silhouette returned. The scent of lilacs and fresh green grass wafted over Torin's face, and the wet strands of hair covering his eyes prevented him from seeing the figure clearly. It pulled him to the edge of the pool and gently brushed his tangled hair away from his face.

A young woman had pulled Torin from the depths of the pool and now she leaned over his rigid form. Long curls of silver hair spilled down over her shoulder in ringlets. Her cheeks and lips were pale in the blue torchlight. On the ridges of her high cheekbones and the end of her sharp chin there were flecks of gold which shimmered as fish scales do in sunlight. All in all, he might have thought her beautiful except that her eyes had no irises or pupils, and it unsettled Torin to see those centerless white orbs directed at him.

The young woman gazed at Torin. "Where did it come from?" Her words seemed to come from her mouth too slowly and each syllable lingered in a soft echo.

A second figure appeared in Torin's vision, similar in appearance to the first but much older. Wrinkles creased the silvery skin around her eyes and her cheeks were gaunt. The smell of cedar wood and the sharp scent of pine sap mingled together as she knelt at the edge of the pool to inspect him. She gazed at Torin's face through her blank white eyes, then pursed her lips and drew her silver eyebrows into a sharp frown. She spoke in the same slow and unhurried manner of the younger woman. "A young *madur*. How strange."

A third figure appeared, similar again yet far older than even the second figure. Her curled hair was a frayed mess strewn with leaves and twigs and her spine curled so that her whole frame hunched forward. With creaking joints, she crouched down at the edge of the pool, the smell of rich soil and damp moss wafting past. "This one is familiar to me. I must have spun his thread."

The young woman looked at Torin then past him into the deep waters below. "How could he have floated up from the well, Moda?"

The middle-aged woman looked back at the youngest and shrugged. "Who can tell, Dotti? The Well of the Tree will do as it will."

"Nonsense," said the elderly woman. She grinned at the one called Dotti, her crooked teeth aglow in the flickering light of the blue torches. "In my time, many odd things have appeared in this sacred pool, and this is hardly the strangest of them."

Moda sat back and crossed her hands in her lap. Without turning toward the elderly woman, she spoke. "Then what could it mean, Amma?"

Young Dotti leaned in toward Torin and frowned. "And what should we do?"

Amma, the elderly woman, shook her head and wagged a gnarled finger at the two others. "So many questions, Dotti. What else could he have come for besides our gleaming thread? What else do we do at the base of our beloved tree but spin and weave and spin and weave? He has come for more thread, for Yg has deemed that it has run short before his time. Moda, hold the *madur* in place. Dotti, fetch as large a stone as you can carry."

Amma leaned over Torin, her wrinkled face hovering over his, then pulled a thin bone needle from the folds of her loose flowing gown. She pinched the needle at its center and held it up over the well. The whole pool began to glow as a shimmering thread materialized and tumbled down from the needle's eye to the rippled surface of the water. Amma leaned further over the pool and reached toward Torin with her wrinkled fingers.

Torin's body had been numb for what seemed like a very long time and so it surprised him to feel the prick of the needle in his stomach. At that instant, it all came back to him: the flash of *Tyrfang's* black steel blade as it spun through the air and the sickening thud as it pinned him to the floor. Amma ran the needle through the wound all the way from his stomach to his back, as if her wrinkled hands could pass straight through his body. Torin felt the needle's sharp point piercing him and the tug of the thread whenever the old woman pulled it tight. Tears welled up in the corners of his eyes and he would have cried out if he still had command of his body.

Dotti returned with a round stone about the size of Torin's head. Amma sat back on her heels and nodded. "Alright Dotti, that should do. He will start wiggling if we keep him here too much longer. Place the stone over him."

Moda helped Dotti center the stone over Torin's chest. He was struck with a sudden panic, desperate by instinct to keep his head above water. There was a twitching in his fingers, life returning, but not enough to command his limbs. On Amma's count, they released the stone. Its heavy weight pressed Torin down beneath the surface of the pool. The three strange women, the light of the flickering torches, and the glimmer of the field of stars disappeared in a splash of blue-lit water and a swirl of shimmering bubbles.

Torin kept sinking, slowly at first then faster and faster until he had descended into that same darkness he had been lost in before. Sensation began to return to his limbs, and he could feel the water rush past his ears and between his fingers. The speed of the swirling stream was like the rush of a river roaring by. The weight of the stone on his chest increased so that his ribs ached. Torin worried they might snap one by one. And just as he thought they might collapse, the weight lifted all at once and he burst from the water into the blinding light of day.

"Torin! Torin, can you hear me?"

Torin floundered for a moment before he realized the water was only waist deep. He pulled his sopping wet hair back from his face and sat up, wobbling. A large figure was lumbering toward him.

"Grimsa!" Torin gasped and steadied himself then shouted with joy. "Grimsa! By the gods, I thought for sure that I was dead!"

Grimsa hauled him up into an embrace and squeezed Torin so that he could hardly breathe.

"By the golden tears of Fyr!" cried Grimsa. "You're alive!"

Hot water swirled at their feet, the mist rising into the cold, crisp air. Torin and Grimsa stood a few steps from shore in what seemed to be a gurgling hot spring the size of a small lake. Thunderous falls rumbled nearby. Behind the bubbling pool rose a dark mountain, curls of steam clawing at the steep cliffs up to its jagged summit. Beyond the mountain, the sky was full of grey clouds lit by the pale morning sun.

Bari jumped up from where he had been sitting along the shore. "By the Mastersmith! I can't believe it!"

Torin blinked and squinted in the morning sun. "Where are we?"

"See for yourself," said Bari. "There is Hjartahall."

Torin saw Thrudnir's mighty hall down the hill. A thin column of smoke rose through the holes in the roof and its gilded pillars shone bright in the light of dawn. When Grimsa released him from his iron-gripped embrace, Torin knelt and dipped his hands in the water.

"Is this it?" said Torin. "The Everspring?"

Grimsa laughed in a deep rumbling voice. "Well, if you're alive, it must be!"

Torin pulled up his tunic where it was torn and stained with blood. There was a deep scar in his stomach, but the skin had already closed around the wound.

Bari shook his head. "The magic of these waters must be potent! That cursed sword ran right through your stomach and pinned you to the floor." He shuddered. "There was so much blood that I had given you up for dead, but Grimsa threw you over his shoulder and ran to the Everspring. He placed you in the water and we waited all through the night until morning. I had nearly given up hope!"

With wide eyes, Torin ran his finger over the scar and recalled the prick of the old woman's thread. "Where are the others?"

Bari motioned toward Hjartahall. "After Azal pulled a draught from the spring, he went back to warm himself and tend to the fire in case you recovered. You'll be keen to dry off and have something to eat, no doubt! We found some of Thrudnir's stores in the back corner of the hall; dried meat and berry preserves."

"What about Wyla?"

Grimsa frowned and looked past Torin. "Just down there." He pointed down the beach to a place at the foot of the mountain cliff. "That cursed creature took her hand." Grimsa paused for a moment and crossed his arms. "If these waters were able to mend your wound, then perhaps they can restore her hand as well?"

Though Grimsa's words were hopeful, his tone was dull and flat. It seemed to Torin that to close a wound and to regrow a limb were two very different things. And if it did not grow back, then Wyla would surely be handed a bag of silver and dismissed from the company of Greycloaks, just like Asa the Fletcher when she lost her leg. Wyla's troll hunting days would be over.

Torin nodded and gave a half smile, though it looked more like a wince. "I'm going to go see her. You've both waited here long enough for me. Warm up by the fire and have something to eat.

I'll come down soon." Grimsa and Bari nodded then started back toward Hjartahall.

There on the stony beach, about a hundred paces away, Wyla lay flat on her back with one bandaged arm tied to her chest and the other draped over her eyes. The image of the Shadowstalker's horrid clacking mandibles closing around Wyla's hand came to Torin's mind as her scream echoed in his memory. He shuddered.

Torin limped as he walked along the edge of the steaming pool, an ache in his right side flaring up whenever he put weight on it. He suspected that his wound would need time to heal, no matter the magic of the spring or those strange women of the well. Wyla did not look up at him as he knelt beside her and then lay down on his back.

For a while they lay there in silence, Wyla with her hand over her face and Torin staring up at the rippled grey clouds above them. The Everspring gurgled with steaming bubbles, as a brisk breeze rose and fell. When it blew down the mountain and across the hot spring, it dragged swirls of steam over Torin and Wyla so that a warm mist coated their faces. If Torin had woken up in that place with no recollection of where he had been, he would have thought that he and Wyla were the last two living souls on earth.

Wyla cleared her throat. "I'm glad you're alive."

"So am I. And I'm glad you are too." Torin paused for a moment then turned his head toward her. "If you hadn't seen through the magic of that creature, we'd all be dead. How did you know that the hanging corpse was an illusion?"

Wyla laid in silence a while longer before she responded. "You saw your father. Grimsa saw Signa. Bari saw his uncle, and I guess that Azal saw Aldrin." She lifted her arm and looked at Torin. "I saw you as clearly as I see you now. But I knew that it couldn't be true because you were there in the hall with me. That's why I woke you from the curse first. I had to make sure you were really alive."

Torin looked back at her with wide eyes. Before he could speak, Wyla turned away and draped her arm over her face again. She shook her head and sighed.

"They'll never let me hunt trolls again."

Torin frowned. "You're the best damn trollhunter the Greycloaks have."

Wyla swallowed and her voice tightened. "Had. As soon as they see my arm, they'll take my cloak and hand me a bag of silver."

Torin did not know what to say, so he said nothing at all. It was vain to hope that the Greycloaks would make an exception as the Greyraven's law strictly forbade it. Wyla could stay in Gatewatch, but Torin knew that her spirit was too wild to be contained within those walls. A life so close to the adventure that lay just beyond them would be nothing but a torturous imprisonment. He turned toward her and inwardly begged the gods for some small comfort to offer. Nothing came to his mind.

Wyla raised her free arm and clenched her hand into a white-knuckled fist. Then she brought it down and struck her face hard with every word. "Stupid! Weak! Useless! Broken!"

Torin scrambled onto his knees and grabbed her forearm before she could strike her face again. Her eyes were squeezed shut and a stream of tears cut pale lines through the splattered blood and yellow dust on her face. Wyla clenched her jaw and sat up to wrench her hand away, but Torin would not let go. Then she screamed a hoarse and ragged cry; it was the breaking of the dam and the rush of the flood.

Once the last echoes faded away, Wyla let herself collapse. Her forehead fell against Torin's chest as her shoulders shook with sobs. Wyla emptied herself of tears as the wind whistled over the dark mountain peak that rose high over the steaming pool.

Wyla sniffed and wiped her bleary eyes with her free hand. "I had a vision of what my life would be." She held a deep breath in her chest. "I was living it, Torin, all through these past two years. Troll hunters, both of us, until we got our Greycloaks. Then we would spend the rest of our lives hunting in the wilds together until we met some glorious end."

Wyla shook her head. "When I learned that Keymaster Signy was your mother I hoped even more that you might stay. I hoped this journey to the Everspring would change your mind. But now that future is gone. It's all gone." She turned to Torin, her jaw tense and trembling. "What do I have left?"

Torin met her steel-grey eyes. "There's still us."

Wyla held his gaze as if to test it, as if to question whether he really meant what he said. Whether those strange women at the well had tied his and Wyla's threads together or if simple chance had drawn them close, Torin could not say. However, when he opened his mouth to speak, she turned away, as if some sudden movement had caught her eye.

"Look," she said. "Across the lake."

Far below them, at the south end of the blue-green lake, an enormous eagle was flying toward Hjartahall. It soared above the rippling surface of the water until it came to the rocky beach along the north shore. Flapping its mighty wings, it rose up the steep bank until it circled over Thrudnir's hall. In a slow spiraling descent, the eagle then came to land on an exposed rafter where a few of the black slate tiles had fallen away.

"That must be Hraesvelgir," said Wyla.

"Then Thrudnir will soon be on his way. Perhaps they'll arrive before the day's end."

The eagle tipped its head from side to side, then disappeared into Hjartahall through a gap in the roof. The sound of some great commotion came from the hall, and they heard Grimsa shouting.

Torin scrambled up to his feet. "By the gods, not again." He offered his hand to Wyla, and she pulled herself up. "I swear I'm going to roast that bird over the fire if it attacks us a second time."

As they descended the first steps down toward Hjartahall, Hraesvelgir emerged through the roof. In its beak it held the horrendous skeletal limb that Grimsa had ripped from the Shadowstalker. The eagle shook its feathers free of yellow dust. A few more stray tiles slipped off the roof and shattered on the ground as Hraesvelgir took flight. With incredible speed, it swooped down the side of the mountain, then pulled up just in time to skim above the rippling waves. With a few more flaps of its wide wings, it reached the other side. It rose up one last time, and then disappeared over the misty waterfall at the south end of the lake.

"With any luck, Thrudnir will be back by nightfall," said Torin.

Wyla clutched her arm and nodded. "And with a bit more luck, perhaps he'll bring food and drink." She stood to face Torin and looked him in the eye. "What was it that you were going to say?"

Torin drew in a breath. He looked down at the bloody bandages wrapped around Wyla's arm. The words that had been waiting to bubble up from his heart had dissipated at the sight of the eagle, and he felt unsure of where to begin.

In the long pause, Wyla caught his eye looking down at the bloody shreds of cloth around her arm. She grimaced and untied the knot, peeling back the gore-crusted fabric.

Torin's stomach lurched as the last of it came away to reveal the stump at the end of Wyla's arm. The blood and grime had been rinsed away. There was no torn flesh, no protruding bone. Smooth skin covered the end of her forearm but there were no fingers; instead, there was a knob of blushing flesh where her wrist had once been.

Before Torin could speak, there came a trumpet blast from across the lake, like the bellow of a mighty war horn. A distant chorus of cheers and clanging metal followed. A crimson banner rose through the mists of the falls. Sewn over the crimson was the runic sigil of Thrudnir, the Mountain King. A whole company of *jotur* on horseback spilled onto the plateau as if they had been waiting for the announcement. The echo of their thundering hooves rumbled all the way across the lake.

"Torin! Wyla!" It was Bari calling as he climbed the steps.

Wyla snatched the cloth over her arm and cast it aside. Her cheeks splotched with red as Torin turned toward her with wide eyes.

"Wyla, I—"

Wyla threw up her hand. "Don't."

Bari called again. "Torin! Wyla!"

Torin looked at Wyla and opened his mouth to speak, but Bari's voice interrupted him.

"Thrudnir's company is already on their way," said Bari. "Soon they'll be coming up the hill!"

Wyla drew in a shaky breath then tucked her handless arm through her sleeve to hide it. "We saw them," she said. "We're coming!"

With that, Wyla turned away from Torin and started down the steps to Hjartahall. Bari's eyes were wide as Wyla pushed past him, her back held stiff.

"What happened?" said Bari. "Did the Everspring heal her arm?"

Torin's gaze trailed after Wyla. He shook his head. "It healed her wound but didn't restore her hand or her fingers."

Bari frowned. "A terrible loss. But surely, she must be glad it healed. An injury like that would take months to heal on its own if it didn't kill her first!"

Torin buried his hands in his hair. "If a trollhunter loses a limb, they can no longer be a Greycloak. That loss is considered their debt of service paid, and they are given a bag of silver to start over somewhere else. Some stay in Gatewatch, but most return to wherever they came from."

Bari stroked his beard. "I see. And where did Wyla come from?"

"Nowhere," said Torin, the word slipping out from his mouth before he had any time to think. "I mean, she was born and raised in Gatewatch. Her father is dead. Her mother is dead. I have no idea what she'll do, but I know she won't stay there. She's too proud to sit by while others tell tales of troll-hunting." He looked at Bari for a moment then turned back toward Hjartahall. "I'm worried for her."

Bari shrugged. "And she always worries about you too. Perhaps you should both just admit how you feel so you can be together and worry about each other for all time." The *nidavel* looked over the northern landscape as if he was searching for something in the distance. "My Uncle Brok would tell me this verse when I was young."

> *As for courage, its parts are three*
> *The first in battle, ne'er to flee*
> *Next in sorrow, a wrong forgiven*
> *Last, in love, one's own heart given*

Torin watched Wyla disappear through the doors of Hjartahall. He turned back to Bari and shook his head. "The *jotur* will arrive soon. We'd better go."

Torin and Bari came to the front porch of Hjartahall just as Thrudnir's host arrived. The Mountain King dismounted and gazed at his beloved hall with a gleaming smile. As he ascended the steps, the *jotur* stretched his enormous arms out wide.

"Torin Ten-Trees, son of Einar, kin of the Greyraven, and descendant of the long-lost *huldur*. You have proven your worth, prince of the forest."

"I'm no prince." Torin said. "And I cannot take credit for slaying the Shadowstalker." He motioned to the others. "Without the efforts of every member of this company we would have fallen to that foul creature."

"Yet it must have been *Tyrfang*, your family's cursed sword, that struck the final wound? What other weapon could have pierced its ivory shell? Regardless, we shall be singing the song of this feat beneath the rafters of Hjartahall when your grandchildren hold their own grandchildren in their arms!"

Thrudnir raised his arms toward the crowd of *jotur*. "I declare here, in front of this mighty host, that these mortals are henceforth to be held friends of the *jotur* for whatever years of life they have left, few as they may be." He turned to the mortal company. "Would you stay and see this mighty hall restored to its former glory, so that we can celebrate your feat with a splendid feast?"

Torin looked to Grimsa and Wyla, to Bari, and then to Azal. Each had a determined look in their eyes. In as loud a voice as he could, Torin called back. "We have been sent by King Araldof Greyraven's closest advisors to draw a draught from the Everspring. We are grateful for your generous offer, but we must return as soon as possible. The Greyraven's death would leave the throne of Noros empty, igniting the fires of war across the realm."

The Mountain King nodded. "Very well. Then you shall be taken back across the Vimur River by my swiftest riders." Five riders immediately lined up at the base of the stairs, Jolvar and Ulfrun foremost among them.

Thrudnir lifted his hands. "In place of a feast, I shall give each of you a red-gold ring. Let it be a sign of our friendship!" His servants brought forth five red-gold arm rings, but for the companions they were large enough to be worn as torcs around their necks. The Mountain King motioned for Torin to step forward.

"My traitorous nephew, Ur-Gezbrukter, named you Mindthorn," said Thrudnir, "And you defended that title well in our *bardagi*. But this feat is deserving of a new title. Here I give you the name Dawnbright, for you have cut through the darkness as the first rays of dawn slice through the shroud of night."

Torin, Wyla, Grimsa, Bari, and Azal all accepted a gold ring from the Mountain King in turn. Meanwhile, each *jotur* rider laid out a soft white fur on their saddle for comfort. Once each companion had a ring of gold around their neck, the giants lifted them up onto their horses. The crowd of *jotur* then waved crimson banners and sounded long curved horns.

Thrudnir continued "Dawnbright, heed this warning! The dark deeds of Lysa the Green Witch are far from concluded. She may have used a great deal of her strength to try and end your life at Ballur's Barrow. However, I have no doubt that she will soon appear again to claim the *huldur* wood and the lands beyond that run down to the sea. Be wary! Lysa will certainly seek revenge, both for the slaying of the Shadowstalker and for the restoration of my beloved Hjartahall. Ym's strength and Yg's wisdom guide you!"

Torin took one last look up at Hjartahall, squinting in the midday light that gleamed off the gilded pillars. The swirling mists of the Everspring framed the hall's towering rafters and the roar of cascading waterfalls rumbled through the air. He wondered how he might describe such a place to those back in Gatewatch, and if they would even believe him if he could.

Torin waved to Thrudnir, and the Mountain King gave a solemn nod. Then the enormous horse that Torin sat on lurched forward and the stony ground below him became a blur beneath its thundering hooves.

20

◇ QUEST'S END ◇

TORIN WOKE TO A GOLDEN LIGHT as the first rays of dawn slipped through a leafy canopy. The rhythmic thump of galloping hooves beat the damp ground below him and the sharp scent of cedar filled his nose. He rubbed his eyes clear of sleep as his mind came into focus.

All at once the forest became familiar to him. He could predict each bend in the trail, and he recognized a few of the larger trees which stood with lofty boughs outstretched, as if to welcome them home. As the trail began to climb upward, Torin knew they had nearly reached the winding path that led to the gate of Stonering Keep.

The towering trees gave way to an open field of dewy grass, rising and falling over earthy mounds. Alpine flowers had bloomed and speckled the hills red and blue and purple. Above it all, far away to the east, stood two jagged summits that Torin knew well: Frostridge Peak and Ironspine Mountain.

The fluttering silver banners of Stonering Keep emerged over the hill. Next came the watchtowers along the wall, those sleepless stone sentinels. Last to appear was the wall itself, that stretching all the way across the valley from north to south. A long horn blast rang from Stonering Keep over the wide-open field.

Ulfrun raised her horn in response and sounded it in a series of short blasts. In uniform motion, each *jotur* rider reached back behind their saddle and let loose a long red banner with Thrudnir's runic sigil sewn in with silver thread. The scarlet fabric trailed back behind the line of horses and fluttered in the brisk morning wind. The riders continued up the slope and stopped only when they came within one hundred paces of the gate.

Jolvar dismounted and the others followed his lead. With one hand on the reins and the other on his hip the *jotur* turned to face Torin. From the saddle Torin nearly stood eye to eye with the grizzled giant.

"Torin Ten-Trees," said Jolvar, "as Lord Thrudnir pardoned your trespassing into Ballur's tomb, I hope you will forgive any misunderstanding between us and your company from our first meeting. Your service to my wise cousin has made him glad. Hjartahall is restored and we *jotur* will rejoice in the thrill of the northern hunt once more."

Torin crossed his arms. "Well, the journey back was certainly more comfortable than the way there. I will forget your insults on one condition: you must swear an oath to remember our friendship if the troll hunters in Gatewatch ever face the threat of doom."

Jolvar let go of the reins and placed his right hand on the knotted silver ring clasped around his left wrist. "On this arm ring given to me by Thrudnir the Wise, I swear that I will not let the *jotur* forget how you and your company came to our aid by slaying the Shadowstalker. If we hear any word of the Green Witch rising against the *madur* of Gatewatch, I will personally lead my kin to battle and fight alongside them."

Torin nodded and gripped the *jotur's* mountainous shoulder. Then he slid off the saddle and felt the dewy grass beneath his feet. Torin's stiff legs ached but he relished the feeling of green turf below him after days spent in the rocky, weathered places of the north. The others had already dismounted, and they were waiting for him a little way up the hill.

The giants climbed back atop their steeds and spun around with their scarlet banners fluttering. Ulfrun blew her horn again, a long celebratory blast. Before they set off, Jolvar stood up in his saddle and waved. "Farewell, strange mortal company. Ym's might and Yg's wisdom to you!" With that, the *jotur* riders pressed their heels into their mounts and disappeared toward the wild wood.

Torin turned toward Stonering Keep. Up on the ramparts he saw three figures, silhouettes outlined by bright rays of sunlight that broke over Shadowstone Pass. Once he stepped under the shadow of the towering gate, he could see their faces. Signa had her arm wrapped around her mother Signy's shoulder, and Aldrin steadied himself against the stone battlement.

As soon as Grimsa caught sight of Signa he burst into a sprint. "Signa, my sweet summer rose!"

She leaned over the battlement and called back. "Grimsa, my burly bear!"

Grimsa stood at the gate and stretched his arms up toward her. "It seems like a year has passed since I last saw you!"

Signa reached down toward him. "My heart ached every moment that you were gone!"

Bari cupped his hands around his mouth and shouted. "And Grimsa's stomach ached at being away from Fjellhall!"

The others laughed as Wyla rolled her eyes. "Gods spare us any more of this love-sick drivel. Open the gate and let us in already before these two break into song!"

The gate creaked as the iron-bound timbers slowly rose. When it had risen to waist height, Signa slipped under the beams, running to meet Grimsa with a wide grin on her face. The huge man opened his arms wide and caught her in a twirling embrace.

Captain Gavring stood in the doorway with a host of Grey-cloaks behind him. "Hail, Torin Ten-Trees! Hail, Wyla White-Blaze! Hail, Grimspear and Bari Wordsmith! Hail, Prince Azalweir of Armeah!" He embraced each one with his burly arms as they came through the gate, even Bari, though the captain had to bend down low to reach the *nidavel*.

Torin was last to greet him. "Hail, Gavring! We have a healing draught drawn straight from the Everspring."

Gavring chuckled. "Thank the gods for that! I was certain we would not see you until the end of summer if we ever saw you again at all. The Lorekeeper gave us a brief account of your journey, at least as far as the mountain hall of those northern giants. It seems the favour of the gods carried you swiftly there and back again!"

"Perhaps," Torin said. "Though it may have had more to do with the *jotur's* favor than that of the gods."

"Nevertheless, here you are! Where is the draught?"

Prince Azal drew out the glass flask that Aldrin had given him and passed it to Gavring. The captain held it carefully in his large hands and raised it up so that the early morning rays of sunlight lit the green tinted glass.

"Looks just like normal water to me," said Gavring.

Torin lifted his tunic and pointed to the deep scar on his stomach. "I admit that I also doubted the power of the Everspring—but look! Just yesterday this wound ran straight through my stomach and out my back."

Gavring frowned. "And the Everspring healed you?"

Torin nodded. "It is a real place, Gavring, a steaming spring among a range of ash-black mountains far to the north. The journey took us well beyond the wild forest and across a wide empty plain."

The eyes of the Greycloaks widened and Gavring's jaw dropped in awe. "Then the tales were true after all! By the gods, I never would have believed it." He turned to the Greycloak next to him and passed her the flask. "Greycloaks, this company has done their part. Now it is time to do yours! Take this flask to the Grey Council in Ravensnest with all speed. Don't delay another moment!"

The Greycloaks shouted in unison and raised their fists high. "Long live The Gatewatch! Long live the Greyraven!"

Signy shouted from the top of the wall. "As for the rest of you, send word to the attendants at Fjellhall to prepare a feast! First we will eat and drink until this company is full and then we will hear the full tale of their adventure in the north." The small crowd that had gathered there hurried out of Stonering Keep into the winding streets of Gatewatch.

Aldrin stepped forward and gripped Azal by the shoulders. "My prince! It seems you were listening to at least a little of what I have been telling you over all these years. How else could you have survived?"

Azal pulled the old Lorekeeper close and squeezed him tight. "I summoned the fire, Aldrin! I spoke the words you taught me, and the flames rose up in front of my eyes."

"A good thing too," said Bari, "or else the Shadowstalker would have dragged us all into the dark corners of Hjartahall and eaten us one by one!"

Aldrin shook his head. "Perhaps that is what your training lacked all these years, a desperate situation! No matter. Now that you know the feel of it, I have no doubt it will come easier."

Azal narrowed his eyes. "How did you get back so quickly, Aldrin?"

The old Lorekeeper grinned. "I arrived late last night, only a few hours before the rest of you. It was that eagle, Hraesvelgir, that brought the news of your success to us. Lord Thrudnir ordered that noble bird to carry me back from Jokulheim, over the northern plain and the wild forest, here to Gatewatch."

Grimsa snorted. "Wait! You got to ride on an eagle while the rest of us clopped all the way on horseback?" The others laughed and a moment later Grimsa's face broke into a smile.

Torin saw Signy looking on from halfway down the stone steps that led up to the gatehouse tower. He turned away from the others and met her near the bottom of the stone stairway.

The corners of her eyes wrinkled as she smiled. There was joy in her face but also a kind of pain in the way she tensed her brow. Torin's heart pounded as he searched for something to say. For a while, they just looked at each other in stillness and silence.

"I am so proud of you, Torin."

Torin felt a lump in his throat at her words. "I'm sorry I didn't say goodbye."

"And I'm sorry I sent the sword along without telling you."

Torin grinned. "Well, it came to good use in the end. Though I'm still not sure I should thank you. It nearly killed me."

Signy's eyes opened wide. "Really?"

"I guess it was my own fault. It was the curse. *Tyrfang* would have been the end of me if Grimsa hadn't pulled it out of my stomach and dragged me into the Everspring."

"Then the sword really does have magic," Signy said.

"More than you know." Torin looked down at the rune-etched scabbard tied to his belt and frowned. "What else do you know about this sword?"

Signy shook her head. "It was a wedding gift given to my father by my mother. She said she came across it while exploring some ruins beneath Stonering Keep before they had been filled in and built over. But that was a long time ago, just a short time after the Battle of Gatewatch."

"That's all she said?"

Signy shrugged. "Nothing more than that. I only kept it hidden away in the hopes that one day you would take possession of it."

Torin looked down at the ground for a moment then raised his eyes to meet Signy's. "Do you think it's in our blood to keep secrets?"

Signy opened her mouth to respond then closed it. The old woman gave a long sigh. "Perhaps."

"I don't want it to be like that," said Torin. "Not between us."

Signy fixed Torin with her steel grey eyes and reached forward to grip his shoulder. "Believe me, I am tired of living in a shroud of secrets."

Torin held her gaze a moment longer, then grinned. "Well then, I've got a few more family secrets to share. Apparently, there are some rather strange relations going back on my father's side."

"Ah," said Signy, "then I suppose I can rest easy knowing that all your strangeness comes from him and not from my side of the family."

Torin paused, still smiling. "I'm glad to be back."

She pulled him toward her and squeezed him tight. "Welcome home, son."

Signy held the embrace a moment longer then stepped back and shook her head. "You smell awful, Torin. You and the others had better wash up before the feast tonight or else no one will have any appetite to eat anything."

"There it is," Torin said. "Pure honesty."

As Torin and Signy walked down the stairs, he looked for the others. It seemed Grimsa had run off with Signa already while Azal and Bari were speaking to Aldrin. He glanced around the wide stone courtyard as he approached them.

"Where's Wyla?"

Azal shrugged. "I don't know."

"Did anyone see her leave?"

Bari looked around then shook his head. "No, I didn't. But if she smells anything like us, she'll be down in the baths, I'm sure!"

Torin thought about it for a moment then nodded. Together they crossed under the gate that led into town and made their way to the underground baths. They sank into the bubbling water and let the steam carry away the stiffness in their backs and the ache in their legs. Keymaster Signy sent one of her hall hands down with fresh clothes for all three of them.

Though they lingered a long while in the underground baths, Wyla still did not appear. Torin left the others to search for her. He emerged from the underground baths in clean clothes, feeling as fresh as the dew upon the grass they had crossed at dawn. From there, Torin followed a familiar path through Gatewatch toward the wide doors of Fjellhall.

Torin paused on the threshold of Fjellhall and ran his hands over the carvings around the doorway. He could hear the crackle of wood burning in the hearth and he smelled the savory scent of bubbling stew, just as he had so many times before. He thought back to the first time he had first stepped into the hall, when he had just arrived in Gatewatch with Bryn and Grimsa. Back then it had seemed magnificent, so tall and wide that he hardly believed such a building could exist. After entering the mountain fortress of Jokulheim and standing under the towering rafters of Hjartahall, it did not seem so large after all. Nevertheless, he wouldn't trade one meal cooked over the hearth in Fjellhall for one hundred days of feasting with the *jotur*.

Torin slipped through the doors and shuffled along the wall as hall hands hurried about their duties. No one had expected them to return so soon and perhaps it seemed that they just finished cleaning up from celebrating their departure. Over the fire there were wild grouse roasting, at least a dozen of them, with hall hands busy basting the golden-brown skin with butter and herbs. Soup was bubbling, bread was rising, and the sizzle of the roasting birds hovered above it all.

There were bundles of brightly coloured flowers spread out along the tables, no doubt the first of spring. Each was bound together at the stems with knotted strands of grass. As Torin thought about the bleak northern plain and the ash-black mountains surrounding Hjartahall, he thanked the gods for the bright colours of those blooms.

Torin expected to find Wyla where she always was, sipping a cup of mead or ale in the back corner and chatting with the other Greycloaks. But the benches along the tables were empty. There was no sign of Wyla anywhere.

Torin stopped one of the hall hands as she was walking by. "Have you seen Wyla?"

"Wyla White-Blaze? Yes, I did. She was speaking with Captain Gavring on the road up to the barracks."

Torin's heart dropped in his chest. Nodding in thanks, he slipped through the bustle of the hall and shoved through the door. Torin raced around the corner and up the crooked streets toward the stables at the north end of Gatewatch. He stopped outside the open stable doors to catch his breath.

Peering in, Torin saw Wyla tossing provisions and supplies over the saddle of a dark-maned horse. She cursed as she leaned against its flank to pin a rope down with her shoulder. With her one hand, Wyla tried to tie the rope into a knot, but the bag slipped and fell to the stable floor. Wyla pounded the seat of the saddle and stepped back. "By Odd!" Then she kicked the ground and let her head fall against the horse's shoulder.

Torin stepped inside. "Let me help."

Wyla jumped, startled at his words, her face burning red. She clenched her jaw and turned back toward the horse. "Help? With what? I'm fine."

Torin hauled the bag over the saddle and tied it down. As he pulled the knot tight, he noticed another bag next to it which clinked as the horse shifted. He had no doubt that it was Wyla's bag of silver.

Torin looked at Wyla. "Where are you going to go?"

Wyla shrugged. "Far away from here. Just like you were going to. Except I am going to leave first." She turned back toward the horse and checked the saddle. "Perhaps I can catch the Greycloaks that left to deliver the draught to Araldof. I guess now you get to watch me ride away."

Torin took a step toward her. "We could go together."

Wyla scoffed. "Where? To Ten-Tree Hall? So I can do what? Laze around the hall barking orders at servants with a set of keys jingling around my waist, while I get fat pushing out children to carry on your name?" She yanked at the straps on the saddle to tighten them. "No, thanks."

Torin frowned. "That had never crossed my mind."

"Well then, what?"

"Lots of things!"

Wyla rolled her eyes. "So, you had thought about it."

Torin rubbed his temples. "Wait! Listen. You could command the guard. The retainers in my father's hall aren't much to look at now but with your help they could become a formidable force. There are always bandits on the road and robbers up in the hills to deal with."

"So, I would whip second-rate farm whelps into shape and hunt down stinking sheep thieves? Sounds thrilling."

Torin shook his head. "Think of it! No trolls to fight, no danger lurking in the shadows between the trees. We would feast in a warm hall and listen to my father tell his most famous tales. We could lay down to sleep without a blade in our hand. For just a while, we would live in peace."

Wyla stepped back and shook her head. "Peace? Who am I talking to here? Only cowards pray for that. I don't know where I'm going, but I promise you this: I will die with a sword in my hand."

Torin cast his eyes down, then looked out beyond the open door. "Have you ever seen the sea, Wyla?"

Wyla stopped for a moment then shrugged. "Not yet. But I will."

"There's a place south of Ten-Tree Hall, about half a day's ride on horseback. You wind through a field of rolling green hills past the barrow mounds of my ancestors. Suddenly the ground falls away and there, at the very top of the Shrieking Cliffs, you feel like you are one of the *asyr* standing in the boughs of the world tree looking down. Far below, the sea foam breaks over the jagged stones in swells of brilliant green before fading into a blue deeper than the sky at dusk."

Wyla paused, the silence between them tense and raw. She wiped her eyes with her sleeve and grabbed hold of the saddle to swing herself up onto the horse. With her good hand, she took hold of the reins and looked down at Torin. For a moment they held each other's gaze, then Wyla spoke in whisper. "Goodbye, Torin Ten-Trees."

Torin stepped back as Wyla galloped by, then he ran to the stable doors and watched as she disappeared into the cobblestone streets of Gatewatch. Some part of his chest was fuller than it had ever been and another part, which had never seemed empty before, gaped wider than the ice-capped peaks on either side of Shadowstone Pass.

Torin decided to stay in Gatewatch a few more days before he departed. Each morning he went walking with Signy through the blooming fields up the valley and spoke with her about a great many things. She told him stories of his grandfather Runolf the Old and of the herbcraft she had learned from her mother, Sigrilinn. For his part, Torin had much to say about Lysa and the fate of the *huldur*.

In the afternoons, he returned to Fjellhall or soaked away the day in the baths with Grimsa, Signa, Azal, and Bari. They told tales and stories, most of which were true, and every one of them had their fill of laughter.

Grimsa and Signa spoke of the journey they would soon take to visit his family. Jarnskaldhus, his childhood home, sat beside the restless sea in the Bay of Noros. Though Signa was excited, Grimsa seemed nervous.

"Well, as I said, I hope you like fish," said Grimsa. "My father and brothers are all fishermen and traders. You'll know it by the smell!"

Signa winced. "I've only ever had river trout and I can't say I'm too fond of it."

Bari smirked. "If you can stand the scent of Grimsa after a long journey, then you'll handle the smell of fish just fine!"

Azal regaled them with tales of Armeah, of his many horse races, and of his father's grand palace. Despite these fond recollections, the prince planned to delay Aldrin in Gatewatch for as long as he could.

"The old man needs time to heal. Besides, he has a cartload of ink and parchment to keep him busy. I don't have anything to look forward to back in Armeah anyway. If my brother is on the throne, he'll surely make me his servant. If my sister manages to thwart him, she'll force me to join the high court. I despise either fate in equal measure!"

As for Bari, the *nidavel* said he would linger in Gatewatch until Torin was ready to depart, so they could walk the road together up valley to Frostridge Falls. There he would turn south and pass through the hidden door beside the thundering waterfalls into the *nidavellish* tunnels which led back to Myrkheim, the city of the Mastersmith.

"Mastersmith Ognir is still searching for the secrets to a lengthened life," said Bari. "I fear that after hearing of our adventure, he will send me north again to Thrudnir in Hjartahall. Any time is too soon for another visit with that *jotur*, if you ask me."

And so, the days passed until the time arrived at which Torin and Bari had planned to set out. They ate a hearty breakfast that morning with the others in Fjellhall and said their farewells at the East Gate. Grimsa squeezed him for what felt like a full minute, then let him go only to give him a second hug just as long.

"That second one is for Einar," said Grimsa. "Pass it along and tell him that Signa and I will come visit Ten-Tree Hall once we're tired of fish. I expect you'll come visit us at Jarnskaldhus sometime this summer?"

Torin nodded and clapped his old friend on the back. "Of course, I will! Just make sure they've got enough mead in their stores for the two of us together." Then he turned to Signy. "Are you sure you won't join me, mother? We could ride together."

Signy embraced Torin tightly then squeezed his shoulders. "Perhaps one day, when Signa has returned from visiting Grimsa's family and she is ready to take up the key to Fjellhall, perhaps then I will finally make the journey to visit Einar and gaze out over the sea."

The weather was fair that day, the breeze crisp, and the sky clear. Torin led his horse down the trail on foot as Bari walked beside him. They walked slowly, enjoying each other's company until they reached the place where their paths diverged.

"Riches and wisdom to you, Mindthorn, Riddlesmith, and Dawnbright," said Bari. "May our paths cross again. Let these be my parting words to you."

> *Copper coins sweet wine may buy*
> *And glint of silver catch the eye*
> *Yet reddest gold looks dull in hue*
> *Beside a friend who's proven true*

Torin bent down and embraced Bari one last time before they parted ways. Bari turned south toward Frostridge Falls and hummed a lively tune to himself as he went. Torin watched his friend until the *nidavel* disappeared behind a grassy hill, then mounted his horse and started up the trail to Shadowstone Pass.

By noon Torin had reached the top of the pass where he lingered a while after eating his midday meal. He looked down over Gatewatch, by then far below him, and to the wild green forest beyond. Then, as the sun began to slip toward the western horizon, Torin climbed onto his horse and started down the long road back to Ten-Tree Hall.

◊ *The End* ◊

◇ AUTHOR BIO ◇

Joshua Gillingham is an author, game designer, and editor from Vancouver Island, Canada. His fantasy trilogy, *The Saga of Torin Ten-Trees*, is a rollicking, riddling, troll-hunting adventure inspired by the Norse myths and the Icelandic Sagas. He is also the co-author of *Old Norse for Modern Times* alongside Ian Stuart Sharpe (Vikingverse Books & Comics) and Dr. Arngrimur Vidalin (University of Iceland), and the designer of the table top card game *Althingi: One Will Rise* set in Viking Age Iceland.

Find more at www.joshuagillingham.ca
or on Twitter – @JoshMGillingham